Carl —
My very good friend
and golf partner.
All the best.

Hank

A LEGACY OF HONOR

BY
HANK MANLEY

authorHOUSE®

AuthorHouse™
1663 Liberty Drive, Suite 200
Bloomington, IN 47403
www.authorhouse.com
Phone: 1-800-839-8640

First published by AuthorHouse 2/24/2009

ISBN: 978-1-4389-4848-5 (sc)
ISBN: 978-1-4389-4849-2 (hc)

Library of Congress Control Number: 2009901790

Printed in the United States of America
Bloomington, Indiana

This book is printed on acid-free paper.

Other Books by the Author

Bahama Snow
Bahama Payback
Bahama Reckoning
Coral Cemetery
Fundamental Behavior
Vengeance

Special Thanks To:

Anne Roberts for introducing me to the Calhoun clan and for the use of her name as Morgan's wife. Among Anne's many wonderful attributes is her generosity to worthy causes such as Canine Companions for Independence. Morgan's recovery with the assistance of his dog is based on an actual happening to a young man I met at a CCI function.

Larry Calhoun and the entire Calhoun family for allowing me to use their names in the story. The names are accurate, but the characters and their relationships are entirely a figment of my imagination. I did, however, use several of the stories Ardyth and Larry related to me about life in Edwards shortly after the turn of the century.

Donna Campbell for her tireless proofreading of my manuscripts, helpful story suggestions, and constant support.

Gretchen Manley for her proofreading and especially her inspiration for all my female heroines.

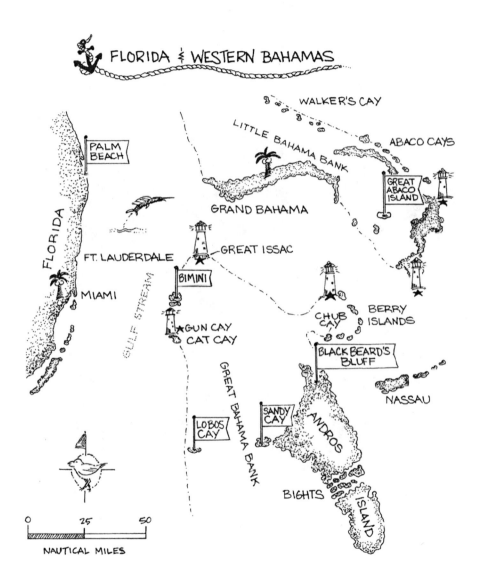

FLORIDA & WESTERN BAHAMAS

WALKER'S CAY

LITTLE BAHAMA BANK

ABACO CAYS

PALM BEACH

GRAND BAHAMA

GREAT ABACO ISLAND

FLORIDA

FT. LAUDERDALE

GREAT ISSAC

BIMINI

MIAMI

GULF STREAM

GUN CAY
CAT CAY

CHUB CAY

BERRY ISLANDS

BLACKBEARD'S BLUFF

NASSAU

GREAT BAHAMA BANK

SANDY CAY

LOBOS CAY

ANDROS

BIGHTS

ISLAND

0   25   50

NAUTICAL MILES

~ 1 ~

"The next pasteboard better not be an ace," Warren Earp said with hard, squinted eyes. "I'd take serious exception if I thought you was dealin' from the bottom of that deck."

The card poised in Johnnie Boyett's hand rolled from his fingers and joined the two aces already face-up on the table. It was the ace of spades.

"You cheatin' bastard," Warren growled as he pushed away from the table, stood, and reached toward the Colt strapped to his hip.

A single shot roared from the Remington Frontier .44 revolver drawn from Johnnie's lap. The lead slug flew unerringly from the eight-inch barrel. A puff of gray smoke twisted into the heavy air of the Dry Gulch Saloon in Wilcox, Arizona. The rank smell of cordite drifted toward the ceiling.

Warren Earp toppled forward, lifeless at age forty-five. His six foot-one inch body bounced on the edge of the round table and thudded to the floor. Drinking glasses, playing cards, coins and bills and a tall whiskey bottle scattered in the grimy sawdust.

"He was goin' fer his gun," Boyett said quickly. "He was goin' to throw down on me. I didn't have no choice."

Shorty Bean raised his hands above the level of the rough hewn bar, anxious to display his lack of a weapon. "I ain't heeled," he said in an even tone. "Whyn't you put up your gun, Johnnie. We don't want no more shootin'."

A puddle of blood began to seep from Warren Earp's starched white shirt. Johnnie Boyett glanced at the leaking body and scanned the room with nervous eyes. He shuffled his worn cowboy boots and pulled at his sweat-stained ten-gallon hat.

"You seen it," he stammered as he swept his hand across the men gathered at the bar. "You all seen he was goin' to draw on me."

The three patrons nodded enthusiastically in concert.

"We seen it, Johnnie," the first said as he reached for a heavy shot glass of amber liquid and with a trembling hand brought the drink to his lips. He drained the contents in a single swallow and slapped the stubby glass on the bar.

"Put the gun away," another man urged. "Marshal Longstreet will be along in a minute. You don't want him seein' you with that pistol in your hand."

As if on cue, heavy footfalls were heard on the wooden sidewalk outside the saloon. A meaty hand clamped the top of the swinging door and pushed it open cautiously.

Marshal Randolph Longstreet tentatively stepped into the stale atmosphere of the saloon brandishing a sawed-off shotgun at his hip. The butt of a heavy revolver protruded from the waist of his pants.

"Drop it," he growled toward Johnnie Boyett.

The shooter deliberately spun his weapon in his hand so the barrel was facing away from the marshal and placed it on the table.

"It was self-defense, marshal," Johnnie said as he raised his hands, palms out, to prove he was no longer armed. "Earp was going for his gun. I jus' beat him to the draw is all."

"We'll let Judge Wallace decide that when he gets here next week," Marshal Longstreet said simply. "What are you doin' in town anyway? Why ain't you off with your herd of damn cows instead of shooting up my town?"

"I done finished my work for the day," Boyett protested. "'Sides, I'm the range foreman. I got a passel of cowboys to ride herd fer me. I don't got to be in the saddle every day."

"Maybe not," Marshal Longstreet said. "But right now you get yourself over to the jail an' set a spell while I talk to these barflies

2

an' see if I can decide what happened. You best be at the jail when I git there. I don't want to have to come lookin' fer you."

Johnnie Boyett's shoulders slumped and he opened his mouth to protest. "You goin' to keep me the whole night? I needs to git back to the ranch."

"You should of thought about that before you got so reckless with your gun," the marshal said. "Now git before I decide to show you the inside of the cell."

Boyett tugged at his empty holster and re-positioned it on his right hip. Without the weight of his six-shooter, the belt felt light and strange. "I'll be at the jail," he said. "Jus' don't be too long with your questionin'."

Longstreet narrowed his eyes and stared unsympathetically at Johnnie Boyett. He flipped the barrel of his shotgun in the direction of the slatted door. "Go on. Git," he muttered.

*   *   *

Marshal Longstreet finished interrogating the bartender and patrons of the Dry Gulch and sat heavily in a wooden chair. He loosened his string cravat and crossed his knee-length black boots at the ankles. Warren Earp's body had been unceremoniously lugged from the saloon by the coroner Jethro Black and two helpers.

"Shorty, bring me a bottle and a clean glass, If you got such a thing behind that filthy bar."

Shorty Bean scooped two shot glasses from the bar and spun a soiled rag around the inside of each. He reached down and pulled a fresh bottle of whiskey from the lowest shelf and ambled toward the marshal.

At the table he pulled the cork from the bottle and filled the two glasses. "Mind if I join you?" he asked softly.

"Go on and set awhile," Marshal Longstreet said as he nodded toward the spare chair. "I ain't in no hurry to go over to Lilly's place and tell the poor girl that Earp was seein' that her boyfriend ain't comin' home tonight."

Bean raised the glass to his lips and paused. "She's 'bout due any time now, ain't she?"

"I think so," Longstreet said with a deep sigh before he hoisted his glass and drained the contents. He licked his lips and brushed the moisture from his heavy mustache with the back of his hand.

Shorty Bean re-filled both glasses and shook his head in wonderment. "Here it is July 6th, 1900. It's a whole new century and these damn cowboys still think it's 1881. When are they goin' to realize the country's growin' up? Gunfightin's a thing of the past, ain't it?"

"Warren's the last of the Earps," Marshal Longstreet said as he stared into the distance. "They got his brother Morgan in Tombstone. Shot up Virgil there, too. Lost the use of an arm."

"All that at the OK Corral?" Bean asked. "I heard them Earps did all the killin' at the gunfight."

"It weren't right at the OK Corral. The fight was in October of '81 and it actually was in a vacant lot beside Fly's Photo Studio near the corral. The Earps and Doc Holliday killed three of the cowboys," Marshal Longstreet said. "Morgan and Virgil was wounded. Wyatt and Doc wasn't even touched. I was still a teenager livin' in Bisbee at the time, right down the road. It was in all the papers and all anybody talked about fer a month."

"So when was Morgan killed and Virgil shot up?"

"Virgil was waylaid a couple of months later, three days after Christmas," Longstreet said nodding his head at the recollection. "Them cowboys peppered him with shotguns as he was coming out of the Oriental Saloon. They shot Morgan in the back whilst he was playing pool at Campbell an' Hatch's parlor the followin' February. Shot him right through the glass in the front door."

"An' now they got Warren," Bean said as he reached for the bottle. "So where's Wyatt off to these days?"

"I done heard he's in Alaska," the marshal said. "Went up there last year to open a saloon. Heard he's doin' right good, too. Place called the Dexter."

Shorty Bean sat without speaking for several seconds. "Wonder if he's interested in the child of his brother?"

"I doubt it," Marshal Longstreet said. "He's old now, maybe near fifty-five. An' he never seemed too concerned with children. Never had none of his own with either of his two wives."

"No easy task raising a child out here, a single mother an' all. And a whore to boot."

Marshal Longstreet stood and knocked some dust from the front of his pants. He tugged on his leather vest and rearranged the pistol in his belt. Snatching the shotgun from the table, he headed for the two swinging doors. "I ain't lookin' forward to this," he said. "That girl surely seemed to love Warren, spite of the fact he wasn't in no damn hurry to make her an honest woman."

~ 2 ~

Marshal Longstreet trudged down the sidewalk, his heels making hollow sounds as they clomped against the boards. He paused at the corner and glanced to his left as if checking for wagon or horse traffic. In reality, he was briefly delaying the painful fulfillment of his duty.

He stepped heavily into the dirt street and his right boot landed in a fresh mound of horse manure. "Sumbitch," he groused as he dragged his soiled foot in an attempt to scrape it clean.

At the next corner he grabbed the wooden post supporting the overhanging balcony and stepped up to the raised slat sidewalk. With a heavy heart he shuffled along the covered passage until he reached Lilly's Parlor of Relaxation. He rapped gently with a single knuckle against the large pane of glass inserted into the upper portion of the door.

After a brief delay the sheer curtain inside the window parted and a broad, painted face appeared. The initial curious expression was replaced with a wide grin. The door opened immediately.

"Land's sake, marshal," Lilly Hampton beamed. "To what do we owe the pleasure of this visit? You're a little early for some sportin', ain't you? You're still on duty if I don't miss my guess."

Longstreet removed his hat and slapped it softly against his right leg. Dust flew from both garments. "It ain't no pleasure this time, Miss Lilly," Marshal Longstreet muttered with bowed head. "I got some news fer that young girl of yours who was seeing Warren Earp right regular."

"You got news fer Samantha James?" Lilly asked with a puzzled expression. "I sure hope it ain't bad. She's been in a sickly way lately with the baby due soon."

"It ain't good," Marshal Longstreet said slowly as he lifted his eyes and engaged Lilly. "You best accompany me while I go see her. She in her room?"

"She is," Lilly said. "An' I don't know if I like this none. What's the matter?"

Longstreet licked his lips and glanced around the salon as if seeking help. A polished piano filled one corner of the large reception area, its surface gleaming in the glow of a tall floor lamp standing beside the player's bench. Heavy chairs filled the other corners. A deep couch backed against the longest wall. Above, a massive framed painting of a reclining nude with lush breasts and wide hips covered the red-flocked wallpaper. In the late afternoon hour, the room was empty.

"Johnnie Boyett killed Warren Earp 'bout an hour ago in the Dry Gulch," Marshal Longstreet said. "I guess you didn't hear the shot."

Lilly Hampton drew a long breath and blew it between her bright red lips. She shook her head and closed her eyes. "Addle brained cowboys," she said with disgust. "If they ain't thinking 'bout diddlin' my girls, they's thinkin' 'bout shootin' somebody."

"You think Samantha is goin' to take it hard?" Longstreet asked.

"Now what do you think, marshal?" Lilly replied in a sarcastic tone. "That girl done fell hard for Earp the first time she seen him. He's a good lookin' man. All the girls hope to marry one of the customers one day an' get out of this life. None of them *wants* to be a whore. It's 'cuz there ain't nothin' else they can do to stay alive."

Marshal Longstreet looked at his hat and shuffled his feet. "I knew she was taken with him..."

"Well, let's git up the stairs," Lilly said slapping her hands on her hips. "This ain't goin' to git any easier if we set here jawin' about it."

*   *   *

7

Lilly pushed the four-panel door open slowly and peered into the sparsely furnished room. She turned to the marshal and nodded. "She's decent. Come on in."

"Hello Miss Lilly," Samantha James said in a weak voice. "You come fer a visit?"

Samantha lay propped against two pillows at the head of a single bed. The sheets and a faded blue blanket were pulled to her shoulders. A small window allowed the rays of the afternoon sun into the tiny room. Dingy white curtains fluttered in the breeze. Dust danced in the muted light.

"How you feelin'?" Lilly asked as she placed a hand on Samantha's forehead. "You still feverish?"

"I'll be fine," the young girl said. "'Cept the baby's been kickin' somethin' awful this afternoon. And the pains been comin' real regular lately. I been thinkin' maybe he's 'bout ready to see what the world's all about."

Lilly lifted a glass of water from the wobbly, three-legged table beside the bed and handed it to Samantha. "Here," she said gently. "You drink this. You need to keep up your strength."

"Hello, marshal," Samantha said, forcing a smile to her pale lips. "What brings you fer a visit? You seen my Warren today? He ain't been around the last few weeks or so. I guess he's been real busy."

Marshal Longstreet lowered his eyes and rubbed his jaw in thought. "Miss Samantha, somethin' real bad's happened."

"What is it, marshal?" Samantha asked. "Ain't no more Indian trouble, is it?"

Occasionally young Apache Indians, bellies awash with alcohol and heads swimming with visions of their hero Goyahkla, whom the Mexicans called Geronimo, slipped from the reservation at San Carlos and shot weapons in the town or burned the barn of a hapless farmer.

Lilly sat on the bed and grabbed Samantha's hand in her own. "No, honey," she said. "It ain't no Indian trouble. An' if we wait fer the marshal to work up his nerve to tell you, it'll be long past suppertime. It's Warren."

"Warren?" Samantha said in alarm as she sat straight up in the bed. "He hasn't done nothin' wrong, has he? He's gonna be a father to our child real soon."

"No, he ain't done nothin' wrong 'cept step in front of a bullet," Lilly said. "He was shot today in the saloon. He's dead, honey. Your Warren's dead."

The last vestiges of color left Samantha's face. Her hand flew to her mouth. She gasped and screamed in agony, the sound of her voice thundering off the thin walls and bounding down the hall. "Warren," she cried. "Warren. I've got to go see him."

Lilly's restraining hand was insufficient. Samantha ripped the covers from her body and swung her legs from the bed. She placed her bare feet on the floor and took a long step toward the door. Suddenly she howled even louder and clutched at her stomach. Without breaking her fall, she collapsed to the floor, rolled to her back, and wailed toward the ceiling.

The exposed sheets on the bed were damp with a blood-tinted liquid. Samantha's gown was stained and dripping. A fresh puddle began to form on the floor.

"Git the doctor," Lilly shouted to the marshal. "Don't jus' be standin' there like some lump of ignorant flesh. Can't you see the girl's in a bad way?"

Marshal Longstreet cast a terrified look at Samantha writhing on the floor, leaking fluids, gripping her abdomen, and shrieking in pain and agony. He departed the room in a single bound. "I'll git the doc," he said as he disappeared from sight.

"An' don't tarry," Lilly yelled at the retreating footsteps.

*   *   *

Doc Hostetler placed his black bag at the foot of the bed and knelt beside Samantha on the floor. The young girl's eyes were rolled to the back of her head and she was groaning and clutching her distended stomach. "We got to git her on the bed," he said. "She's gonna be deliverin' soon."

Lilly motioned to the three young prostitutes huddled in a corner of the room. "Give us a hand movin' her to the bed," she commanded.

"Is she gonna be okay?" one of the girls inquired in a trembling voice. "She's startin' to bleed real bad."

"Grab her feet," Lilly said sharply. "Marshal, take hold of her arms. Let's get her off this cold, hard floor."

Samantha was wrestled awkwardly to the bed and flopped on the soiled sheets. Marshal Longstreet retreated to a corner of the room and leaned against the wall.

"One of you girls fetch the Widow O'Brien," Lilly ordered sharply. "She's had some experience birthin' I hear. She might be more help than you children. You may spend your nights practicin' how to make these babies, but you surely don't know nothin' 'bout bringin' 'em into the world."

One of the ashen-faced girls departed the room, glad to be away from the gruesome scene.

Doc Hostetler lifted Samantha's knees and spread her legs. "You push, girl," he said in a soothing voice. "This child of yours needs help."

Lilly turned to the remaining girls and pointed to the door. "Git some hot water," she said. "Lots of it. And bring some towels. Lord o' mercy. Make yourselves helpful. She's your friend, ain't she?"

The girls vanished through the door.

"I don't like what I'm seeing," Hostetler said in a concerned tone. "There's somethin' bad wrong with this girl."

"Is she goin' to make it?"

"I don't know," Doc Hostetler said sadly. "But we got to git this baby out of her if the child is to live."

"Push, Samantha," Lilly said as she gently laid her hand on the groaning girl's cheek. "Do this thing for your child. Push!"

Tears of grief and pain ran down Samantha's cheeks. "Warren," she called. "Warren! What am I gonna do without you?"

"Never you mind about Warren," Lilly chided. "You got to think of your baby. Push. Push hard."

"My baby," Samantha said. "Don't let nothin' happen to my baby."

"Then push," Lilly coaxed. "You can grieve for Warren the rest of your life. Right now you got to pay attention to this birthin' business."

Samantha struggled to focus her eyes on Lilly. Her face was blanched and clammy. "I don't feel right," she said in a distant voice. "I feel plumb tuckered all of a sudden. You take care of my baby if somethin' goes wrong, won't you Lilly?"

"Push, darn you," Lilly said. "Quit talkin' foolishness."

Doc Hostetler dipped his hands into the bowl of hot water brought by one of the girls. He dried them with a towel and positioned himself between Samantha's legs. "If she can help a little, I think this baby is about on the way."

Samantha gritted her teeth and closed her eyes. Her breathing slowed and her cries of anguish ceased. Summoning all her strength she pushed and pushed until her baby's head appeared and the doctor was able to lift the boy from her body.

The blood clot that had originated in her womb passed through her lungs and entered her aorta. Her heart immediately pounded in wild arrhythmia. Moments later the beating ceased. Samantha James was dead at the age of eighteen.

*   *   *

"That's a handsome boy," the Widow O'Brien said as she entered the room and saw Lilly holding the infant in her arms.

"He surely is," Lilly agreed before tilting her head toward the bed where Samantha lay beneath a sheet. "Except he ain't got no mother or father to care for him."

The widow turned toward the bed and slowly shook her head. "What happened? Why did she die?"

Doc Hostetler released a long sigh and shrugged. He was a conscientious man who cared about his profession, but he was among the ninety percent of doctors in the country at the time with no college education. "Maybe she was so grieved about the boy's father getting himself shot she didn't want to live. Maybe a blood clot went to her head. I've read about it in the medical journals. It happens sometimes when women are birthin'. Nobody seems to know why."

"Who was the father?" the widow asked. "I didn't hear about a shooting."

"It happened just this afternoon at the Dry Gulch Saloon," Marshal Longstreet said. "Johnny Boyett shot Warren Earp. He was the father."

"Was he going to marry the poor girl?"

"All these cowboys say they'll marry the girls," Lilly said with a disgusted smirk. "Then the girls get in the family way an' the cowboys want nothin' more to do with 'em."

"Warren Earp," the Widow O'Brien repeated as she reached for the infant and held him lovingly in her arms. "I've seen him around. He was a nice looking man."

"And Samantha was a beautiful girl," Lilly said with a shrug of her shoulders. "But none of that helps this little tyke now."

Widow O'Brien looked at Lilly for several seconds before speaking. "I'll take him," she said simply. "I'll give him a home and raise him."

"That would be most neighborly of you," Doc Hostetler said.

"I wonder what to name him?" the widow said slowly as she gently rocked the infant. "Did the girl ever talk about names for her child?"

"Never around me," Lilly replied. "I guess since he's gonna be your boy, you can call him whatever meets your fancy."

"I heard Warren talk fondly about his brother Morgan who was killed in Tombstone," the marshal said. "Maybe you could call him Morgan."

"That's a good name," Doc Hostetler said. "But I'd advise against Earp for a last name. Seems like everybody with that name winds up gettin' shot at some point."

Lilly looked at the child in the widow's arms. "The boy seems to have arrived a little early because of his father's death. That might be a fitting last name."

"Yes," Widow O'Brien said with a positive nod of her head. "That would be appropriate. Come along young Morgan Early. Let's find you some milk for supper."

Lilly turned to Marshal Longstreet. "Did Warren have any money in his pockets when he died?"

"The coroner turned over four hundred-fifty dollars to me," Longstreet replied. "I don't rightly know what to do with it 'cept pay for the funeral expenses. Earp didn't have no relatives around."

"Well, he sure got a relative now," Lilly said with a shrug. "You give that money to the widow. She'll need it with the boy. It's more than the town pays her in a year to teach their runny-nose kids how to spell and do sums."

"That sounds fair," Marshal Longstreet agreed.

"An' send over Earp's horse an' saddle an' guns," Lilly continued. "I doubt this unforgivin' country will outgrow them things before this poor boy is old enough to need 'em."

~ 3 ~

Morgan Early attended school every day of his life. Lorraine O'Brien was the schoolteacher in Wilcox, Arizona, and without the benefit of a baby sitter, she carried her son unfailingly to the little red building where she conducted classes.

By the time Morgan was four he was able to read. His appetite for learning impressed even his doting foster mother. The boy devoured each book she placed in his hands. As he grew, Morgan read every one of Widow O'Brien's extensive collection including studies of ancient history, Shakespeare's numerous plays, geography, treatises on the planets and stars, political thought and the history of the fledgling United States of America.

Morgan was particularly fascinated by biographies of famous warriors from Odysseus and Ulysses to the heroes of the American Civil War such as Stonewall Jackson, Ulysses S. Grant, Robert E. Lee and the incomparable cavalryman George Armstrong Custer.

Numbers came easily to the boy. He was able to recite multiplication tables long before the other students his age had gained such mastery.

"You will speak proper English," his foster mother cautioned from infancy. "I won't tolerate sloppy speech in my house. 'Ain't' isn't a word. Gerunds have the letter 'g' on the end, and you will pronounce them correctly. Dropping the 'g' only displays one's ignorance and doesn't save time."

Morgan's keen curiosity with the written word and his ease with mathematics did not preclude his interest in the outdoors. He grew quickly and by age twelve he was approaching five foot-eight inches and one hundred fifty pounds of solid muscle. Marshal Longstreet unselfishly invested countless hours teaching the lad to shoot his father's rifle with uncommon accuracy, and draw his father's Colt Peacemaker with amazing speed. Together they spent many days in the wild outskirts of town hunting and fishing. At the conclusion of each day, meticulous care was paid to cleaning the weapons.

"You must respect and care for your pistol and rifle," the marshal cautioned. "Dirt and neglect can cause these wonderful weapons to jam and fail."

Morgan became an accomplished horseman. He practiced galloping full speed and shooting from the saddle both over his horse's head and beneath his neck. He could toss his hat to the ground while fully loping, slide the animal to a complete stop, spin the beast within its body length, and retrieve his hat from the ground at a full run in the opposite direction.

Morgan's inquisitiveness never ceased to amaze and delight the Widow O'Brien. Nights were spent during and after dinner in lively conversation. "Why did the Greeks believe in so many gods?" the boy asked on one occassion.

"If the Roman Empire was so strong, why were the barbarians finally able to conquer Rome?" Morgan demanded another night.

"I think the greatest achievement of our Founding Fathers was decreeing the state must remain forever separate from the church," Morgan pronounced another evening as he and his foster mother sat on the porch and watched the sun drop over the Galiuro Mountains. "If religion rules the state, how can the people change their government?"

The Widow O'Brien nodded with contentment and merrily engaged the boy in a spirited debate about the subject.

*   *   *

Shortly after Morgan's fourteenth birthday, the Widow O'Brien sat the boy down after dinner one night in August to discuss their future. "The mines here in Wilcox have just about played out," she explained. "Several have flooded and others have yielded less

15

and less in recent years. Families are leaving and the town can no longer afford to pay me the same salary to teach the fewer students that remain in the school."

"What's that mean, Mother?" Morgan asked with concern. "I can continue to bring in some extra money after school. Maybe now that I'm almost grown I can earn even more."

Morgan had worked in the afternoons for the town blacksmith learning to shape horseshoes and other metal objects and discovering the effects of heat on steel. When a sprinkling of motor driven vehicles began to arrive in the new state of Arizona, the smithy added automobile repair to his business and Morgan became a capable mechanic. In the summers he worked cattle on a nearby ranch and quickly developed top cowboy abilities.

The Widow O'Brien tousled Morgan's hair with a loving hand and smiled. "You've been very helpful with the money you've earned. Not many boys your age bought and paid for their own boots and britches and a new McClelland saddle. But I've decided we're going to move. There's a town in Colorado named Edwards that has offered me a job teaching for forty dollars a month. I answered their advertisement and received their reply today. They want us there to start the new school year in September."

Morgan settled back in his chair and looked up at the darkening sky. Stars were shining increasingly brighter as the sun's rays melted beyond the horizon. Vermillion clouds paled to gray before disappearing in the night.

"Maybe it's good we're moving," the boy concluded after a long pause to reflect on his foster mother's words. "I've read about many wonderful places in the world. I've studied powerful and important men. Perhaps it's time to see more than just the desert around Wilcox, Arizona."

The widow nodded and slapped her knee as if to punctuate the decision. "We'll inform the people of Wilcox tomorrow. Then we'll begin packing. The entire journey will be more than eight hundred miles and we should start soon if we're to be there for the beginning of school."

"How will we travel?" Morgan asked. "With your books and other possessions it will be difficult to manage a train. I'd like to take my horse, too."

"I'll drive the buggy and you ride your horse," the widow replied. "The buggy is sturdy enough for the trip. We should find decent roads and trails most of the way. And I've always wanted to go by the Grand Canyon."

Morgan's eyes lit with excitement. "Can we really see the Grand Canyon?"

"Yes, darling," the widow said enthusiastically. "I understand the photographs in the books do not begin to do it justice."

*   *   *

Morgan reined his buckskin horse at the bank of the San Pedro River and looked back for his foster mother. A small cloud of dust plumed in the distance where the single horse buggy, loaded with books, clothes, water and an emergency supply of food, trudged along the dirt stagecoach road.

Excitement tingled through Morgan's body. He found it difficult to refrain from putting the spurs to his mount and dashing toward... toward his future. The mountains of Colorado beckoned in his imagination. He had ridden into the Dragoons less than ten miles northeast of Tombstone on several hunting trips, but those peaks were small compared to the massive ridges of Colorado that towered into the sky up to fourteen thousand feet.

The Widow O'Brien drew alongside Morgan and halted the buggy. The settlement of Benson was visible across the wooden bridge spanning the San Pedro River. A diminutive trickle of water meandered in the center of the wide ravine.

"Let's water the horses," the widow said. "Then we'll proceed on another hour or so and look for a campsite. We don't want to exhaust the animals their first day on the trail. They need to build their strength."

"I just want to ride and ride and ride," Morgan said with a wide grin as he dismounted and secured his horse to the rear wheel of the buggy. "I can't remember ever being so excited."

"I know, Morgan," the widow said easily as she lifted the bonnet from her head and shook her hair in the breeze. "I feel the same way starting a new adventure."

"Are you sad we're not taking a train?"

"No, darling," she replied. "I suspect we'll both be taking many trains in the future. It's certainly the fastest way from place to place. But I'm enjoying the country from my buggy without the noise and smoke. This way of travel may be coming to an end with the motor coaches taking over. I may never have the opportunity again."

Morgan poured water from a canteen into his hat and placed it beneath his horse's muzzle. The animal drank noisily, splashing drops on Morgan's arm with his flapping lips.

"We made about thirty miles today," Morgan said as he refilled his hat and walked toward the buggy horse. "We should be in Tucson tomorrow."

"Maybe I'll let you escort me into town for a proper dinner," the widow said with a delighted smile. "You've never taken a lady to dinner before."

Morgan lowered his head and felt a flush of blood tint his face. "No, Mother," he said. "Once Becky Montgomery tried to kiss me behind the blacksmith's shop, but I never took her to dinner."

"I suspect you'll have no trouble with the ladies, Mr. Early," Widow O'Brien said gently. "No trouble at all."

~ 4 ~

Morgan sat with his foster mother at the junction of the Colorado and Eagle Rivers. Their fire crackled and spit in the center of their campsite.

The two horses were loosely tied off to the buggy and happily munched on tall tufts of grass sprouting from the red soil. A clear sky gradually began to lose its vivid blue hues as the last rays of the sun receded behind the mesas to the west.

"With luck we should make Edwards by tomorrow in the late afternoon," Widow O'Brien said as she flipped the two sizzling trout in the iron skillet that was balanced on three rocks at the edge of the fire.

"It's been a wonderful journey, Mother," Morgan said as he reclined against his saddle and savored the cooking smells. "I still can't believe the size and magnificence of the Grand Canyon. I think it must be the most spectacular place in the world."

They had camped on the south rim of the Grand Canyon for two nights, marveling at its immensity and grandeur. Morgan had ridden his horse all the way down to the river and back, one mile below, with two other male travelers, while his foster mother had enjoyed the company of their wives at the campsite.

"Yes," she agreed, "the Grand Canyon is breathtaking. But Monument Valley must rate highly as well."

Morgan and Lorraine O'Brien had ridden through the quintessential western landscape with mouths agape as they passed each towering red rock protrusion reaching majestically skyward from the desert floor.

Morgan shrugged his shoulders and opened his palms to balance the answer. "It was simply spectacular," he nodded. "You're right. How can one choose between two such phenomenal sights? Can I rate them both number one?"

The widow and her foster son had traveled northward across the flat land west of the Colorado River until they reached Grand Junction. The land remained open with steep buttes visible in the distance. An acceptable dirt road paralleling the Union Pacific railroad tracks wended through the valley toward Glenwood Springs, and many other wagons and the occasional motor coach passed in each direction. They stopped in Glenwood for an afternoon to bask in the hot springs, and Morgan found an immediate affinity for the water. He quickly learned to swim and reveled in his newfound ability to hold his breath, open his eyes, and swim long distances underwater.

The widow recalled Morgan's instant comfort in the water and laughed. "I didn't realize I was raising a fish."

Morgan joined the merriment. "I want to swim in the ocean some day," he said with a grin. "Maybe sail off to some beautiful island."

The fourteen-mile stretch of the narrow Glenwood Canyon kept their eyes roaming along the soaring red rock cliffs that flanked the banks of the Colorado.

"Glenwood is not nearly as huge as the Grand Canyon," Morgan remarked. "But in a way it's almost as impressive because the walls are so close at hand."

"I had heard of the canyon," the widow said. "But I didn't realize it would be this spectacular."

The sound of a dry branch cracking in the distance suddenly riveted Morgan's attention. "What's that?" he said quickly as he jumped to his feet. "Is somebody out there?"

A man advanced with upraised arms from behind a large boulder. "No shoot," he said. "No shoot."

"Advance slowly," Morgan called as he flipped the slotted leather thong from the hammer of his Colt and loosened the weapon in its holster. "I want to see those hands as you approach."

The man stepped cautiously toward the campfire. He pointed to his nose and then the sputtering pan of fish. "Is good, no?" he said.

"Who are you?" Morgan asked. "What do you want?"

The man stood several inches taller than Morgan. He was powerfully built under his heavy coat, dark green cotton shirt and thick britches. His hair was long and scraggly and unwashed. He leaned forward and released a long drool of tobacco juice to the ground. His few remaining teeth were stained brown. A pungent odor of dried sweat drifted toward the fire.

The man formed binoculars with his hands and then pointed to the flat top mountains to the north. "I done see you come."

Widow O'Brien stood and extended a hand in welcome. "Are you hungry?" she asked. "We might be able to share some of the fish Morgan caught this afternoon."

"Good," the man grunted. "Hungry. Only damn sheep I eat."

"Sheep?" Morgan repeated. "You've been eating sheep?" The area around Wilcox was cattle country. People ate beef or the occasional wild antelope. Sheep had not come to the new state of Arizona.

"Damn sheep," the man acknowledged. "Sheep." He again pointed to the flat tops.

"That must be lonely work," Widow O'Brien said as she placed a piece of crisp fish on a plate and passed it to the man's outstretched hand.

"Me and sheep, only," the man admitted.

"I think I've heard of shepherds in this area. Are you from Spain?" Widow O'Brien asked. "Do you speak Spanish?"

The man blew on a hot piece of trout and forked it into his mouth. "*Espanol un poco*," the man said holding his index finger an inch from his thumb. "English a little. *No mucho Espanol*. Basgue. *Norte del Epana*."

Morgan sat again beside the fire and gathered his plate of fish. He didn't replace the leather thong over the Colt's hammer. Something about the sheepherder was troubling. His young senses remained on alert as the Basque stared at his foster mother with a strange gleam in his eye and a cruel set to his jaw.

21

"You're welcome to more fish," Morgan said. "But those sheep of yours must be missing you about now. If you're to return to the flock before full dark, perhaps you better be going soon."

The shepherd turned his head slowly toward Morgan. The man's mouth opened to reply, but he changed his mind and looked Morgan over silently. His eyes narrowed and Morgan felt a disturbing sense of discomfort as he witnessed raw hatred flashed in his direction.

"I go," the shepherd said as he scooped the last of his fish into his mouth. "Maybe again I see you." There was no friendliness in his hard voice. "Where you go?"

Widow O'Brien started to speak, but Morgan interrupted. "Denver," he said. "We're going to Denver."

"Hmm. Denver. Far," the Basque acknowledged with a long wave to the east. "But maybe so, I see you again."

With a final, strange grin directed at Widow O'Brien, the man stood, rearranged his trousers, and trudged off toward the looming hills to the north.

"I didn't like that man," Morgan stated when the Basque finally disappeared. "He looked at you in a weird way."

Lorraine O'Brien gathered the dishes and began to wipe them with a moist rag. "Don't fret, Morgan. He's probably not used to the company of a woman."

Morgan tapped the butt of his Colt with his fingers and drew a deep breath. "His manners better improve substantially if he ever hopes to join our campfire again."

*   *   *

Morgan awoke in the morning and placed dry sticks on the embers of the fire. He filled the coffee mug with fresh water and set it between two rocks to catch the rising flame.

Widow O'Brien stirred in her blanket and looked at the cloudless day breaking overhead. "That trout was wonderful last night," she said. "I'm sure we have time if you want to walk to the river and catch some more."

Morgan stood and looked to the north. The tall hills, cut flat high above, stretched as far as he could see from west to east. There was no sign of a single living person.

"Are you sure you'll be okay if I leave the camp for an hour or so?" he asked. His unspoken concern about the Basque was evident in the tone of his voice.

"Everything will be fine," his foster mother said. "I'll just busy myself packing the wagon while you're fishing."

Morgan walked to the buggy and retrieved his fishing rod and tackle box. "I shouldn't be too long," he said. "Hopefully the trout will be hungry this morning."

"Have fun," Widow O'Brien called with a wave as Morgan headed for the Colorado River.

The Basque watched from hiding as the broad back of the adolescent disappeared down the slope toward the riverbank. Then he advanced toward the camp with a grotesque expression of lust on his rough, unshaven face.

~ 5 ~

Morgan approached the Colorado River and studied the patterns of swirling water created by the rocks and boulders in the river. He looked back. The campsite was lost to view by the steepness of the bank. The cascading water created a cacophony that drowned all other noise.

He doffed his boots and entered the shallow edge of the river facing upstream. Ahead he noticed water pouring over and around a large rock. An eddy of relative calm circled slowly in the lee of the obstruction. Morgan made several false casts to peel line from his fly reel. He snapped the rod back, hauled line with his left hand, and fired the rod forward, again hauling to accelerate the line. The dry fly sped forward, rolled over gently, and landed softly seventy feet ahead, just behind the rock.

Within a fraction of a second a fat rainbow trout rose from the pool beneath the rock and inhaled the fly. Morgan squeezed the fly line against the rod with his index finger and sharply raised the rod. The tiny hook set in the corner of the rainbow's mouth. The fish broke the surface of the water and danced in the morning sunlight, pulling slack line through Morgan's left hand. When the line became taut, and the fish was "on the reel", the carefully crafted reel immediately spun backward as the trout sped into the current.

Morgan added cautious pressure to the revolving reel with his fingertips, carefully seeking to slow the run of the powerful fish without breaking the line. The rainbow leaped twice more and

Morgan gently steered the fish downstream and wound furiously with the reel handle. After several minutes of give and take, the fish began to tire. Morgan was able to retrieve line and finally lift the spent fish from the river.

"You're a beauty," he said with undisguised admiration of the rainbow's glorious colors and courageous battling ability. "You're nearly two feet long."

Morgan continued upstream, casting to likely holding places in the river. He caught three more rainbows and a large German brown trout before glancing at the sun and deciding to head back to the camp. Morgan considered fishing a wonderful diversion as well as a splendid source of food, and he was quickly developing into an extremely competent angler.

*　　　*　　　*

Morgan climbed the bank and headed for the campsite. "I caught five fish," he called when he was close. "They're all big ones, too."

His foster mother failed to respond. Usually the Widow O'Brien yelled a congratulatory reply when Morgan announced his presence as he returned to camp.

A disquieting feeling swept over Morgan. He increased his pace and shouted. "Mother! Where are you?"

His question was greeted with silence.

Morgan broke into a run, his tackle box and creel full of fish bouncing from his hip. Where would his foster mother have gone? There would be no reason for her to leave the campsite.

Near the smoldering fire Morgan saw his foster mother. She was prone on the ground. Her skirt was hefted above her waist. Her undergarments were tangled around one ankle. Was she sleeping, Morgan wondered? The widow never slept during the day. Why were her clothes disheveled? A strange, uncomfortable feeling invaded Morgan's soul.

Morgan slid to a stop and knelt beside the widow. Her head rested against a rock. Blood coated the rock and pooled in the surrounding dirt.

"Mother," Morgan screamed. "What's the matter?"

He reached behind her neck and gently lifted her head from the ground. Her eyes were closed and her head lolled from her shoulders.

Tears welled in Morgan's eyes. He pulled his foster mother to his chest and saw that his hand was covered in blood. Her body was limp. No breath escaped her lips.

"Mother," he howled again. "What happened? I should never have left you alone."

Morgan's tears turned to wracking sobs. His eyes flooded and he squeezed his foster mother as if he could force life back into her flaccid body with the strength in his arms.

He held his lifeless mother, kneeling in the dirt, rocking her in his arms, for almost an hour until he could cry no longer. His tears were exhausted, but his sorrow was just beginning. Then a new emotion crept into his soul. Morgan desperately wanted to understand what had happened. If another person had harmed his mother...

He gently placed the widow on the ground. He smoothed her skirt and stretched it over her legs, averting his eyes from her nakedness. His gaze fell to her hands. Both were clenched tight. Blood covered the fingers of one hand. Residue of skin appeared under the broken nails. A patch of cloth was clutched tightly in the other hand.

Morgan pried the fingers wide. He looked at the torn swatch. It was heavy cotton. The color was a deep green.

He gasped. The Basque had worn a cotton shirt of exactly this color.

The widow O'Brien had instilled a kind and gentle heart in Morgan Early. She had stressed the need for understanding and compassion when dealing with other humans. Forgiveness was emphasized, for people were never perfect and generally required consideration when they behaved poorly.

But Morgan carried warrior blood in his veins. Two of the Earp brothers, James and Virgil, had fought in the American Civil War. All the Earps had carried weapons throughout their adult lives. Virgil, Wyatt and Morgan had been peace officers in Dodge City and Tombstone. Warren, the youngest Earp, Morgan's father, had died at the point of a pistol.

Morgan's natural instincts welled to the surface. Revenge dominated his thinking. He was still a boy. He was inexperienced and untested in the skills of combat. But he knew how to handle a pistol and a rifle. He could track animals. Being alone in the wilderness didn't scare him. At that moment he knew he would never forgive himself if he didn't avenge the death of special woman who had raised him from birth, loved him unconditionally, and given him the best education she was able to impart.

~ 6 ~

Morgan scratched out a meager grave in the rocky soil and buried his foster mother beside the Colorado River. He fashioned a cross of sticks cinched together with a length of rawhide and jammed them into the shallow red ground.

He gathered a large group of flowers and placed them around the grave marker. Fresh tears returned as he looked at the completed site and realized with a terrible suddenness he would never again hear the sweet voice of the widow O'Brien. He had felt her warm touch for the last time. Morgan Early, at the age of fourteen, was truly alone in the world.

Morgan's tears soon dried and his heart steeled itself for the mission he selected. He would hunt the Basque who had killed the widow and take his life. That the man was older, more experienced, taller and stronger mattered not the least.

He hitched his horse to the back of the buggy and drove the rig to the dirt road near the railroad tracks. He halted and jumped from the wagon. As he waited he checked his possessions. His Winchester was missing. The shepherd was now armed with an accurate rifle and was even more dangerous. Morgan's resolve increased. The rifle had belonged to his father. He abhorred theft and he wanted it back.

A train chugged past, black smoke pouring from the tall, conical stack as the engine labored to climb the slope eastward. Passengers waved from the open windows and Morgan returned the greeting with a desultory salute.

An hour later a man and a boy near Morgan's age clomped by in a buckboard.

"Hello," Morgan called. "I see you're heading east."

The man reined in his team and pressed the tall brake handle with his right foot. "Which way you headed?" he asked. "Seems to me you ain't made up your mind yet."

"Oh, yes sir," Morgan replied with a definitive nod. "I've made up my mind about my direction. But I would like to impose upon your good nature for a large favor. Where I'm headed I can't take this buggy. If you would be kind enough to take it east a ways, I'll pick it up in a day or two when I'm finished with my business."

"We have a place in Edwards," the man said. "My name's Con Ira Calhoun. I'm known as Con, and this here's my son Buddy."

"Edwards?" Morgan repeated. "My mother is supposed to teach school there this year."

Con Ira Calhoun opened his hands in acknowledgement. "Then your mother's Lorraine O'Brien. We're all waiting on her to arrive. The ladies have a social planned when she settles in. What's your name?"

Morgan looked down and shuffled his feet in the dirt. "Morgan Early," he said grimly. "The widow was my foster mother. But there won't be any need for a social. She won't be teaching there. She... she won't be teaching anywhere."

The searing pain of speaking about his foster mother choked Morgan, and he couldn't frame the words to announce her death.

Con Calhoun looked puzzled. "She won't be takin' the job at the schoolhouse?" he asked. "We got such a nice letter from her. She seemed mighty anxious."

Morgan sniffled tears and mopped his eyes with his sleeve. "She...she..."

"Did something happen to your mother?"

Morgan could only nod. Words stuck in his throat.

"What happened, Pa?" young Buddy Calhoun asked, tugging at this father's shirt. "What happened to the new teacher?"

"Is she dead, son?" Con Calhoun asked. "Did your mother die on the trip?"

Morgan dropped his head and turned away. His hands went to his face and he nodded again before releasing a flood of hot tears.

"What's so important you can't come to Edwards with us?" Calhoun asked. "We can put you up at the farm until you figger what you want to do."

Morgan turned to face Con Calhoun. He brushed his eyes dry and shook his head. "I'd be powerfully obliged if you would take my rig with you. I'll be along in a couple of days. There's something I must do before I continue traveling."

Calhoun looked at Morgan carefully. "How old are you, son," he asked.

"Fourteen."

"Does this something have anything to do with your mother's death," he asked. "Was she killed? Are you lookin' for revenge against somebody?"

Morgan looked pleadingly at Con Calhoun without speaking. A deep sadness pervaded his soul. "I'd be much indebted to you if you would take my rig," he said after a long pause.

"If it's killin' you have in mind," Calhoun said. "I'd advise letting the law handle the matter."

"I haven't seen any law in the last couple of days," Morgan replied with a simple shrug.

Calhoun nodded. "You're right. Law's scarce around here. But you're just a boy."

"I may not be a boy next time I see you," Morgan said.

*   *   *

Morgan secured the load on the buggy. He transferred some jerked beef and extra .45 caliber shells to his saddlebags and filled his canteen.

Young Buddy Calhoun scrambled from his father's wagon and jumped to the seat of the widow O'Brien's buggy. He released the brake and took up the reins.

"I hope to see you soon," he said with heartfelt enthusiasm. "Maybe we can be friends."

"That would be nice," Morgan said with a genuine smile. He jabbed his foot into the buckskin's stirrup and slung into the saddle. "I'd like that."

"You be careful, son," Con Calhoun called as Morgan reined his horse toward the north and nudged his spurs into the animal's flanks.

"Thanks, Mr. Calhoun," Morgan said as he waved over his shoulder and headed for the flat tops.

~ 7 ~

Morgan Early returned to the campsite and dismounted. He walked toward the large rock the shepherd had emerged from and found his boot prints. The trail headed straight north.

Morgan remounted and rode a mile to the west before turning toward the looming hills. A prudent man might cover his back trail and spring an ambush if he was expecting to be followed.

The sun was bright overhead and Morgan's buckskin was soon lathered in sweat as he pushed higher. Morgan steered his mount along subtle swales and depressions in the landscape that afforded cover from roving eyes above. He rode through aspen groves when they sprang on the hillsides and maintained concealment in the periodic stands of lodgepole pines. Sign of deer and elk littered the myriad game trails that twisted across the terrain. He observed bear scat in several places. Morgan was young, but he was extremely bright and well schooled by Marshal Longstreet.

A babbling stream snaked along the edge of a field of tall aspens. Morgan jumped from the buckskin and allowed the animal to drink heartily. He pulled several swallows from his canteen and refilled it with the cool mountain water.

Two hundred feet above his head the land flattened. Morgan looked down to the valley floor below and saw the Colorado River, the railroad tracks and glimpses of the rudimentary road running between Edwards and Glenwood Springs. A tiny cloud of dust marked the passage of a motorcar. Morgan estimated he was near the summit.

He swung into the leather and heeled the buckskin. When he was twenty feet from the leveling of the land, he halted, dismounted, and tied his horse firmly to a stout bush. Removing the restraining thong from the Colt's hammer, he eased up the remaining slope and crouched behind a jagged rock.

The flat tops were aptly named. A vast meadow of rich grass undulated gently as far as Morgan could see. Trees were noticeably absent. The wind blew from the west and cotton balls of cloud scudded across the sky. A mile and a half in the distance Morgan discerned a disruption in the landscape. Something unnatural interrupted the flow of the countryside. Slight movement provided a clue. The area of white plunked on the verdant ground was a large, tightly grouped, flock of sheep.

Morgan nodded silently and a small smile cracked his lips. A new sensation stirred in his blood. The initial inkling of the warrior he was to become began rising to the surface.

"When I find the man with a torn shirt and scratched face, those sheep will require a new caretaker," he vowed to the wind.

*　　　*　　　*

Night fell and Morgan huddled in his blanket beside the small stream, his McClelland for a pillow. Buck grazed happily nearby. He looked at the stars, seemingly brighter in the rarified air of the mountains, and plotted his move. The lack of natural cover was a concern. Night would become his ally. He turned over and set his mind to awaken two hours before dawn.

Morgan's eyes popped open abruptly at four o'clock. The sky was black to the east, but a quarter moon hung in the western sky providing a trace of illumination. A rustler's moon: sufficient light to steal cattle but not enough for the sheriff to follow your trail.

He saddled the buckskin, rolled his blanket and refilled his canteen. Quietly he swung into the saddle, the only noise being the creaking of stiff leather. Morgan nudged the horse ahead and within minutes they climbed over the mountain face and headed across the flat top toward the last sighting of the flock of sheep.

Morgan reined his animal after traveling a mile. He tied the horse to a shrub in a shallow depression in the ground and proceeded on foot. When he had moved another quarter mile he halted and bent his ear to the wind. A faint sound of animal noise drifted from the west. The smell of dung and musky hide scented the air.

Crouching low, Morgan scurried ahead directly toward the location of the flock. He calculated the shepherd's camp would be on the other side of the sheep. That would place the Basque above the noise and smell of his charges and allow Morgan to approach from the downwind side.

Morgan descended into a wide swale, crossed the depressed ground, and then rose on the far side. He dropped immediately to his knees. The flock was fifty yards ahead. His presence was still undetected, but his heart rate jumped. He had lost sight of the sheep crossing the swale and arrived near the flock sooner than he had anticipated.

He backed into the lower ground and began to circle to his left, maintaining a greater distance from the flock. When he was certain he had cleared the animals, Morgan continued west, searching for signs of a camp. A faint whiff of smoke tickled Morgan's nostrils. An almost imperceptible glow of nearly extinguished embers caught his eye.

Morgan crept silently toward the vestiges of the campfire. He placed each boot tentatively on the ground before moving forward, careful not to scrape a rock or snap a twig. Silence was his cover and concealment on the barren landscape. Dawn was not far away. The first hint of light painted the sky to the east with a thin stroke of gray.

*   *   *

The initial throaty growl erupted into an ear-piercing series of yaps and barks. The sheep dog dashed at Morgan's feet and attempted to clamp on to his ankle with slobbering jaws. Morgan kicked at the attacking animal and made solid contact with its head. The dog stumbled backward and whimpered before resuming its frenzied yowl.

"You stop," a deep voice called from the camp. "You move slow this way."

34

The sudden attack of the vigilant sheep dog had startled Morgan. His plan to sneak undetected into the camp was aborted. He possessed no contingency. He spread his arms and ventured forward.

A man rose from beside the fire and shed a blanket from his shoulders.

"Hold right there," the man said before turning to the dog and calling it to heel. "That's a good boy. Good dog."

Morgan stopped. The dog sat at the man's left leg, trembling, a low growl rattling deep in its throat.

The man reached down and set several dry sticks on the fire. Loud crackles followed and a flame soon licked at the cool morning air. "What you want?"

Morgan kept his arms apart. "I'm just passing through," he said.

A footstep behind Morgan froze him. A sudden jab in the kidney with the point of a rifle barrel riveted his attention. How had he been so stupid not to anticipate the presence of a sheep dog around a flock? Why hadn't he considered the possibility of two men sleeping at the camp?

"Move," the voice behind him demanded.

Morgan stepped forward with the assistance of two more cruel stabs with the rifle.

The campfire was ablaze. Faint sunlight crept over Morgan's shoulder. The features of the man standing in the camp became distinguishable. It was the Basque. He turned slightly and three deep, angry red scratches were discernable high on his left cheek. His green shirttail, hanging outside his trousers, was torn near the placket.

"Another starvin' cowboy come to steal our vittles," the man behind Morgan said with a laugh. "I say we string him up as an example to his kind."

Morgan saw the Basque standing by the fire. The man reached down and lifted the stolen Winchester from the ground. Morgan understood immediately his inexperience and stupidity was about to cost him his life. He was a boy, arrogant enough to think he could prevail over a man who had survived on the land for many years. His death would be fitting proof of his folly.

35

"No tree on this flat top," the Basque snarled. His eyes narrowed and recognition crossed his face. "I know this boy. You come kill me?"

"You killed the finest woman who ever walked the face of the earth."

The Basque suddenly lifted his head and laughed. "What you do? You a little boy."

"I plan to send you where you sent my mother. Maybe she'll forgive you. I can't."

The sheepherder behind Morgan shifted his rifle. The barrel rested briefly against Morgan's side to steer him toward the fire. Morgan seized the opportunity. He stepped backward, toward his assailant, inside the end of the weapon, and turned. His left fist crashed into the man's jaw at the same time the rifle fired.

The force of the blow caused the man to drop the weapon and clutch his face. The report of the round sent the Basque standing by the fire ducking to his left.

Morgan completed his spin. He rotated to face the Basque and heard the sound of his father's Winchester as a round was jacked into the chamber. The Basque lifted the weapon to his hip.

Morgan's right hand flashed. One moment there was no Colt in his grip, and then the Peacemaker was there as if levitated from the holster. The hammer was magically drawn. Morgan fingered the trigger and pulled.

A heavy .45 caliber slug ripped through the Basque's chest. The man's heart exploded. Morgan held the trigger and fanned the hammer twice more with the palm of his left hand. Two more rounds tore into the shepherd's upper body as he toppled forward and crashed on to the snapping flames of the campfire.

Morgan turned to the second sheepherder, extended his arm to its full length, and trained his Colt on the man's forehead. He calmly clicked back the hammer with his thumb. "I have no quarrel with you," he said. "Your friend killed my mother yesterday. He didn't deserve to live."

The shepherd nodded as he spit blood to the ground and wiped his mouth with a filthy sleeve. "So you were the ones he watched comin' through the valley," the man said. "I wondered where he disappeared to yesterday."

"Now you know," Morgan said. He walked to the body of the Basque where it lay covering the fire, the man's girth having extinguished the nascent flames. "He stole my father's rifle. I'll have it back. I can't abide a thief either."

"You'll get no argument from me," the shepherd said. "He was no friend. I'm just workin' with him. Feel free to go. I won't shoot you on the way out of camp."

Morgan shouldered the Winchester and turned south. "I'm sorry to double your work load," he said as he began walking back to his buckskin. "But I'm not sorry about that woman killer smoldering in the fire."

~ 8 ~

Morgan Early loped his horse along the southern shore of the Eagle River. He crossed Squaw Creek and Lake Creek, both draining from their respective valleys to the south. A sign hanging from a tall wooden arch announced the entrance to the Brett Ranch.

A quarter mile farther along the dirt road Morgan turned south and slowed at the winding road leading to the Calhoun farm. He crossed the property, reined the buckskin and dismounted. He tied the horse to the hitching post in front of the house. The front door opened and a young girl emerged.

"Daddy don't hanker to no strangers," she said with a stern look on her face.

Morgan looked up as he loosened the cinch from beneath Buck's belly. "If I'm at the right place, I don't think I'm exactly a stranger. I met your father yesterday down the road."

The girl allowed a wide smile to spread across her face. "So you're the boy Buddy was tellin' me about," she said. "He never got your name. What do they call you?"

"Morgan. Morgan Early. And what's your name, if I may be so bold as to ask?"

The girl shook her blonde pigtails and placed her hands on her hips. "I'm Ardyth," she said. "Ardyth Calhoun."

"Well, Ardyth, you're certainly a lovely one when you take that scowl off your face."

"My, Mr. Early surely talks pretty. But who says I'm interested in your opinion?" Ardyth said as she turned and stomped from the porch.

Morgan knitted his eyebrows in bewilderment. What had he said that upset the girl? Didn't he say she was pretty? He shook his head and shrugged his shoulders. His small amount of experience with girls generally left him perplexed.

"Hello, young man," Con Calhoun boomed as he rounded the house and approached on foot. "I wasn't rightly certain I'd ever lay eyes on you again after yesterday."

"I appreciate that you cared for my rig," Morgan said extending his hand in greeting. "I hope it wasn't too much of a burden."

"No trouble a'tall. Buddy enjoyed the chance to drive it."

Morgan glanced toward to west. The sun was the width of two hands above the tops of the mountains. Darkness would be approaching in a couple of hours. "If you'd direct me to my buggy, I'll move off your property and set a camp. I wouldn't want to impose further on your kindness."

Calhoun looked closely at Morgan. He hesitated then spoke in a lowered voice. "Did you...finish your business back there on the flat tops?"

Morgan scraped a toe along the ground and then nodded slowly as he cast his eyes downward. "Yes, sir," he said. "I finished."

"I don't recall that Winchester in your saddle boot when you was on the road back there. That a new acquisition?"

"It was my father's. It was misplaced for a while, but now it's back where it belongs."

"What do you plan to do? Have you got relatives anywheres?"

"No, sir. I'm down to me."

Calhoun rubbed his chin in contemplation for several seconds. "Can you cowboy? I might need a hand here on the farm."

Morgan tilted his head and thought a moment. He had some money. He and the widow had left Wilcox with almost seven hundred dollars. The wagon was of no further use to him. He had considered selling it and the horse, which should garner another hundred or more. The widow had some personal possessions that without the wagon would be impossible to carry. The school might enjoy the books. But he had no idea where to go.

"I've had some experience in the saddle in Arizona," he answered. "I think I can handle whatever you require."

"I can pay thirty dollars a month," Calhoun said. "That includes room and board for both you and your horse. Winters can come mighty early in the mountains. It ain't no time to be travelin'."

"I guess you get some snow here," Morgan said. "I've never seen snow. It might be a nice change from the desert."

Calhoun laughed. "If you stay, you'll see snow. That I can guarantee. Some years we'll get five hundred inches."

"I have no place in mind at the moment," Morgan said. "I think I'll accept your offer, and I thank you kindly."

"Good," Calhoun said with a bright grin. "You'll be beddin' down in the bunkhouse over yonder. Let me show you where to stable your horse."

*   *   *

Con Calhoun jogged his horse beside Morgan's buckskin as they headed south up the Lake Creek valley. He led a mule carrying coffee, slabs of bacon and extra blankets. Broad green pastures spread west before butting against a steep rise that towered sharply above the stream. Tall lodgepole pine trees edged the cliffs and pockets of aspens were scattered on the lower slopes.

The aspen leaves were bright gold and shimmered in the stark sunlight. Morgan could hear their gentle rustle in the fall breeze. The air was cool and Morgan was wearing a fleece coat that had just arrived from the Sears, Roebuck store in Chicago.

"We got 'bout four hundred head up there on the summit," Calhoun said. "We best be gettin' 'em down where we got the feed before the snows gets 'em."

Fifteen-year-old Buddy Calhoun rode near his father. "You reckon we'll have trouble finding the herd, Pa?" he asked. "Las' year they was scattered all to hell and gone."

The boy's father cast a stern look. "Don't you be lettin' your Ma hear none of that language."

Buddy nodded, sufficiently chastised. "Yes, Pa," he said.

Since Morgan Early's arrival on the farm, Buddy had felt a competition for his father's attention. He had increased his efforts to act and sound grown. Although he was a year older than Morgan, he felt less mature, less capable. His resentment of Morgan's presence became more difficult to conceal.

Con Calhoun and the two boys rode in silence for three more hours, steadily ascending the mountains along the creek. Morgan reveled in the scenery. The scattered mountain ranges of Arizona were completely different in size, contour and vegetation.

In late afternoon they broke out of a deep pine forest on the ridgeline and reined their horses. A vast grassy field stretched for miles to the south. In the distance, mountain peaks, dusted white from recent snowfalls, scratched the sky.

"How high are those peaks?" Morgan asked.

Con Calhoun pointed. "Near fourteen thousand feet," he replied. "That there is the Mount of the Holy Cross, the source of the Cross Creek which drains into the Eagle River above Minturn where all them Mexicans live."

"What's the Holy Cross?" Morgan asked.

Calhoun turned in his saddle. "The east side of the mountain has intersecting ravines in the shape of a cross. The snow stays in the ravines all summer and you can see the cross showin' all white against the mountain face fer miles away."

"Come on, Pa," Buddy said. "Let's git after them cattle. I seen the Holy Cross before."

Con Calhoun shook his head before gesturing to the west. "Buddy, you ride down that edge of the meadow an' push the cows toward the middle. Me, I'll ride the other side. Morgan, you stay in the middle and try to bunch the critters into a herd."

Morgan nodded his understanding and squeezed Buck's flanks with his knees to start him off.

"You boys keep alert," Calhoun yelled. "The bears an' lions are active this time o' the year."

Buddy spurred his horse and called back. "Ain't no need to worry, Pa. I kin handle myself plenty good."

Morgan Early eased his buckskin through the tall grass. He stood in his stirrups and looked around the vast meadow. Cows were scattered as far as he could see. He nudged his horse toward several milling animals and cut sharply around them to tighten them into the beginning of a herd. When the cattle were bunched he wheeled behind and began driving them down the center of the meadow.

Morgan turned to his right and saw Buddy darting his horse in and out of the edge of the pine forest. Cattle were drifting from the trees toward the grassy field. Suddenly Buddy's horse reared on its hind legs, shook its head and released a long, panicked whinny. Buddy flew from the back of the horse as the terrified animal dug in his hoofs and fled.

Without hesitating, Morgan spurred the buckskin toward Buddy. Holding the reins slack in his left hand to give the horse his head to run, Morgan reached for his Colt and pulled the thong from the hammer.

Morgan couldn't see Buddy. The boy was on the ground, lost to view by the tall, yellow grasses. Above the thunder of the buckskin's hooves and the snorting of his labored breathing, Morgan thought he heard a scream of fear and pain.

At the edge of the meadow, Morgan pressed his heels forward in the stirrups and hauled back on the reins. The horse locked his rear hoofs and slid to a stop.

Buddy was down. His cries of fright pierced the thin mountain air. A full-grown mountain lion was mauling the boy with slashing claws.

Morgan jumped from the saddle, Colt in hand, but could not shoot for fear of hitting Buddy. He leapt at the snarling animal and smashed his revolver against the broad, tawny head. The lion ceased his attack and disengaged his grip from the terrified boy. The big cat turned toward Morgan. Long teeth framed a vermillion tongue and drooling mouth. The enraged lion roared, reared on its hind legs, and sprang at Morgan.

The mountain lion's front paws brushed past Morgan's shoulders. He felt the hot breath of the animal on his face. Saliva gushed past the exposed teeth and splattered his chest.

Morgan rolled with the attack and raised his Colt. Thrusting the barrel directly under the mountain lion's throat, he pulled the trigger as he fell backward. The bullet splintered the animal's brain before shattering through the top of its skull.

The weight of the large lion, and the thrust of the leap, slammed Morgan to the ground. His breath rushed from his lungs, and he gasped for air as he struggled to heave the lifeless carcass from his chest.

"Buddy," he managed in a weak voice. "You okay, Buddy?"

Buddy Calhoun lay curled in a ball, moaning and crying. The shoulders and front of his heavy coat were lacerated. Blood was visible beneath the garment.

Morgan crawled to the boy's side and gently turned him over. His face appeared unscathed.

"You'll be okay," Morgan said gently. "I think you're mostly scared."

"You...you saved my life," Buddy whimpered. "I'll never forget that. Never!"

"You take it easy," Morgan said. "I hear your father riding hard this way. We'll get those wounds cleaned and you'll be as good as new."

Fresh tears welled in Buddy's eyes. He reached for Morgan's hand and squeezed it. "Thank you," he said.

Morgan wiped blood and bone splinters from his forehead. "I just figured us cowboys have to stick together," he said. "If the situation was reversed, I'm sure you'd do the same for me."

~ 9 ~

Con Calhoun removed the long Bowie knife from his scabbard and handed it to Morgan. "Slice that cat's stomach open," he said. "We'll leave the carcass for the bears an' wolves an' coyotes. Might help to keep 'em away from us in the night."

Morgan nodded and walked to the mountain lion. He drove the huge knife into the cat's massive rib cage and sliced downward. The razor-sharp blade split the tough hide, exposing the cat's stomach and intestines.

Con Calhoun gathered two long poles from the edge of the woods. "We need to make a sled for Buddy. He won't be ridin' for the next few days."

The ends of the two poles were lashed to the sides of the mule, and blankets were slung between them to form a stretcher. Buddy Calhoun was hoisted onto the makeshift rig.

"We'll move a couple miles south and make camp by that spring pond in the center of the meadow," Con Calhoun ordered. "We should be fer enough from the lion that the scavengers don't give us no trouble."

"I'll ride ahead and start a fire," Morgan said. "You'll want to clean those wounds with some hot water the first chance you get."

"Good idea," Con Calhoun said. "I've some salve to rub on the cuts. Buddy can rest up a few days while we form the herd. He should be ready to ride when we drive 'em home."

44

Buddy Calhoun gave a wan smile and a small wave from the back of the sled. "I'll be okay," he said in a shaky voice.

Five days later, with a hint of snow in the crisp air, Con, Buddy and Morgan Early trailed four hundred thirty-five summer fattened cows to the lower range of the Calhoun farm. Buddy's heavy clothing had ameliorated the worst of the claw attack by the big mountain lion. His wounds were bloody and painful but not deep. His father had washed them and applied salve liberally. No infection appeared imminent. The boy rested by a fire during the round up and silently endured the discomfort during the ride home.

Morgan marveled at the magnificent mountains. During the day he contemplated a life in the area, but when evening fell and the temperature dropped precipitously, he longed for warmer climes. Shivering in his blanket, nestled close to the fire, Morgan thought of his foster mother's geography lessons. Florida repeatedly popped into his mind. Wasn't it always warm there? Were there cattle in Florida he could work?

*   *   *

Two weeks later, on a Saturday in early October, twenty inches of snow fell during the night in the Eagle River valley. Morgan awoke in the bunkhouse, tossed three lumps of coal into the potbelly heater and tugged on his boots. He stepped outside and gasped. The bitterly cold air seared his lungs. The wind knifed through his long johns and grated against his bones.

The journey to the outhouse was torture. Snow cascaded over the tops of his boots and froze his feet. Mucus crusted in his nostrils. Blowing flakes landed on his head and stuck to his eyebrows. He rubbed his hands together frantically in a futile effort to bring warmth. Morgan was too cold to enjoy perusing the Christmas cards from previous years tacked to the walls of the outhouse as decoration.

Dressed in double layers, Morgan plowed through the mounting drifts toward the Calhoun house. He flapped his arms on the porch to remove snow from his clothing and stomped his feet to restore circulation to his limbs.

Inside, Mrs. Calhoun served Morgan a steaming mug of tea. "Drink this, child," she said firmly. "I'll have a heaping plate of eggs and bacon in a minute."

Con Calhoun appeared and smiled at Morgan. "You was wonderin' if you'd see any snow," he said with a laugh. "What do you think about this little storm we had last night?"

"Mr. Calhoun, I don't see how I can take this weather," Morgan replied.

Sixteen-year-old Ardyth Calhoun appeared at the breakfast table. Morgan jumped to his feet at her arrival. She kissed her mother and father on the cheek and smiled brightly at Morgan.

"I know how you can pass some of the time," she said with a mischievous twinkle. "There's a dance tonight at the school house. You could accompany me there if father will allow it."

Morgan's eyes opened wide in astonishment. Ardyth had barely acknowledged his presence since the first day when they met on the porch. His duties kept him busy, and he initially took his meals in the bunkhouse, but on the occasions when Morgan and Ardyth's paths crossed, she treated him with disinterest at best and often with disdain.

Following the cattle round up and drive from the high country, the story of Morgan's brave act to save Buddy from the mountain lion changed the dynamic of his relationship with the family. Con Calhoun treated him almost as a second son. Mrs. Calhoun insisted Morgan take his meals at the family table, and Buddy, though older, warmed to Morgan like a big brother. Ardyth was the last to drop her indifference.

"I've never been to a dance," Morgan protested. "I've never danced before."

Mrs. Calhoun brushed her hands against her apron and spread them wide in acknowledgement. "Well," she said. "Then I think it's high time you learned, young man."

"Then it's okay if Morgan takes me to the dance?" Ardyth said looking hopefully between her father and mother.

The Calhouns exchanged glances. Con gave an imperceptible nod and Mrs. Calhoun replied. "I think it's a splendid idea."

Morgan gulped and looked around the table with trepidation. An apprehensive smile broke the edges of his mouth.

*   *   *

Hot coals were wrapped in canvas and placed on the floor of the sleigh to warm their feet. Buddy Calhoun with sister Ardyth and Morgan Early flanking him, waved to his parents and snapped the reins. "Git along," he called to the two horses attached to the rig.

"Have fun," called Mrs. Calhoun.

The three teenagers clomped across the expanse of the Calhoun property, above the town of Edwards, toward the one room red schoolhouse where Morgan's mother was to have served as teacher. A replacement had been recruited from Salt Lake City to instruct the fifty-four children of the twenty families that resided near the town.

The runners of the sleigh squeaked along the dry snow, and a bell attached to one of the horse's collars clanged merrily. The school was only a mile from the Calhoun house, and Buddy reined the animals and tied them to a post next to the building. Inside, carbon lights burned brightly and the warm glow, along with the sounds of the band, filtered invitingly under the wooden door. An iron stove stuffed with split logs snapped with heat.

Lela Richards shouted a greeting to her classmate Ardyth when the three youngsters entered the school. "So you brung your boyfriend after all," she said. "You done nothin' but talk 'bout him fer a month now."

Ardyth looked at Lela and scowled. "I ain't been doin' no such thing at all," she protested through her blush of embarrassment.

Morgan looked at Lela Richards. She was the largest young girl he had ever seen, easily topping two hundred fifty pounds. What had she said? Had Ardyth been talking about him? Did the huge girl call him Ardyth's boyfriend? In Morgan's mind, Ardyth barely knew he existed. For the millionth time since his foster mother's death, Morgan lamented her murder. Who could he ask about the confusing behavior of Buddy's sister? Would he ever be able to understand girls?

"Put your coats over there on the table," Ester Klack, the evening's chaperon, instructed. "It's plenty warm inside."

Morgan doffed his heavy coat and looked around the room. The band consisted of three men standing in the corner, one playing the bass, the second a banjo and the third a fiddle. They broke into a lively rendition of the Turkey Trot.

"If you ain't gonna dance with your boyfriend," Lela Richards said to Ardyth, "I'll give him a whirl around the floor."

"But I don't..." Morgan's protestations were in vain. Lela seized his hand and pulled him to the center of the room.

"Jus' you watch me," Lela said as her feet began to flash lightly to the beat of the music. She grabbed his hands with her massive fingers and began to move him to the rhythm.

Lela Richards was shockingly nimble on the dance floor. Her bulk appeared to float above the rough boards of the schoolhouse, and her feet maintained perfect time to the music. Morgan watched her feet for a moment and immediately began to imitate her movements. He felt energized and excited moving to the beat of the band.

"I don't know if I'm doing this right," Morgan said excitedly, "but it sure is fun."

"You're doin' jus' fine," Lela assured him.

Morgan looked around at the other dancers. Some maintained the rhythm but looked clumsy. A few never managed to stay with the beat. Lela was clearly the most proficient dancer of the group. A wide grin spread across her face as she turned and swayed to the music.

In the corner Morgan spotted Ardyth Calhoun with her back to the dancers. She was pointedly ignoring the action on the floor. The song ended and Morgan looked at Lela. "That was fun," he said. "Thank you for showing me the dance."

Lela glanced quickly around the room before leaning toward Morgan and planting her copious lips on his mouth. "That's not all I would like to show you. You let me know if Ardyth doesn't want to take good care of you."

Morgan stepped back and looked curiously at Lela. What did this enormous girl mean by that remark? Why was she so bold to kiss him on the lips? What did Ardyth have to do with him? Morgan suddenly felt extremely uncomfortable and well out of his realm.

"I think I better be getting back to Ardyth," he said. "After all, it was her idea to bring me to the dance."

"Of course," Lela said with a wink. "But don't forget what I said. You're going to grow up to be a right handsome man. You're gonna want a real woman."

Morgan turned and walked toward Buddy who was nibbling on a piece of cake at the refreshment table. "That Lela sure can dance, can't she," Buddy said between bites.

"I don't understand her," Morgan said. "She heaped a big kiss on me right on the floor after the dance."

Buddy laughed. "Billy Carter lives over yonder in Squaw Creek," he said. "He tol' me him and his brother was sportin' with Lela las' summer up by the beaver pond."

"Sporting?" Morgan repeated. "I guess I don't know what you mean."

"You know," Buddy prompted. "Sportin'. Spoonin' with her."

Morgan shrugged his shoulders. "I wish my mother were alive," he said. "There's a whole lot about women I guess I need to know."

Ardyth assiduously kept her attention away from Morgan. "Is your sister mad at me?" he asked Buddy.

"I think you made her jealous dancin' with Lela," Buddy replied. "She don't want to admit it though."

"How did I make her jealous?" Morgan asked. "Lela dragged me out to dance."

Buddy handed Morgan a steaming glass of warm cider. "Try some of this," he said. "It ain't bad."

Morgan sipped the hot drink and sighed. He didn't feel inadequate often, but at the moment his confusion was overwhelming.

~ 10 ~

Winter gripped the Eagle River valley and held its clutches tight for six months. The sky remained slate gray for weeks at a time. The temperature dropped below zero at night and rarely rose above twenty during the day. Snow dumped on the area two or three times a week, some storms accumulating two feet or more.

Morgan rose every morning to a chilly bunkhouse. After breakfast he fed the pigs and chickens, mucked the stalls and brought water and grain to the horses. He milked the dairy cows and loaded the overflowing jugs on a wagon for delivery to the Denver and Rio Grande train platform in Edwards where the product eventually was sold in Denver.

In the afternoons, he rode toward the lower pasture and swept fresh snow from the piles of feed that the longhorns munched on throughout the winter. He became adept at estimating the size of the herd to determine if rustlers or predators had visited the cattle over night.

The intense work built hard muscles on Morgan's frame, which grew two inches during the winter. Mrs. Calhoun's excellent cooking and heaping portions supplied the necessary fuel to power his growing body.

In early April a final storm blanketed the valley with two feet of wet snow, but the next day a cloudless, blue sky shown brightly and temperatures soared into the fifties. The ground softened, ice seemed to disappear from the creeks and river, and within days green grass was visible poking from clear spots in the meadows. Colorful wildflowers dared emerge from their slumber, and Morgan's customary cheerfulness returned.

"I found a dead steer today," he reported to Con Calhoun at dinner. "It was at the far end of the pasture."

"Any idea what happened?" Calhoun asked.

"It looks like a bear," Morgan said. "I noticed tracks in the wet ground near the carcass."

"Seems early for a bear to be about," Calhoun said. "You sure?"

Morgan nodded.

"If we lose another head, we may have to go huntin'," Calhoun said. "Them bears usually stick to the berries an' such. But if they git a taste of the cattle, they may keep killin'."

"I'll keep a sharp eye out," Morgan promised.

"I know you will," Calhoun said. "You're the best hand we've ever had on the spread, even if you're the youngest by near ten years."

Morgan lowered his head, uncertain how to respond.

Ardyth glared at Morgan and remained silent. She had hardly spoken a word to him since the dance.

"Mr. Calhoun," Morgan began. "When I took the milk to town yesterday, a man approached me and asked if I could fish. I said I knew something about fishing."

"I suspect you do," Calhoun said. "You seem to know a great deal about many things."

"Well, he said the miners up in Leadville would pay fifty cents a pound for fresh trout. I was wondering, with the days getting longer, if I could catch some fish and sell them after I finish my chores for the day."

"How you goin' to git these fish to Leadville? That's a fer piece up the valley. Near 'bouts thirty miles."

"This man said he would buy the trout from me there in Edwards and deliver them himself."

Mrs. Calhoun wiped the corners of her mouth with her napkin and spoke. "I think that's a splendid idea," she said. Turning to Con she continued. "Let the boy make some extra money. He works plenty hard fer the thirty dollars we pay him. He deserves more if you ask me."

Con knew when he was defeated. He turned to Morgan and tapped him fondly on the forearm. "Jus' so your chores are finished," he said. "No slackin' off with your duties."

"No, sir," Morgan assured Con Calhoun. "I know the farm comes first.

Morgan ordered fifty fish hooks from Sven Stephenson at the general store in Edwards. They arrived from the Eagle Claw factory in Denver the following week. Using readily available barnyard hackles, he fashioned colorful fishing flies with lengths of string and waded Lake Creek and the Eagle River late afternoons after his work was complete at the farm.

Fishing was excellent. The rainbow and brown trout were ravenous after the long winter and Morgan was able to catch at least fifty pounds of fish every evening. The twenty-five dollars was almost his month's salary, and Morgan fished five days a week as the days grew longer and the weather more mild.

*   *   *

"I think we have bear trouble," Morgan told Con Calhoun one afternoon in mid-June as he was completing his chores. "I found another mauled steer."

"Did you see the tracks?" Calhoun asked.

Morgan pursed his lips and nodded. "There was clear sign."

"You ever hunt a bear?"

"I saw several when my mother and I rode here from Arizona, but I never hunted one."

"You know the difference between a black bear and a grizzly?" Con asked.

"I know the difference," Morgan said. "I've never actually seen a grizzly, though."

"Let's hope it's a black," Calhoun said soberly. "Them grizzlies can be plumb mean critters. Hard to take down."

"When do you want to go after this bear?" Morgan asked.

"First thing in the morning. I don't want to lose no more stock to this animal."

"I'll be saddled at first light," Morgan said.

Con Calhoun looked at Morgan before speaking. He had come to regard the young man as almost a second son. Lying in bed at night the farmer's thoughts occasionally flickered to the possibility of Ardyth and Morgan married and working the land together with Buddy. His daughter's apparent disdain of Morgan was bewildering, but perhaps it was simply a symptom of her youth. Was she not attracted to the young man's good looks and diligence?

"Buddy will stay here and work the farm," Calhoun said. "You and I will hunt this bear. But I want you to take extra care. I wouldn't want nothin' to happen to you."

Morgan hesitated before replying. This was the first instance Con Calhoun had voiced paternal concern. His cautionary timbre was strangely disturbing.

"I'll be careful," Morgan said suppressing his anxiety.

That evening he sat for an hour after dinner and cleaned and oiled his Colt and Winchester.

*   *   *

In the morning Morgan and Con Calhoun spurred their horses into a gentle trot and headed for the herd. Patchy ground fog hovered in the shallow depressions of the meadow. The sun shone brightly with the assurance of another splendid day in the mountains, but the night's chill remained in the air.

The two rode in silence, content with the hearty breakfast inside their stomachs and warm in their heavy coats and scarves wrapped around their throats.

Morgan loosened his reins and allowed Buck to pick his own way through the scattered cows when they reached the herd. The buckskin appeared to enjoy veering toward a munching cow and forcing it to startle and skip out of his path. At the far perimeter of the herd, Morgan reined his animal and dismounted. The mutilated carcass of a steer lay in the trampled dirt.

Con Calhoun stopped and swung from his saddle. He studied the area around the fallen cow before dropping to one knee and pointing to the ground. "That there is one big bear," he said with a gentle whistle. "The print's as big as I've seen in these parts."

"He looks like he's headed up there," Morgan said as he walked carefully along the paw path.

53

"This bear likely lives up yonder in the forest," Calhoun said. "Once he got a taste of that first steer back a while, he decided he wanted nothin' more of berries. We'll be hunting him in his own forest, will be my guess."

Morgan nodded and returned to the buckskin. He placed his hand on the butt of the Winchester and pulled it from the saddle boot. With polished ease he jacked a round into the chamber and checked the safety. "How do you want to proceed?"

Con Calhoun stared at the forest and pointed to the mountains rising to the south. "You ride the edge of this here meadow up toward the ridge yonder," he said. "Look for sign that the bear has come out of the trees. I'll head into the forest a piece an' see if I can pick up his trail."

Morgan paused. "Shouldn't we stay together? Wouldn't it be safer?"

Calhoun shook his head immediately. "If that bear is in them trees, he could jump at any time. I don't want you gettin' hurt."

"But if the bear is in the forest, and I'm in the meadow, I can't help you," Morgan protested.

"Likely I'll drive him out of the trees up yonder and you'll get a clear shot," Calhoun responded. "You jus' keep yourself alert, son."

Morgan tarried before swinging into the saddle. "Are you certain we shouldn't stay together?"

"Be safe, boy," Calhoun said as he motioned for Morgan to mount the buckskin.

~ 11 ~

Trepidation filled Morgan as he slowly picked his way along the edge of the meadow, climbing steadily south toward the mountains beyond. He nosed Buck into the thick pine forest several times and pulled the horse to a stop. Tilting his head into the wind, Morgan strained for sounds of Con Calhoun working his way through the trees. The loud creaking of leaning lodgepoles rubbing against other pines high overhead masked all other noises.

Morgan exited the forest and swung the buckskin back toward the north at an easy lope. He feared he had moved too far ahead of Calhoun and would not be in position to render assistance if the man were to encounter the bear. Reentering the pines, Morgan vectored through the edge of the forest at a fast walk, peering deep into the darkness with increased anxiety. Progress was slow in the heavily wooded area. Morgan now feared he was too far behind. He dropped the right rein across the right side of Buck's neck and steered the horse back toward the meadow.

Clear of the tall trees, Morgan squeezed his knees and the buckskin broke into a trot. At the sound of the frenzied whinny from Con Calhoun's horse, Morgan buried his spurs into Buck's flanks and sprinted ahead to the edge of the forest. A gunshot split the thin mountain air. Morgan leapt from the saddle before his horse had slid to a halt, drew the Winchester from its boot, and ran into the forest toward the sound of the fired weapon.

Low lying bushes pulled at Morgan's pumping arms as he dashed toward the sounds of a furious struggle. A deep growl rolled through the pine trees. The heavy beat of panicked hooves grew louder. Suddenly Con Calhoun's horse burst into view and Morgan was forced to leap from the path of the horrified animal as it sprinted through the forest, white foam flying from its bared teeth.

"Shoot," Morgan yelled as he regained his footing and continued running in the direction of the thrashing and grunting ahead. "Why aren't you shooting?"

The sharp scent of copper filtered through the pines. Morgan immediately knew the smell of fresh blood. He slowed and fought to control his panting. The forest was momentarily silent except for the sound of Morgan's labored breathing. But Morgan knew the bear was close. Why wasn't Calhoun working his gun? Why had he only fired once?

A small clearing opened. Morgan skidded to a stop and saw the answers to his questions. Con Calhoun lay twisted on the ground, his head barely attached to his shoulders. A huge pool of blood surrounded the mangled remains. Deep slashes split the bare chest. Calhoun's sidearm rested beside his outstretched hand.

An unearthly roar snapped Morgan's attention from the grotesque carnage at his feet. He looked up to nearly twice his own height into the bloody jowls of an upright grizzly.

The bear shifted his weight from hind leg to hind leg and rolled his furry arms in front of his massive chest. Two long, curved fangs framed an upper jaw of sharp teeth. Red tinted saliva drooled from a hairy lower jowl.

Morgan's breath caught in his chest. His heart raced like a jackhammer, thumping wildly, audibly, beneath his breast. Panic threatened to overwhelm him. Certain death stood, towering over him, mere feet away.

Morgan knew panic would kill him. He fought to remain rational. He willed his body not to run, for escape by foot from a bear was impossible. Attempting to climb a tree was suicide. He drew himself to his full height, shouldered the Winchester quickly but deliberately, and sighted the bear's throat. The temptation to rapid fire was enormous. But a wounded animal, enraged by pain and confused by gunfire, would be vastly more dangerous. His only hope for salvation was composure and deliberate, yet unhurried, aim.

Morgan squeezed the trigger. The heavy slug bored unerringly upward through the grizzly's windpipe and shattered against the lower stem of the brain. All cerebral activity ceased. The bear stood, seemingly bewildered. Gravity lowered its arms. Morgan worked the lever of the Winchester without taking his eyes from the animal and pumped another round into the chamber. He sighted and fired again. The second bullet entered the bear's right eye socket and exited through the top of the skull.

The grizzly turned in slow motion and appeared poised to step forward. The heavy rear paw was unable to lift from the ground. The bear closed his jaws. A strangely quizzical expression wrinkled its face as the creature toppled forward with a loud crash. Dust and loose leaves jumped from the matted dirt of the forest floor and then settled silently beside the inert carcass.

*   *   *

Morgan wrapped Con Calhoun's mauled body carefully in a blanket and secured it tenderly across the saddle of his horse. Death had been instantaneous. The bear had raked an enormous claw across Calhoun's neck, lacerating the skin to the windpipe. Gnarled tissue and strands of sinuous muscle alone held Con's head to his body.

Morgan inspected Con Calhoun's pistol. Rust surrounded the cylinder and clung to the hammer. A second shot was impossible because the weapon's cylinder was unable to revolve. Marshal Longstreet's advice to scrupulously maintain his firearms was brought back with chilling impact.

He found Calhoun's horse nonchalantly grazing in the tall grasses on the edge of the forest. The animal had put the encounter with the bear completely out of mind. Morgan was unable to do the same. Sadness pervaded his soul. Con Calhoun had been a kind and fair employer. His attitude toward Morgan had always been friendly and open. Following Morgan's intervention with the mountain lion, Calhoun's manner had warmed significantly. More recently, the man had treated Morgan in an almost paternal fashion.

Sadness was not the entirety of Morgan's feelings, however. He felt an acute sense of failure and shame. He had failed to protect his foster mother, and a murderous sheepherder had killed her. Now he had failed to prevent Con Calhoun's gruesome death at the claws of a grizzly bear.

What good was he if he couldn't help the most important people in his life? Why did the few people who cared for him have to die? The world seemed suddenly unfair and cruel. How was he to tell Buddy that his father was dead and the blame was his? What words could he possibly use to explain to Mrs. Calhoun that he had failed to defend her husband and that she was now a widow?

Morgan mounted the buckskin and headed north toward the farm with the reins of Con Calhoun's horse in hand. The lashed roll that was Calhoun's body bounced gently with the animal's gait, a sickening reminder of Morgan's inadequacy and failure.

~ 12 ~

The depressing pall of gloom hung over the Calhoun household for several weeks. Mrs. Calhoun had assured Morgan repeatedly the death of her husband was not his fault. "You're just a boy," she said sympathetically. "You were just fifteen last week. What could you have done? We live in a cruel land and terrible things happen to good people. You can't blame yourself."

Morgan was not assuaged. He was unable to forgive himself. He would not allow his age to be an excuse.

Buddy was distraught. He loved and respected his father. But in a strange way he seemed to welcome the opportunity to accept the role of household leader. Any residual feelings of the jealousy toward Morgan he had initially harbored immediately disappeared as Buddy quickly came to understand he was now titular head of the family.

Ardyth continued to limit her interaction with Morgan to snide put-downs or outright displays of dislike. She hinted at times that Morgan's inadequacies were solely responsible for her father's demise.

Morgan wasted little time dwelling on the girl's puzzling behavior. His state of confusion about young women was already overwhelming. Further deliberation about Ardyth Calhoun's attitude would only produce more questions than answers.

The splendid weather of July arrived in the valley, and Buddy hired Jesse Brett from the neighboring ranch to help move the cattle into the high country for grazing. Jesse's family owned the ranch immediately to the west of the Calhoun farm. In their main house resided the first telephone in Edwards. The absolute marvel of the instrument was a source of wonder to all who witnessed it in use. The utility of the device was another matter; there was nobody within fifty miles to call.

Buddy, Jesse and Morgan drove the herd south into the mountains for three days until the lush grasslands of the higher elevations were reached. Diminutive streams trickled from the melting snow in every dale, plenty of water to keep the cattle slaked as they fattened on the rich growth of the meadows.

With the cattle settled for the summer, the three boys returned to the Calhoun farm. Morgan planned to continue fishing commercially for trout. He had amassed more than two thousand dollars selling his catch in Edwards. He had no plans for the money, but his limited experience in the world had taught him life was far more satisfying for those who had money than for the impecunious.

*   *   *

Late in August a stranger halted his horse at the Calhoun house and called to Ardyth sitting in the rocker on the porch.

"We're lookin' for a hand to help with a problem we got up the flat top way," the man said as he drooled a long spittle of tobacco juice to the ground. "You got anybody on this here farm ain't feared of some hard ridin'?"

Ardyth Calhoun suppressed her disgust at the sight and manners of the ruffian seated in his saddle outside the hitching post. She opened her mouth to explain that they only had one employee and that since the death of her father he and her brother had struggled to keep up with the chores. But then an idea dawned.

That confounded Morgan Early! Why did he have to be so handsome? Why did he have to be so good at everything he attempted? He had saved her brother's life. He had killed a grizzly bear, which was a feat the entire valley acknowledged was unprecedented. He rode effortlessly and shot unerringly. He was able to look at a trout stream, discern where the fish lived, and cast within inches of the spot.

Ardyth had fought her initial attraction unsuccessfully. Within a week of Morgan's arrival she secretly acknowledged she might be in love with the youngster. But she pondered how to initiate a romance. It would be unseemly to throw herself at a man, especially when he was two years younger! So she held herself aloof, not daring to show her feelings, afraid to allow Morgan the advantage of knowing she cared.

Then there was the night of the dance! Ardyth would manage to maneuver Morgan to the dance floor. He didn't know how to dance! The situation was perfect. She was a good dancer, and she would be in control. But then that brazen hussy Lela Richards had dragged Morgan to the floor and practically seduced him! Ardyth knew what the fat girl was offering, and it wasn't just dance lessons. There were rumors Lela had allowed a few of the boys in school to remove her knickers and see her privates. How could Ardyth compete with that?

Her fascination with Morgan had evolved into anger with her inability to find a way to interest him without looking desperate or foolish. Her thoughts often turned to seeking ways to castigate him for his good looks and for her failure to find a way to begin a relationship. Now perhaps an opportunity had arrived to punish Morgan by sending him off on a dangerous mission.

Ardyth stepped closer to the porch railing and looked at the scruffy man. He sat his horse nonchalantly, one knee wrapped around the saddle horn, both feet on the same side. A menacing pistol hung low on his right hip, the holster tied to his leg with leather thongs. His clothes were worn and dusty and his shirt was stained dark under the arms. "We have a hand we might lease out to you," Ardyth said casually.

The man puckered and fired another glob of tobacco juice at the ground. "He any good?"

"He killed a grizzly," Ardyth said, slightly annoyed at the pride that inadvertently crept into her voice.

"Yeah?" the man said, unimpressed. "Pretty far south for a grizzly to roam, ain't it? How long a shot?"

Ardyth straightened her back and snickered. "'Bout five feet," she said. "Close enough to feel his breath."

The man looked skeptically at Ardyth. "Sounds like a tall one to me."

"Men from the town set out and found the bear next day," Ardyth said firmly. "They said it was a grizzly all right. And the shootin' happened like I said."

The man lifted his eyebrows. "How old's this hero of yours? This ain't no work for some old timer."

"He was fifteen last month," she said.

"Ha," the man laughed. "A damn boy."

Ardyth's true feelings for Morgan welled to the front. Her plan to send him off on a dangerous mission to chastise him for his inattention abruptly morphed into a desire to have this saddle tramp understand that the focus of her affections really was a wonderful and resourceful cowboy.

"He's the best hand you'll ever ride with," she said simply. "Never you mind about his age."

"Well, I might be able to use him for a week if he's as good as you say," the man concluded. "I'll pay you twenty dollars if you'll turn him loose."

"That's cash," Ardyth said firmly. "We don't offer credit to strangers in these parts."

The man nodded. "Cash," he said. "You tell him to meet me at the Eagle tomorrow evening. Me and the other boys are camped where the Squaw Creek comes into the river."

"I'll tell him," Ardyth agreed. "Who should he ask for?"

"My name's Jethro Pardon. If your boy shows up and does good, I'll send him back with the cash."

*   *   *

Morgan rode the buckskin slowly west along the dirt road paralleling the Eagle River. His eyes scanned the water, imagining likely hiding places for trout, but his mind was back at the Calhoun farm. Why had Ardyth insisted he join a group of strangers to perform dangerous work? She mentioned he would receive twenty dollars for his efforts, but the money was to be handed over to Mrs. Calhoun. Was the Calhoun farm so desperate for cash that they needed to rent him out like a mule? Twenty dollars was significant; it would pay for three weeks of his labor. Hard cash was not a common commodity in the West, but he had never noticed a circumstance where the Calhoun family was unable to pay for things they required.

After an hour's ride down the river, Morgan nudged his mount into the hills to the south and moved to higher ground. He dismounted in a grassy swale and secured Buck to a small aspen. He proceeded on foot to the crest of a sharp rise and settled on his stomach. Below, where Squaw Creek tumbled into the Eagle, a fire licked the air from a pit of rocks.

Morgan extended the copper-plated spyglass Con Calhoun had given him and trained it on the camp. Three men sprawled around the warmth drinking coffee from tin cups. A fat chicken hung above the fire from a skewer suspended between the crotches of two "Y" shaped sticks.

Morgan studied the men. All carried tied-down side arms. Rifles rested against near-by trees. Three able horses were tethered to a rope stretched across the gap between a pair of tall aspens.

All three wore mustaches; Morgan had yet to require a shave. Their clothes were worn and smooth but serviceable. The saddles were well used but in excellent condition. These men were not saddle tramps; they were well fed, mature and experienced.

Returning to the farm never entered Morgan's mind. His employer had issued instructions and he saw his duty to carry out the assignment. Fear was not a factor. Morgan was certainly younger than these men, obviously less experienced, and possibly smaller. But he now stood almost six feet tall and weighed close to one hundred-seventy pounds. He had not met the man who physically intimidated him.

Curiosity crept over Morgan. The farm work was rewarding but increasingly dull. Riding, hunting and exploring new terrain excited him. The encounter with the mountain lion had occurred so quickly Morgan had not had time to become afraid. Would he have reacted the same way if he had time to think? The confrontation with the grizzly was spurred by his desperate desire to save Con Calhoun. But when facing the enormous beast, Morgan's response had remained calm and calculated.

Morgan closed the telescope, slid back down the rise, untied the buckskin, and swung into the leather. With a gentle squeeze, he pointed the horse toward the camp.

63

~ 13 ~

Morgan waited until a motorcar passed, the exhaust popping and spitting, before easing the buckskin across the dusty road. He ambled toward the campsite and halted twenty yards from the men.

"Hello the camp," he called. "I'm coming in. I'm looking for Jethro Pardon."

A man stood and waved Morgan toward the fire. "I'm Pardon. You the boy from the Calhoun farm?"

"Name's Early. Morgan Early. I understand you're in need of a hand for a while."

Pardon pointed to the three horses tethered beyond the camp. "Unsaddle your mount and hitch him over yonder," he said. "Then join us at the fire."

Morgan secured Buck and walked toward the seated men. He extended his hand to Jethro Pardon. "Pleasure to make your acquaintance."

"Likewise," Pardon replied. "That there's Tommy O'Shea an' the skinny one's Ike Sproul."

"Nice to meet you," Morgan said shaking hands around the circle.

"You're a might young, ain't ya?" O'Shea asked. "Your momma know you're goin' off with us?"

Morgan looked at O'Shea for several seconds before answering. "My mother's dead," he said simply. "Both of my mothers."

The men exchanged glances. Jethro Pardon coughed nervously and looked at Morgan. "You had much time in the saddle?"

"I can manage," Morgan responded. "What are we going to be doing up on the flat tops, rounding up cattle?"

"You ever been on them flat tops?" Ike Sproul asked.

"Just once," Morgan replied. "I was only there briefly and it was mostly dark."

"That there's a strange place to be roamin' around in the dark," Tommy O'Shea observed. "What was your business that took you there at night?"

Morgan looked at his boots and shook his head once. "It was a personal matter," he said at last. "I resolved the issue and departed soon after."

"Well," Jethro Pardon said with a small laugh, "we won't be roundin' up no cattle. It's sheep we're after this trip."

"Sheep?" Morgan repeated. "We're going to round up sheep?"

Pardon motioned for Morgan to sit. "We've been hired by a group of cattle men to clear the flat tops of sheep. These men want that land fer to graze their beef. They want those damn sheep herders and their woolly animals off that range."

"Who owns the land?" Morgan asked.

"Whoever is a settin' on it," Pardon said firmly. "It's government property by rights, but these men want to fatten their herds there. The sheep dippers have beat them to it, an' now they want to change that."

Morgan scratched the side of his head in confusion. This was the first time he had encountered a legal dispute, and he was unclear how his involvement would be beneficial. "So we're to go up there and tell the shepherds to vacate the land? Why should they listen to us?"

Tommy O'Shea stifled a laugh and reached for the fixing of a smoke in his shirt pocket. He deftly sprinkled tobacco from a drawstring pouch on a curled strip of paper, wet one edge, and rolled the cigarette closed with his fingers. He drew a stick from the fire and lit up.

"They'll listen," he said confidently.

"That there bird's 'bout done, ain't it?" Ike Sproul observed. "How 'bout we eat and git some shut-eye. Tomorrow's likely to be a long day."

Jethro Pardon lifted the chicken from the fire and began quartering it for the men with a large knife. "We may be dinin' on mutton tomorrow," he said with a smile. "There's likely to be plenty to go around."

*   *   *

Morgan Early slept fitfully. He was looking forward to the impending adventure on the flat tops, but he was uncertain about his participation. He assumed he was needed as an extra hand to assist with the herding of the sheep after the shepherds agreed to allow their stock to be removed from the mountain.

Why would the shepherds acquiesce to the removal of their flock? Were the cattlemen willing to pay the shepherds to vacate their established grazing grounds? Perhaps the owners of the sheep and the cattle interests had reached an agreement earlier. The details of the negotiations were certainly no concern to Morgan. He was merely a rented hand passed along by his employer.

Dawn broke and Morgan heard Pardon throw several new branches on the embers. A fresh pot of coffee was set on a stone near the burgeoning fire, and the men wandered to the river to relieve themselves before breakfast. Ike Sproul threw a rasher of bacon into a fry pan, and soon Morgan's stomach was growling with hunger from the pleasant smell.

"You stay near me," Jethro Pardon said as Morgan chewed on a fat slab of pork. "I'll tell you what to do."

Morgan nodded with his full mouth.

The fire was doused with the remains of the coffee. O'Shea kicked dirt over the coals. The men slung their saddles over the backs of their horses and mounted. A general feeling of excitement pervaded the air. The men seemed anxious to begin their day. Pardon led them off at a fast trot down the road toward the west.

Where the Eagle River met the Colorado, the men turned and rode north for three miles before heading up a logging road toward the flat tops. They climbed steadily for another hour and a half until the land leveled and the magnificent, verdant pastureland was

66

visible stretching endlessly to the west. A stream trickled from a small rise and flowed across the trail.

"We'll rest and water the horses here," Pardon instructed. "This afternoon, be ready for some hard ridin'."

Morgan extended his looking glass and scanned the horizon. "I can see two distinct flocks of sheep a couple of miles off," he reported to Jethro Pardon. "Care to have a look?"

Pardon took the telescope and panned across the grass. He studied the terrain carefully for several minutes before compressing the instrument and handing it back to Morgan. "We'll hit the flock to the south first," he said. "There's a ridge not but a half mile from the animals that should suit us fine."

Morgan looked at Pardon and wrinkled his forehead in question. "What does the ridge have to do with talking to the shepherds?"

"You'll see, boy," he replied. "Just keep within shoutin' distance of me when we're ridin'. I'll let you know where to push those critters."

Morgan walked back to the buckskin and jabbed his left boot into the stirrup. In an easy motion he swung into the saddle and pulled his hat tight on his head.

Ike Sproul spurred his mount and whacked his hat across the animal's flank. "Let's go, boys," he yelled. "This here's where the fun starts."

The three men dashed across the rolling meadow straight for the nearest flock of grazing sheep. Morgan gave Buck his head and within seconds he was racing beside the others at a full gallop.

Jethro Pardon waved to Ike Sproul and motioned for him to swing wide behind the sheep. Tommy O'Shea rode inside Sproul with Morgan forty yards farther to the left. Pardon completed the rank on the left flank. The sheep began to run as the riders swept closer in a disciplined formation.

The two shepherds, milling on the fringes of the flock, looked up in panic at the thundering riders. One drew a pistol from a sash wrapped around his waist and brought the weapon to a firing position. Ike Sproul snapped three shots from his revolver; the third managed to strike the hapless shepherd in the leg and caused him to drop to the ground.

The terrified sheep bolted from the closing riders. Bleats of frenzied panic mixed with the pounding of thousands of feet that resonated from the fleeing animals. Tommy O'Shea pulled his pistol and fired into the air, adding to the fright of the sheep.

Morgan looked ahead and quickly understood the meaning of the ridge. The sheep were to be driven over the cliff to their death. Discussion with the shepherds was never part of the plan. Pardon and his men were hired to kill every sheep on the flat top. How could he have been so naïve and not understand the true intentions of these men? He cursed his youth and lack of sophistication. He had been enlisted in the slaughter of countless innocent animals for the benefit of some nameless cattle owners who coveted the range.

Morgan urged Buck forward. The fleet horse quickly passed Pardon's mount and swung around the left flank of the racing flock. With another burst of speed the buckskin turned the front edge of the panicked sheep and steered them parallel to the looming ridge. Morgan continued racing between the sheep and the cliff, pushing the fleeing animals away from their doom.

Ike Sproul slowed his horse as the frantic flock turned inside and began to circle away from the precipice. Tommy O'Shea watched helplessly as two thousand sheep thundered past his bewildered mount.

"What do you think you're doin'?" Pardon screamed at Morgan when he reined beside Morgan's slowing buckskin.

"You were going to push those sheep over that abyss," Morgan yelled from his saddle. "Is that your way to negotiate the use of this land?"

Ike Sproul slid his horse to a stop beside Pardon. "Shoot the kid," he screamed. "What is he, some sheep herder himself?"

Jethro Pardon pointed to Morgan. "Yeah, that's the way we handle these stinking sheep in cattle country. They ain't nothin' but a bunch of hoofed locusts."

"I know that killing somebody's stock is wrong," Morgan growled. "I know that running innocent animals over a cliff is wrong."

"Boy, you got a lot to learn 'bout this here country," Pardon said. "We been paid to rim-rock these sheep an' we're gonna finish the job."

Morgan heeled Buck around so the three men were in front of him. He lowered his right hand and flipped the leather thong from the hammer of his Peacemaker. "You'll do no such thing with me alive."

Ike Sproul leaned back in his saddle and laughed. "You think you're man enough to put a stop to this?"

"Perhaps not," Morgan admitted. "But I'm man enough to try."

"You're gonna gun us all?" Tommy O'Shea said in amazement.

"I guess not," Morgan replied. "But I'll get a couple of you before you get me. Who wants to be first?"

Jethro Pardon turned to the other men. "Now hold on," he said. "Nobody wants it to come to..."

Sproul's hand lifted from his holster. He had drawn his pistol. He cocked the hammer of his revolver and took aim at Morgan across the pommel of his saddle. He never squeezed the trigger.

Morgan's hand blurred and his Colt discharged a single round into Sproul's forehead. The man's horse reared and the rider slid from the saddle, dead before striking the ground.

Without pause Morgan swung the weapon and trained it on Tommy O'Shea whose hand was reaching for his pistol.

"I wouldn't advise it," Morgan said.

O'Shea withdrew his hand slowly and placed it carefully on his thigh.

Morgan looked at Pardon and O'Shea. "Ease those gun belts from your waists with your left hands," he said. "Don't give me a reason to use this again."

Morgan pointed to O'Shea. "Sling those belts over Sproul's saddle horn. Then jack all the rifles clear and stuff them in his saddle boot. I'll leave the mount and the iron by the little stream where we watered the horses. My advice is to bury your friend and don't follow me too closely."

"How we gonna explain this to the men who hired us?" Pardon said. "They'll be mighty put out we didn't get the job done. Every sheepherder on the flat tops will be laying for us now. With just two of us, we can't run no sheep."

"It's a nasty business you signed up for, Pardon," Morgan said. "I'd ride away from it. Head up Montana way. Join an honest outfit."

69

Tommy O'Shea looked hard at Morgan. "I best not see you again," he said. "I'll kill you."

"That's what your partner Sproul had in mind," Morgan said with a shrug. "The notion didn't work out too well for him."

"Go on an' leave," Pardon said. "We'll put Ike in the ground. I ain't hankerin' to follow you. Maybe I'll do as you say an' look at Montana. I suspect it's healthier up that way without you around."

"Just remember," Morgan said as he pointed Buck back to the east, the reins to Ike Sproul's horse, laden with gun belts and rifles, in his hand. "Your friend brought the trouble on himself. I don't relish taking another man's life. But I'm not ready to cash in my own chips just yet either."

~ 14 ~

Morgan Early rode down from the flat tops and turned south at the Colorado River. He walked the buckskin along the bank until he located the camp where his foster mother had been murdered a year earlier. His grief had not abated. The easy joy he found in each day, the delight he felt experiencing life, was forever tempered by the loss of the widow O'Brien.

He searched for her grave and was surprised that he had difficulty locating it. The crudely constructed cross marking the burial position was gone. Animals had trampled the ground. A full winter of shifting snow followed by a spring of rain and sheeting water had obscured the site. Morgan's sadness amplified.

Why did violence and death seem to follow him? Was there something about his character that attracted aggression? Was Morgan responsible for the people he loved losing their lives? His mother had died fighting to bring him into the world. His foster mother had died making a journey she thought would bring them both a better life. Con Calhoun had died because he positioned Morgan in a safe place while he hunted a grizzly alone in the forest.

Morgan had taken the life of a man attempting to kill him in a fit of passion. He didn't regret his action. Killing in self-defense was one of the most widely accepted codes of the West. But why was Morgan thrust into those precarious positions? Couldn't there be a life without the necessity to shoot others in order to survive?

Morgan made a cold camp and chewed on some jerked beef as the sun inched below the mountains. Pardon and O'Shea had kept their word. They had busied themselves with the burial of Ike Sproul and did not appear eager to follow. Perhaps Tommy O'Shea would hunt Morgan at a future time, but the threat could not dictate Morgan's life. He wouldn't run from the territory.

Winter was approaching and Morgan pondered another six months in the mountains. The snow was something he could accept, but he didn't relish the biting mornings when the temperature sank toward zero. Perhaps he should leave for a warmer clime before the snows blocked the pass to Denver. How far must he travel before he escaped the bitter weather? Florida again popped into his thoughts. Could he ride Buck all the way? Did the train go there? He had a sizeable stash of money. Surely he could afford a ticket.

In the morning he would ride to Edwards and inquire at the station depot. He wasn't expected back to the farm for a week; half a day spent in town wouldn't be unreasonable.

What would he say to Ardyth? Why had she leased him out to a stranger so easily? Would she demand the promised twenty dollars? Morgan rested his head against his McClelland, wrapped the blanket around his shoulders, and pondered these and myriad other questions as he sought sleep beneath a full sky of bright stars.

*   *   *

Morgan rode Buck through Edwards along the rutted main street and reined his mount at the railroad station. The occasional motor coach puttered past among a smattering of horses and buggies. He waved to Mr. W.H. Wellington who was making one of his fourteen weekly trips by buckboard between Edwards and the railroad station, the only mule route in the United States. Morgan dismounted and stepped up to the platform. A sack of newspapers sat bundled on a bench. The front-page headline screamed in large, bold letters.

WAR RAGES IN EUROPE
CONFLICT NOW ONE YEAR OLD
GERMANS APPROACHING PARIS

Morgan studied the words and reflected on his geography lessons with the widow O'Brien. Europe was a relatively small place compared to the vastness of America. A concerted effort by the Germans might result in the capture of Paris within a short period of time. Could that lead to an invasion of the United States? How many ships would be necessary to bring an invasion force across the wide Atlantic? Morgan doubted the feasibility of such an occurrence, but so many things baffled him lately that he wouldn't have been surprised if the German army arrived on the shores of America before Christmas.

Shaking his head, Morgan approached the stationmaster's window. "Can you tell me if I can purchase a ticket to Florida on the train?"

The stationmaster looked at Morgan. "You thinkin' of leavin'?" he asked. "I hear tell they think the world of you at the Calhoun spread."

Morgan blinked and swallowed. Who could have been bragging about him? It certainly wouldn't be Ardyth. Mrs. Calhoun seemed to like him well enough, but she had never expressed her approval. Buddy was more like a younger brother in spite of being a year older than Morgan.

"I...I just had a notion that maybe the winters would be a little easier," Morgan said with a shrug.

"I can sell you a ticket to Denver," the stationmaster said. "From there you can take a train to Atlanta. After that, I'm sure there's trains to Jacksonville and Miami. I even hear you can take a train to Key West. You wouldn't never know it by the looks of this backwoods junction, but the country's all growed up. All you need is some money."

Morgan nodded. "Can I carry my horse? I expect I'll need him when I get to Florida if I find a job working cattle."

"That ain't no problem," the man replied. "Most of the trains carry a stock car or two. You jus' got to pay."

"Thanks," Morgan said as he stepped away from the window.

A cool northwest breeze brushed against Morgan's face, reminding him of the approach of winter. He shivered slightly recalling the mornings he traipsed to the outhouse with snow filling his boots. He recalled chipping at the ice in the water basin before he could brush his teeth. Was Florida really always warm? Did it never snow?

*   *   *

Morgan angled Buck toward one of his favorite spots on the Eagle River. His fishing gear was back in the bunkhouse, but he wanted a few moments to sit by the river and reflect before he returned to the Calhoun farm. He tethered the horse to a stout willow near the edge and sat in the shade of a broad overhanging branch. He removed his boots and socks and dangled his feet in a cool eddie. The murmur of the tumbling water was mesmerizing, and Morgan felt the tension from the past two days leaking from his body. He closed his eyes and allowed his mind to drift away from his nagging thoughts.

"Now ain't you the lazy one," Lela Richards laughed as she slid down the embankment and landed with a thump beside Morgan.

Morgan jumped with surprise at the sudden appearance of the large girl. "Why Lela," he managed. "What...what are you doing here?"

"I seen you ridin' down here from up the road," Lela said. "I jus' thought you might be needin' some company."

"I was just catching my thoughts before heading back to the farm," Morgan said.

Lela looked directly into Morgan's eyes and ran her tongue slowly over her lips. "What kinda thoughts you been havin'?" she asked in a slow, drawn-out voice. "You been thinkin' 'bout me any?"

Morgan felt his breath stick in his throat. His mouth dried and he swallowed once to summon moisture. "Not so much," he stammered. "I've been busy at the farm and then Ardyth sent me off to the flat tops."

"The flat tops?" Lela repeated. "Why there? That's sheep country. Cattle and sheep don't mix."

"I found that out," Morgan said. "I'm just sorry I had to ride all the way up there to learn the lesson."

Lela shook her head and laughed. "That Ardyth," she said. "She sure has a different way about her. If I was a little beauty like her, I wouldn't be sendin' you off on no fool's errand like that."

Morgan nodded. "Maybe she had her reasons..."

He never finished his sentence. Lela leaned over, touched his face with a soft hand, and placed her full lips on his. Her tongue gently parted his mouth and began to aggressively explore the inside.

Morgan felt heat rise from his groin and his head grow dizzy. A strange sensation swept over him and he wrapped an arm around Lela and lowered her tenderly to her back. He returned her kiss and probed her mouth tentatively with the tip of his tongue.

Lela's busy fingers unbuttoned her blouse and removed Morgan's shirt. Her ample brassiere fell away and Morgan stared in fascination at her swelling breasts and erect nipples before lowering his head and covering them with kisses.

"Help me with these knickers," Lela panted as she squirmed and pulled at her last remaining garments.

Morgan tugged his pants past his ankles before relieving Lela of her clothes. He gazed at the large girl lying completely exposed beneath him. He rubbed his hand experimentally down her rotund stomach and between her legs, increasingly self-conscious of his growing tumescence.

Lela reached for Morgan and guided him lovingly into her. "I can tell you ain't had no experience with sportin' before. Let Lela show you what you been a-missin'."

Morgan could only mutter his consent as his breath tightened and every fiber in his body began to tingle with surging waves of passion.

~ 15 ~

"Where have you been, child?" Mrs. Calhoun cried when Morgan rode up to the house and dismounted. "I've been worried to death. You've been gone three whole days." She nervously scrubbed her hands in her apron.

Morgan hitched Buck to the railing and looked a question at the frantic woman. "Didn't Ardyth tell you?" he stammered. "She sent me off with some men to the flat tops."

"She did what?" Mrs. Calhoun screamed. "She had you rim-rocking sheep for those scallywag cattle ranchers down valley?"

"They started to run the first flock over a ledge, but when I understood what they were doing, I turned the sheep away."

"They let you save the flock?" Mrs. Calhoun asked incredulously.

Morgan shuffled his boots in the dirt and looked down. "They weren't happy with my interference," he said after a pause. "But I think we agreed there would be no more attempts to kill sheep."

"I...I'm not sure I completely understand what happened up there," she said. "Are you telling me you convinced the men to stop that disgusting rim-rocking?"

"Yes, Mrs. Calhoun."

"Was anybody hurt?"

"A man lost his life," Morgan admitted. "But there's nothing for the law to examine."

"Mercy sakes. I'm sure glad you wasn't hurt. What's with that daughter of mine sendin' out a boy such as yourself with some rough men like those."

"I'm sure Ardyth didn't mean any harm."

Mrs. Calhoun wiped her palms and smoothed the apron. "Are you hungry?" she asked with a sigh. "I don't expect the vittles were the best while you were ridin' around them flat tops and back."

"I could use a hot meal," Morgan agreed. "I'd like to wipe my horse down and get him fed. Then I'd like to wash up first."

"Go on ahead. I'll send Ardyth out to the bunkhouse in a while with some supper. After I give her a piece of my mind fer sendin' you off on some fool errand, that is."

Morgan untied the buckskin, loosened the cinch, and led the horse toward the barn and a good helping of feed.

*   *   *

"Morgan?" Ardyth called gently at the door to the bunkhouse. "You in there?"

"Come in," Morgan replied.

"You ain't mad at me, are ya?" Ardyth asked in a meek voice as she pushed through the door holding a heaping tray of food covered with a large red and white checkered cloth.

"You can set my dinner on the little table," Morgan said gesturing to the rough-hewn piece of furniture.

"You are mad, ain't you?"

Morgan peeled the cloth from the tray and inhaled the pleasing aroma drifting upward from the steaming platter of beef, potatoes and carrots.

Ardyth placed her hands gently on Morgan's arms and turned him to look into his eyes. "You can't be mad at me," she said. "I just won't allow you to be mad at me. That's final."

Morgan licked his lips in thought and pulled away to sit at the wooden bench. He lifted a fork and carefully pronged a piece of beef toward his mouth. "I'm not so much mad," he said before taking a bite. "I'm confused."

Ardyth sat opposite Morgan and placed her elbows on the table. Her hands cupped her chin and she smiled. "You men," she said with a firm shake of her head. "You're just so ignorant about women. You think you know everything, but you're such children when it comes to the important things in life."

Morgan chewed silently in thought and then reached for a potato.

"Can't you tell how I feel about you?" Ardyth asked in a plaintive voice. "Does everything have to be spelled out for you men all the time?"

"From the day I arrived, you acted as if I were lower than dirt," Morgan said. "I guess I understand how you feel about me."

Ardyth slapped her hands on the table in disgust. "That's what I'm talkin' 'bout," she said. "Right there. You don't have any idea about women."

"I'd have to agree," Morgan said. "And if I thought I was close to understanding, you certainly have been able to prove me wrong."

Ardyth stood and walked quickly toward the cabin door. She slid the wooden latch across the sill into the metal receiver, locking the door. She slowly returned to Morgan's side of the table and stood beside him. Her hands fell to his neck and she began to knead his shoulders provocatively.

"You men," she repeated in a husky voice with a brief chuckle. "You'll have time to eat later."

Morgan looked furtively at the door to the bunkhouse. "Are you sure it's safe? Your mother or Buddy..."

"Don't you worry about them," Ardyth whispered in Morgan's ear. "Stand up so I can get you shed of those breeches."

Morgan stood and began to unbutton Ardyth's dress. Within moments they were both naked and falling on the blankets covering Morgan's cot.

*   *   *

Ardyth nestled her head in the warm crook of Morgan's shoulder. Her free arm rubbed his hard pectorals and then dropped down to traverse his rippled abdomen. Her fingers tickled between his legs.

"For such a youngster who doesn't know nothin' 'bout women," she said with a broad smile, "you certainly were pleasin' on your first try."

Morgan kissed Ardyth warmly on the lips and remained silent. His mind whirled with the events of the last forty-eight hours. He had been temporarily banished from his job on the farm for no reason he could decipher. Then two women sexually devoured him in the same day. Lela was not entirely a surprise as she had strongly hinted at the possibilities on the dance floor. Ardyth's behavior had been a total shock. She was right; his level of understanding of women bordered on non-existent.

Morgan would have guessed Ardyth disliked him at best and abhorred him at worst. Instead, she professed her love and claimed she felt that way from the day he arrived on the Calhoun property. It was a very confusing situation for a boy only recently fifteen years old.

"I better get back to the house," Ardyth giggled in Morgan's ear. "I'll tell mother I was apologizing for sending you up to the flat tops. I never thought that dirty cowboy was a rim-rocker."

Morgan swung his legs from the cot and reached for his shirt. "I'll finish my supper," he said. "I guess I've worked up an appetite by now."

Ardyth dressed hurriedly, kissed Morgan and walked for the door. "You sleep tight," she said. "I believe in the comin' days you're goin' to need all your energy."

Morgan nodded. "I realize with just Buddy and me to work the farm, there'll be plenty to do."

Ardyth laughed and shook her head as she unlocked the door. "Men," she chuckled again. "Men!"

~ 16 ~

The days gradually grew shorter and a chill pervaded the morning air. The aspen leaves turned a golden yellow and whispered the coming of winter as they shimmered in the afternoon breeze.

Morgan fished most evenings after completing his chores at the farm. His pile of money grew rapidly and he wondered about the prudence of keeping such riches in cash. There was no bank in Edwards, and he considered asking for a day off to take a train to Denver and deposit his earnings in a bank.

Buddy and Morgan successfully drove the cattle down from the high pastures at the end of the Lake Creek valley. The animals had put on substantial weight over the summer feeding on the rich grasses, and Mrs. Calhoun contemplated selling part of the herd to the army that was gearing up to send troops to France to fight the Germans.

Most evenings, following dinner in the main house with her mother, Morgan and Buddy, Ardyth excused herself to retire to her room. From there she exited her window and dashed to Morgan's arms in the bunkhouse, showering him with hugs and kisses as she entered.

The first night in October, venom replaced her recently acquired sweetness. "You dallied with that fat cow Lela, didn't you," she screamed as she slammed the door shut and marched toward a bewildered Morgan.

Morgan opened his mouth, but Ardyth pointed a warning finger. "I don't want to hear no lies from that mouth," she growled. "Did you and Lela do some sportin' by the river?"

"I...we...it wasn't like that at all," Morgan attempted. "I never..."

"Lela told me herself," Ardyth yelled. "I saw her in town today and she said how happy I looked. I told her 'thank you' and she said it was about time I took my knickers off for you."

"Lela said that?" Morgan stammered. "How would she...?"

"She said she could see it in my eyes that we was sportin'. She said she can always tell."

"I don't know how..."

"Then she said it was lucky for me I made up my mind because you and her had done it by the river and that she was the first time you had ever done it and that by rights you and her should be doin' it now," Ardyth spewed breathlessly.

Morgan stood motionless. His mind spun with the implications of Ardyth's words. "But she followed me to the river," Morgan began cautiously. "I didn't invite her..."

"So she ain't lyin'," Ardyth yelled. "You and her did do it."

"Just once," Morgan said holding his hands up defensively. "And we never did it again after that."

Ardyth dropped her head in her hands and burst into tears. "You... you bastard," she mumbled between her fingers. "How can I go on livin'? Lela will tell the whole town she and you was sportin'."

"But I don't understand why that matters to you," Morgan said softly. "There was only that one time and that was before I knew..."

"Men," Ardyth grumbled. "I just knew it. You've ruined my life. Here I am not yet eighteen years old and my life is over. I might as well die right now."

Morgan approached slowly and placed his hands on Ardyth's shoulders. "What can I do?" he asked in a plaintive voice. "I didn't mean to hurt anybody, especially you."

"You've got to leave," Ardyth said firmly, pulling her face from her palms. "Leave the farm tomorrow."

Morgan stepped back and looked wide-eyed at Ardyth. "You want me to leave?"

"Yes, it's the only way. I can't have people think I was sharin' a boy with that Lela. Who would ever marry me and raise a family?"

"You mean you want me to leave for good," Morgan said in disbelief. "You don't want me to work on the farm any more?"

A fresh wave of tears overwhelmed Ardyth. Her body racked with sobs. "Yes. You've got to go. Leave at the first light. The sooner you're gone maybe people will start to forget."

Morgan retreated to his bunk and flopped on the mattress in complete bewilderment. Ardyth's reversal of behavior toward him since the incident on the flat tops had come as a total surprise. He welcomed her advances for the physical thrill, but almost as compelling was his happiness at no longer being treated with barely disguised contempt. Mystifying was her incessant blathering about "we" and "us" in the future. Terrifying were her periodic references to their children.

Did he love Ardyth? Morgan wondered privately if he could properly define the word. He eagerly anticipated their trysts in the bunkhouse, but he didn't dwell on Ardyth in her absence. Could they even be described as friends? What did they share beyond the moist tussles on his bunk in the evenings? Shouldn't a couple be friends before they became physically involved? For the millionth time, Morgan longed for the warm comfort of the Widow O'Brien. How he pined for the lost opportunity to ask her about these perplexing mysteries in his life.

"I'll pack my things and be gone before breakfast," Morgan said. "You won't have to worry about me disgracing you again."

Ardyth walked toward Morgan and stood defiantly before him with her arms crossed. Suddenly her hand flashed and Morgan felt the sting of her palm on his cheek.

"You've ruined my life," she said as she sniffled back a fresh spate of tears.

Morgan dropped his head as Ardyth stomped to the door and walked into the night.

~ 17 ~

Morgan Early crested the steep rise and reined his buckskin. To the south a tall range of mountains appeared in the distance, covered at the summit with the vestige of a recent dusting of snow. The closest peak boasted a prominent white cross planted in the face of the rocky slope. Heavy snow clung in the cross-shaped fissures turning the natural feature into a surreal religious artifact.

Ahead a small stream gurgled from a spring in a wet, grassy depression and trickled toward the east. Morgan noted the direction of the flow and nodded with understanding. He had just crossed the Continental Divide.

A train labored toward him in the distance and two motorcars fought for proper combustion in the thin air as they struggled to attain the summit. Morgan patted his mount affectionately and nudged him forward. He had never ridden in an automobile. He had never taken a train ride. He could appreciate the utility of each mode of transportation. Speed and comfort and shelter from the elements were compelling, but Morgan was reluctant to distance himself from the tactile proximity of the land afforded him on horseback. Also, he acknowledged, he had no place to go and the rest of his life to get there. What was the hurry?

Three days later he trotted off the front range of the Rocky Mountains and approached Denver. Automobile traffic grew significantly heavier. The buildings of the city loomed toward the sky and once inside the perimeter they appeared to block much of the daylight. Noise assaulted Morgan's ears. Trolleys clanged down the middle of the thoroughfare; motor coaches whined and backfired as they jostled for position on the congested streets. Buck shied and raised on his rear legs at the most egregious noises.

*   *   *

Morgan had awakened before first light, saddled the buckskin, and walked his mount toward the house. Mrs. Calhoun was asleep and Ardyth conspicuously absent. Buddy was banging around in the kitchen as Morgan entered.

"Coffee?" he asked as he wrapped a heavy cloth in his hand and removed a smoking pot from the fire.

"I'm leaving," Morgan said simply. "It's been a real pleasure and privilege to work here on the farm."

Buddy turned and stared at Morgan in disbelief. His jaw opened but no words emitted.

"Ardyth told me I had to leave," Morgan said. "She wanted me gone from the farm this morning."

"Wait a minute," Buddy managed as he stood dumbfounded with the coffee pot in hand. "My sister doesn't own this farm herself. What's my mother have to say about you leavin'?"

Morgan held up a hand in self-defense. "I don't know what Ardyth said to your mother, but if she tells me to leave, I don't see what choice I have."

"We need you to help with the work," Buddy protested. "Besides, you've become almost like a brother."

"Your sister doesn't see it that way," Morgan said with a shrug. "You can always hire another cowboy."

"I'm goin' to wake mother. You can't leave without her knowin' it."

Morgan shook his head and held out a hand to stop Buddy. He didn't particularly want to leave the Calhoun farm. He had enjoyed the work and was appreciative of the opportunity. But the work had become stale and repetitive. The prospect of another brutal winter in the mountains was of no appeal. Ardyth's puzzling behavior, in spite of her tantalizing evening visits, had the capacity to become loathsome. Morgan thirsted for a new adventure in a warmer clime. He wanted to go to Florida and experience life there.

"I couldn't be comfortable here knowing Ardyth wants me off the property," Morgan said. "If I've done something to offend her, perhaps it's best I go."

"What could you have done? She barely recognizes you exist."

"Your sister may be more complicated than either of us understands."

"You're packed?"

"I'm packed," Morgan said with obvious sorrow in his voice. He extended his hand and opened his left arm.

Buddy and Morgan hugged. Tears misted the eyes of both young men.

*   *   *

Morgan halted a nervous Buck in front of the massive Cattleman's Bank in Denver. He wrapped the reins around a thick supporting column and left his mount standing between two dusty black motor coaches. He untied his saddlebags, slung them over his shoulder, and entered the august building. It was without question the largest structure Morgan had ever seen.

"May I help you, young man?" the cashier inquired behind a fence of steel bars.

"I'd like to leave some money with you," Morgan replied.

"Do you have an account with us?"

Morgan shook his head. "I've never even been to Denver before."

"Why don't you step over to that desk," the cashier said. "That's Mr. Fillmore, our vice president. He can assist you opening an account."

Morgan took the proffered seat in front of Mr. Fillmore's massive oak desk. Half an hour later he left the bank with documentation proving he was the bearer of an account worth five thousand, four hundred dollars. The funds could be transferred to any recognized bank in the United States by presentation of a letter above Morgan's signature with the proper account numbers and codes. Three hundred dollars remained in Morgan's pocket for the journey to Florida.

"Where will you stay in Denver?" Mr. Fillmore asked when they had concluded business.

Morgan shrugged. "I only just arrived an hour ago. What do you suggest?"

"Try the Brown Palace," Fillmore offered. "I think you'll find it acceptable."

Morgan thanked Fillmore and exited the bank. Buck was immensely relieved to see his master.

"I don't blame you, boy," Morgan said as he swung into the saddle. "I don't know if either of us are cut out for big city life. I think we'll prefer Florida."

At the entrance to the Brown Palace Hotel Morgan stepped from the saddle and looked up at the ornate building reaching to the sky. Polished marble columns flanked massive dark oak doors carved with ornate figures in relief.

A uniformed doorman dashed to Morgan's side. "Welcome, sir," he saluted. "We have a wonderful stable around the corner for your steed. Should I lead him there for a nice rubdown and full helping of oats?"

"He'll be well cared for?" Morgan asked as he removed his saddle bags and extra clothing rolled behind the saddle. "I want only the best for Buck. We've traveled far in the last few days."

"Never had a complaint yet," the doorman replied. "From the horses I mean," he added with a grin.

Morgan slapped his denim pants with his broad brimmed hat and watched as the dust flew into the air. He brushed his red cotton shirt until most of the grime of travel was removed. He looked sheepishly at the doorman taking the buckskin's reins.

"You'll find all the most modern conveniences in the hotel," he reported. "A bath tub you could swim in with all the hot water necessary."

Morgan looked a question at the doorman. He had never bathed inside before. The idea of an indoor facility had never entered his mind. Wisely he held his ignorance to himself and entered the lobby.

"Do you have a room for the night?" Morgan asked at the desk.

The clerk peered over the counter. "Will you be staying just one night?" he asked.

"I think so," Morgan replied. "I'm not sure how this city life will agree with me. I'm hoping to purchase a train ticket to Florida."

"Very well," the clerk said. "We have a nice room on the third floor with full bath. The cost will be ten dollars."

Morgan blinked at the price. Working at the farm would require more than a week's labor to earn that much money. Leaving the hotel would be embarrassing. He planned to stay only for the night. "I'll take it," he said.

"Do you have bags?"

"Only what's slung over my shoulder."

The clerk smiled. "Must be nice to travel so light. Most of our guests arrive with steamer trunks."

"If I knew what a steamer trunk was," Morgan said with a chuckle, "maybe I'd have one."

"The dining room and bar are over there in the Grand Salon," the clerk said as he handed Morgan his room key. "Enjoy your brief stay."

"I hope to," Morgan said. "Thanks."

~ 18 ~

Morgan entered the Grand Salon and looked around with undisguised awe. White onyx wainscoting covered the twelve-foot high walls. Huge Ionic columns sprouted in the corners. An immense central medallion was overlaid on the slatted wood ceiling. Lush purple carpeting spread across the floor and white clothed tables were lined row upon row, dining utensils and napkins arrayed in perfect order before each satin covered chair.

Across the far wall stretched a long bar. The top glistened in the electric lighting that gently washed from dim bulbs enshrouded with curved green lenses. Stout barstools covered with deep blue leather stood in a row against a polished foot rail. Shiny brass spittoons were interspersed among the legs of the stools. Morgan stood aghast at the richness of the room. The dingy, dusty, dirty towns of Edwards and Wilcox seemed a million miles away.

White coated waiters hustled around the room seating and serving male guests dressed in tailored suits with cravats neatly tied around their necks. Ladies wore colorful silk dresses cut low in the front to accentuate their swelling breasts.

Morgan wandered slowly toward the bar. He eased a leg around one of the vacant stools and sat, supremely conscious of his worn trail clothes.

"Where you from, cowboy?" the bartender asked as he wiped the area in front of Morgan with a damp cloth.

"Edwards," Morgan replied as he motioned around the room with a finger. "This certainly is a fancy place."

"I reckon there's none finer all the way to Chicago. What can I get you to drink?"

Morgan paused. He had never tasted liquor. Con Calhoun and some of the other men in Edwards occasionally made a home brew that they drank from jugs in the evenings, but Morgan had never been invited to join them.

"I understand you have cold drinks," Morgan said.

"I can draw you a cold beer. We have a chill machine in the basement. You might like it."

"I'll try one," Morgan said. "I've never had a hot bath before tonight and that was pretty agreeable."

The bartender pulled a long, wooden handle and filled a glass with foamy beer. "Just yell when you're ready for another."

Morgan took a tentative sip and licked the residue from his top lip. The temperature of the drink was refreshing. The taste was pleasing.

Sitting on the bar was a stack of papers. Morgan picked one from the pile and read it with interest.

WE NEED YOU GRINGO
The last adventure it's here!
Join the Mexican revolution.
Be proud to ride with Pancho Villa.
Enlistments taken in Juarez, Mexico
January 15, 1915
VIVA VILLA   VIVA LA REVOLUTION

Morgan motioned to the bartender. "Is this real?" he asked. "Is there really a revolution in Mexico?"

"Haven't you heard? It's real," The bartender replied. "I hear they pay pretty handsome, too."

Morgan sipped on his beer and read the bulletin again. The brew seeped into his bloodstream and his thoughts wandered to his foster mother's books about ancient heroes and dramatic battles during the War Between the States. He looked around the room and tried to imagine himself dressed as the Brown Palace patrons filling the Grand Salon dining area and lining the bar. He contemplated living in Denver and weaving through the tooting and sputtering motorcars astride Buck. He sniffed and recalled the noxious fumes spewing from the exhaust pipes of the automobiles.

Perhaps he would ride south to Mexico and see first-hand what a revolution was all about. The United States of America was formed after a revolution; perhaps Mexico was following a similar course in history. Florida wasn't going anywhere. He and Buck could always board a train and head east. Meanwhile...

The bartender approached and lifted Morgan's empty mug. Without asking he refilled it and set the chilled beer on the gleaming counter. "You have a woman with you?"

Morgan shook his head slowly. "No. A woman is the reason I'm here. She threw me off the farm."

"What did you do to raise her ire?"

Morgan smiled and raised his shoulders. "I guess I made her jealous," he replied. "I haven't had much luck understanding women in my life."

"If you're interested, there's a place where understanding isn't required."

Morgan wrinkled his forehead in confusion. "Now I don't understand you."

"You just wander two blocks to Market Street and look for Jennie Rogers' Hall of Mirrors. If you have a little money in your pocket you might find yourself an expert on women by morning. Ask for Squirrel Tooth Annie if she's available."

Morgan lifted his beer mug and pulled deeply on the contents. He had been thinking about Ardyth's bunkhouse visits the last two days as he huddled by a fire in the mountains. In spite of her crazy talking, they were undeniably pleasurable. Perhaps a dalliance in Denver would prove interesting.

The bartender pointed to the recruitment flyer. "If you're serious about joinin' up," he said, "Juarez ain't that hard to find. Just ride south along the mountains and keep the Castle Rock to your left. Go through the Springs an' on down to Albuquerque. From there you pick up the Rio Grande. It runs right into Juarez."

"I was thinking about Florida," Morgan said. "I've had enough of the cold weather for a while. But I don't believe it snows in old Mexico, and the revolution sounds like it could provide some excitement."

"Then you should go to Jennie's Hall of Mirrors before you push off. I don't believe old Mexico will provide the likes of her stable of women."

~ 19 ~

Late on the fourteenth afternoon after leaving Denver, Morgan slowed the buckskin at the bank of the Rio Grande. The horse reached a cautious hoof into the muddy river before hopping into the water. Across the narrow stretch of river a large collection of adobe huts stood shimmering in the baking rays of the slanting sunlight. Morgan reached down and scooped a handful of water, which he splashed on his face. He untied his kerchief and soaked it thoroughly before lashing it around his neck.

On the old Mexico side of the river Buck jumped on the shore and broke into a trot toward the town. He looked forward to having the saddle removed, a rubdown and a tall pile of oats.

The ride from Denver was without major incident. The terrain east of the Rockies was essentially flat. A hard-packed wagon trail wound south a mile from the slopes, and Morgan never encountered motorized traffic. The occasional buckboard jostled past but the lack of fuel precluded the use of automobiles.

Morgan was able to reflect on his decision to leave the city. His brief stay in Denver confirmed his preference for the outdoors. How could he earn a living in a city? He was well read and intelligent, but his lack of a formal education would certainly be a detriment if he applied for a job in a bank or a business establishment.

His night at Jennie Rogers' Hall of Mirrors had been a complete revelation. Morgan was pleasantly shocked at the inventiveness and energy displayed by the young girl Squirrel Tooth Annie. Ardyth had been a willing partner but lacked the imagination and raw vigor Morgan experienced in his upstairs room in the Hall. He shook his head for the hundredth time at the memory as he rode along and reflected on his continuing amazement at women and their behavior.

Morgan wondered if he would actually meet Pancho Villa when he arrived in Juarez. Was this man Mexico's George Washington? Morgan was unfamiliar with the history of Mexico. The Widow O'Brien did not possess any books devoted to the subject. It would be interesting to learn the factors that initiated Villa's uprising. Would Morgan have a heroic role in the formation of a new Mexican government? The thought was exciting to contemplate.

The barrel of a German Mauser rifle thrust around the corner of the closest adobe as Morgan approached the cluster of buildings that was Juarez. "*Alto,*" the droopy mustachioed Mexican growled.

Morgan reined Buck and held his hands clear of his waist, away from his Colt. "I'm looking for Pancho Villa," he said wondering if the man would understand his English.

"*Los Federales, tambien,*" the man laughed. So are the Federal troops. "*Que quiere?*" What do you want?

Morgan slowly reached with his left hand and withdrew the recruitment poster from his shirt pocket. "Is this where one joins the revolution?"

"So," the Mexican nodded. "Another gringo wants to become a Mexican hero."

Morgan shrugged. "I hear Pancho Villa pays well."

"Oh, yes," the man said with a bemused smirk. "We are all millionaires in the revolution."

"Where can I find Villa?"

"This way. But keep your hand from that gun. The general is suspicious of new recruits until they prove themselves."

The Mexican turned and walked toward a low-roofed building with hitching posts flanking the entrance. A dozen horses stood secured to the railing. The single word *CANTINA* was hand painted above the door in faded letters.

"Tie your horse. But don't make any fast moves," the Mexican warned.

Morgan entered the dim saloon and squinted to see in the reduced light. A cloud of cigar smoke hovered against the ceiling. The strange smell of tequila assaulted Morgan's nostrils. He stifled a cough and looked around the room. Men slouched in every available chair circling the several round tables. Bottles and glasses were scattered across the tops.

"That's far enough, gringo," a voice barked from a corner. "How do you call yourself?"

"Early. Morgan Early."

"What's your business in Juarez?"

"I came for the last adventure," Morgan said quoting the recruitment poster. "I want to see what this revolution is all about."

"So...you want to be a soldier in Pancho Villa's army."

"That's right."

"You're a might young, ain't ya?"

"I figured I was old enough."

"You know how to handle that hardware you're packin'?"

Morgan nodded once. "Are you Villa?"

A tall man emerged from the darkness. "I'm Captain Julio Cardenas, General Villa's bodyguard. These are some of *Los Dorados*, the golden ones."

Morgan took a step forward and extended his hand. "My pleasure, Captain."

"*Viva la revolution,* Early. Welcome to Mexico. Tomorrow we show you how to make war."

*   *   *

At dawn the fifty members of the elite cavalry unit *Los Dorados*, along with Morgan Early, galloped south from Juarez. The men were a rough collection of peasants, idealistic and opportunistic soldiers of fortune, enlisted men of defeated enemy units and four gringos generally reticent about their reasons for being in Mexico. A coterie of photographers and journalists accompanied the *villistas*.

The combatants were heavily armed with American made weapons, supplied by the United States, and wore bandoliers of rifle ammunition across their chests. All featured heavy mustaches in salute to their leader.

Slightly before noon Captain Cardenas raised his right hand signaling a halt. The soldiers reined their horses and dismounted beside a large tent erected in the shade of a stand of palm trees. The *villistas* assembled in front of the tent, the forward ranks kneeling in the sandy soil.

Francisco "Pancho" Villa, nicknamed *El Centauro del Norte*, stepped from the tent and scanned the faces of the assembled soldiers of his *Division del Norte*.

Morgan looked closely at the famous revolutionary. He was less than forty years of age with a round, unlined face. His mustache flared to the width of his full cheeks. He wore a hat with a wide, circular brim that was pushed back on his head. His pants and long sleeved, three-button coat were tan, and he wore a bow tie around his neck. Twin leather bandoliers of rifle bullets crisscrossed his chest. His dark eyes shone brightly beneath thin brows.

"Tomorrow we strike the railroad train on the Mexican North Western Railway," he said in a booming voice. "There will be *Federales* on the train guarding a shipment of guns and ammunition for the army of General Obregon, the lapdog of President Carranza."

The *villistas* cheered the news. It had been several weeks since they had seen action and the inactivity had been boring.

Pancho Villa smiled at the reaction. "*Si, amigos*," he said gleefully. "Tomorrow we kill *Federales* and further our glorious revolution."

With a long stick Villa drew railroad tracks in the sand. "Here is the track," he said. "Here is the station at Guzman. We will blockade the tracks at this position to halt the train. We will attack the train when it stops there. I want all *Los Dorados* on the north side of the tracks. We can't be shooting at ourselves. You hold your fire until given the signal to shoot. Nobody is to escape, but if a *Federale* wants to surrender, bring him to me. We can always use extra troops."

Captain Julio Cardenas stepped forward. "Feed and water your horses. We ride toward Guzman in one hour. Tonight we will camp outside of town and be ready at first light for the battle."

Morgan returned to his horse. A light-skinned man fell into step. "You're the new gringo?" the stranger asked with a smile.

"That's right," Morgan replied. "I just rode into Juarez yesterday."

95

"Have you fought before?"

Morgan pondered his response. "This is the first army I've been a part of," he said. "What about you? How long have you ridden with Villa?"

"About a month. We fought Obregon's soldiers at Celaya and got chewed up pretty good."

"Were you hurt?"

"I was lucky. I didn't get hit, but a couple of my friends were killed."

Morgan winced. "Were you scared?"

"Yes. But I was excited, too."

Morgan reached out his hand. "My name's Morgan."

"I'm Bill Winters. Maybe we can be buddies. It helps to have someone when the bullets start to fly."

Morgan nodded. "What brought you down to old Mexico? Did you see the recruitment poster talking about the adventure?"

"I saw it," Bill Winters said. "My parents were killed in an automobile wreck. They got stuck on a train track and got hit by the train."

"I'm sorry," Morgan said. "That must have been terrible."

Bill Winters sighed deeply at the memory. "The bank came and took the farm house. They wanted to send me off to some cousins in Philadelphia; so I just up and ran away down here. At least I get a peso a day. Villa promises to divide up the big haciendas after the war is won and give it to his soldiers."

Morgan whistled. "I was headed for warmer climate when I saw the poster in Denver. I guess my curiosity got the better of me."

"It looks like you'll be getting' your curiosity satisfied real soon," Winters said with a chuckle.

~ 20 ~

Morgan lay beside Bill Winters in a sandy ditch forty yards from the railroad tracks. He cradled his Winchester in the crook of his arms to keep it from the fine dust that pervaded the ground beneath him. Marshal Longstreet's long ago caution about keeping his weapon free of potentially jamming grit echoed in his ears. The sun beat through the back of his shirt and heat rose from the scalding desert into his chest. His mouth was dry and his lips felt cracked.

"This revolution sure is excitin', ain't it," Winters said with a small laugh.

Morgan nodded his agreement. "What time's the train due?"

Winters shrugged. "About an hour ago, but keep in mind we're in old Mexico. Nothin' happens here in a hurry."

A rotund Mexican scrambled along the gully on his hands and knees. His sombrero was pulled tight on his head, almost obscuring his face. His black mustache wobbled under the gigantic hat as he repeated his message to the men waiting in ambush. "*El tren esta llegando. El tren esta llegando.*" The train is arriving.

Morgan peered above the edge of the trench. Four Mexicans hauled heavy logs from a position down the swale and placed them across the tracks.

To the south a faint column of black smoke appeared on the horizon. Morgan cocked his ear to the gentle westerly breeze but was unable to hear the engine. He tipped his hat back and wiped perspiration from his forehead. His vision seemed blurry with the shimmering air hovering above the desert floor and the sweat in his eyes. Would he be able to shoot straight when the fighting commenced? He closed his eyes and blotted his face against his shirtsleeve. Had he made a monumental mistake coming to old Mexico? Would he live to see Florida one day? He rubbed his fingers against his palms. To his surprise they were dry. He felt the excitement build in his stomach as the train approached and the first sounds of the chugging of the engine reached his ears.

Morgan eased the leather strap from the hammer of his Colt. He slid the Peacemaker from his holster, flipped open the gate and twirled the cylinder. The weapon was "cowboy loaded" with five rounds; the hammer rested on an empty position to prevent accidental discharge if the revolver were dropped or bumped. Morgan slipped a .45 caliber shell from his gun belt and inserted it into the blank hole. He reasoned caution could suffer for the possible benefit of an additional round in the firefight.

"She's a comin'," Bill Winters said with obvious glee.

To his right Morgan studied the experienced Mexican soldiers. Their rifles rested in the dirt. Their bandoliers of ammunition slung across their shoulders were caked with grime. He hoped their carelessness didn't cost him his life.

"There's a lot of cars to that train," Winters said with a waiver of concern. "I hope them cars ain't full of *Federales*."

"They wouldn't be sending an ammunition train without guards," Morgan said flatly. He jacked a round into the Winchester and thumbed the safety to the off position. "I hope we have enough firepower to stop them."

The noise from the engine built quickly as the massive wheels of the train rolled relentlessly over the steel rails. Huge clouds of dark smoke belched from the tall, funnel-shaped smoke stack. The ground trembled with the rapid approach of the thundering machine. Morgan's eyes widened involuntarily as he stared at the awesome locomotive, its coal car immediately behind and twenty-five boxcars in tow.

Suddenly the churning wheels locked in position as the engineer spotted the stack of lumber blocking the tracks. Sparks flew from the hardened rails as the wheels slid, without rotating, along the metal surface. The whistle screamed from atop the engine. White steam cascaded from beneath the carriage of the engine as excess energy was bled from the boiler. The protruding "cow catcher" nose of the engine smashed into the blockade. Splintered wood exploded into the air and the locomotive jolted to a halt.

The train's whistle ceased screeching. A momentary wave of silence fell over the expanse of desert.

Suddenly the doors of the boxcars flew open and the reports of one hundred rifles filled the air. Mexican *Federales* leaped from the train behind the smoke of their initial volleys.

Morgan gasped in disbelief when the firing began. The individual shots came so frequently they sounded nearly constant. One of *Los Dorados* to his right slumped face first to the sand. Morgan reached out and rolled the man to his back. Bloody sand slid down the incline; a dribbling red hole appeared in the center of the man's forehead.

"Any ideas?" Bill Winters shouted over the dim of combat. He lay on his side with his head below the level of the trench.

"Why aren't we returning fire?" Morgan asked.

"You want to stick your head over that rise?"

"It's that or die here when they charge," Morgan replied simply. "If we don't stop them now, we won't stop them."

Morgan slid to his right. He pushed the dead Mexican *villista* to the top of the gulley and positioned the body as a bulwark across the lip. Within seconds two bullets jolted the inert soldier. Morgan inched his Winchester across the man's back and slithered into firing position. Targets were plentiful. He sighted on a crouched *Federale* approaching the ditch and squeezed the trigger. The man looked at Morgan in confusion then fell dead.

Morgan swung the rifle toward another soldier, ratcheted a fresh round into the chamber, and pulled the trigger. The solid impact lifted the man from his feet, and he flopped to the ground in a cloud of dust.

"Fire your weapon," Morgan yelled at Winters as he discharged a third bullet into an approaching *Federale*. "You've got to shoot."

Morgan killed four other Mexicans, and then slid down into the ditch. He scrambled twenty yards to his right and fell to his knees beside three of *Los Dorados* huddled below the lip of the depression.

99

He grabbed the first man roughly by the arm and dragged him to the top of the culvert. "Shoot," he screamed as he pointed his Winchester at the train. "Shoot!"

Morgan snapped off three quick rounds, killing two more men and sending a third diving for the safety of the train's wheels. The two *Dorados* in the ditch crawled to the top and began to return fire. For the moment, no *Federales* threatened to overrun the *villistas* in their positions.

Morgan moved farther along the depression. Some *Dorados* were at the lip and firing. Three men were slumped across the edge. Blood trickled from beneath the prone bodies. He stopped where *Dorados* were below the top and cajoled and prodded them to firing positions. Where the *villistas* fought back, the *Federales* hugged the relative safety of the train.

Morgan looked behind his position. Pancho Villa and Julio Cardenas were riding back and forth on horseback, thirty yards from the ditch. Bandoleers of bullets crisscrossed their chests, and they brandished their rifles and yelled unheard orders into the fusillade of fire.

Morgan approached the farthest *Dorado* position opposite the end of the train. A ragged group of five *villistas* was gathered delivering sporadic return fire at the *Federales*. One of the men was a weathered, older appearing, gringo. Another sat with a shocked expression on his face, a hand across a pulsing wound in his neck.

"You speak Spanish?" Morgan asked the gringo as he tumbled to his knees.

"Yes," the gringo said. "I speak Spanish."

"Tell these men to follow me," Morgan said. "We're going to run toward the rear of the train and attack up the length of it."

"Who the hell are you?" the gringo said. "You're kinda young to be givin' orders, ain't ya?"

Morgan looked hard at the man. "I'm just another gringo like you. But I'm telling you; if we stay here we'll all die. When they figure out they can take us, they'll charge and overrun us. We've got to do something first."

The old gringo surveyed the battle developing in front of their position. He scratched his haggard beard as his eyes confirmed Morgan's assessment of the situation.

"You probably ain't far from wrong, youngster," he said. "There's a passel of Federals aboard that train. More than we planned on seeing."

"*Que dice?*" a short, chubby *Dorado* asked the gringo. What is he saying?

In Spanish the gringo quickly explained Morgan's plan. The *villistas* babbled among themselves for several seconds before Morgan pulled his Colt and fanned it across the gathering. "Move," he yelled at the men. "Move or die right here."

The men hesitated. Morgan prodded the closest man roughly in the neck with the barrel of his Peacemaker.

The gringo spoke sharply. "*El esta correcto,*" he said, "*Vamanos.*" He's right. Let's go.

The men mounted the top of the ditch. Morgan crouched and ran behind them, directing them in the flanking maneuver toward the last car in the train. A *Federale* peered around the corner of the open door of the boxcar and fired. One of the Dorados clutched his arm and howled in pain. Morgan snapped a shot that burrowed into the *Federale's* leg. The man toppled from the rail car.

The group dropped to the desert floor at the railroad tracks, panting with equal amounts of exhilaration and fatigue. They were ten yards beyond the last car in the train. Morgan pulled rifle shells from his pocket and reloaded his Winchester. *Los Dorados* followed his lead.

"Tell them to keep moving," Morgan instructed the old gringo. "Don't stop until we're past three cars. Then we'll reload and continue. Do you understand?"

The gringo nodded and translated. The men signaled their comprehension.

"Go," Morgan yelled as he jumped to his feet and moved rapidly along the first boxcar, firing at every *Federale* he surprised along the way.

*   *   *

Emboldened by the decreased fire from the *Federales*, more of *Los Dorados* crawled to the top of the trench and engaged their enemy. As Morgan and his small band swept along the train, eliminating the resistance, the *villistas* recognized the maneuver and increased their fire into the cars ahead, diverting *Federale* attention from Morgan's threat approaching from their flank.

Half an hour later, *Federale* troops in the first three boxcars realized their plight and threw down their weapons. Pancho Villa, *El Centauro del Norte*, completed his great victory by capturing and recruiting into his *Division del Norte* nineteen new conscripts along with two tons of ammunition, eight machine guns and several artillery pieces.

Morgan sat heavily against one of the massive engine wheels and drank deeply from a canteen. Bodies of both armies were strewn in the sand, their limbs akimbo where they collapsed in death. Several soldiers groaned with painful wounds. "*Agua, agua,*" moaned from parched lips.

A photographer wandered around the scene firing a bulky box camera at the gruesome detritus of the battle. Another man scribbled furiously in a large notebook.

Bill Winters dropped beside Morgan and removed his hat. "You're crazy," he said reaching for the water. "I figured you caught one after you left me in the ditch."

"We were all going to die if somebody didn't do something," Morgan said. "Those *Federales* would have wiped us out if we didn't keep them down."

"You asked me before if I was scared," Winters said. "Were you scared?"

"I got very concerned when I saw the number of *Federales* on that train," Morgan replied. "But after that I don't think I had time to be scared."

Captain Julio Cardenas pulled his horse to a halt and dismounted. "Hey, gringo," he said with a large grin. "You're a good fighter! Where you learn that?"

Morgan shrugged. "It just made sense to me. I guess I wasn't ready to die in some sandy ditch in Mexico quite yet."

~ 21 ~

Pancho Villa's victorious band stripped the train of its ammunition and weapons. The machine guns were loaded on horse-drawn carts and the artillery pieces were coupled to buggies and pulled backwards toward the *villista* refuge of Juarez.

Bill Winters approached Morgan who was busy cleaning his Winchester. "You don't have to worry about using that for a while," he said. "We're headed back to Juarez."

Morgan looked up. "What makes you think Juarez is so safe?"

Winters laughed. "Villa is the provisional Governor of Chihuahua. He's the law in the whole state, including Juarez."

Morgan raised his eyebrows. "I didn't know that."

"He even prints his own money. That's how we get paid. He rides over to San Antonio in the United States and has them print pesos."

"It seems to pay to be Governor," Morgan said with a smile. "I wanted to learn about the revolution; I guess I'm getting the education."

Los Dorados, led by Captain Cardenas and accompanied by the photographers and journalists, mounted and rode slowly back to Juarez. The wounded rode in ammunition carts. Pancho Villa saluted his *Division del Norte* and trotted off in the opposite direction. The rumor among the men was that important political matters demanded Villa's attention and further campaigns were to be temporarily suspended.

*   *   *

In Juarez the men rested and waited. January and February passed with no military operations undertaken. Morgan had time to reflect on several matters. There was something about living on the edge of civilization, far from a large city, far from crowds of people, far from the congestion of motor coaches that appealed to him. The air seemed to carry an extra snap of excitement. There was a constant uncertainty and challenge to living that turned a key to Morgan's psyche and opened a door to his free and adventuresome spirit.

Morgan spent many hours pondering the battle for the railroad train. He had read about the heroes of various battles, but he had never studied the tactics and strategy employed by the commanders. Why had the *Federales* not exploited their numerical superiority and immediately overwhelmed the entrenched *Dorados*? Why had many of the *Dorados* not laid down suppressing fire at the train? Many of the men had not fired their weapons until pushed to the top of the ravine.

The flanking maneuver Morgan initiated was neither brilliant nor original. But *Los Dorados* had engaged their enemy in a firefight without thought to encirclement and rolling up a flank. Why wasn't Villa or Cardenas directing the men to victory?

The technicalities of martial engagement continued to intrigue Morgan. Could he lead men in combat? Would he ever have the opportunity?

*   *   *

Morgan and Bill Winters hunted in the neighboring mountains and took long rides into the desert. They cleaned their weapons and tended their mounts. They practiced shooting from various poses including prone, sitting and standing. They fired from galloping horseback and rehearsed jumping from the saddle and immediately coming to a fighting position. The other *Dorados* idled their time in the many cantinas, listened to the music of well-tuned instruments, participated in the nightly *bailes* or dances with the local *senoritas*, munched on simmering frijoles and piping hot tortillas, and drank tequila until completely inebriated.

In March of 1916 Pancho Villa returned to Juarez with three hundred additional men to strengthen his *Division del Norte.* He assembled his troops and outlined his plan. They were to attack the small city of Columbus, New Mexico. The United States had changed its policy toward Villa and his revolution. Previously Villa had enjoyed the support of the United States and received arms and ammunition. Now President Woodrow Wilson decided to support the Mexican President Carranza, believing this policy would be the best way to expedite establishment of a stable Mexican government. There would be no more weapons for the *villistas*. Further, the United States was to allow the movement of constitutionalist troops on U.S. railroads.

Pancho Villa was livid. He railed against the treachery and deceit of the American president. He accused the Americans of deliberately supplying defective bullets that cost the lives of many of his soldiers. He was particularly enraged by the constitutionalists' use of searchlights, powered by American electricity, to help repel a *villistao* night attack on the border town of Agua Prieta. He vowed to teach the United States a lesson they would not soon forget. He would invade United States territory and kill Americans.

Morgan Early's blood ran cold. He would never participate in an expedition against his own country. He would quit *Los Dorados* and proceed to Florida. His involvement with Pancho Villa's revolution was at an end.

At the conclusion of Villa's tirade, Morgan walked to the general's tent and asked permission from the guard to enter.

Morgan stood rigidly in front of Pancho Villa who was sitting at a small table with his boots resting on a chair. Captain Julio Cardenas sat beside him. A half consumed bottle of tequila resided next to a pair of filthy glasses brimming with the amber liquid. The general's cot and a standing rack for his clothes were the only other items in the tent.

"*Eres le gringo nuevo, no?*" Pancho Villa inquired. You're the new gringo aren't you?

"*Si,*" Morgan said.

"*Mi dicen que eres un soldado excelente,*" the General continued. I hear you are an excellent soldier.

"*Gracias, generale.*"

"*Que quieres?*" What do you want?

"*No puedo luchear encontra de los Estados Unidos,*" Morgan said. I can't fight against the United States.

"*No puedes luchear?*" Captain Julio Cardenas screamed as he leaped to his feet from his chair.

"*No encontra de mi propio pais,*" Morgan said. Not against my country.

"*Entonces eres un traidor de la revolucion,*" Cardenas yelled, shaking his finger at Morgan. Then you are a traitor to the revolution.

Morgan blinked in disbelief. "*Liberame de las fuerzas armadas. He luchado bien para ti, pero no puedo luchear encontra de mi propio pais,*" he said. Just release me from service. I have fought well for you, but I can't fight against my own country.

"*Sargento,*" Julio Cardenas yelled. "*Tire a este hombre en la estacada. El sabe nuestro plan de ataque hacia los Estados Unidos. Si se escapa, podra informales a sus compatriotas.*" Throw this man in the stockade. He knows of our plan to attack the Unites States. If he escapes, he will warn his countrymen.

The sergeant snatched Morgan's Colt from his holster and seized him roughly by the arm. "*Vamanos, amigo. Es las estacada para ti.*" Let's go, friend. It's the stockade for you.

"You speak pretty good Spanish," Julio Cardenas said with a smirk in accented English. "You've learned well while you've been in my country. But I'll tell you this in your language so there's no mistake. When I get back from this battle, I will see you hung."

Morgan was unceremoniously thrown in one of the Juarez jail cells. The tall metal door clanked shut with a heavy finality and the bolt snapped closed with a forbidding conclusiveness.

A dank odor of rotten food and stale sweat pervaded the small space. Morgan walked to the tiny window and pulled experimentally on the steel rods. They were immovable. He flopped on the meager mattress covering the narrow cot and raised a thin cloud of dust. The smell of mold and urine assaulted his nostrils.

*   *   *

Villa's *Division del Norte* departed with great enthusiasm the next morning. Morgan watched from the window as the *villistas* moved toward the northwest and the United States. They were well armed and carried a huge cache of ammunition. The artillery pieces behind the wagons were formidable weapons to precede an assault. He closed his eyes and fought to maintain control of his jangling emotions as he pictured his countrymen under siege from the approaching army.

*   *   *

A week later the first of Pancho Villa's army straggled back to Juarez. Word of the attack spread through the town like a roiling tsunami. The guards at the jail chattered incessantly about the debacle. The *Division del Norte* had attacked a detachment of the 13th United States Cavalry stationed at Camp Furlong near Columbus, New Mexico. Nineteen Americans had been killed including nine civilians. Following the initial battle with the American cavalry, the Mexicans had shot up the town of Columbus and burned many of the buildings to the ground. Several more civilians were killed as the Mexicans rode through the town shouting "*viva Villa*" and "*muerte a los Americanos.*"

The Mexicans had suffered enormous losses of men and material and were eventually driven across the border leaving many to die on the battlefield. Those *villistas* able to walk or ride hobbled with their wounds back to Juarez.

Bill Winters suffered two non-fatal bullet wounds but managed to escape the scene before finally collapsing from his horse at a small hacienda twenty miles from Juarez. A sympathetic family nursed him for a month until he regained enough strength to ride. At the beginning of April, Winters appeared in the darkest hour of the night at the stockade window in Juarez.

"Hey, hero," he whispered. "Wake up. You still alive?"

Morgan rolled from his cot and sprang to the bars. "Bill," he called in a low voice. "Is that you? I heard you got it in the raid."

"I got hit," Winters replied. "Twice. But I was lucky. The bullets passed through and my horse found somebody to nurse me back to health."

"I guess Villa's attack on the United States didn't work out too well," Morgan said with obvious joy in his voice. "The attack was the talk of Juarez for a week."

"Take this rope," Winters said. "Wrap it around the bars and tie it tight. Then get your boots on. I'm going to get you out of there."

"Why?" Morgan asked with heavy sarcasm. "I'm getting to love the food and the accommodations are first class."

A moment later Morgan heard Bill Winters deliver a heavy slap on the flank of a horse. The rope snapped tight and the bars in the small window exploded outward. Morgan dove through the opening and rolled to a stop beneath his buckskin's hooves.

"Ride," Winters yelled as he untied the rope from his saddle horn. "If Villa finds us, we're dead men."

Morgan vaulted into the saddle and spurred Buck. His heart soared with unrestrained joy as the wind rushed past his face for the first time in a month.

~ 22 ~

Morgan Early and Bill Winters ducked their heads beside the straining necks of their mounts and galloped into the night without looking back. Morgan could not suppress a broad smile and the feeling of unmitigated glee as Buck's pounding hooves carried them far from Juarez and the confines of the depressing, loathsome jail cell.

They reined to a controlled trot after the initial four mile dash to safety and the horses, lathered and panting, adjusted to the measured pace that would carry them until dawn.

When the sun broke above the horizon, and it was evident no Mexican soldiers were in pursuit, the two Americans halted at a small stream and watered their horses.

Bill Winters reached into his saddlebag and withdrew Morgan's Colt Peacemaker and holster. "I took this from the guard after they arrested you," he said. "I know how much you favor it."

Morgan strapped the belt around his waist. "Thank you," he said. "It was my father's. I've felt naked without it."

"Did you hear that the *Federales* shot Villa while you were in the stockade?"

"Really? Is he dead?"

"They got him in the leg," Winters said. "He's hiding out in a cave somewhere in the Sierra Madres. The U.S. Army is after him. Some general named Black Jack Pershing is leading the troops. I heard the news from a couple of Americans when I was riding back to rescue you from your upcoming lynching."

Morgan shook his head. "I guess I wasn't privy to that gossip in the hoosegow."

Winters laughed. "The United States didn't take kindly to the raid on Columbus. They're calling this the Punitive Expedition. They're after Villa, and they won't be happy until they find him."

"How about Captain Cardenas," Morgan asked. "I overheard one of the guards say he was hiding out in a hacienda in San Miguelito. I guess that's why he didn't return to Juarez to hang me."

"I wonder if the U.S. Army would like that information," Winters said with a broad smile. "Cardenas was determined to string you up for treason."

Morgan smiled. "Let's find this General Black Jack Pershing. Cardenas was so eager to see my neck stretched; I wouldn't mind returning the favor."

*　　*　　*

Morgan and Bill Winters rode toward the encampment of the United States Punitive Expedition. Two guards with Enfield rifles halted them and demanded they dismount. "What's your business?" one of the soldiers called.

"We're here to see the general," Winters shouted back.

The two guards exchanged glances and smiled. "The general don't have time to converse with a couple of saddle bums."

"He might make time if the saddle bums could lead him to the leader of *Los Dorados*," Morgan replied. "He isn't too busy to capture Captain Julio Cardenas, is he?"

"You two Americans?" the second guard shouted. "This ain't some Mexican trick, is it?"

"We're Americans," Morgan yelled. "And unless you want to incur the wrath of your general, you better let us talk to him. We hear he's not having much success running Pancho Villa to ground."

"Come ahead slow," the guard motioned with his rifle. "And keep those hands a good distance from your sidearms."

*　　*　　*

General Black Jack Pershing looked up from the desk in his tent when Morgan and Bill Winters were admitted. His tan uniform was sharply creased and the stars on his epaulets highly polished. A flat brimmed, four point, campaign hat with a patent leather chinstrap sat on the seat of a nearby chair. An American flag hung from a varnished pole in one corner. A gold eagle adorned the top of the shaft.

"The corporal tells me you have information about Julio Cardenas." he said.

"That's right," Bill Winters nodded.

"Who are you? And what are you doing in Mexico?"

"My name's Morgan Early, lately of Colorado."

"And you?"

"Bill Winters. I came down to join the revolution and make some money until the Mexicans took up arms against my country. Now we're headed back."

"And what do you know about Captain Cardenas?"

Morgan stepped forward. "I know where he is."

"Can you lead my soldiers to him?"

"Yes."

General Pershing turned to a sergeant. "Get me Lieutenant Patton."

The sergeant saluted smartly and wheeled on his heel. "Yes sir. Right away, sir." The soldier disappeared.

A few minutes later a tall, thin, youthful 1st lieutenant appeared, cracked his heels together and saluted the general. "Lieutenant Patton reporting as ordered, sir."

"At ease, Georgie," General Pershing ordered. "These two boys seem to think they can find Julio Cardenas for us."

George Patton spread his legs and locked his arms behind his back. His posture was rigid, his uniform custom tailored, and his knee-high, mahogany cavalry boots spit shined to a mirror finish. A single revolver was strapped to his waist in a covered leather holster.

Morgan almost laughed upon hearing the lieutenant's high-pitched, squeaky voice, which was so out of context to the man's strict military bearing.

Georgie Patton turned to Morgan Early. "We've been looking for Cardenas and Villa for a month," he said. "How is it you know where that Mexican bandit is located?"

"My friend and I have been in Mexico since last fall," Bill Winters replied. "We've come to know a little of their habits and whereabouts."

"You can lead me to Captain Cardenas?"

"Yes, lieutenant," Morgan said.

"And is he with soldiers? How many men will we need to take him?"

"There might be a few soldiers at the hacienda with him," Morgan said. "But all of *Los Dorados* that survived the raid in New Mexico are still hanging around in Juarez. Villa and Cardenas don't have any more soldiers. A few good men should be sufficient to take him, and we can make better time."

"How can you be so certain of the troop strength of Villa's army?" General Pershing asked.

Bill Winters stepped forward and pointed to Morgan. "This young man was a hero in a battle against a train-load of Federals. Many of Villa's men think he saved them from certain death. He knows what's going on."

Black Jack Pershing nodded and motioned for Lieutenant Patton to continue.

Patton pulled a gold watch from his pocket and flipped the cover open. "Get some supper and sleep. You look like you've been undernourished for a while. Tomorrow at first light, with the general's permission, you'll take me after this Captain Cardenas."

"It's a fair ride," Morgan said. "Do you have a good horse?"

"We'll take automobiles," Patton said. "It'll be faster."

"I've never ridden in a motor coach before," Morgan said. "I look forward to the experience."

"Have you killed Mexicans before? You look a little young for this work."

Morgan tilted his head side-to-side. "You won't find me a burden," he said in a low voice.

*   *   *

Sergeant Fulton cranked the engine of the open-topped Dodge to life when Lieutenant Patton approached. "All the vehicles have sufficient gasoline for the round trip?" Patton asked the soldier.

"Yes, sir," Fulton replied. "The tank is full and we've got two spare canisters strapped to the back of each."

"Excellent, sergeant," Patton said in his incongruously high voice. "What about weapons?"

"All the men have rifles with plenty of ammunition," the sergeant answered. "The two civilians chose to keep their own side arms and Winchesters."

Lieutenant Patton turned to Morgan and Bill Winters. "Get in," he ordered. "Let's see if your information on Captain Julio Cardenas is correct."

Morgan gingerly tested the integrity of the running board with one foot before stepping into the back seat. He looked at Bill Winters and shrugged. "I saw a bunch of these motor coaches in Denver when I passed through," he said. "I wasn't too impressed at the time. Maybe riding in one will change my mind."

"I hope my horse isn't watching me get aboard this thing," Bill Winters said. "He might be a trifle jealous."

"How long will it take us to get to this hacienda?" Patton asked.

"How fast can this contraption travel on a dirt road?" Morgan replied. "By horse it's an all day ride if you push hard."

Lieutenant Patton rubbed his jaw in contemplation. "A competent horseman can cover thirty miles or more in a single day without hurting his animal. We should be there in an hour."

Bill Winters turned and looked at Morgan. "An hour?" he repeated incredulously. "I guess our horses have seen their day."

"Except if this thing decides to quit running," Morgan observed. "It may not be as easy to nurse along as a horse."

~ 23 ~

A long plume of dust spiraled behind the three Dodge open touring automobiles carrying the ten soldiers from the 6th Infantry Regiment and Bill Winters and Morgan Early as they sped across the parched desert road south into old Mexico. In the distance, peaks of the Sierra Madres reached 10,000 feet into the sky. Along the valley floor dirt and cactus and sage stretched as far as the eye could see.

After an hour of travel, Morgan reached toward Lieutenant Patton and tapped him gently on the shoulder. "Tell the driver to pull over here," he said. "San Miguelito is just ahead, and I believe the hacienda is down below this next rise."

The three Dodge autos halted on the top of a gentle hill. Lieutenant Patton opened the door of the Dodge and stepped off the running board. He pulled a pair of binoculars from a leather case and rotated the focusing wheel until satisfied with the view.

"The hacienda appears deserted," he said without removing the lenses from his eyes. "You sure Cardenas is here?"

Morgan exited the automobile and stood beside Patton. "I can't be certain, but the recent talk in Juarez was that Cardenas was here."

Patton lowered the binoculars and turned to Sergeant Fulton. "Have the men double check their weapons," he ordered. "We'll proceed at normal speed toward the hacienda. The second car will move down the rise, swing to the left and halt one hundred yards from the building. The third will do the same on the right."

"Yes, sir," Sergeant Fulton replied.

"Tell the drivers to wait for my signal before proceeding closer," Patton continued as he waved the sergeant off toward the other vehicles and replaced the binoculars in front of his eyes.

"The men understand your orders, sir," Fulton said when he dashed back to the lead automobile.

"Let's move out," Patton said sharply as he walked with long strides toward the Dodge.

Morgan and Bill Winters drew their pistols from their holsters and spun the cylinders to check for rounds. They levered cartridges into their Winchesters and removed the safeties.

A tingle of excitement swept over Morgan. At the railroad he had initially been nervous and uncertain how he would behave when the battle commenced. Shooting the sheepherder who had killed his mother was a calculated act of necessary revenge. Killing the rim-rocking cowboy was pure, unthinking, self-defense.

When he discovered he was able to remain focused and function at a high level of efficiency during the chaotic frenzy around the train, he had thrilled at the revelation. The rush of adrenaline as the conflict raged, the noise of the gunfire rattled in his ears and the smoke drifted over the scene, was more powerful than any previous emotion he had experienced. He was anxious to relive the thrill.

The three Dodge touring cars motored down the rise, bumping over small animal holes and flattening brittle clumps of brush. Half way down the hill the two following cars broke off and swept around a perimeter before halting the prescribed distance from the mud-brick structure. Patton's lead vehicle rolled through an opening in a split-rail fence surrounding the hacienda and stopped.

Lieutenant Patton stood and called toward the front door. "Hello the house."

He was answered with a single shot from a Mauser rifle that shattered the windscreen of the Dodge. Patton dropped like a falling rock to the relative safety of the vehicle's front seat.

"Where did that shot come from?" he screamed. "Did anybody see the shooter?"

Morgan jumped from the back seat and crouched behind the Dodge. Bill Winters followed.

A second shot followed that plowed into the passenger side door with a metallic splat.

"The window beside the front door," Morgan called. "I saw the smoke from the rifle.

Morgan and Bill Winters rose above the level of the automobile and fired four rounds apiece as fast as they could reload fresh shells into their chambers. Glass shattered in the upper panes of the window and the curtains hanging on the sides fluttered as the bullets passed through on their way into the house.

"Get out of the car," Morgan hollered to Patton. "You're a sitting duck in there."

"Give me some covering fire," Patton yelled.

Morgan and Bill Winters stood again and unleashed a hail of bullets at the open window. Lieutenant Patton tumbled from the front seat and crawled around to the back of the Dodge.

"Fire," he called in the direction of the two automobiles flanking the hacienda. "Fire."

A fusillade of bullets pummeled the front of the house, splintering the heavy front door and bursting the remaining window panes. No return fire came from the hacienda.

"They're going to make a break out the back," Morgan said definitively. "Tell those soldiers to hold their fire so they don't kill us by mistake."

Lieutenant Patton lifted his lanky body to a crouch and waved his arms vigorously. "Cease fire," he yelled in his squeaky voice. "Cease fire."

"Let's go," Morgan said nudging Patton.

The lieutenant looked a question at Morgan.

"Come on," Morgan said. "Around the back if you want to catch Cardenas." He sprinted away from the Dodge and headed for the rear of the hacienda.

Georgie Patton followed closely in Morgan's wake.

They ran directly for the shelter of a watering trough and slid to a stop. Both men hugged the ground and peered around the edges of the low, wooden basin.

Behind the rear of the hacienda a fenced corral held several horses. A small barn occupied the far side of the compound. An upper level was visible through a wide, hinged-panel opening above the entrance. Piles of feed stood on either side.

A door flew open at the rear of the hacienda and three men dashed across the open ground. Lieutenant Patton fired three wild shots with his ivory handled pistol. The bullets dug tiny holes in the dry earth behind the feet of the fleeing Mexicans.

One man took refuge behind a stack of grain. Recognizing that the three shots had emanated from the trough, the Mexican sighted his rifle at Patton's end and fired. The first bullet burrowed in the ground six inches in front of the lieutenant's head and splattered his face with sand and pebbles. The second passed completely through the flimsy structure and a tiny stream of water immediately poured on Patton's right shoulder.

"They got us pinned down," Patton called to Morgan at the other end of the trough.

"Fire that pistol," Morgan yelled back.

The lieutenant reached around the corner of the trough and emptied his weapon at the barn. He withdrew his arm and rolled to his back, frantically reloading his pistol. The stream of water continued to douse the back of his neck.

A shot roared from the upper level of the barn and plunged into the trough. A small wave of water crested the lip and soaked the ground. Morgan inched around the corner of the low cover and sighted his Winchester with deliberation. He fingered the trigger and applied gentle pressure.

The brim of a hat appeared in the upper opening of the barn. A face followed. The muzzle of a rifle poked around the corner. A man's shoulder was suddenly visible. Morgan took a half breath and eased his finger against the warm metal of the trigger. The weapon roared. The bullet flew unerringly. A Mexican tumbled from the balcony of the barn.

"You got one," Patton yelled.

"Shoot," Morgan replied.

Patton lifted his eyes above the level of the trough. A man dashed from the safety of the barn toward the horses in the corral. The lieutenant squeezed his trigger six times in rapid succession.

The man stumbled, clutching his wound, before hopping on one leg toward the nearest horse.

"Stop him," Patton called. "I've got to reload."

Two shots burst from the feed piles beside the barn offering cover fire for the escaping Mexican.

A third shot sounded. Morgan removed his hat and placed it atop the trough. A bullet buried into the wood nearby. Morgan reached up and flipped the hat to the ground. He paused several seconds then spun to his knees and aimed the Winchester. He fired once and jacked a fresh round into the chamber.

A scream of agony drifted across the corral from the feed pile. The sound of pounding hoofs immediately replaced the cry of pain. The Mexican wounded by Lieutenant Patton dug his heels into the flanks of a horse and headed for the far end of the corral. A trail of blood was visible leaking down the man's leg as he exhorted his mount to greater speed.

Lieutenant Patton stood and fired three times. Morgan stood and shouldered his Winchester. He drew a careful bead on the fleeing Mexican, swinging the weapon across his chest to match the speed of the horse. He depressed the trigger smoothly. The bullet crashed into the man's head flinging him from the panicked animal. The mortally wounded Mexican slammed heavily into the ground just as the horse vaulted the upper railing of the corral and escaped into the wild of the parched desert.

~ 24 ~

"That's Captain Cardenas," Bill Winters said as he pointed to the Mexican in the sand at the edge of the corral.

Lieutenant Patton stood proudly beside the fallen revolutionary and brandished his pistol. "I got him in the leg," he said in his alto voice, raised an octave by the excitement of the battle.

"That's true," Morgan acknowledged.

"I felt like I spent most of my time re-loading," Patton continued. "These six shooters sure gobble up the ammunition."

"You might consider carrying two pistols," Morgan suggested. "That way you'll have twice the rounds and a back-up if the first jams."

Lieutenant Patton nodded slowly as he contemplated the idea. "Two pistols," he said pensively. "Yes, that would be quite a statement."

Bill Winters pointed to Patton's revolver. "Is that a pearl handle?" he asked.

Patton laughed. "Only a pimp in a whore house would carry a pearl handled pistol," he said. "It's ivory. But I like your friend's suggestion. It will soon have a companion on the other side."

Sergeant Fulton scurried up to the lieutenant. He held a silver sword proudly in his hand. "Sir," he said excitedly. "I found this in the hacienda. Ain't it a beauty?"

"That sword belongs to Cardenas," Bill Winters said. "I've seen him wear it on numerous occasions."

119

Patton reached for the sword and hefted it aloft. The silver of the handle and the long blade glistened in the bright sunlight. "It's a wonderful trophy of war," he said. "I'll keep it as a memento of this glorious day." He pulled his Sam Browne belt away from his uniform and slid the sword down beside his hip. He caressed the polished knob and smiled broadly.

"You might be interested in the captain's saddle," Bill Winters said. "It's loaded with silver, too. I don't know how much his horse likes carrying it around, but it sure is pretty."

"Sergeant," Patton called. "Search the barn until you find this silver saddle. I want it. Cardenas has no further use for it."

"Yes, sir," Fulton said before dashing away toward the barn.

Turning to one of the soldiers, Patton pointed to the two Mexican bodies lying near the corral. "Gather those dead men and strap them to the fenders of the Dodge. Get Cardenas, too. I want to present them to General Pershing."

*   *   *

The entourage of Dodge automobiles slid to a halt at the American camp. Lieutenant Patton jumped from the lead vehicle and dashed toward Black Jack Pershing's tent. He snapped a sharp salute at the soldier guarding the general's quarters. "Inform the general I have returned with Captain Cardenas," Patton ordered.

The soldier disappeared inside the tent returning moments later with Pershing in tow.

"You've returned, Georgie," General Pershing said with a tight smile. "Where is Cardenas?"

"If you'll accompany me around the back of your tent, I'll show him to you."

"Carry on," Pershing said with a flip of his hand.

The two officers rounded the tent and approached the vehicles. Morgan and Bill Winters were lounging near the rear of the first Dodge, carefully remaining upwind of the bloated bodies tied to the front fenders. Insects began to swirl around the rapidly decomposing carcasses in the harsh Mexican sun.

General Pershing pulled up quickly upon witnessing the swollen bodies. He swiped at his nose as the first whiff of rotting flesh assaulted his nostrils.

120

"One of these poor creatures is Cardenas?" the general asked as he turned from the gruesome scene.

"Yes, sir," Patton replied. "These two men confirm his identity."

"Congratulations, lieutenant," General Pershing said. "Well done."

"These two men deserve thanks for their accurate information leading us to the hacienda," Lieutenant Patton said. "We would have never found Cardenas in the middle of all that desert."

Black Jack Pershing looked in the direction of Morgan and Bill Winters. "The United States is indebted to you for your assistance."

Morgan nodded his appreciation. "Captain Cardenas vowed to hang me for treason," he said simply. "Leading your men to him was only a fair return."

"Treason?" Pershing asked. "What was your treasonable offense?"

"I refused to join the attack on Columbus," Morgan said. "I told him I wouldn't participate in any action against my country."

General Pershing rubbed his jowls in thought before speaking. "You would have been an enemy of your own country if you had joined Villa in the raid."

"Yes, sir," Morgan said. "I told him I couldn't abide that notion. He disagreed."

Lieutenant Patton stepped forward and placed a paternal hand on Morgan's shoulder. "This young man would make an excellent soldier, general. He was courageous under fire and has an innate understanding of tactics. He's an excellent shot as well."

"Thank you, lieutenant," Morgan said. "But I think I'm headed to Florida where I understand the weather is always warm."

"You heard correctly," General Pershing said. "But perhaps Lieutenant Patton is right. We could always use a good scout in the army. Would you be interested?"

"I'm afraid not," Morgan replied. "Beside, I don't see much of a war to fight. Pancho Villa was wounded by Federal troops a couple of weeks ago. I heard he's hiding in the Sierra Madres. But you'll never find him. You could run around this desert for the rest of your life and never discover Villa."

"There's a war in Europe," Lieutenant Patton said. "It can't be long before the United States joins the conflict."

Morgan looked between General Pershing and Lieutenant Patton. "Does it snow in Europe?" he asked with a smile.

"I believe it does," Pershing replied.

"Then I thank you again, but I think I'll stick to my plan. I've seen enough snow to last me a lifetime."

"When will you two leave?"

Morgan turned to Bill Winters and shrugged. "Tomorrow, if we can draw some rations and feed for our horses."

Lieutenant Patton turned to Sergeant Fulton. "See that these men are well supplied for their journey."

A commotion was heard approaching. A small gaggle of reporters and photographers hustled around the corner calling excited questions.

"Lieutenant Patton...we heard you killed Cardenas?"

"Can we get photographs of the bodies?"

"Can we see the sword?"

"Stand beside the dead and hold up the sword, please lieutenant."

Bill Winters and Morgan Early shared a look and walked slowly away with Sergeant Fulton. The enlisted man shook his head and whispered over his shoulder. "Glory hound. He may be a capable officer, but he's going to get a lot of good men killed to advance his career."

~ 25 ~

Morgan Early bid farewell to Bill Winters at the railroad station in Denver. Buck was safely ensconced in one of the stock cars with an enormous pile of hay and oats at his disposal. Water sloshed in buckets hanging from one of the wooden slats enclosing the car.

"Are you sure you don't want to see Florida?" Morgan asked as he shook his friend's hand and patted him firmly on the shoulder.

"No thanks," Bill Winters said with a sorrowful expression. "I'll miss you, but I think I'll try California. I've heard good things about that state."

"Well, don't do anything foolish like join the army," Morgan laughed. "I think we've had enough fighting for a lifetime."

"And you should follow your own advice," Bill said. "I don't know much about soldierin', but if ever I've seen a natural warrior, it would be you."

The train whistle sounded from the engine ahead. A chubby man in a blue suit with a round hat walked down the tracks swinging a lantern. "All aboard," he yelled. "All aboard for points east."

"Don't worry," Morgan said as he mounted the steps to the passenger car. "I didn't like those army uniforms anyway. They were too drab."

*   *   *

123

Morgan pressed his face to the filthy window of the swaying car as it approached Miami. The ride had been uncomfortable, hot and dreary. Morgan's ticket purchased a place on a hard, wooden bench. Sleep was nearly impossible as the train clacked and clattered across the endless junctions of the iron rails. Food at usury prices was only available at the various stops along the route. Dodge City, famous booming cattle town of twenty-five years ago, was a row of desolate wooden structures, lining a dirt street, on the verge of collapse. Wichita was smaller and more forlorn. Open top automobiles ground along the dusty avenues, honking at the horse drawn buggies. Visiting the stock car and keeping the buckskin in feed and water became the main diversion of the trip.

Oklahoma City appeared to be growing as the discovery of oil and its accompanying riches spawned a building explosion of brick houses, hotels and gaudy saloons. Motor coaches outnumbered buckboards. Little Rock and Birmingham were sleepy towns shaded by huge willow trees where the inhabitants appeared to proceed about their business in slow motion.

Tallahassee was the first stop in Florida and Morgan fought his disappointment. Moist heat from the Gulf permeated the air, and apart from the apparent unlikelihood of snow, there was little to hold Morgan's interest. The land was flat making him yearn briefly for the beauty of the Rocky Mountains in summer.

The station in Jacksonville overlooked a vast river emptying into a limitless sea of blue. "Is that the Atlantic Ocean?" Morgan asked the conductor in wide-eyed astonishment.

"Yep, son," the conductor replied. "That's the Atlantic. We'll go away from it as we head for Orlando, but from West Palm Beach down we'll be only a few miles to the west at any one time."

Morgan sat back on the bench that had been his home for the three days of the ride and closed his eyes. Images of the maps in the widow O'Brien's books flashed into his mind. How wide was the Atlantic? How long would a steam ship take to cross to Europe?

Morgan opened his eyes and shook his head. Europe? There was still a war raging in Europe. Hadn't he had enough of being the target of men firing bullets? He closed his eyes again and reflected on his encounters with men shooting at him. Was it strange that he felt such excitement during those times? Why did he never fear that he would be hit by any of the flying lead? What combination of synapses and muscles and nerves permitted him to draw and fire his pistol with such unerring accuracy in the heat of a conflict? What instinct allowed him to see the correct strategic maneuver that eluded other men during the chaos and confusion of a battle?

Was he meant to be a soldier?

Service to his country would be the highest calling he could imagine. But during his six-month enlistment in Pancho Villa's army, he had experienced only one battle, and *Los Dorados* had only engaged their enemy twice. Listless drilling or simple boredom dominated the remainder of the time. Was that a worthwhile and exciting life?

"Next stop, Miami," the conductor shouted as he walked briskly through the passenger car.

Morgan put on his wide-brim hat and gathered his roll of extra clothes. He stretched his back and reached upward to loosen his muscles. He was one month from his sixteenth birthday and already stood half an inch over six feet tall. He had filled out to nearly one hundred eighty-five pounds during his stay in old Mexico. He had shaved for the first time in Denver the night before his departure. His blonde hair fell to his collar and his blue eyes sparkled with the excitement of experiencing a new life. He was alone in the world except for his horse. His only blood relatives, uncles Virgil and Wyatt Earp, both now residing in Southern California, did not know of his existence. As far as Morgan knew, his natural mother did not have a living parent or sibling. The nearest human being he could call by name was two thousand miles away in Edwards, Colorado, and she probably wouldn't speak to him.

He walked to the stock car to saddle his buckskin horse and prepare to exit the train. There was a distinct jaunt in his step and a smile on his youthful face.

*   *   *

Morgan walked Buck down the wooden ramp and stared at the pandemonium unfolding before him at the train station. Women in long white dresses stood demurely holding parasols while gentlemen, immaculately clothed in linen suits and white starched shirts with broad neckties, pointed to piles of trunks and organized the loading of Cadillac motorcars.

The sun beat down from a cloudless sky, but a cooling breeze drifted across the flat landscape to the east. Soaring palm trees lined the hard-packed streets of sand and crushed shell.

Morgan mounted the buckskin and weaved his way through the throng of arriving and departing passengers. Miami appeared more far more densely populated than he had expected. Automobiles predominated along the avenues leading to the station and the only horses in evidence were pulling carts loaded with piles of fruit and vegetables.

West of the railroad tracks individual hovels baked in the mounting heat. Laundry flapped in the gentle wind on line stretched between palms. Black women with scarves wrapped around their heads scratched the arid soil of pitiful vegetable gardens. Morgan reined his mount toward the east.

Four and five story buildings sprang from the land as he approached the shoreline. Hotels appeared with wide verandas facing the water. Stores selling clothes and paintings displayed their wares behind large glass windows. Across a wide-open bay a long strip of sand stretched with white buildings aligned along the shore. Where were the ranches? Morgan had noticed predominately wet marshland west of the tracks as the train puffed south from Orlando. He had been told that cattle were a large industry in Florida and he wouldn't have trouble securing a job. Was that a lie?

Activity appeared to the south near the water and Morgan nudged Buck in that direction. He dismounted at a ramshackle wharf and looked down. A single mast sailing vessel was tied to the pier. Two shirtless men, their ebony skin glistening with the efforts of their labor, were carefully unloading large, pink shells and strange looking spiny animals with long wiggling antennae.

Morgan watched in fascination as the bounty appeared from the hold of the boat and was carefully recorded by a white man with a pad and pencil.

"What are those things?" Morgan inquired of one of the men on the boat when he paused to wipe his brow with a filthy rag.

"Them's lobsters," the man said with a broad smile. "Ain't you never et one?"

"I've never seen one," Morgan said with a small grin. "Where do they come from?"

"We catches 'em on da bank," the man replied.

"The bank?" Morgan repeated.

"It be out dere, beyond dat beach on da other side of da bay," the man said smiling.

Morgan looked in the direction of the man's pointing finger. "I can't see the ocean from here."

"It be dere, an jus' about forty miles dat away it get shallow and you find dese lobsters and sponges and turtles and conch. Dats where we live."

"You live in the ocean?"

The man threw back his head and roared with laughter. "Boy, you don' know much about nothin' about da ocean."

Morgan dropped his head and shrugged.

"We lives on Bimini. It's an island out dere. Not even a day's sail. Da water so beautiful it bring tears to your eyes."

Morgan looked back to the west. His eyes scanned the burgeoning landscape of Miami. Automobiles zoomed up and down the streets. People scurried through the congestion. Noise hung in the air. The rap of hammers and the rip of saws promised more buildings and more crowding. The weather was wonderful, but Morgan wondered how he could earn a living. Like Denver, everyone seemed dressed for commercial activity that he knew nothing about.

"Are there motor coaches on this Bimini?"

"Ain't got a one."

"Could I book passage on your boat to this Bimini? I think I might find it more to my liking than what I see of Miami."

"Dat ain't no problem, mister. We take you dere if you can pay."

"Can I bring my horse?"

"Ain't no law against a horse on a sailboat," the man said with a roar of laughter. "He be welcome."

~ 26 ~

"My name's Ashley," the first Bahamian said as he extended a massive brown hand toward Morgan. The man stood over six feet tall with bunched muscles in his arms and a thick neck that flowed from his ears to the ends of his shoulders. A wide gap separated his two front teeth that were almost permanently on display with his constant smile.

"I'm Morgan Early."

"Where you from?" Ashley asked. "Seems like da ocean be a big mystery to you."

Morgan smiled. "I was born in Arizona," he said. "My foster mother and I moved to Colorado a couple of years ago. I spent half a year in old Mexico before taking the train down here."

"Ain't much ocean in dem parts o' da world I 'spect," Ashley observed. He was dressed in tattered shorts, a sleeveless shirt bleached almost white from countless douses of salt water, and brown leather shoes with the toes cut open to accommodate his wide, flat feet.

"Who's your friend?"

"Oh, dats Cecil. He don't take to talkin' too much, but when it comes to da sea, I don't want no other man wid me."

Morgan waved a salutation to Cecil and smiled. "I'm Morgan," he said.

"Go get your horse, an' we'll load him up," Ashley said. "Soons we get our money from da man, we needs to make for da inlet. Da tide be startin' to fall."

Buck walked down the ramp leading to the sailboat with trepidation. His nostrils flared in question the moment he inhaled the first strange scent of salt water.

"Easy, boy," Morgan soothed. "It'll be okay."

The buckskin snorted and stamped a front foot to display his anxiety, but Morgan's firm hand and gentle voice calmed the horse. Trust built over the years allowed the animal to step fearfully aboard the wooden deck of the thirty-five foot vessel.

"Keep him in da aft dere jus' ahead o' da tiller," Ashley said. "He get to wanderin' forward, we won't be able to come about without knocking him wid da boom."

Morgan led Buck to the designated area and lashed the halter to an upright portion of the railing. He wondered what Ashley meant about Buck becoming an impediment, but he held his questions. Ashley and Cecil were busy untying their boat from the pier and preparing the sail on the tall mast.

"Haul da sail," Ashley called the moment the boat was two feet clear of the pier. Cecil pulled vigorously on a rope and a gigantic triangle of cloth leapt up the mast. The boat did not immediately react, but moments later the breeze snapped the sail open and the craft heeled to starboard.

Morgan gasped a small breath when the boat inclined. How far would it lean? For an instant he wondered if they would tip over. Buck whinnied once. His eyes appeared to open wider. But the boat held steady. The angle of the deck was not as severe as Morgan had anticipated.

Ashley stood behind Buck at the tiller and grinned even wider. "Don't you worry none," he said to Morgan. "You in good hands wid us." He patted the buckskin on the haunch and laughed. "You neither, horse. Ain't nothin' to fear on da ocean in dis good boat."

Ashley steered the sailboat easily across Biscayne Bay and masterfully negotiated the rock jetties lining the inlet. He was forced to tack once against the east breeze, but the falling tide swept the nimble craft swiftly toward the ocean.

"Dats Miami Beach," Ashley said pointing to the north. "Dey say one day it be full of hotels an' people from da north."

Morgan looked with fascination at the ocean unfolding before the boat. Along the beach the water curled and crashed against the shore. The waves washed up on the white sand and turned it momentarily tan before retreating back to the sea. Off the beach the water changed to a bright green and then, farther out, transformed to a radiant blue.

The bow of the boat rose slowly and eased gently over the first swell pushing from the east. Morgan found the sensation comforting and exhilarating. He steadied himself against the rail and looked at Buck. The horse stood calmly, swinging his head back and forth to absorb all the new sights and sensations.

"We gots ourselves a sea horse," Cecil said as he moved back from the mast and rubbed Buck's muzzle affectionately.

Ashley laughed. "You don't say much, Cecil," he said. "But you sure gots a sense of humor."

Morgan smiled and nodded in appreciation of the joke he didn't understand.

*   *   *

The vastness of the Atlantic impressed Morgan in spite of his understanding of its size. He had studied the maps in widow O'Brien's Atlas with fascination, tracing imaginary journeys in his mind, moving his finger slowly to simulate the time required to travel the distances represented. But Morgan's virtual voyages could not prepare him for the reality of the ocean. There was nothing as far as the eye could see except gently rolling hills of water.

Ashley positioned Morgan at the tiller and allowed him to steer. He pointed at the sail. "We be sailin' to da wind," he explained. "You gots to keep da boat pointed to da east cuz' dats where we goin'. If you head too high, da sail drop its wind an' we stop. So jus' keep pointin' as high as da wind will allow. We go dis way for an' hour, den we tack and go another hour in da other direction. Ain't nothin' to it."

With Ashley's powerful, practiced hand on the tiller, there *was* nothing to it! Under Morgan's unskilled guidance, keeping the sailboat properly trimmed and the sail full was a constant battle of tiny adjustments.

"We be dere sooner if you sail in a straight line," Cecil observed with a bemused expression.

Ashley laughed. Morgan concentrated harder to master the challenging new skill. The sailboat relentlessly cut through the waves as the sun fell into the horizon behind and turned the heavens a brilliant vermillion.

*   *   *

Dawn broke with a suggestive pale hue before the sun burst above the ocean surface and ignited the day with a glorious array of blues. The ocean appeared cobalt. The sky brightened from robin's egg to indigo. Morgan shook sleep from his eyes and stood. Buck was drinking happily from a wooden bucket of fresh water.

"Good mornin'," Ashley called from the helm. "Ain't much farther 'till we be in Bimini."

"I slept soundly," Morgan said. "The motion of the boat must agree with me."

"Maybe you ain't a mountain man after all," Cecil observed. "Maybe you a man o' da sea like us."

"You should have awakened me for my shift," Morgan said. "I feel badly that you had to steer all night."

"Ain't no big ting," Ashley said with a broad smile. "You was lookin' so peaceful, I didn' want to disturb you."

"Well, I thank you," Morgan said. "I guess I needed the sleep."

Ashley pointed ahead. "See where da sky be takin' on a little green color?"

Morgan looked and nodded. "I see what you mean."

"Dat's da shallow water. Dats da reflection off da flats. You can always tell when you approachin' da bank by da color o' da sky.

A dark smudge soon popped from the horizon slightly to the north of the boat's course. The outline of trees became apparent.

"Dat's da pines," Ashley explained. "Dey be coverin' da north end o' da Island."

More dry land quickly stretched toward the south from the heavy groove of pine trees. A glistening beach bordered the length of higher ground. The purple-blue of the deep water gave way to turquoise and then gleaming white as a sand bar extended from the south end of North Bimini. Tiny wavelets lapped over the shallows, and Ashley adroitly sailed his vessel around the south end of the sandbar and up a narrow channel between the bar and the beach.

Morgan sat back against the rail and absorbed the stunning beauty of the entrance to the Bimini harbor. Three huge creatures swam effortlessly ahead of the boat. Long, narrow tails trailed behind their graceful, undulating bodies.

"Dem's eagle rays," Cecil said. "You can always tell by da white spots on dere backs. Look at dere heads. Jus' like da bird."

Morgan looked into the pale, crystal clear, water. The beaks of the animals looked like the eagles he had seen soaring in the sky above the magnificent mountains.

Cecil lowered the sail as Ashley guided the sailboat into a shallow cove and gently drifted the bow into the soft sand of the beach.

"We be home," Ashley said smiling. "Now alls we got to do is find a place for you an' your horse to live."

"Dat shouldn't be no problem," Cecil added. "Plenty o' people willin' to rent a room. But we gots to do some-ting 'bout dem clothes. Dat cowboy get-up and boots ain't gonna work on Bimini."

~ 27 ~

Morgan stood barefoot in the shallow water of Porgy Bay just north of Alicetown in the Bimini harbor. The six months he had spent on the island had bronzed his skin and hardened his physique. He had grown another inch and added ten pounds to his chiseled frame. His short sleeve shirt, stiffened with countless salt-water washes and bleached by the sun, exposed the bunched muscles of his arms. His blonde hair had lightened to streaked platinum.

He lifted a hand and waved to Alrick Brown standing ready to sail the thirty-foot sloop Morgan had purchased shortly after arriving in Bimini. Morgan had hired twenty-one men for a sponging operation that was about to embark on another voyage.

"Good luck," Morgan called. "I'll see you in a week."

"Don't worry none, Master Morgan," Alrick yelled. "We get 'em again, like always."

"I know you will," Morgan shouted with an exaggerated salute. "You fellows are the best."

Percy Hinzey, the mate on Morgan's sloop, pulled the anchor line and Stanley Davis, cook for the fleet, hauled the main sheet aloft. Alrick grasped the tiller and glanced back at the string of ten dinghies tied in a line to the transom. Percy and Stanley, along with the eighteen other Bimini men huddled on the foredeck, would handle the small boats in pairs when the sponging procedure commenced.

The sloop departed the Bimini harbor and turned north, circling the island and then entering the vast stretch of the Great Bahama Bank just below North Rock. Alrick sailed east over waters he had previously fished, until he arrived some twenty miles from Bimini in an area he suspected was ripe with sponges. He anchored the sloop, and the men boarded the dinghies and dispersed over the grounds searching for saleable sponges. The first man was the sculler who maneuvered the tiny craft over the shallow water with a single oar. The bowman knelt in the bow of the dingy and scanned the sea floor through a round bucket fitted with a glass bottom. The hand-held device allowed perfect, undistorted, visibility.

When the bowman spotted a sponge, he scooped it up with a long-handled shaft fitted on the end with a two-pronged hook. "I gots one," the bowman called as he stood and hauled the sponge aboard. "It be a good velvet."

Velvet and wool sponges were highly prized for their softness. The reef, hardhead and yellow sponges were less valuable and considered non-commercial.

Morgan had made the initial two trips on his new sloop learning the details of sponging and understanding how much could be accomplished in a single day's operation. He hired Bimini men willing to work diligently and paid them above the average wage. In the very difficult times of the Great War, virtually all trade with the islands had been cut off, and the natives had to rely on their ingenuity to survive. Morgan had no trouble staffing his sponging operation.

When the dinghies were loaded with sponges, they returned to the sloop. Velvets and wools were piled together; all other varieties were kept separate. The small boats continued to fish day after day, with the mother sloop moving to keep the fleet over fresh bottom, until the larger boat was full. Rudimentary meals were served aboard the sloop, and the men slept under the stars with only canvas tarpaulins for cover.

When the sloop was finally overflowing with sponges after six or seven days at sea, Alrick Brown ordered the men to tie their dinghies in a line to the stern and sailed back to Bimini.

Once more in the protection of Bimini harbor, the sponges were unloaded and placed in fenced areas along the shoreline to soak.

After a week in the "kraals", where the tide swept across twice a day, the sponges were removed and beaten with wooden bats before being washed and dried in the sun.

Ready for sale, Morgan counted his inventory as Alrick and Percy loaded the sloop for departure to the Nassau Sponge Exchange where they would be sold to the highest bidder.

"I figure about ten thousand pounds this trip," Morgan said studying his notes when the loading process was complete. "And I think the quality is excellent."

Alrick would sail to Nassau with the load of sponges, which would be sorted on the dock into lots according to quality. A "wharfage" charge of one-half percent of the gross proceeds would be deducted by the broker for landing the crop on the dock. Another five percent "brokerage" commission was deducted for conducting the sale of the sponges. A final two percent was charged for "drayage" to the warehouse by horse and buggy. The final product would be pressed into bales with protective burlap and wired tight for shipment to the United States or Europe. Alrich would finally leave Nassau with the net proceeds in cash according to the Sponge and Turtle Fisheries Act of 1905 that mandated payment in cash to protect the fishermen from the clever nefariousness of the businessmen in Nassau.

"Me an' da fellas sure appreciate da chance to work wid you, Morgan," Alrick said. "Tings ain't so good on da island dese days as you know."

"I understand," Morgan said. "When you get back I want to talk about another idea I have. I was riding Buck around the north end of North Bimini a few days ago and found some areas I think we can plant with sisal. When the sponge season slows down, what do you think of doing some farming?"

"I don' know nothin' 'bout farming, Morgan," Alrick replied. "Most of us Bimini men consider the sea our home."

Morgan laughed and opened his arms in acknowledgement of Alrick's remark. "I don't think I could ever make you a farmer, but we could put some of the women to work planting, cultivating and harvesting sisal. We could even make rope. I heard the Andros Fibre Company has hundreds of women working on their plantation. I want you to oversee the operation for me when you aren't fishing."

"Dat be good puttin' da women to work," Alrick replied. "But where you gonna be? You ain't tinkin' 'bout leavin' Bimini, is you?"

Morgan shook his head. For the last several weeks he had wrestled with thoughts of returning to Florida and joining the military. Many of the Bimini men including Benjamin, Uriah and Edwin Rolle and Alaric and Herbert Saunders had joined the British West India Regiment and were serving in Europe and Africa. Other men had left the island and were engaged in contract farming in Florida to feed the military, which was expanding for an expected entrance into the war.

Morgan's brief experience with Pancho Villa's army had inspired an appreciation for the bonding that he saw among men committed to a common cause. Villa's ragtag group of turncoats, peasants and hired gringos wasn't an exemplar of a professional army, but still the men had displayed deep fraternal feelings that Morgan found lacking in his life.

In the evenings, sitting on his porch, Morgan imagined brave men in creased uniforms ready to attack cowering Germans. Trumpets in perfect harmony announced every charge. Glorious explosions painted the sky but no American soldier fell. Enemy bullets always missed their targets. Advance was the only direction. Glory and adulation from appreciative young French girls with fresh skin and red lips followed each battle.

Morgan dreamed of repulsing the enemy at the gates of Paris, pushing the Germans back, and the final triumph of victory. Bimini would again be prosperous and free trade would propel the population of the island from bare subsistence to a modicum of prosperity.

But what army could Morgan join? Would the English allow him to serve with their forces? Could he join the French army without a syllable of the language in his repertoire? Rumors suggesting the United States might join the fracas had circulated for a year. How much longer could his country hold out before coming to the aid of its closest ally?

"I might leave Bimini for a while," Morgan finally announced to Alrick. "But I'm going to leave the sloop for you to continue working until I return. I'll purchase the land to grow sisal. You'll be able to feed your family and keep a little money while I'm away."

"I don't knows if I likes dis," Alrick said with genuine sadness in his voice. Morgan had become more than an employer. The two young men had become close friends.

"I'll come back," Morgan said. "Things will be better. There's just something I feel I have to do."

"It must be important if it means leavin' here," Alrick said fighting back a tear. "I hopes you knows what you're doin'."

Morgan swallowed his emotion and blinked. "I do, too," he said at last. "I do, too."

~ 28 ~

Word that the United States had declared war on Germany on April 6, 1917 reached Bimini two days later when a sloop returned to the island from Miami.

"Da United States done joined da war," Bahamians repeated until there wasn't a single inhabitant who hadn't heard the news. "Da war be over befor' long now!"

Morgan and Alrick were informed of the monumental event the moment they moored the boat after a sponging trip.

"We're leaving for Miami with the morning tide," Morgan announced. "I'm going to leave a letter with Commissioner George Sherman granting you unrestricted use of the sloop and the sisal farm. You should be all right while I'm away."

"You goin' off to fight in da war, ain't ya?" Alrick protested. "Why you want to do such a fool ting as dat?"

The question had haunted Morgan during many sleepless nights. The widow O'Brien had told him his father was the youngest brother of the famous frontier marshal Wyatt Earp. Marshal Longstreet had told Morgan about the gunfight in Tombstone in 1881 in detail during several of their hunting expeditions. He knew how his three uncles, Virgil, Wyatt and Morgan and a dentist friend named John Henry Holliday had stood virtually toe-to-toe with four cattle thieves and exchanged pistol shots for almost a minute. But the story of the shooting had never resonated with Morgan. It was an event from another era involving people he had never met.

Nevertheless, Morgan understood he shared blood with these men who had stood bearing weapons in several of the mining camps and cattle towns of the old west to bring law and order to the community. Was this genetic connection the ingredient in his make-up that now pushed him inexorably toward the war in Europe? Had the blood of his father and his uncles inevitably dictated his involvement with Pancho Villa's army? Would Morgan have avoided the deadly confrontation with the murderous Basque if he were not, in reality, an Earp by birth?

Morgan looked at Alrick and released a long sigh. He shook his head and lifted his shoulders in apparent bewilderment. How could he explain his feelings when he wasn't certain of his own motivations? He had read about the celebrated killers John Wesley Hardin and Billy the Kid in the dime novels that flooded the country hungry for titillating stories of the old west. Morgan's killings hadn't brought him joy, but he hadn't regretted his actions either.

Duty was a difficult concept to articulate, but Morgan knew he felt an irresistible obligation to serve his country in the war. He understood the hardship the conflict had brought to Bimini and the friends he had made on the island. If he could help alleviate some of the suffering by bringing the war to a close, that would be a worthwhile endeavor.

"I just feel like it's the right thing to do," Morgan finally answered simply. "I'm an American. My country is at war."

"Dere be plenty men to go," Alrick said. "Why you gots to go?"

"Take good care of old Buck for me," Morgan said. "He's the oldest friend I've got in the entire world."

"A lot of foolishness," Alrick concluded with a final shake of his head.

*   *   *

Morgan waved his hand toward Alrick before slinging his pack over his shoulder and walking from the wharf toward the main street of Miami. Only after he turned did he wipe the tears from his cheeks and sniffle back his emotions. Would he ever see his friend again? Would he ever again see the island of Bimini he had come to love?

139

Strangely, as he fought the heartbreaking emotion of his departure, his spirits began to soar with the thoughts of the adventure on which he was about to embark.

The bustle of the city and the energy of the scurrying people soon lifted the gloom from Morgan's mood. He approached a policeman standing on a corner busy waving automobiles through an intersection.

"Where can I find a place to join the army?" Morgan called over the din of the traffic. "I just heard the country's at war."

"Over by the train station a few blocks west of here," the constable replied. "From what I hear there's lots of young men signing up these past few days."

"Thanks."

Morgan adjusted his pack and lengthened his stride to dart between two approaching motor coaches. He jumped to the edge of the sand street and headed for the station where he had arrived nearly a year earlier.

A large American flag festooned the entrance to a small shed adjacent to the station. A soldier sat behind a desk inside the open door. A stack of papers and a Bible resided at his elbows. The man's uniform was a drab olive color. His shoes were dull and tarnished. Sweat stains marred the limp shirt.

Morgan peered inside and looked around the bare room. "Is this where I join the army?" he asked.

"That's right, sonny," the soldier replied in a bored voice. "All's you got to do is sign these here papers."

"It's that simple?"

"Ain't nothin' to it."

Morgan advanced toward the desk and reached for the proffered pen. He turned the paper and lowered his hand to affix his signature. Inexplicably, he hesitated. He looked at the soldier sitting behind the desk and raised the pen from the document.

The loud crunching of heels grinding smartly into the path outside the shed grasped Morgan's attention. He looked out the door and opened his eyes wide in surprise. A tall, erect, soldier walked smartly past. His uniform pants were sky blue with a 1-1/8th inch red "blood stripe" running down the side. His blouse was darker blue with a standing collar. Polished emblems featuring a globe with an eagle and an anchor glistened on either side of his neck, the "bird and ball" in Marine parlance. Four rows of ribbons adorned his left chest and three prominent chevrons stood out on each arm. His shoes were polished to a mirror finish and a shiny belt encircled his trim waist.

"Who's that?" Morgan asked.

The soldier looked up and waved a dismissive hand. "That's a fancy pants Marine."

"Do they fight?"

"They consider themselves the best fighters of all the services. If it's fightin' you want, maybe that's the outfit for you."

"Marines," repeated Morgan. "I don't think I've ever heard of them."

"Go talk to the man," the soldier said. "They don't take just anybody."

"Thanks," Morgan said. "I think I will."

Morgan walked to the Marine recruiting office and knocked tentatively on the door. "Are you taking new Marines here?"

The sergeant looked up and smiled. "We take young men here and make them Marines," he said. "Most don't make the Corps, but those that do, they belong to the best outfit on earth."

"Do I get to wear a uniform like yours?" Morgan asked. "I sure admire what you're wearing compared to that soldier."

"I'll have one in your size ready when you get to boot camp in Parris Island," the sergeant said.

"Paris Island?" Morgan said. "You'll send me to boot camp in France?"

"If you make the Corps, you'll get to France soon enough. But boot camp is in Parris Island, South Carolina. Before you get a crack at the Hun, you'll need to become a Marine first."

"I'd like a chance to try."

"How old are you, son?"

"Seventeen."

"You'll have to get your parents to sign for you," the sergeant said. "Eighteen is the minimum age."

Morgan looked down and closed his eyes. "They're dead."

"Both of them?"

Morgan nodded without speaking.

"You'll have to come back when you're eighteen."

Morgan shook his head. "I don't think I want to wait. I'll join the army," he said. "I'll lie and tell them I'm eighteen."

The sergeant looked at Morgan. He had served in the Marine Corps for fifteen years, experiencing combat in Nicaragua. He had seen recruits in training and in the field. Something about this young man struck him as exceptional material for the Corps. To surrender such a candidate to the army seemed to be a foolish loss for the Marines over a mere technicality.

"Where it asks when you were born, put down 1899," the sergeant said simply.

Morgan spun the paper and signed his name to the recruitment form. After raising his right hand and swearing allegiance to the United States and the United States Marine Corps, he was officially a boot on his way to Parris Island.

"You were just kidding about the uniform, I guess," Morgan said as shook the sergeant's hand.

The sergeant smiled. "I was kidding. Before you can wear the uniform of my Marine Corps you'll have to prove that you're worthy. But I'm guessing you'll do just fine. Good luck, son."

~ 29 ~

Morgan Early stepped to the Recruit Depot dock on Parris Island, South Carolina, from the ferryboat that had transported him the short distance across Beaufort Sound from Port Royal. Forty-nine other bewildered young men who, along with Morgan, would make up Recruit Platoon #7, hustled on to the weathered wooden structure and began looking around dubiously. The date was April 14, 1917.

"What the hell you civilian pukes lookin' at?" screamed a starched corporal from the steps of a battered bus parked at the end of the dock. "Get on this bus, double time."

Fifty pairs of feet immediately began running for the bus. "Move! Move! Move!" the corporal yelled as he slapped a baton into his palm impatiently.

Within seconds the bus was loaded with sweaty young men. The door slammed shut and the driver accelerated away from the pier.

"We got about a three minute drive to the Recruit Depot," the corporal announced. "When this door opens you people will double time off the bus and fall in on the deck. Place your grubby civilian feet on the yellow footprints painted on the hardtop. Heels together and toes apart, forty-five degrees. You will stop acting like runny-nose, spoiled, soft civilian slobs immediately and start learning to be Marines."

Morgan looked at the boy seated beside him and smiled. "I wonder what's made this Marine so mad," he said extending his hand in greeting. "My name's Morgan."

"Corky Jones," the short, squatty recruit replied as he took Morgan's hand. "I'm from Hilltop, Kentucky."

Morgan nodded. "I guess I'm from Arizona, but lately I've been living on an island off Florida."

"How 'bout that," Jones said. "I ain't never been on an island."

"You're on one now," Morgan said. "And it looks like this is our home for the next three months."

"All right, maggots," the corporal shouted from the front of the bus. "We're here. All's I want to see are assholes and elbows when this door opens. You're about to meet your lord and master."

"We goin' to church?" Corky Jones called out with a grin as he started down the isle.

"You don't talk unless spoken to, puke," the corporal snarled as Corky stretched a truncated leg to descend the steps. With a vicious shove the corporal propelled Corky Jones out of the bus. The pudgy recruit skidded to a halt on the hard surface in a tangled heap.

"Get up, maggot," a new voice growled. "Fall in."

"I jus' did fall in," Corky Jones protested from his prone position. "I got to do it again?"

"Feet on the yellow footprints! Feet on the yellow footprints!"

Fifty boys, the oldest not yet twenty and most just eighteen or younger, scrambled to locate a free set of painted footprints and adjust his feet to the Marine Corps' position of attention, heels touching and toes apart.

"ATTENTION!" bellowed Staff Sergeant Hill.

The recruits of Platoon #7 stiffened in various, disparate, erect postures.

"My name is Staff Sergeant Hill," the medium height, broad-shouldered Marine barked in a commanding voice. His light blue trousers with the blood stripe were perfectly pressed. His tan shirt was starched and creased, and his tan necktie was concisely knotted between the tabs of his stiff collar.

"I will be your drill instructor for the next twelve weeks. Many of you will not last twelve weeks," Sergeant Hill stated. "I will not allow an unworthy recruit to pollute my beloved Corps."

Fifty boys shifted uncomfortably in their positions.

"The first word out of your mouth at all times will be 'sir'," Sergeant Hill barked. "Am I understood?"

Several of the boys managed a meek "yes."

The sergeant dashed from his position in front of the assembled platoon and pressed his face against the nose of one of the boys in the front row. "What did you say, maggot?"

The boy replied in a loose Texas twang. "I said 'yes'."

"I told you the first word out of your mouth was to be 'sir', didn't I?"

"That's what you said," the tall, slim, gangly boy replied.

"Drop down and give me twenty," Sergeant Hill bellowed.

"Twenty what?" the Texan asked with genuine confusion spread across his gaunt face.

"Twenty push-ups, moron," the sergeant shouted. "And I better not see that back sag or that butt in the air. I want Marine Corps push-ups."

"Okay," the boy said as he bent over and lowered his hands toward the ground.

"You," Staff Sergeant Hill said to Morgan standing next to the Texan. "Do you get it yet?"

"Sir," Morgan said sharply. "Yes, sir."

"And how about you, the dumpy one there?" Sergeant Hill called to Corky Jones. "You get it?"

"Get what, sergeant?" Corky stammered.

"The first word out of your mouth is always 'sir'," Sergeant Hill repeated, exasperation building in his voice. "Now you give me twenty."

"Sir. Yes, sir," Corky Jones managed as he dropped to his knees and fell forward on his hands.

"How about the rest of you civilian maggots? Do you get it?"

"Sir. Yes, sir," several of the recruits managed.

"I can't hear you," Sergeant Hill called in a sing-song voice.

"Sir! Yes, sir," fifty voices sounded in unison.

"That's better. Now listen up. You stand at attention with your shoulders back, your stomachs pulled in; your hips are thrust forward, your thumb and forefinger lay along the seam of your trousers and your eyes are straight ahead. Do I make myself clear?"

"Sir! Yes sir!"

"All right. ATTENTION! Pull those shoulders back. Suck those guts in. Get those hands positioned. And stop those eyeballs from flyin' around."

"Sir! Yes, sir!"

Sergeant Hill approached Corky Jones who had managed to complete six push-ups and was lying panting on the ground.

"Off the deck, maggot."

"Sir, yes, sir," Jones said in a weak voice with sweat running from his nose.

"What's your name, puff-ball? Come to attention."

"Sir. Corky Jones, sir."

"You want to leave now? You want to be my first D.O.R?"

"Sir. I don't rightly know what a D.O.R is."

"D.O.R!" Staff Sergeant Hill spat the letters slowly. "Drop on request. Leave Parris Island and go directly to the army."

Comprehension swept slowly over Corky Jones. "Sir. No sir. I don't want to go home. My Pa, he'd tan my hide if I was to shame him like that."

"You best get squared away, recruit. I don't think I want you in my Marine Corps."

"Sir. I'll get squared away, sir," Corky Jones said earnestly. "I don't want no D.O.R."

Staff Sergeant Hill retreated to his position in front of the platoon. Five rows of ten boys stood on fifty pairs of painted footprints in a ragged semblance of attention.

"When I say 'fall out', you take one step back with your left foot, pivot one hundred eighty degrees on your right toe and run for the first building behind you. Find a cot and put your civilian junk on top. You will have one minute to accomplish that and return to this position. Understood?"

"Sir! Yes, sir!"

"FALL OUT!" Staff Sergeant Hill bellowed.

Pandemonium ensued as fifty boys attempted their first formation dismissal and charged off to the recently constructed barracks that would be their home for their stay on Parris Island.

~ 30 ~

Morgan Early lay on his cot and stared up at the springs holding the mattress above his head.

Staff Sergeant Hill had just turned the lights off and led the fifty exhausted recruits in singing the first stanza of the Marine Corps Hymn.

> From the halls of Montezuma,
> To the shores of Tripoli.
> We fight our country's battles
> On the land as on the sea.
> Admiration of the nation,
> We're the finest ever seen.
> And we glory in the title
> Of United States Marines.

Then he had slammed the hatch shut.

"Hey Texas," Morgan whispered to the boy in the upper bunk. "I'm Morgan. What's your name?"

"Slim," the recruit said. "Slim Hitchins."

"Quite a day," Morgan said with a small laugh.

"You can say that again," Slim called back in a low voice. "I ain't no greenhorn when it comes to workin' on the ranch. But I ain't never been this tired in all my days." Tired came out *'tarred'*.

When the recruits had reassembled on the footprints after depositing their bags on a bunk, Sergeant Hill had shouted 'ATTENTION'. The platoon alternated between 'attention' and 'at ease' until the boys achieved a modicum of military bearing.

They were next run to the supply building and issued olive drab, twill, fatigue uniforms, underwear, socks, boots, and soft hats. The platoon then double-timed back to the barracks, discarded their civilian clothes, stowed them away in a wooden footlocker, and dressed for the first time in Marine Corps issued clothing.

Corky Jones observed to Morgan his uniform looked like a tent draped on his pudgy body.

"You'll get the hang of it," Morgan said reassuringly.

The recruits then attempted to march for the first time to the mess hall where they were fed heaping portions of chicken and mashed potatoes and told to drink three glasses of water. Twenty minutes after sitting at long tables for lunch, they were roused from the mess hall and herded to the barbershop for a military haircut.

"Jus' a touch off the top, if you don' mind," Corky Jones requested of the barber seconds before the sharp hand-held clippers removed his mane within an eighth of an inch of his scalp.

"Them barbers don't have a lick of sense about fashion," Corky confided to Morgan in formation after their turn in the chair.

"No talking in ranks," Sergeant Hill had bellowed. "Give me twenty, butter-ball."

"Sir. Yes, sir," Corky Jones shouted out before falling to the ground to commence his punishment.

"Nomenclature!" Sergeant Hill had screamed. "This is the Marine Corps. The recruit who can't keep his mouth shut is doing push-ups on the 'deck'. Doors are 'hatches'. The latrine is the 'head'. Your helmet is a 'cover'. You salute only when 'covered'. You salute officers. I am not an officer. I am your D.I., your drill instructor. Am I understood?"

"Sir! Yes, sir!"

"Back to the barracks. Take five for a head call. Then back here double-time. We're heading to the grinder to learn to march. FALL OUT!"

On the grinder, the enormous blacktop expanse behind the barracks, Staff Sergeant Hill began the laborious process of teaching Platoon #7 to march.

"Every command has two parts," Sergeant Hill had instructed. "The first part is the preparatory command. 'FORWARD' alerts you a command is coming. The second command is the command of execution. That command tells you what to do. 'MARCH' means start marching. Do you understand?"

"Sir. Yes, sir."

"When I want you to stop, the preparatory command is 'PLATOON'. The command of execution is "HALT'. Is that clear?"

"Sir. Yes, sir."

"You always start off on your left foot. When I give the command of execution 'HALT', I will give it on your left foot. You will take one more step on your right foot and bring your left foot to a halt beside the right. Understood?"

"Sir. Yes, sir."

"FORWARD...MARCH."

Forty left feet advanced. Ten right feet moved forward.

"Your other left foot, maggots. Do it again."

"FORWARD...MARCH."

Recruit Platoon #7 moved off in a semblance of order.

"LEFT...your LEFT...your LEFT, RIGHT, LFFT," Sergeant Hill called in a surprisingly harmonious cadence.

Morgan marched with his shoulders back and eyes straight ahead. The nearly simultaneous movement of the recruits sent a mild chill of excitement through him. He began to feel the power of the group and the initial sense of teamwork and coordination.

"Dig those heels in," Staff Sergeant Hill called. "I want to hear you together. Dig 'em in!"

The platoon responded. A crisp, crunching sound, surprisingly concurrent, accompanied the sergeant's cadence call.

"LEFT...LEFT...your LEFT, RIGHT, LEFT.

"PLATOON...HALT!

"LEFT...FACE.

"RIGHT...FACE.

"FORWARD...MARCH.

"TO THE REAR...MARCH."

Platoon #7 had marched until chow time. After chow they ran ten laps around the grinder on the way back to the barracks. Inside, Staff Sergeant Hill had instructed the recruits how to make their beds ('racks' in Marine Corps parlance) complete with hospital corners, stow their uniforms in their lockers and spit shine their boots.

The gentle sounds of snoring now resonated through the barracks. Fifty thoroughly spent boys, their first day on Parris Island complete, fell rapidly into deep, untroubled sleep.

(The Marine Corps Hymn at the beginning of the chapter is the version used before 1919.)

~ 31 ~

At precisely 0500 hours, Sergeant Hill opened the hatch of Platoon #7's barracks and entered. His uniform was perfectly pressed. He was freshly shaved and showered.

He removed the lid from the galvanized trashcan standing nearby and reached his baton inside. With a rapid rotation of his hand he ran the baton around the inside of the empty can several times. The unexpected clamor in the silence of the barracks was ear shattering.

Fifty recruits jolted awake in various stages of fright and disorientation.

"What the hell..." Corky Jones managed. "Don't nobody have no proper manners in the morning?"

"Out of those racks," Staff Sergeant Hill hollered. "You have fifteen minutes to brush you teeth, get dressed and fall in for chow."

Winslow MacIntosh 3rd dropped to the deck beside Morgan from the adjacent bunk. "I'll have to tell father about the despicable lack of courtesy around here," he said. "Imagine being awakened in such barbaric fashion."

"What time is it?" Morgan asked. "I feel like I just went to sleep thirty minutes ago."

"It's 5:00 AM, paleface," Cochise Birdsong said with a smile on his ruddy, wide face as he rolled out of the bunk below MacIntosh. "Time to get up and start learning how to scalp Germans."

Ira Silverstein yawned and swung his narrow feet to the deck. "Fifteen minutes?" he said with a small laugh. "I'm from New York. What'll I do with the other seven minutes?"

Recruit Platoon #7 managed to finish their rituals in the head, dress and fall in outside their barracks for chow within the allotted time. Staff Sergeant Hill ordered 'ATTENTION', and the recruits locked their heels together, pulled back their shoulders and stiffened with their hands properly positioned along their trouser seams.

"RIGHT...FACE"

"FORWARD...MARCH"

Platoon #7 marched off to breakfast in the muggy darkness of the South Carolina morning.

The next two weeks proceeded at the same frantic pace from reveille at 0500 until lights out at 2200 hours. Rigorous physical training with push-ups, sit-ups, squats, and running followed morning chow. The recruits marched in the morning and again after lunch. The platoon ran along the sandy trails near the Beaufort Sound, gradually increasing the distances covered as their young bodies hardened, unused muscles strengthened and civilian fat melted away.

Commander's time in the barracks was built into the training schedule to allow the recruits to clean their uniforms, sew buttons and shine shoes and belt buckles. The young men used the opportunity to acquaint themselves with their fellow mates.

"Have you fellows noticed the number of empty racks is growing?" Morgan said to Corky and Slim as they were busy bringing a fine luster to the toes of their boots with saliva and polish.

"Now that you mention it," Corky said, "there's a decided decrease in our numbers. Where's everybody gone that we don't know nothing about?"

Corky's pudgy body had begun a transformation that necessitated the reissue of his uniform in a smaller size. "Maybe the Hun been sneakin' around capturin' us before we can git to France and kick them back to Germany."

Ira Silverstein sat at the foot of Morgan's bunk. "Our platoon may be shrinking," he said. "But have you noticed the number of platoons is growing? It seems like boys are arriving every day."

On April 6, 1917, when the United States declared war on Germany, the Marine Corps consisted of 462 officers and 13,214 enlisted men. By the end of the war, those numbers had increased to 2,431 officers and 70,489 enlisted men.

Cochise Birdsong joined the group and began to sew a button on his blouse. The needle passed through the garment and stabbed him in the finger. "Damn," he said in exasperation. "My grandmother could make a whole dress out of an antelope hide, and I can't replace a single button without drawing blood."

"Where are you from?" Morgan asked as he laughed at Birdsong's comments.

"A little place called Turkey Creek in Arizona. You ever heard of it, Morgan?"

"I was born in Wilcox," Morgan said. "It was a mining camp until the silver ran out. But I never heard of Turkey Creek."

"You didn't miss much," Birdsong said sadly. "Turkey Creek ain't nothin' but a dead end. That's why I'm here."

*   *   *

Recruit Platoon #7 stood at ease in front of the Parris Island armory. Staff Sergeant Hill walked slowly in front of his charges holding a rifle horizontally in his hands.

"Every man in the United States Marine Corps is a rifleman," he said firmly. "Every cook, every machine gunner, every truck driver, every officer, every desk clerk in the Marine Corps is a rifleman. No man will be sent overseas who has not qualified as a 'marksman'. Understood?"

"Sir. Yes, sir."

"This rifle is a bolt-action Springfield M1903. It fires a caliber .30-06 150-grain round at 2,800 feet per second. It weighs 8.7 lbs. and holds five rounds in an internal box magazine. This weapon is your best friend. It is more loyal than your mother. It is more beautiful than your girlfriend. You will know the nomenclature of every piece that comprises this rifle. You will be able to fieldstrip your Springfield and reassemble it blindfolded. You will be able to fire it with complete accuracy at distances of 500 yards. Are there any questions?"

"Sir. No, sir."

"You will enter the armory single file. You will sign for your weapon when it is issued. Memorize the serial number. Fall in outside the armory with your rifle. We will double-time to the rifle range when everyone has his weapon. We will learn the various firing positions of the Springfield rifle. We will "click-in" from each position. We will practice firing without ammunition until each of you masters the firing positions. Only then will you be allowed to fire live ammunition."

*   *   *

Morgan knelt on the deck of the barracks with his Springfield in front of him. Winslow MacIntosh 3rd, Cochise Birdsong, Ira Silverstein, Slim Hitchins and Corky Jones sat cross-legged, completing a tight circle around the weapon.

"How do you know so much about this weapon?" Cochise asked. "You ever owned one before?"

"No," Morgan said. "But I've had some experience with rifles. I guess it just comes easy to me."

"Well, I've never even seen a rifle except in a magazine," Ira Silverstein said. "In New York a tire iron or a knife is the most popular weapon."

Winslow MacIntosh 3rd looked down his patrician nose and sniffed. "I've fired shot guns at birds, but this contraption has too many parts. Show us again how to take it apart."

"Okay," Morgan said. "We'll go real slowly this time. You call out the names of the parts as I take them off the rifle."

Corky Jones shook his head. "I don't know how I'm supposed to tear that thing apart when all's I got at the end of my hands are ten thumbs."

"You better learn," Cochise Birdsong said with a laugh. "Otherwise you'll be back in Hilltop with your Pa beatin' on your behind."

"Oh Lord," Corky Jones sighed. "Don't remind me."

"Okay, here we go again," Morgan said as he carefully began to disassemble the Springfield. He retracted the bolt, removed it from the weapon and held it aloft. "What is this called?"

*   *   *

154

Morgan stood behind the line with the other members of Recruit Platoon #7 as they waited their turn to fire live ammunition. Another platoon was stretched in front of him in the prone position. Down range, large target boards appeared before each shooter, each one raised independently on pulleys by members of a recruit platoon working from deep pits in the sandy soil.

"LOCK AND LOAD," called the range officer. "Five rounds slow fire."

The recruits on the line retracted the bolts of their Springfields, inserted five rounds of live .30-06 ammunition into the weapon from a stripper clip, and closed the bolts.

"ALL READY ON THE FIRING LINE," bellowed the range officer.

The recruits snapped the safeties on their rifles to the "off" position. Morgan experienced a strange harmony with the snick of metal against metal.

"FIRE."

The sound of three dozen high-powered rifles split the air. For most of the recruits on the range it was the first time they had heard gunfire. To Morgan Early the sound was eerily comforting. Thoughts of hunting with Marshal Longstreet a decade earlier filtered through his mind. The thrill of the adrenalin-charged encounters with the Mexican *Federales* while serving with Pancho Villa returned with the sharp snapping of firing pins against loaded steel casings followed by the crack of exploding gunpowder.

The buttery workings of a precision engineered weapon held an endless fascination for Morgan. The smooth interaction of the finely honed parts was as beautiful as a sunset over azure waters. The calm, dispassionate deadliness of a rifle was a tribute to man's ingenuity to create a tool capable of conquering his surroundings.

But the recruits on the firing line had much to learn about marksmanship. Following each volley, the target was quickly lowered, a square of red tape was stuck over the entry point, and the target raised so the recruit could see where his shot landed.

Bullets that that failed to hit the target were greeted with an enthusiastic waving of "Maggie's drawers" from the pit, a red flag attached to a raised pole.

"You recruits ain't never gonna git to fight the Hun if you don't learn to shoot straight," the range officer shouted when he scanned down the firing line and witnessed the plethora of red flags fluttering back and forth from the pits.

* * *

Staff Sergeant Hill stood behind Morgan Early as he assumed the Marine Corps standing firing position. The sergeant stared at the target down range through powerful binoculars. Morgan had hit the bull's-eye of the target with each of his first ten rounds from both the prone and sitting positions.

"I ain't never seen a recruit hit bull's-eye his first thirty rounds," Sergeant Hill whispered to another D.I. standing nearby.

"I ain't never seen it any time," the drill instructor replied in a soft voice. "I ain't sure I could do it."

"FIRE," the range officer called.

Morgan eased the butt of the Springfield into his right shoulder and gently rested his cheek on the wooden stock. The leather rifle strap was looped around his left arm. His left hand firmly held the weapon beneath the barrel. He looked through the rear barrel-mounted sight and centered the black ring of the target in the raised front sight. He inhaled calmly and released half his breath. He smoothly squeezed the trigger while the rifle remained absolutely motionless in his grasp. The 150-grain bullet flew unerringly down range and passed through the target paper in the center of the bull's-eye.

Morgan retracted the bolt, ejecting the spent round, and ratcheted the bolt forward, ramming a fresh shell into the chamber. The entire process consumed less than one second.

Sergeant Hill lowered the binoculars and shook his head in disbelief. "The Marine Corps has us a natural born killer," he muttered to himself as Morgan fired another round into the center of the target.

* * *

Morgan Early graduated from the U. S. Marine Corps boot camp at Parris Island on July 15, 1917. Recruit Platoon #7, originally fifty strong, contained thirty-one members deemed sufficiently fit by Staff Sergeant Hill to join his beloved Corps.

The recruits had been subjected to intense physical and psychological stress during their twelve weeks on the island. The drill instructors had hiked the boys to exhaustion, forced them to complete simple tasks such as dressing and preparing for chow with insufficient time allowed. The entire exercise was to weed out the recruits who might break or falter in combat.

The boys had been indoctrinated in Marine Corps history to inculcate the tradition of victory in battle. They had learned to march to instill the concept of working together as a platoon.

The recruit program at Parris Island had produced a group of boys with hardened bodies, a keen sense of Marine lore, and a determination to serve their country with distinction. They had learned to shoot the Springfield rifle, but they had not yet learned how to wage war. That would be the job of the non-commissioned and commissioned officers awaiting them in Quantico, Virginia.

Between April, 1917 and November, 1918, 239,274 young American boys applied to join the United States Marine Corps. A startling 177,419 were rejected for medical reasons. Another 1,125 were under age and their parents refused to sign a waiver. Morgan's status as an orphan and his dishonesty at the recruitment office in Miami kept him from adding to that number. Another 373 declined to take the oath of allegiance to the United States. Approximately 60,000, or roughly one quarter of those seeking to join the Marines, made the Corps.

~ 32 ~

Morgan Early stepped off the train in Washington, D.C. with Corky Jones, Slim Hitchins, Ira Silverstein, "Chief" Birdsong, Winslow MacIntosh 3rd and Michael Houlihan, a nineteen-year-old Irish lad from Nashville, Tennessee. The boys looked around in wonder at the broad streets and massive government buildings. It was the first trip to their nation's capital for any of the young recruits.

They were dressed in their service A uniforms with green trousers, khaki long-sleeved shirts and neckties, web belts, spit-polished black shoes and green coats. "Marksman" badges adorned the left breast of every coat save Morgan's; his badge signified "Expert".

Large olive canvas "sea" bags where slung over each shoulder containing toiletries, boots, physical training gear, and "utility" uniforms for wear in the field.

"You ever see such big buildings?" Michael Houlihan marveled. "You could fit all of Nashville in just a couple of 'em."

Ira Silverstein laughed. "Guess you country boys never seen New York. Why, we got buildings so tall they block the sun."

Cochise Birdsong's eyes opened wide in wonder. "You white boys sure like your teepees big," he said. "What happens when the buffalo move on? How do you knock these things down and follow the herd?"

"Come on, Marines," Slim Hitchins said. "There's the bus across the road. I see a corporal 'bout ready to bust a gut if we don't start to hustle."

Loaded with recent graduates of Parris Island, the bus wound through the bustling streets of Washington, crossed the Potomac River and headed south. The steamy heat of summer had invaded the area, and the boys removed their twill coats and cupped the moist air into the open windows of the bus with their hands.

"I certainly hope this frightful weather turns," Winslow MacIntosh 3rd said. "My shirt is nearly soaked through. I'll have to write father to increase my uniform allowance."

"We could use a little wind to cool things off," Slim Hitchins added. "In Texas the wind blows hard enough to knock the fleas off a hound dog."

"Maybe they'll let us fight with just war paint," "Chief" Birdsong said with a shrug. "Be a lot cooler than these heavy cotton outfits."

"By the time we git to fightin'," Corky Jones drawled, "it might jus' be winter time. All this trainin' jus' to kill some Hun. Ain't it getting' tiresome?"

Morgan shook his head slowly and shrugged. "I imagine the best trained army will be the one winning this war. I don't think these Hun are going to be push-overs."

*　　　*　　　*

"My name is Gunnery Sergeant Kidd. I will be your platoon sergeant for the next eight weeks. You have all graduated from Parris Island. You are Marines. There is no need to call me 'sir'. I am not an officer. But I am going to teach you how to fight. I am going to teach you to kill. And I am going to teach you how to survive."

"I like the survival part," Winslow whispered.

Gunnery Sergeant Kidd stood stiffly erect in front of the new Marines standing at attention. His dress blue uniform was sharply creased and pressed. His black shoes reflected the afternoon sun pounding on the hard clay of the Quantico Marine base on the shores of the Potomac thirty miles below Washington. The area above his left breast pocket was adorned with three rows of colorful ribbons.

"At my command, fall out and get squared away in your barracks. The next two months are going to be busy."

"We ain't been busy so far?" Corky Jones hissed under his breath.

"FALL OUT."

       *   *   *

"There's a German machine gun nest on the crest of that hill yonder," Sergeant Kidd said to the young Marines gathered at his feet deep in the forest of the Quantico Marine base. "Your job is to take that hill and eliminate that gun emplacement. Who wants to give it a try?"

"I'll do it, Gunney", Morgan said rising from his haunches and stepping forward.

Heavy foliage hung from the dense clusters of trees on the hillside above the ravine where the Marines were huddled. They had hiked from the barracks in the morning covering eight miles of twisting trails in less than two hours. Their utilities were soaked with sweat. Their packs cut into their shoulders. Their boots were heavy with the red clay soil of the Virginia forest.

"All right, Early," Gunnery Sergeant Kidd replied. "It's your squad. Plan and execute the attack."

Morgan scanned the anxious faces of his comrades. They were participating in their first simulated combat maneuver. Rimmed steel helmets were strapped under their chins. Springfield rifles loaded with blank ammunition were nervously held in their hands. Web gear hung from their shoulders supporting packs and entrenching tools. Laced leggings encircled their lower legs above their sturdy combat boots.

"Secor, Brown, Murray, Hauser, Smith and Louden," he said quickly pointing at each of the boys. "You fellows advance on line to the base of that rise. Keep good intervals. Don't bunch up. Stay spread out. If the machine gun opens up, hit the dirt and take cover. If it doesn't open up, stop and take cover fifty yards from the crest. Don't get closer. Understand?"

The designated boys nodded.

"When you're in position, lay down a steady base of fire on the gun emplacement. Don't panic. Don't shoot too fast. Just enough fire to keep their heads down," Morgan said firmly. "Got it?"

"Got it," several of the boys said.

"I'm going to flank the machine gun with Houlihan, MacIntosh, Silverstein, Hitchins, Jones and the Chief," Morgan continued.

"When you hear us start to shoot, double your rate of fire for sixty seconds. Then stop. I don't want to get shot by you boys just yet."

Strained laughter greeted Morgan's comment.

"Check your watches," Morgan concluded. "We should be in position to charge from the flank about five minutes after you get to cover. Any questions?"

The boys shook their heads.

"Give us a one minute head start around the side of the hill," Morgan said. "Hauser, you're in charge of this group. Keep them apart and on line. Good luck."

"Yes, sir," Bill Hauser said as he unconsciously brought his right hand to his helmet and snapped a salute at Morgan. "Oh...I almost forgot...you aren't an officer."

The boys in Bill Hauser's group looked sheepishly about, momentarily captivated by Morgan's command presence and his firm seizure of authority.

"Remember," Morgan cautioned. "One minute and then you move out."

"Right," Hauser confirmed.

"You six," Morgan ordered as he swept his hand across the crouched boys selected to accompany him, "let's go."

*   *   *

Morgan led his six comrades in a low crouching run around the far edge of the hill. He gripped his Springfield in his right, downhill, hand and trained his eyes toward the summit of the rise. If the gun emplacement was invisible to him, he felt certain he was below the eyesight of the cadre Marines acting as German machine gunners.

He glanced at his watch. Ninety seconds had elapsed. Hauser's men should be on their way up the hill. Would the machine gun open up as soon as the advancing Marines were visible, or would the gunners wait until the targets were closer?

RAT-A-TAT-TAT-TAT. RAT-A-TAT-TAT-TAT. RAT-A-TAT-TAT-TAT.

Three short bursts of machine gun rounds barked from the top of the hill. Hauser's men were under fire.

Within seconds individual shots rang from barrels of the Springfields at the base of the hill. Hauser and his men had taken cover and were returning fire.

"Don't stop," Morgan urged his compatriots as he continued to race around the base of the hill. "Keep up the pace."

"Don't you see the length of these legs?" Corky Jones panted in Morgan's wake. "I got's to take two steps to ever'body else's one."

"Move, move, move!" Morgan commanded as he quickened his pace and angled up the side of the hill.

Within minutes Morgan and the six boys had gained position on the side of the rise at the same elevation as the machine gun crew. Ira Silverstein breathed heavily through his mouth. His chest heaved with the exertion of the scramble up the side of the hill.

"I didn't know there were this many trees in the whole country," he said. "When the war is over, I'm never leaving the city again."

Cochise Birdsong squinted across the forest at the sound of the machine gun.

RAT-A-TAT-TAT. RAT-A-TAT-TAT. The machine gun rattled more fire at Hauser and his group at the base of the rise.

"Say the word, general," he whispered to Morgan. "That gun's getting' to be an annoyance."

"All right," Morgan said in a calm voice. "Stay spread out. Fire slow so you don't run out before you get to the gun emplacement. Just enough to keep their heads down. Most important thing is to keep moving. Don't stop for anything. Got it?"

"What do we do when we get there?" Winslow MacIntosh 3rd asked.

"Kill 'em," Corky Jones said simply. "They's the reason I had to run all the way up this dad gum mountain."

"Let's go," Morgan said shaking his head at Corky's humor.

The seven boys burst from their hiding place and raced through the forest toward the chattering machine gun, firing their Springfield rifles from the hip. Slim Hitchins released several loud screams of "hee haw."

Covering fire from the group of young Marines at the base of the hill rose in volume briefly before falling silent as Morgan and his comrades swept closer to the machine gun.

The cadre Marines handling the machine gun were taken completely by surprise by the swiftness and direction of Morgan's flanking assault. They tried to swing their weapon to bring fire against the rushing boys, but the sides of their log emplacement blocked the gun barrel.

Less than a minute after commencing their charge, Morgan's six boys surrounded the machine gun position and menacingly brandished their weapons at the three cadre Marines.

"You German boys don't look so tough now," Ira Silverstein laughed as he pointed his rifle at the head of one of the defenders. "You wouldn't last five minutes in my old neighborhood in New York."

Gunnery Sergeant Kidd and the rest of the Marines at the base of the hill double-timed up the slope and approached the gun emplacement.

"Lower them rifles, boys," Gunnery Sergeant Kidd ordered. "Even a blank can do damage if you hit somebody in the face."

Winslow MacIntosh 3rd grinned widely at the Gunnery Sergeant. "How'd we do, Gunney?" he asked. "Not bad for the first time?"

"Unload those rifles," Sergeant Kidd ordered. "Fall in on the trail down by the ravine. Take five and grab a drink. Then we're hiking to the next problem. Take off!"

"No appreciation for a job well done," MacIntosh grumbled in a low voice. "Very poor employee relations, I must say."

"Early!" Gunnery Sergeant Kidd barked when the boys had begun walking down the hill. "Report to the company commander after you clean up when we get back to the barracks."

"Aye, aye, Gunney," Morgan replied. His confusion was evident in the tone of his voice.

~ 33 ~

Captain Jim Bennett sat in starched utilities behind a metal desk in the headquarters of what was to become Able Company, 1st Battalion, 6th Regiment of the 4th Brigade of the 2nd Marine Division.

"At ease, private," he said as Morgan Early stood at attention before the desk. Neither Marine had saluted, as both were "uncovered", without hats or helmets. Morgan was dressed in fresh utilities with spit-shined black shoes and a polished brass buckle clasping his web belt.

An open manila folder was spread in front of the captain. His eyes scanned the top page. He turned to the second page and grunted once in admiration.

"You shot 'expert' at P.I.," the captain said with a nod. "Not many shoot 'expert'."

"Yes, sir," Morgan confirmed.

Captain Bennett looked up. "Where'd you learn to shoot?"

"Sir, I guess I had a rifle in my hand from the time I was a boy. A kindly sheriff in Arizona taught me to shoot. Many days if I didn't shoot straight, my mother and I didn't eat."

"You finished at the top of your recruit platoon," the captain continued.

"Yes, sir," Morgan said with eyes straight ahead and his hands clasped behind his back. His feet were properly positioned eighteen inches apart.

"Gunnery Sergeant Kidd told me how you took charge of the squad today with one of the combat problems," Captain Bennett said as he leaned back in his chair and wiggled a pencil between his fingers. "The Gunney said you were very impressive."

"Thank you, sir."

"The Gunney doesn't believe this simulated problem was the first time you experienced combat. He says you were too calm, too knowledgeable and too poised. He's never seen a new Marine act like you acted today."

"Thank you, sir," Morgan repeated.

"Is the Gunney right, Private Early? Have you been in combat before?"

Morgan licked his lips and drew a breath. The silence in the room was deafening. "Yes, sir. I've been under fire before."

"Where?"

"Mexico, sir," Morgan said. "I served in Pancho Villa's army before he attacked the United States. Before the raid on Columbus, New Mexico, I resigned."

The captain wrinkled his forehead in disbelief. "Villa allowed you to resign? I didn't think anybody resigned from his army."

"No, sir," Morgan said. "I resigned and Villa jailed me. But a friend helped me escape and we made our way to General Pershing's camp. That was the last I saw of Villa."

Captain Bennett laughed. "Don't tell me you served with Pershing."

"No, sir. My friend and I just helped the general a little. We knew where Captain Cardenas was hiding, and we led a squad to find him."

"Successfully?"

"Yes, sir. We found Cardenas and killed him. That is, a young lieutenant named Georgie Patton took the credit."

"I heard about Cardenas' death. I never heard about this Lieutenant Patton."

"Yes, sir."

Captain Bennett stared at Morgan for several seconds before speaking. "The Gunney tells me the other members of the platoon respect you."

"I try to help where I can, sir."

165

"The 2nd Division will be sailing to France soon. I don't know when we'll get a crack at the Hun, but when we do, I'll need the best non-commissioned officers to lead the men."

"Yes, sir."

"These Germans are warriors. They've fought throughout their history. Battle is in their blood. They won't be easy to defeat."

"Yes, sir."

Captain Bennett stood. "I'm promoting you to corporal. You'll take over the first squad of the 2nd platoon. That's your squad. Make me proud, son." He extended his hand in congratulations.

Morgan swallowed once before words escaped his mouth. His mother had depended on him, and he had allowed her to die. The Calhoun family had depended on him, and he had allowed Con Ira to be killed by a bear. Ardyth Calhoun had loved him, and he had disappointed her so badly she couldn't allow him to remain on the farm. How could he be expected to lead his friends into combat and save them from certain death at the hands of the Hun?

"Sir, I..." Morgan began nervously.

"The proper Marine response," Captain Bennett said with a broad smile, "is 'aye, aye, sir'."

Morgan stiffened. "Aye, aye, sir." He took the captain's hand and shook it firmly.

*   *   *

"Do we got to salute you now?" Corky Jones asked with a loud chuckle.

"Astonishing," Winslow MacIntosh 3rd added with a smile. "Birth and education must count for nothing in this organization."

Morgan sat silently on his rack sewing the twin chevrons on the sleeve of his khaki, long-sleeved, Service A shirt. "I'll expect a little respect from you leather-necks, now," he said laughingly.

Michael Houlihan leaned on one elbow and looked at the ceiling of the barracks. "This reminds me of a gal I knew back in Nashville. Says 'if I do what you're asking me to do, will you respect me in the morning'?"

Ira Silverstein rolled his eyes. "You got them broads in Tennessee, too?"

Houlihan nodded. "So I says, 'what's the difference? I don't respect you now'."

Cochise Birdsong stood and walked past Morgan on his way back to his bunk. "You just lead me to the Hun when we get to France, Morgan. You do that, you'll have my respect."

*   *   *

New Marines, fresh from Parris Island Recruit Depot, cycled through the Quantico Marine training base in eight-week segments until the 2nd Marine Division stood at full strength of nearly 30,000 officers and men.

The Marines were hiked over the dirt roads and steep forest trails of the military reservation until their feet were inured to the pain and pounding. Twenty-mile hikes became easy strolls to the hardened bodies of the young Marines.

The boys battled each other with padded pugil sticks to simulate close combat conditions. They charged straw dummies and thrust bayonets into the hay mannequins with blood-curling screams. They threw hand grenades, fired machine guns and practiced with their Springfields until they could sustain a twenty round-per-minute rate of fire, loading five shells from a stripper clip four times in the sixty-second period.

They assaulted hills in frontal formation and practiced flanking maneuvers. They dug trenches and defended fixed positions. They bivouacked in the forest and learned to pitch tents and dig latrines. They practiced night maneuvers using compass bearings in the pale light of the summer moon.

On September 23, 1917 the 1st Battalion of the 6th Regiment, including Corporal Morgan Early's Able Company, sailed on the *Henderson* from New York City. The ship landed in St. Nazaire, France, on October 5, after surviving two near misses from German submarine torpedoes.

The battalion encamped at the Bourmont training area and remained there until March 14, 1918 when they were moved to Verdun. It required the apparent imminent success of the German Ainse Offensive, the brainchild of General Erich Ludendorff, to finally bring the United States Marines into the First World War after eight months of inactivity in France. By June 1, 1918, the Germans were pushing toward Paris and had reached a position a mere thirty miles from the French capital. The French forces, exhausted from four years of struggle, were collapsing in the face of the onslaught.

The U.S. Marine Corps 2nd Division finally received orders to fill the hole created by the crumbling French forces and halt the German drive on Paris. "Can they hold?" French corps commander General Jean-Marie Deugoutte asked. "General, these are American regulars. In a hundred and fifty years they have never been beaten. They will hold," was the reply by division commander Major General Omar Bundy.

~ 34 ~

Corporal Morgan Early stood in the rear of the *camion* and peered over the forward cab. The rickety truck was barely making headway toward the forward battle lines. A mass of humanity choked the road, attempting to flee the front in the opposite direction. Downtrodden women, old men and babies wandered away from the advancing Germans clutching a few precious possessions to their chests.

"*Beaucoup d'allemands,*" they yelled at the Marines who were weaving through their midst in the *camions*. Many Germans.

Battle-weary French soldiers, dazed and shell-shocked, their weapons long ago discarded, staggered along the road away from the advancing enemy. Many of the troops displayed bloody bandages. All showed a hollow, defeated look on their gaunt, dirty, faces.

"*La guerre est fini,*" they called to the American Marines. The war is over.

Morgan sat heavily between Chief Birdsong and Ira Silverstein. He held his Springfield upright with the tips of his fingers. The smoothness of the wooden stock and the precision of the oily barrel and receiver calmed his nervousness. He looked at his comrades and smiled encouragement. They had been in France waiting for the opportunity to engage the enemy for many months. Their time to prove themselves was now at hand.

The *camion* stopped. Shrill whistles sounded. "Squad leaders, assemble your men!"

"All right," Morgan shouted. "Out of the truck. Form up on me."

Able Company, 1st Battalion of the 6th Regiment took up a position just north of the village of Lucy-le-Bocage on the Paris-Metz highway. Morgan ordered his squad to begin digging defensive trenches. Paris stood nearly deserted only thirty miles to the southeast.

Captain Lloyd W. Williams strode past Morgan's position. "How's it going, Corporal?" he inquired.

"We're dug in, sir," Morgan replied. "We'll hold. My squad will do their duty."

Stragglers from the 43rd French Division stumbled toward Able Company's lines. "You better leave this area," one French soldier advised as he helped a comrade with a bloody, mangled leg. "The Germans will be coming this way soon."

Captain Williams snapped his reply. "Retreat, hell! We just got here!"

Morgan smiled and saluted the young officer. "I'll pass the word, sir. My men will enjoy your comment."

*   *   *

On the morning of June 2, 1918, the Germans unleashed a ferocious artillery barrage on the Marine lines. Heavy shells whistled through the air and landed with precise accuracy on the newly dug positions.

"Keep your heads down," Morgan screamed.

Private Bill Hauser risked a curious peek over the rim of his concealment. A piece of shrapnel whistled through the damp morning air and decapitated him. His head fell to the bottom of the foxhole and landed on Casey Brown's left foot. The young Marine retched his breakfast, screamed in horror and collapsed against the headless body of his comrade.

The merciless barrage pounded the Marines for more than an hour. The screech of incoming rounds and the ear-shattering burst of the explosions frayed nerves already stretched raw with the unknown of combat and the uncertainty of their own mortality.

"Stop!" Casey Brown shouted to the sky. "We're all going to die. I can't take any more shelling."

Brown's face beneath the dirt and scruff of a day-old beard was blanched. His eyes darted wildly without focus. A dribble of saliva escaped his lips. "I've got to get out of here."

Morgan had never experienced artillery, but he knew the barrage couldn't last forever. Gun barrels overheat; ammunition runs low. The shelling would stop and the infantry would attack.

"Stay in your hole," Morgan shouted to Casey Brown as another volley of high explosives tore the ground in front of their position and sent clumps of dirt flying high into the air. The impact of the detonations shuddered the earth at Morgan's feet.

"I can't stay," Brown moaned over the din of the shelling. "We're all going to die."

Morgan peered over the edge of his trench in the direction of the panicked Marine. Casey Brown's face appeared above the rim of his hole, bloodless and contorted with terror. His jaw hung slack and his tongue lolled from his mouth.

"Don't," Morgan managed to shout before another round of German artillery whistled toward their concealment.

Casey Brown launched from his hole and began to run toward the rear. His rifle remained in his position. His helmet flew from his head. The frenzied dash to safety lasted three steps before a Mauser round struck Brown's left knee. Moments later a stream of fire from a German Maxim machine gun ripped across the young Marine's back. Private Casey Brown plunged to the ground without a sound. He would endure artillery shelling no longer.

Shortly after the last round exploded into the raw earth, the German foot soldiers began to inch toward the Marine lines. Morgan scurried behind his squad whispering encouragement. "Don't waste your ammunition," he called in a low voice. "Make sure you have a target."

"Do we have to wait until we can see the whites of their eyes?" Chief Birdsong asked with a wry grin.

"You're a good shot," Morgan snickered. "When you can put one between their eyes, do it."

Michael Houlihan turned to face Morgan. "This situation sort of reminds me of the time I was waiting for a girl I knew to come home from a date with a friend of mine. I was hiding in the bushes..."

"Corporal, order that Irishman to shut up," Slim Hitchins grumbled. "If he don't quit talkin' an' start shootin', he'll be tellin' his lies to the Hun."

"When the Hun start firing," Morgan warned, "don't duck down. You've got good cover. Keep shooting. Not every bullet they send your way is going to hit something."

"Is it okay to duck when they start throwing tomahawks?" Cochise Birdsong asked.

"That's the time to fix your bayonet and charge, Chief," Morgan replied.

"FIRE!" screamed Morgan when the Germans were within range.

The accurate rifle fire of the American Springfields poured into the German ranks. The deadly spray of Marine machine guns interspersed among the ranks of the riflemen mowed the advancing Germans down and halted the assault.

Enemy bodies piled in front of the Marine positions. Morgan rested his Springfield against the earthen wall of his trench and sighted toward the Germans. A distinct helmet shape appeared behind a fallen tree. The dome was taller than that of the Americans', and the rim was more steeply sloped.

Morgan waited. The helmet lifted. A forehead was suddenly visible.

Morgan squeezed the trigger. A hole appeared above the nose of the enemy soldier. The head flew backward and disappeared. Morgan swung his weapon and scanned the terrain for another target of opportunity.

*　　　*　　　*

Night fell on the Marine lines and the intense shooting of the day slowed to an occasional single shot. The German advance had been halted. The Hun had suffered enormous causalities. Their recent battlefield success at the expense of exhausted, disheartened French troops was over. The foe they now faced was fresh, anxious for combat, well equipped and excellently commanded. Never again in the present conflict would they be so close to Paris.

Morgan walked his position. "Anybody hit beside Hauser and Brown?"

"What happened to Hauser?" Corky Jones asked. "I didn't hear nothin' about him."

"I was in the hole next to him," Ira Silverstein said. "He stood up to take a look, and his head flew off."

"Jesus," Winslow MacIntosh 3rd whistled under his breath. "An outright ugly situation. What about Brown? How'd he get it?"

"Brown panicked," Morgan said simply. "He ran from his hole while the shells were falling and the Hun cut him to ribbons with one of their Maxim machine guns."

"I saw his body," Slim Hitchins said as he reclined against the splintered stump of a tree. "The Hun butchered him."

"Brown was the one always said how tough he was," the Chief remarked with an expression of distain. "Always braggin' how he was goin' to lick the Hun once we got into action."

"That's a lesson for everybody," Morgan said. "Keep your heads down when the shells are falling. Do not panic. The Germans won't be attacking. They don't want to run under their own barrage."

Ira Silverstein dabbed at his cheek with the sleeve of his utility shirt. "The bastards shot me," he grumbled when he saw blood appear on his uniform.

"Our first Purple Heart winner in the squad," Slim Hitchins said with mock reverence. "Congratulations."

"I've had worse scratches from a woman's fingernail," Silverstein said as he spit blood that had dribbled into his mouth. "But I guess a Purple Heart is better than the Royal Order of the Mattress Cover Hauser and Brown won themselves."

"Talkin' about women's fingernails," Michael Houlihan said. "Reminds me of a girl I knew had these nails so long she could scratch your back from across the room. What a tigress she was!"

"That's it?" Cochise Birdsong asked. "She just scratched your back?"

"She turned me over and asked if I wanted anything else scratched," Houlihan continued. "My little friend took one look at those claws and wouldn't come out of hiding. Them nails scared him to death!"

"Where do you make up all these lies?" Jones asked.

"I swear it's the truth."

173

"Chow will be here in a while," Morgan said. "Clean those weapons and clean them well. Tomorrow you'll be using them again; make no mistake about that. These Germans aren't licked yet."

"Squad leaders to the company headquarters!" The word passed rapidly through the area. "On the double!"

"Watch the boys," Morgan called to Chief Birdsong. "Make sure they work on those rifles. I guess we're about to find out what's going to happen tomorrow."

"Yes, sir, corporal," Cochise Birdsong replied with a flip of this fingers from his forehead.

~ 35 ~

Captain Jim Bennett stood in front of a map hanging from the rear flap of a tent. Three second lieutenants and a Gunnery Sergeant represented the four platoons of Able Company, 1st Battalion, 6th Regiment. The fourth officer had been killed that afternoon defending the company position against the onslaught of German infantry.

Morgan's platoon leader was 2nd Lieutenant Peter Gross who had been drawn from the senior ranks of enlisted men and commissioned an officer in the Marine Corps' accelerated expansion program immediately following the declaration of war of April 6, 1917.

Morgan and eleven other corporals commanded the three squads that comprised each of the four platoons.

Captain Bennett scanned the men hunched in front of him. "I want to congratulate all of you for a job well done these last few days. This was the first combat for most of you, and the company performed well. We didn't yield an inch of terrain to the Hun."

Murmured "thanks" sounded from the Marines.

"Today we defended," Captain Bennett continued as he slapped the map with a bayonet. "Tomorrow we attack."

The officers and non-commissioned officers looked at one another with clenched jaws. The action in the trenches and foxholes had been relatively straightforward. The shelling had been horrific, and some men had lost control of their nerves and panicked. "Shell-shocked" was a word the Marines heard for the first time from the

175

corpsmen attending the boys incapacitated by fear of the falling shells. French soldiers had been seen wandering aimlessly with rosary beads in nearby woods saying prayers in the midst of the whistling artillery barrage. But when the shelling lifted, the Marines had only to remain in their positions and shoot at the attacking Germans. There had been no maneuvering necessary. No military decisions were required.

Tomorrow would be different. The platoon leaders would be required to make command decisions. The ultimate responsibility for the success of the action and the lives of the individual Marines would, as always, fall on the shoulders of the squad leaders.

"Bouresches, gentlemen," Captain Bennett said simply with the tip of the bayonet pointing at the tiny French town on the map. "Right here on the highway to Paris. The town has a railroad station that our command needs for re-supply. Tomorrow Able Company will take Bouresches."

*　　*　　*

At dawn on the morning of June 6, 1918, Morgan nudged Private Cochise Birdsong. "Wake the squad," he ordered. "Get some food in them and have them take care of business. Fall in on me at 0545."

Able Company hiked the mile and a half from their defensive positions to the outskirts of Bouresches. A chill tinged the morning air and patches of fog clung to depressions and shell holes in the ground. Brick homes and wooden barns appeared faintly two hundred yards ahead. No movement was discernable in the town.

"I haven't had my morning coffee, corporal," Winslow MacIntosh 3rd complained in jest. "It's uncivilized to require a man to work without a proper breakfast."

Morgan smiled at the private's levity. MacIntosh had acquitted himself admirably in the defensive battle against the attacking Germans. He would prove to be a valuable member of the squad.

Lieutenant Peter Gross, 2nd platoon leader of Able Company approached Morgan as the Marines stood uncertainly beside the road leading into Bouresches.

"The captain has set up four machine guns on the edge of the wooded area just below the town to cover our assault. Able Company

176

will jump off at 0745 and advance on the town; 2nd platoon will have the left flank. Your squad will take the left position of the platoon."

"Aye, aye, sir," Morgan said. "We'll be ready."

"Do you have enough hand grenades, corporal?"

"Yes, sir," Morgan replied. "We were issued three grenades each last night."

"Good luck, Early," the lieutenant said. "I'll see you in the town."

"Good luck to you, sir,"

*   *   *

Morgan looked at his watch and lifted his eyes toward the town of Bouresches. The sun was above the horizon and shined brightly on the roofs and windows of the buildings. No human was visible walking the streets. Silence reigned over the pastoral village. The Germans occupied the town and railroad station. Were they asleep? Had they spotted the Marines approaching on foot? What were they waiting for before firing?

"One minute," Morgan called to his squad. "Check those weapons again. And remember to keep moving forward. Do not stop until you reach the town."

At precisely 0745 the angry rattle of heavy machine guns sounded from the Marine positions. Lead poured from the ventilated barrels as shells were fed into the weapons from belts of ammunition. Windows in the town shattered as the gunners raked the openings in an attempt to keep the Germans from firing at the advancing Marines.

Brick buildings puffed with red powder as bullets dug into the walls sheltering the defending Hun. Barn doors splintered as well-aimed covering fire bored through the wooden slats and sought the enemy lying in wait inside.

"Move, move, move!" Morgan yelled over the din of the growing battle as he urged his squad through an orchard toward the left edge of the town.

Sporadic rifle fire dug tufts of dirt at the feet of the Marines. A German Maxim machine gun hammered from a corner window. Branches snapped and leaves flew from several trees between Morgan's squad and the hamlet.

177

"Get down," Morgan called. "Fire at that window."

Cochise Birdsong threw his body into a prone firing position and took careful aim at the source of the automatic weapon fire. He snapped off five accurate rounds that whistled through the opening in the window. MacIntosh and Silverstein fired at the same location. Several bullets penetrated the house; others crashed into the frame and windowsill sending chunks of wood spinning into the air.

"Up!" Morgan shouted. "Keep advancing while they've got their heads down."

The squad stormed across the last of the orchard and approached the nearest building. Each Marine flattened his back against a wall, away from a window, as he had been taught in training.

Michael Houlihan leaned against the wall beside a doorway. Slim Hitchins stood on the other side of the entrance. Houlihan pulled the pin on a hand grenade and nodded. Hitchins spun around to face the door and kicked it open with a heavy boot. Houlihan lobbed the sputtering grenade through the opening.

Both Marines flattened against the wall away from the entry. The blast reverberated through the opening. Dust and powder billowed through the passageway. Without hesitating, Houlihan and Hitchins spun through the doorway before the smoke had settled and sprayed rifle rounds around the inside of the house.

A loud groan greeted the Marines from a corner of the interior. A wounded and dazed German muttered through blood-flecked lips.

Private Houlihan answered the enemy soldier with a bullet to the forehead.

Morgan burst into the house and looked momentarily at the dead German. His expression did not change. He felt neither sympathy nor hate for the man who had been trying to kill him as he had advanced across the orchard toward the town. Emotions in combat could be potentially dangerous. Acting impulsively because of anger or fear or fatigue could lead to fatal mistakes.

A German Maxim machine gun rattled from a room upstairs.

Morgan pulled a hand grenade that he had attached to the web shoulder strap supporting his pack and rushed to the stair landing in the next room. "Hitch, come with me," he called. "Houlie, watch the windows in the back. There may be Germans jumping from the top floor in a few seconds."

Michael Houlihan stripped five fresh rounds into his Springfield. "Send 'em my way, corporal," he said with a grin. "I'll show them a merry Irish reception."

Morgan stepped carefully up the steps until he could see into the rooms at the top of the stairs. Slim Hitchins followed at his heels.

Two Germans crouched beneath a window facing the field the Marines had advanced across minutes earlier. One soldier clutched the handle grips of a Maxim machine gun. His finger was paused above the trigger. The second German held a belt of ammunition ready to feed into the chamber of the deadly weapon.

Two other Germans sat in the corners of a second window pointing their Mausers at Marines advancing on other buildings in the town. Single shots rang from their rifles. The gunner behind the Maxim unleashed a stream of bullets at a group of attacking Marines.

Morgan used the deafening cacophony of the gunfire to mask the sound of the hissing grenade which he rolled into the room. He ducked as the tiny bomb tumbled across the hard wood floor and came to rest behind the oblivious Germans. The explosion was a total surprise. Hot shards of steel fanned across the room, tearing through the filthy uniforms and sinking into the soft flesh of the enemy soldiers.

Morgan poked his head above the level of the floor. The machine gunners had died instantly. One of the riflemen, blood pouring down his face from a vicious wound in the forehead, turned and attempted to fire in the direction of the stairs. Morgan fired from the hip and pumped a round into the German's head. The man fell forward with a loud clump against the slatted floor. The second rifleman, wounded in the back and shoulder, gathered his weapon and leapt from the window. A whoosh of air announced his encounter with the dirt below. Seconds later two shots from Private Houlihan's Springfield sounded, signaling the German's demise.

"You sure you wasn't a cowboy one time in your life, corporal?" Slim Hitchins asked Morgan as they descended the stairs. "That was sure quick shootin'."

Morgan looked at Private Hitchins and returned a wry smile. "I was a cowboy," he said. "But that seems like a long time ago."

"Well, if you take a hankerin' to the saddle again, I could always use you at the ranch in Texas."

"Thanks," Morgan said. "When this war is over, I think I'll be returning to the little island I found off Florida. The peace and quiet look awfully good compared to the noise and lunacy in this part of the world."

"You lads all right?" Michael Houlihan asked.

"We're fine," Private Hitchins replied. "The corporal killed three of the Hun up there."

"I guess the fourth didn't enjoy your company," Houlihan said. "He came sailin' down to the garden and tried to flee the party. He didn't make it too far."

"Nice shooting," Morgan observed as he reloaded his Springfield. "Now let's keep moving."

The three Marines exited the house and crossed the street. Ira Silverstein walked down the cobbled path leading two Germans with their hands clasped behind their necks. The vaunted enemy soldiers looked young and scared. Peach fuzz covered their dirty faces. Their uniforms were threadbare and baggy.

"This is more like my kind of war," Silverstein said. "Fightin' in the streets. I didn't know much about that woods work the other day."

"What you got there, Ira?" Michael Houlihan asked.

"These Hun don't look so tough up close," Silverstein said. "I found 'em behind that house over there. I'm takin' 'em to the captain."

"Good work," Morgan said. "Maybe they can tell us something about the German defenses."

"They don't look old enough to know much," Silverstein said. "They look even younger than we do. By the way, the captain wants to see you, Morgan. Lieutenant Gross is dead. He got it comin' across the orchard. I guess he stopped and a Maxim got his range."

"The captain wants to see me?" Morgan asked.

"Yeah. I heard he wants you to take over the platoon," Silverstein said as he rudely goosed one of the Germans in the rear with his rifle barrel to get him started toward the company command area.

*   *   *

When June 6, 1918 ended, the Marines had captured the hamlet of Bouresches and advanced to the edge of Belleau Woods. The fighting for the town had been a series of house–to-house battles, driving the defenders from their positions, singly and in pairs, with hand grenades and rifles. The Marines suffered the costliest day of fighting in their history since the founding of the Corps in 1775, incurring nearly 1,100 casualties.

But the worst of the carnage was yet to come. The capture of Belleau Woods awaited the Marines of the 2nd Division.

~ 36 ~

Michael Houlihan sat tipped on the back legs of a chair in the tiny kitchen of one of the houses in Bouresches. His boots rested on the scratched table in the center of the room. A bottle of cognac was clutched in his right fist, and he gleefully lifted the potent liquid to his lips and drank heartily.

"I tell ye lads, a wee sip will change your entire outlook on life," he said with deep philosophic thought. "If a man wasn't supposed to drink, why were the ingredients put on God's green earth?"

"Pass that bottle again," Corky Jones said with an outstretched hand from the floor of the kitchen. "I thought liquor only came in a jug made in the back of Grandpa's cabin in the woods. This stuff ain't half bad."

"I dread to think what would happen if I were to have you ignorant wretches to dinner at father's house," Winslow MacIntosh 3rd expounded as he reached for another pull on the cognac bottle. "Between the fine French wines and the liqueurs and the Courvoisier after dinner, your uneducated pallets would be overwhelmed with the sensuous delights."

Cochise Birdsong wiggled his fingers calling for the bottle to be passed his way. He sat cross-legged against the far wall of the small room. "Cour...what? I guess you white men only allowed us redskins to drink your rejects. I never heard of that Cour-stuff you're talkin' about."

"Courvoisier, Chief," MacIntosh 3rd repeated with exaggerated politeness. "I must introduce you to the pleasure some time."

"Don't knock yourself out," Birdsong said with a shrug. "I wouldn't want to put you to any bother."

Winslow MacIntosh 3rd took a second long pull on the bottle before passing it up to Michael Houlihan. He leaned his head back and closed his eyes in contemplation. He took a breath and spoke softly. "I must admit that in spite of your lack of social graces and apparent ignorance of life's finer things, I find you comrades among the best company I have ever enjoyed. I will take you all home to father after the war. He'll find you all...intriguing."

Ira Silverstein entered the room and placed two additional bottles of cognac on the table. "Rejoice, boys. Nobody goes home thirsty tonight."

"You're a good man, Silverstein," Michael Houlihan said. "Even if you ain't Irish."

"No, I ain't a drunken Irishman. I'm Jewish and proud of it," Silverstein said with a chortle. "In my neighborhood we always say 'if it weren't for liquor, the Irish would rule the world'."

Houlihan laughed and shook his head. "I can't deny the truth of that. Every Irishman I know is a sot at the end of the day."

"My family don't do so bad in the drinkin' department up in them hills of Kentucky," Corky Jones said. "'Cept we don't buy it. We make it."

"All this talk of drinkin' reminds me of a girl I knew back in Tennessee," Michael Houlihan began in a wistful tone. "Ugliest gal you ever could imagine. Why, she was so ugly, her mother had to tie a lamb chop around her neck to get the neighborhood dogs to play with her."

"She was that ugly? We don't even have Indians that ugly," Chief Birdsong noted.

"What's that got to do with drinkin'," Corky Jones asked. "I thought we was talkin' about drinkin'."

Michael Houlihan cracked the seal on another bottle of cognac. "I'm getting to the drinkin' part," he said. "One night I get into some of my parents secret stash and as I'm wanderin' around this girl pops up out of nowhere. And I looks at her real good, and I say to myself 'she ain't so ugly as everybody says. I think I'll see if she wants to join me in the back of the shed'."

"Did she go with you?" Corky Jones asked anxiously.

"She did," Michael Houlihan confirmed. "And it wasn't half bad. But when I wakes up in the morning, she's back to the ugliest girl you ever seen. I take one look at her and I want to run, but she's asleep on my arm."

"So what did you do?"

"I didn't want to wake her, so I chewed off my arm like an animal in a trap and lit out of there like a scalded cat."

Cochise Birdsong burst out in a deep laugh, spitting cognac across the room. "Houli, you got some imagination."

The other boys joined the hilarity. The third bottle of cognac was soon opened and passed around with enthusiasm.

Slim Hitchins ambled into the house. He folded his long legs and slumped into a corner. "You boys hear the news?"

"The war's over?" Ira Silverstein asked with an inebriated grin.

"They made Morgan sergeant. He's in charge of the platoon now that Gross is dead."

"The boy can fight," Ira said seriously. "That's okay with me."

"Yeah," Chief Birdsong said. "He might even get us through this war with our scalps still attached. How many we lost in the company so far?"

"Near twenty-five percent," Corky Jones said. "An' next we gots to take that woods away from the Hun. I hear they's dug deeper than whale vomit on the bottom of the ocean."

"What's the name of the woods, anyway? I never heard tell of it," Slim Hitchins said.

"Bell-Oh-Woods," Michael Houlihan said before taking a long slug on the bottle. "Some French name. An' after we take it, probably nobody will ever hear of it again."

~ 37 ~

Sergeant Morgan Early, platoon leader of the 2nd platoon, Able Company, 1st Battalion, 6th Marine Regiment sat slumped on the outskirts of the hamlet of Bouresches. A smattering of officers and non-commissioned officers, leaders of the other eleven platoons in the three battalions that comprised the regiment, huddled with Morgan. Colonel Jeffrey Taub stood in front of the men and looked down with sad eyes and a grim expression.

The Marines had assaulted Belleau Woods every day for the last twelve. Minimal ground had been wrested from the well-hidden Germans determined to hold their positions in the deep forest. The fighting had been fierce and bloody. The defenders were dug in among the numerous fissures, crevices and caves that littered the thick woods. Their Maxim machine guns had cut into the Marine ranks with appalling effectiveness.

Artillery barrages prior to the attacks had minimal effect on the Germans. The Hun were able to burrow into safe shelters beneath the numerous boulders and in the maze of caves to avoid the exploding shells.

Advances had been counted in yards as Marines attacked fixed positions with rifles and bayonets, wading through relentless fire from the terrifying Maxim machine guns and the accurate Mausers.

The sounds of battle of the automatic weapons and the exploding hand grenades had often been drowned out by the screams of the wounded calling for help. After one terrible day of savage conflict more than two hundred ambulances had been required to carry the fallen Marines to the field hospitals in the rear.

Despite such heroic efforts, the woods remained firmly in German hands. The Marines had to finish the job, and Colonel Taub had to order the action.

"Gentlemen, I wish to make the next assault on Belleau Woods the last one necessary," Colonel Taub began. "At 0300 tomorrow morning, June 23rd, we will unleash an artillery assault of maximum intensity that will continue until 0500 hours. At that time 2nd Battalion will assault the woods from the south and 1st Battalion will sweep across from the east. Good luck to you and your men. I know you'll make me and the Marine Corps proud of you tomorrow."

Morgan returned to his platoon after receiving his specific orders. His Springfield rifle felt heavy on his shoulder as the strap rubbed his skin raw beneath his filthy utility shirt. He stroked his fingers, nails cracked and dirt embedded, across his chin and noticed a stubble of beard. Did he need to shave again? Hadn't he just shaved three days ago?

The colonel had mentioned a date during his briefing. Was tomorrow June 23rd? That meant he had a birthday coming soon. How old would he be? The Marine Corps thought he was eighteen, but in reality he wouldn't be eighteen for another two weeks. In his brief years he had seen more death, suffering, blood, butchery and inhumanity than most men could witness in a dozen lifetimes.

Fatigue pulled at Morgan's shoulders. Resignation to his own death settled in his heart. Would the war never end? Would he ever see the purple of the ocean and the turquoise of the flats again? Would he ever feel clean and rested and healthy? Would he ever awaken to the gentle lapping of wavelets against a coral shore instead of the pounding of bombs, the rattle of machine guns and the tortured cries of battered and dying men?

How many of his men had he lost to the Germans? Hauser was dead. Brown was dead. Murray was alive but would walk with one leg the rest of his life. Louden was dead. Secor had an arm torn from his body. A corpsman had bandaged him, but would he live?

Replacements had arrived. Morgan had learned their names but deliberately refused to befriend anyone. He needed to command them, but he didn't care to make a close acquaintance. Why acquire a new friend only to have the Germans rip his body apart with bullets and then have to feel sad for the loss? The replacements died at a much quicker rate than the experienced boys, anyway. They didn't know an incoming shell from an outgoing. They didn't know the peculiar whirl of a friendly short round destined to land in Marine trenches. They didn't know the sound of a Maxim from a Marine machine gun. They couldn't distinguish the crack of a friendly Springfield from an enemy Mauser. They died quickly for their ignorance.

*   *   *

In the pre-dawn darkness, aided by the lingering smoke from the massive, two-hour artillery barrage, and patches of clinging fog, the Marines' stealthy approach to the dreaded woods was concealed. Morgan ordered his platoon to affix their bayonets on their rifles and form a skirmish line. Shoulder to shoulder his Marines plunged into the thick forest of the former hunting preserve.

Able Company advanced slightly more than one hundred yards before the German defenders realized the ground attack was underway.

The sustained chatter of a Maxim machine gun erupted twenty yards in front of Morgan's position. A replacement that had joined the platoon two days before caught the burst squarely in the chest and flew backward, lofting his rifle over his head with his final death throe.

Morgan dove behind a large rock. One second later Winslow MacIntosh 3rd landed on top of him.

"Sorry, sergeant," MacIntosh said as he spat dirt that had wedged into his mouth during his landing, "I didn't know this establishment was occupied."

Morgan rolled over and peered around the rock. Bullets splattered above his head and shards of granite rained on his helmet. He pulled his body behind the shelter and looked right and left.

"Jones," he called to the Marine crouching to his left. "When I throw this grenade, you charge that machine gun nest."

"Any other favors I can do fer you sergeant?"

"Yeah," Morgan called. "Pass the word to those on your left to do the same."

"Okay."

"Houlihan, is that you to my right?" Morgan shouted. The Irishman had awakened from the squad drinking bout two weeks previously vowing to never touch alcohol again. It had required all of twenty-four hours to rescind his pledge.

"I've got Ira with me," Michael Houlihan called. "We goin' to charge that gun?"

"After I throw a couple of grenades."

"Well get tossin'," Silverstein yelled. "Them Hun are getting' better at shooting all the time."

Morgan pulled a hand grenade from a satchel slung around his neck. He passed it to MacIntosh and took another for himself. "Don't bounce it off a tree," he said seriously. "We've got enough lead flying our way from the Hun."

"You seriously underestimate my athletic ability," MacIntosh said with genuine hurt in his voice. "Did I ever tell you about the time I caught a fly ball in center field and threw out the runner from third?"

"Only about a dozen times in the last year," Morgan replied. "I just hope you haven't lost any of your accuracy during this unfortunate interruption in your glorious athletic career."

"I quite agree."

"Ready?"

The two Marines pulled the pins on their hand grenades and scrambled into position behind the rock.

"Throw!"

The two sputtering bombs lofted through the air on a straight line for the chattering Maxim that was concentrated on a target to Morgan's right. The explosions sounded simultaneously. A moment later Morgan and MacIntosh spun around their rock concealment and charged the German position. Michael Houlihan and Ira Silverstein rushed the trench from the right, and Corky Jones stumbled through the dense underbrush with his stubby legs on the left.

The Maxim machine gun loader was dead, a drooling vermillion sponge the only vestige of his face. The grenade had flung its shrapnel directly into the German's visage. The gunner, blood oozing from his nose and ears due to the concussion of the blast, reached a trembling hand for a pistol. Morgan leapt into the trench and thrust his bayonet into the German's heart. He pulled the trigger of his Springfield to facilitate removing the long steel blade from the enemy's body, blowing a wide hole in the man's back.

Ira Silverstein and Michael Houlihan bounded over the earthen parapet and landed in the trench as two Germans charged with Mausers ready to fire from the hip. Ira Silverstein parried the first German's thrust with the barrel of his Springfield and swung the butt of his weapon into the man's face. The German's jaw ratcheted from its hinges and the enemy soldier dropped his rifle and clutched his face in agony with two hands. The young Marine ended the German's pain, and his life, with one rifle round to the throat.

Michael Houlihan side-stepped the second German's rifle barrel and the two warriors locked together in a momentary clasp, neither willing to step back and expose themselves to a bullet or bayonet.

Winslow MacIntosh 3rd ended the bizarre entanglement with a sharp thrust of his bayonet into the German's kidney. The enemy dropped his rifle and stood limp and bewildered as he reached in vain for his wound. Michael Houlihan stepped back and fired a round into the German's chest.

Corky Jones righted himself from a stumble five yards from the German position and leapt toward the trench. His left foot caught the edge of the rampart and he toppled head over heels into the chest of a German soldier rushing down the dugout position. The two soldiers collapsed to the bottom of the trench, their rifles crashing beside their tangled bodies.

"I knew these little legs would be the death of me one day," Corky Jones bellowed as he felt frantically for his rifle without taking his eyes from the German determined to kill him.

The German seized his Mauser from beside his feet and raised it to his waist. Corky Jones, groveling in the heavy dirt of the trench on his knees, realized his perilous predicament. He reared back on his haunches, launched his squatty body forward, and thrust his helmeted head into the German's face. Cartilage snapped as the steel helmet smashed into the German's nose and drove splintered shards of bone into the man's brain.

Corky Jones rebounded from his impact with the German's head and rolled to a sitting position. He grasped his Springfield from the dirt and pulled the weapon to his shoulder. He sighted the rifle on the enemy's chest. The German had ceased breathing.

"No need to waste good ammunition on no dead man," Corky Jones panted as he heaved himself to his feet.

~ 38 ~

"Everybody okay?" Morgan asked when he turned to survey the scene on either side of him.

"The Hun sure seem attached to this place," Winslow MacIntosh 3rd said uneasily. "Although the appeal escapes me at the moment."

RAT-A-TAT-TAT. RAT-A-TAT-TAT. RAT-A-TAT-TAT.

Two German Maxims opened fire on the trench from a well-concealed position thirty yards ahead. Dirt flew from the embankment piled on the edge of the trench. Trees and scattered rocks, crevices and ravines separated the new nest of Hun from the Marines.

"Who has hand grenades?" Morgan asked when the guns ceased rattling bullets overhead.

"I got a couple left," Corky Jones volunteered. "Who wants 'em?"

"Can you throw?" Morgan asked seriously. "Otherwise give them to MacIntosh.

"I can throw if you can move them trees out of my way," Corky Jones protested. "I never seen such obstacles to allowin' a man to do his job."

"All right," Morgan said. "Silverstein and Houlihan lay down covering fire from the trench. "Jones and MacIntosh come with me. When we get within twenty yards of the next Hun position, let go with a grenade. As soon as they explode, charge before they recover."

"An' what if I hit a tree?" Corky Jones asked.

"Catch it on the way back and throw it again, you ignorant hillbilly," Winslow MacIntosh 3rd said without hesitation.

"All right." Morgan said. "Let's go."

Under a hail of well-placed Springfield fire, Morgan, Winslow MacIntosh 3rd and Corky Jones slithered forward, moving from rock to crevice to fissure until they were within hand grenade range of the next German position. They lobbed sputtering grenades at the firing Maxims and after allowing the flying shrapnel to pass, stood and charged the entrenched Germans.

Ira Silverstein and Michael Houlihan dashed from the first trench at the sound of the explosion and rushed to join their comrades.

A pair of Mauser shots, lost in the shattering commotion of the battle raging throughout the woods, whistled unnoticed through the trees. The first lodged in Ira Silverstein's right lung; the second punctured his stomach. The young Marine halted in mid-stride. Complete bewilderment swept over his brain. What happened? Nothing hurts. Why don't I feel right?

Ira Silverstein looked down at the front of his tunic and noticed an incarnadine liquid bubbling from his chest and abdomen. Is that blood? Is it mine? Suddenly he experienced an enormous thirst. Water! I need water!

"Morgan," Ira called, wondering why his voice was so weak. "Morgan. Where are you? Why ain't you here now?"

Morgan vaulted into the smoking German trench just as an enemy soldier was struggling to regain his feet after the explosion of the three grenades. He landed on the German's chest and thrust his bayonet into the man's gaping neck. There was no need to fire the rifle to dislodge the sharp steel from the soft flesh.

Winslow MacIntosh 3rd landed with a heavy thud in the bottom of the trench and turned to his right. A German soldier was taking aim with his Mauser. The Marine fired from the hip, downing the enemy before he could release a round.

Michael Houlihan paused at the top of the parapet and looked desperately for Morgan. "Sergeant," he called when his eyes fell on Morgan standing over the dead German. "I think Ira is hit."

"Get down," Morgan called.

His warning was too late. A Maxim chattered from a clump of trees ahead. The hot lead stitched across Michael Houlihan's mid-section. The young Irishman was dead before he tumbled into the trench.

"That reminds me of a girl I knew back in Tennessee. She was drop-dead beautiful. I was dying to take her behind the shed. If she had slept with me, I'd have killed myself with joy."

"Houlihan, where do you get all these lies?"

"If I'm lyin', I'm dyin'."

Michael Houlihan had told his last tall tale to amuse the boys in the squad.

Corky Jones fell to his knees at the edge of the trench. He had stumbled twice during the twenty-yard run toward the German position and twisted his ankle the second time.

"Where have you been?" Morgan asked. "Were you hit?"

"I'm okay," Corky Jones said. "Except I think I broke my ankle."

"Get in this trench. The Hun just shot Houlihan when he was standing up there where you are. He told me they got Ira, too."

"Yeah," Corky Jones replied. "I heard Ira call out when I was running this way."

"Where was he?"

"Back there," Corky Jones said pointing in the direction of their charge.

"Stay here," Morgan ordered. "I'll be right back."

Morgan swung over the edge of the embankment and retraced his steps toward the first trench. He found Ira Silverstein doubled over in agony beside a tree stump.

"Water," Ira moaned. "Morgan, I'm sure glad you're here. Give me a drink of water."

Morgan straightened the young Marine and looked at the frothy blood bubbling from his chest. He recognized the lung wound immediately. The hole in Ira's stomach seeped blood just above his web belt. Water was the worst thing to give a man with a stomach wound. He held Ira's limp body against his own chest. Why does he have to die? Why couldn't I have saved him? How many more of my friends will I see killed? Couldn't I have been a better Marine and helped my comrades stay alive?

"Water," Ira moaned weakly. "I'm so thirsty."

Morgan pulled his canteen from his web belt and unscrewed the cap. He held the container to Ira's parched lips. The young Marine from New York was going to die. A little water wouldn't change that fact.

"Here," Morgan said gently. "Drink this. You'll feel better."

"I'm going to die, aren't I?"

"Corpsman!" Morgan shouted. "Corpsman! Over this way!"

"Don't let me die," Ira pleaded as he coughed blood that dribbled over his chin and ran down his soiled neck.

"You aren't going to die," Morgan said reassuringly. "There's a corpsman on the way. I'll stay with you."

"I feel cold," Ira said in a weakening voice.

Morgan wrapped his arms around the young Marine and pulled the limp body to his chest. He looked upward through the trees and allowed his mind to wander from the explosions and rifle shots and rattle of the Maxim machine guns and screams of the wounded. Puffy clouds scudded across the robin's egg blue sky. The sun dappled the churned soil and rocky terrain as it penetrated the leafy canopy of the dense forest.

The juxtaposition of the serenity overhead and the violence on the ground overwhelmed Morgan. His eyes misted with tears as he thought of Michael Houlihan's tattered body falling into the muck at the bottom of the trench, Ira Silverstein dying in his arms, Bill Hauser headless in his foxhole, and Casey Brown running in terror as bullets ripped into his back.

"You hit, sergeant?" the corpsman asked as he slid to a stop on his knees.

Morgan shook his head to clear the fog of melancholy that had descended on him. "I'm okay," he said vaguely. "But you've got to save this boy. We went through basic together."

"Are you sure you're okay?"

Morgan blinked and looked curiously at the corpsman. "I'm sure. Why?"

"This Marine is dead, sergeant. You're holding a corpse."

Morgan's shoulders slumped. His head dropped and tears leaked from his red eyes.

"He was just talking to me," Morgan protested weakly. "He can't be dead."

"Get hold of yourself, sergeant," the corpsman said shaking Morgan by the shoulder. "You might be the company commander now. I was just over by the 3rd platoon area. Captain Bennett's position was overrun by a counter-attack. He's either dead or a prisoner."

~ 39 ~

"Who's in charge here?" Morgan asked when he reached the 3rd platoon's area of operation.

"The lieutenant's dead," Sergeant Tucker said. "I guess it's me."

"What happened?"

"We pushed the Hun out of three trenches and were advancing when they counter-attacked. Captain Bennett went down and we got overrun. They killed four of my men and shoved us back with bayonets. That was about one hundred yards forward of our position now."

"Was the captain hit?"

"I couldn't tell," Sergeant Tucker replied. "I saw him spin around and fall, but I didn't see any blood. Then the Germans overwhelmed us. There must have been twenty of them."

"I need a runner," Morgan said. "Send one of your guys to 2nd platoon and have Privates Birdsong and Hitchins report to me here."

Sergeant Tucker waved one of his Marines away after repeating Morgan's instructions.

"What's your plan?"

"I'm going back to your position and find the captain. As soon as I have him, I'll throw hand grenades. When you hear the explosions, bring your men up on the double."

"You're going alone?"

"If we attack, and the Germans have the captain, they'll kill him. If he's hit in the woods up there, and we attack, he'll probably get killed by our own grenades or rifle fire. I've got to sneak in there if he's to have a chance."

Cochise Birdsong and Slim Hitchins trotted from the woods and stopped in front of Morgan. "What's going on, sergeant?"

"Captain Bennett is up there somewhere," Morgan explained. "I'm going to find him."

"Why don't we jus' tell the Hun to send him back?" Private Hitchins asked reasonably. "They probably got enough officers of their own. They don't need one of ours."

"That's an excellent idea," Birdsong added. "The only problem is we don't speak German. How are we gonna ask?"

Morgan smiled in spite of the seriousness of the situation. "You two have enough ammunition and hand grenades?"

"We loaded up before we ran over here," Slim Hitchins replied. "We figgered you weren't inviting us to no church social."

"You two move up with Sergeant Tucker's men when you hear my grenades," Morgan said to Birdsong and Hitchins. "I want those Germans pushed back beyond their present positions. And have a corpsman with you in case the captain's wounded."

"We're down to about eighteen in the platoon," the sergeant said.

"With my two men you've got twenty," Morgan said. "Don't stop until you get past me. I don't look forward to eating sauerkraut the rest of the war."

*   *   *

The midday sun blazed through the diminished canopy of branches and leaves that had escaped shearing from the innumerable artillery barrages of the past two weeks. The uneven ground was as rough as a storm churned ocean, with deep holes and piled dirt littering every inch of terrain. Rocks and boulders dotted the landscape. Crevices and ravines slashed into the earth. The faint smell of cordite lingered in the air.

Morgan carried his Springfield in his right hand. His bayonet, sharpened and honed to a razor edge, was firmly affixed. Hand grenades hung from his shoulder web straps. He had discarded his steel helmet; the protective device was heavy and hot and difficult to keep on the head when running. If it fell against a hard object, the resounding noise would certainly alert any Germans within earshot.

The gnarled and scarred topography of Belleau Woods was ideal for stealthy advance. Morgan dashed from rock to fissure keeping a low profile and shielding his body from possible sight by Germans ahead. A moan of agony sounded in front and to his left. Was it an American calling out in pain or a German? Hand grenades sounded one hundred yards to his right. Machine guns barked long bursts of deadly fire. Single shots rang out in the woods from other individual battles along the line of advance. Morgan's focus remained steadfast.

He huddled behind a boulder and listened. The guttural sound of voices drifted over his head. How far away were the speakers? He did not comprehend the language, but undoubtedly they were German this far in front of the Marine lines.

Morgan picked up a rock and threw it to the left of the voices. He waited.

"*Fritz? Bis du das?*" Is that you?

At the sound of the voice, Morgan stood and rushed forward. He hoped he wouldn't have to fire and reveal his position.

The German was standing in his foxhole, searching for his comrade where Morgan's rock had landed. Morgan covered the fifteen yards in less than two seconds. He leaped forward and plunged his long bayonet into the German's chest before the enemy soldier could bring his Mauser to bear.

"*Fritz?*" the German groaned in complete surprise. Shock and confusion contorted his face. "*Eh, das bist du nicht.*" Hey, that's not you.

Morgan twisted the Springfield in his hands, wrenching the bayonet in the German's chest, ripping vital organs and facilitating the removal of the blade. He raised his boot and shoved against the German's stomach, freeing his rifle from the enemy's dying body.

A long depression in the terrain slashed forward, and Morgan slithered on hands and knees toward the German lines until the crevice shallowed. He flattened his body in the last of the cover and looked around. Sporadic rifle fire whistled through the air on both sides. Crumpled bodies of dead Marines and Germans littered the landscape. Several of the downed warriors were without arms and legs.

A long groan of anguish and confusion sounded ten yards to Morgan's left. The voice did not betray pain.

"Where am I?" the bewildered soldier cried out.

The caller was a Marine. Morgan scrambled toward the voice and rolled the disoriented man toward him. It was Captain Bennett.

"What happened?" Morgan whispered.

"I...I was running...we were running...toward the German position and then...and then I don't remember anything."

Morgan looked at the captain's helmet lying in the dirt nearby. A concave dent was plainly visible in the front of the steel dome. An enemy bullet had clanged off the captain's helmet and rendered the officer unconscious. This explanation coincided with Sergeant Tucker's report that the captain spun and fell although he didn't see any blood.

"Can you move?" Morgan asked.

"My knees feel weak, but I guess I can move a little."

"Throw your arm over my shoulder. I want to get you to that little ditch over there."

Morgan pressed the captain into the ravine where any flying shrapnel from his grenades would pass overhead. He handed Bennett a Springfield he had retrieved from a fallen Marine.

"Fire this when the grenades explode. If we can keep the Hun busy for a couple of minutes, Sergeant Tucker and his platoon will have an easier time of their assault."

Captain Bennett nodded his comprehension although his eyes still appeared glazed and his reactions sluggish.

Morgan pulled three hand grenades from his web straps. He lined them in front of his defensive position. The occupied German trench was twenty yards ahead. He selected three open lanes without tree interference.

"Get ready," he said calmly.

Morgan pulled the pin on the first grenade and tossed it toward the Germans. Before the first sputtering bomb detonated, the second and third were airborne. The three explosions sounded within a second of one another. Cries of agony and surprise sounded from the German trench. Before the Germans could fire a shot, Morgan emptied a five round clip from his Springfield at enemy soldiers visible above the rampart of the position.

"Fire," he shouted to Captain Bennett as he pushed a fresh clip of bullets into his weapon and sighted toward the German lines.

Shouts and rifle fire emanated from the woods behind Morgan's cover. Privates Birdsong and Hitchins led the charge of the 3rd platoon across the rocky, undulating terrain. Sun flashed off steel bayonets as the energized Marines dashed toward the German positions.

Several stunned defenders rose and fired their Mausers at the approaching Marines, but the aggression displayed by the attackers struck fear in the Germans. Singly and then in numbers they vaulted the trench and began to run away.

The conquest of Belleau Woods was nearing completion.

"Sergeant Early," Captain Bennett said slowly as the Marines sprinted past after the retreating Germans. "I'm recommending you for a commission to 2nd lieutenant. I'm also putting you in for the Navy Cross."

"I was just doing my job, sir," Morgan protested.

"I know," the captain said nodding with understanding. "I've watched you since Quantico. You have natural leadership and the men respond to you. You innately understand tactics. The Corps needs officers like you."

"Thank you, sir," Morgan said.

"And you saved my life, lieutenant," Captain Bennett grinned. "I'll never forget that."

*   *   *

On the morning of June 26, 1918, after nearly a month of the most vicious fighting in the entire war, the following message was sent to 2nd Division headquarters. *"Woods now entirely U.S. Marine Corps."*

The cost to capture the woods was horrific. Dead, wounded and missing Marines numbered 4,298. No German fatalities were ever calculated, but undoubtedly they exceeded the Marine numbers by a significant amount. One thousand six hundred Germans were taken prisoner.

Private Michael Houlihan, the Irish boy from Tennessee who loved to spin a yarn, was wrong when he said nobody would ever remember the name of the woods after the Marines took it from the Germans. The French, delighted that the Marines had saved Paris from the advance of the Germans, bestowed upon them numerous awards and accolades. In addition, they gave the woods the sobriquet *Bois de la Brigade de Marine*. In 1923 a monument was dedicated at the site to the slain in the battle. Belleau Woods became an icon of U.S. Marine Corps lore only to be eclipsed a quarter century later by the words Guadalcanal, Tarawa and Iwo Jima.

*   *   *

At 11:00 in the morning of November 11, 1918 an armistice was declared ending the bloody Great War. Following a brief duty in Germany with the occupational forces, 2nd Lieutenant Morgan Early, winner of the Navy Cross, the Marine Corps' second highest honor, was discharged and sent back to the United States. The date was January 29th, 1919, the day the Eighteenth Amendment to the U.S. Constitution, known as the Volstead Prohibition Act, was certified which prohibited the use and distribution of alcoholic beverages in the country.

~ 40 ~

Alrick Brown steered the thirty-foot sloop toward the pier in Miami and anxiously looked at the people gathered. Suddenly tears of joy flowed down his mahogany cheeks when he saw Morgan Early waving from the shore.

"You alive!" Alrick screamed as he tossed Morgan a bow line. "I done prayed for your soul ever' night you was gone."

Morgan stepped aboard his boat and hugged his friend enthusiastically. "There were many nights I dreamed about returning to Bimini. I wasn't always sure it would happen. Thank you for thinking of me."

"What was it like over dere? We heard you whipped dem Hun real good."

Morgan lowered his eyes and shook his head slowly. "They were good soldiers," he said after a pause. "We didn't really whip them. I think they were a little tired by the time we got into the fight."

"Was you scared?"

"It's...it's a little hard to talk about," Morgan said slowly. "Sometimes the month in combat seems like it was a long, frightening nightmare. I saw things I could never have imagined. Boys were blown apart, their heads and legs and arms ripped off, their insides hanging out as they cried for their mothers. And still the others fought on until finally the enemy retreated. We were all scared, but most of us were able to overcome the fear and do our jobs."

"You was a Marine, wasn't you? We heard you was made an officer. There was news in the paper here in town a few months back."

Morgan nodded and waved his hand dismissively. "They made me an officer," he said simply. "For some reason, I guess I'm good at the war business. But I hope that's the last I see of it."

"I's proud of you," Alrick said. "Welcome home."

"How were things on the island?"

"We done got by," Alrick said with a shrug. "We caught lobsters and sold 'em here in Miami. An' we grew plenty sisal and made rope like you said. Dat turned out pretty good. At least nobody was throwin' no bombs at us."

"I'm glad," Morgan said. "I know the war was difficult for everyone here, too. But I have an idea that I think will make us plenty of money."

"Now you be talkin', Morgan," Alrick said with a bright smile that exposed his white teeth. "Let's get off dis pier and head for home. You can tell me all about it on the ride over."

*   *   *

Three weeks later, with two thousand dollars in cash withdrawn from a Miami bank, following a transfer of all his funds from his account in Denver, Morgan and Alrick sailed to Man-O-War Cay in the Abaco chain of islands two hundred miles northeast of Bimini. Morgan's liquid assets totaled nearly nine thousand dollars, counting the money he had earned in Mexico and his Marine Corps salary, which included combat pay for serving in France and bonuses for his battlefield commission and Navy Cross award.

Morgan and Alrick pulled to a gentle stop at a wooden dock in the protected Man-O-War harbor and tied the sloop securely before stepping ashore.

"Where can we find Mr. Albury?" Morgan asked the first Bahamian he encountered.

"Mr. Albury done be in his boat shed over yonder," the young man replied, pointing to a large wooden structure one hundred yards down the waterfront.

"Thank you."

Morgan and Alrick walked briskly along the beach until they arrived at the designated building. The shed was almost eighty feet long and forty feet wide. Two massive doors stood wedged to the sides of the structure by large, pink conch shells, leaving the rear of the shed open to the water. The stern of a sailboat under construction was visible just inside the building. The craft was propped on its keel by slanted shafts of wood.

A man was busy sanding the sleek hull in preparation for paint. Other workers scrambled around inside the boat screwing planking in place to form a deck.

"Is Mr. Albury here?" Morgan asked one of the men.

The Bahamian paused from his labors and wiped perspiration from his brow. "Mr. Albury be workin' on da mast in da front of da shed."

"May we enter?" Morgan asked.

"Don't see no reason why not, if you want to talk wid Mr. Albury."

Morgan and Alrick stepped into the shed. Morgan looked at the flowing lines of the small sailboat that undoubtedly would be used to gather sponges or conchs or lobsters by an enterprising Bahamian. The belly of the boat was generous and the draft appeared minimal, allowing use in the shallow waters of the Bahamas. The workmanship was impeccable. Morgan ran his hand along the hull noticing the tight joints of the planks and the smooth fairing to produce a fast, reliable vessel.

"Are you Mr. Albury?" Morgan asked when they approached a tall, thin white man affixing a bronze track along a mast resting horizontally on a pair of sawhorses.

"I'm David Albury," the man replied. "How may I help you?"

"My name is Morgan Early, and this is my partner Alrick Brown. We'd like you to build us a couple of boats."

David Albury wiped his hands on a rag and the men shook hands.

"Nice to meet you, Early. What did you have in mind?"

"I need a speedboat and I need a barge," Morgan said simply. "I'm hoping I can interest you in my projects."

"Young man, I build sailboats. I've never build a motor boat and a barge...well I don't know if I'm interested in building a barge."

Morgan smiled and nodded with understanding. "I thought that might be your reaction, Mr. Albury. But I see you are a craftsman, and I'm hoping you might be challenged by the opportunity to build a quality speedboat."

David Albury rubbed his chin in thought. "And what are you thinking about for an engine in this motorboat of yours?"

"I believe Mr. Albury be workin' up some interest in our speedboat," Alrick said with a gleam in his eye.

"I want a boat thirty-five feet long," Morgan said. "And it has to be fast. I need at least forty miles an hour; fifty would be better. I found a man in Miami who can sell me a Liberty V-12 aircraft engine with 450 horsepower. That should be sufficient, if you can keep the weight down and still make a strong, safe hull."

Albury released a slow whistle. "Fifty miles an hour," he repeated. "And how much fuel would the boat need to carry? What kind of range do you need?"

"Two hundred-fifty miles," Morgan said quickly.

"You seem to have worked all these calculations out," Albury said with a smile.

"We done our homework," Alrick nodded.

"And what about the barge?"

"I want a barge 100 feet long and 40 feet wide," Morgan answered. "A canvas cover would be sufficient and a small shack for one man to live aboard while he watches our inventory."

David Albury looked at Morgan for a long moment. "You seem rather sure of yourself," he said. "But you look very young. How old are you?"

"I'll be nineteen this coming July."

"And I assume you have sufficient funds for these projects," Albury said.

"I do," Morgan said reaching in his pocket. "In fact I've brought money for a substantial deposit if you agree to build both vessels."

"I'm not too excited about the barge," Albury said. "That's hardly a challenge."

Morgan shrugged his shoulders. "It's both or none," he said. "Consider the speedboat a test of your nautical experience and the barge a chance to reward your pockets."

Albury extended his hand. "I'll begin building the barge immediately," he said. "And I'll draw up plans for the speedboat hull. When can you get the engine here?"

Alrick looked at Morgan and flashed a wide grin. "How 'bout two weeks," he said turning to David Albury. "We done got da engine on order already."

"May I ask what you plan to do with these two vessels when they're finished?" Albury asked. "I don't think you're going lobster fishing."

Alrick Brown shook his head. "Ain't you heard? The United States is gonna quit wid da liquor. Dey jus' passed da law an' it go into effect next January 29th. We figger those folks ain't gonna want to quit like the government say; so we plan to supply 'em all they can afford."

David Albury threw back his head and laughed. "You two are going to smuggle cases of liquor into the United States?"

"We'll smuggle some and sell the rest to anybody who wants to run over to Bimini and buy," Morgan said. "That's where we'll anchor the barge."

"I believe you young men have come up with an idea that will make you a lot of money," David Albury said. "If any of your customers needs a fast motorboat, I hope you refer them to me."

"I'm sure we can agree to that," Morgan said. "As long as that consideration is reflected in the price we pay for the first one."

*   *   *

Late that afternoon, Morgan and Alrick caught the falling tide and sailed down the Sea of Abaco. They exited Man-O-War Channel and headed south toward the town of Nassau on New Providence Island, one hundred miles distant. Mid-morning the following day, they entered the rock-lined harbor through the west entrance and pulled their sloop against one of the several wooden wharfs on Bay Street, across the harbor from Hog Island.

The sun shone intensely on the vibrant waters of the protected harbor, and the turquoise colors glistened bright against the sandy beach bordering the narrow island where the residents of Nassau grazed their livestock.

The two enterprising young men walked confidently down the dirt and crushed shell road of the Bahamian capital town. Street vendors hawked fresh fish from straw baskets covered with seaweed. Women sold conch meat recently gouged from shiny, pink shells that were then tossed to the water's edge behind their stand. Ramshackle bars of driftwood and tarpaper offered cheap rum drinks to anyone interested in wasting the hot afternoon in inebriated stupor. They paused at the modest building owned by Clifton Bethel that dispensed liquor in bottles to the Bahamian inhabitants of the island. A general malaise hung over the sleepy town in the heat of the noon sun.

Morgan entered the squalid store and peered around the dim structure. The floor was dirt. A decrepit counter crossed the room, and three shelves were tacked to the wall displaying dusty bottles of Scotch whiskey and rum imported from Jamaica. A curtain covered the rear half of the shed and a dark face appeared when a gnarled hand parted one side.

"What you boys want, some liquor to drink?"

"We're looking for Mr. Bethel," Morgan said politely. "Are you the proprietor of this liquor store?"

"I'm Bethel," the man said cautiously as he wandered from behind the closure. "What can I do for you?"

Alrick Brown stepped forward and presented his hand. "I'm Alrick Brown," he said. "And this here is my partner Morgan Early. We'd like to talk to you about purchasing some liquor."

"What you see dere on da shelf is what I gots to sell," Bethel said with a shrug. "Grab what you want."

Morgan shook his head twice and smiled. "Actually, we're not interested in a bottle or two," he said. "We'd like to talk to you about purchasing cases of Scotch and rum. Initially we will need one hundred cases, but I can visualize taking one thousand cases very soon. Within a year we could buy in lots of five thousand cases."

Clifton Bethel leaned back and laughed. "Either you boys are plumb crazy or dis be some kind of a joke. Ain't nobody can drink dat much liquor, and we gots some pretty good drinkers here in Nassau."

Alrick Brown looked directly at Bethel with a solemn expression. "We be serious," he said. "Da United States done pass a law against drinkin'. But dat ain't gonna stop dem people over dere. We plan to sell 'em all dey can handle."

Bethel's eyes opened wide. "Maybe so, but how you gonna afford to buy all dis Scotch? You know a case done cost me almost $30 from England after the tax been added here in Nassau. Where you gonna get three thousand dollars to buy one hundred cases?"

"We'll pay you $33 for each case in advance," Morgan said. "We want you to make a profit so you'll keep the supply coming when we need it. If that sounds fair, I think we should discuss our first order. We have a barge being built that we'll operate from Bimini, and we have a fast boat being built that we can use to run to Miami."

"When you need dese first hundred cases?" Bethel asked. "It take time to get Scotch from England."

"The law takes effect next January 29th," Morgan replied. "Can you have merchandise here by the beginning of January?"

"Dat I can do," Clifton Bethel answered. "It ain't yet March."

"Good," Alrick said. "Our barge be completed by then. We'll load it with da Scotch and tow it to Bimini so we be ready jus' when dem people in Miami start to get real thirsty."

~ 41 ~

February 15, 1920, broke fresh and clear in Bimini. A cold front had passed through the island from the northwest three days previously with twenty-five mile per hour winds churning the Gulf Stream into an angry maelstrom of ten-foot waves. Behind the front a gentle southeasterly breeze flattened the ocean and made for ideal boat passage to Miami.

Morgan and Alrick started their sleek, black hull Albury speedboat *Belleau Woods* and idled slowly from the North Bimini harbor, around the south end of South Bimini, and entered the protected bay of Nicholas Harbour in the southwest corner of the island. They approached their anchored barge *Thirst Quencher* and hailed Rudy Dames who had taken up residence on the vessel to protect their precious cargo of Scotch. Morgan shut off the engine.

"Yo, Rudy," Alrick called from the bow of *Belleau Woods* as they came alongside. "Rouse yourself on dis beautiful mornin'. We gots to go to work."

Rudy Dames appeared from the small hut at one end of the barge, yawned and stretched his arms wide. "You gonna make your firs' run to Miami today?" he called with a grin. "Looks like a good day to cross."

"We done tol' dem boys in Miami when we was dere las' week to be lookin' fer us the first good day to travel," Alrick said.

"How much you gonna charge dem boys?" Rudy Dames asked. "You puttin' in a lot of work to git da liquor from England and deliver it to Miami."

Morgan grinned. "They agreed to our price of $135 per case," he said. "And that's what you're going to charge when they send their own boats over here."

Rudy Dames knitted his dark, bushy eyebrows and extended his ten fingers into the air. One-by-one he counted off the profit to be made from the one hundred cases aboard the *Thirst Quencher.* "Dat's...dat's...jus' a minute. Dat's one thousand dollars profit on dese hundred cases of Scotch."

Alrick Brown beamed with joy. "No," he said didactically, "dat's *ten thousand dollars* profit on dese one hundred cases of Scotch."

"Lordy me," Rudy Dames said shaking his head in wonder. "I hope dem Americans never change dat law dey jus' passed."

"I agree," Morgan said. "Now get busy loading thirty of those cases aboard *Belleau Woods*. We've got some thirsty customers in Miami waiting for us."

*   *   *

Morgan and Alrick had taken delivery of *Belleau Woods* in late December. David Albury had crafted a magnificently efficient hull of double mahogany planking with a sharp fifty-eight degree entry that sliced through the waves effortlessly. Internal sloping chines cascaded the wake down and away from the hull for a dry, smooth ride. Aft of the forward section the bottom twisted to a flatter configuration culminating in a gentle fourteen degree V shape at the transom that carried the boat high and flat in the water for maximum speed and fuel efficiency.

The hull had been painstakingly sanded until it was smooth and fair. The black paint had been meticulously applied in seven individual coats until it shone a rich ebony with the reflected sunlight from the water.

The foredeck, engine box and forward seat were carefully fitted teak with eight layers of varnish, each lightly sanded until the finished surface was as smooth as satin.

The engine installation was simple, robust and designed with ease of repair firmly in mind. With the teak box removed, the entire

Liberty V-12, with its myriad belts and hoses used to adopt the engine to its marine environment, was exposed and readily serviced if needed.

A tachometer, speedometer, oil pressure gauge and water temperature gauge were neatly clustered in a polished chrome panel set into a glistening teak dashboard. A teak steering wheel, chrome throttle and a chrome clutch lever completed the mechanical package in front of the driver's seat.

The initial sea trial had astounded everyone who witnessed the boat in the water. At maximum engine speed, *Belleau Woods* screamed through the protected Sea of Abaco on the west side of Man-O-War Cay at fifty knots or fifty-eight miles per hour. With the engine turning at more sedate revolutions, the boat cruised at forty knots or forty-six miles per hour. Morgan and Alrick were ecstatic.

The *Thirst Quencher* had been launched early in January and immediately towed to Nassau. It was loaded with the one hundred cases of Scotch that had arrived from England and had been stored in Clifton Bethel's modest liquor warehouse. The barge was then towed the one hundred thirty-five nautical miles to South Bimini and placed at anchor in the calm waters tucked in the southwest corner.

*   *   *

Morgan turned the ignition key and pressed the start button. The Liberty V-12 re-fired. The water-cooled exhaust burbled from the twin chrome pipes protruding from the teak transom.

"Good luck," Rudy Dames called as Morgan eased *Belleau Woods* from the barge.

"We be back in a few hours," Alrick called. "Don't you be touchin' dat Scotch whiles we're gone."

"Don't you fret none," Rudy shouted back. "I knows you got 'em counted. If I want a drink, I'll buy it like ever'body else."

Morgan turned *Belleau Woods* west and exited the Great Bahama Bank in the deep cut just north of Pickett Rock. The water turned from emerald green on the bank to turquoise and then cobalt as the depth dropped from twenty feet to one thousand. He immediately sensed the gentle swell of the open ocean under the bow. He advanced the throttle and felt the boat lift as it rapidly gathered speed before settling on a plane at thirty knots or thirty-four statute miles per hour.

Gossamer wings of aerated spray flew horizontally from the chines before slashing back into the ocean. An abbreviated rooster tail formed in the distance behind the transom as the wake crashed together from the corners of the hull.

Cumulus clouds drifted lazily across the blue sky, propelled by a gentle trade wind that forecasted the coming summer breezes.

Morgan glanced at the compass floating freely in a gyro mechanism on the dashboard, unaffected by the motion of the boat. Miami lay forty-three nautical miles at 279 degrees magnetic to the west. At thirty knots, they would be in Miami in exactly an hour and a half. He settled down in the teak helm seat, scanned the gauges, and, satisfied the Liberty was operating at the proper temperatures, began to enjoy the exhilarating ride.

The first trace of the Miami skyline crested the horizon after an hour and ten minutes of running. The tallest buildings initially appeared as a smudge above the water but quickly gained definition as *Belleau Woods* rapidly approached the shore.

"You tink dem boys will be at the meeting place?" Alrick asked.

Morgan nodded affirmatively. "They'll be there," he said. "As much money as we'll make on these cases, they'll make more. I estimate the ultimate drinker will pay over thirty dollars per bottle or about four hundred dollars per case."

Alrick blew a long, slow whistle. "Dat's sure a lot of money."

"Yes, it is," Morgan said nodding. "But if the demand is there... Alrick, do you see that boat ahead?"

Alrick Brown stood and squinted into the rushing air pouring over the windscreen. A vessel of approximately one hundred feet, with a distinctly military appearance, loomed against the background of Miami. The mid-morning sun beaming over *Belleau Woods'* stern illuminated the menacing cutter perfectly. "Dat looks like one of them Revenue Cutter Service boats I seen around Miami," he said slowly. "You tink they be lookin' for us?"

"They're headed on a direct course for us," Morgan said. "They're moving fast, too."

"Dem boats carry guns, I do believe," Alrick said pensively. "What you tink we should do?"

Morgan pursed his lips in contemplation. Continuing their present course would certainly invite an interdiction at sea which at the least would result in loss of their cargo if not incarceration and seizure of the boat. Running back to Bimini would risk alienating their customers and destroying a nascent business relationship. Timely delivery of the Scotch was imperative if they were to be relied upon as trustworthy suppliers.

Morgan turned the steering wheel abruptly to port and *Belleau Woods* began a graceful one hundred-eighty degree maneuver away from the shoreline.

"We ain't gonna deliver the Scotch?" Alrick asked with concern. "We done promised them guys in Miami."

"We're going to keep our promise," Morgan said as he looked over his shoulder and eased the throttle back, allowing the cutter to reduce the distance between the two vessels. "But we have to be clever about it."

"Dey gonna catch us if we keep dis speed," Alrick observed after studying the closing rate of the trailing boat.

"We have to lure them far enough offshore so that when we make our dash back to the coast, they won't be close enough to see where we land," Morgan explained. "We have to slow down. They must believe they're able to catch us, otherwise they won't keep pursuing."

Alrick brightened as Morgan's plan became clear. "I jus' hope dey don't start shooting," he said. "We be fast, but we can't outrun no bullets."

"I won't let them close enough to find our range," Morgan said.

The coastline of Miami began to fade from view. Morgan ran through a quick calculation. If the cutter could make twenty-five knots and *Belleau Woods* fifty, they would cover twice the distance the cutter could make in the same amount of time. To have the cutter more than eight miles behind them, and thus beyond the horizon and unable to see the shore when Belleau Woods entered Biscayne Bay, Morgan would need to initially lure the cutter more than sixteen miles out to sea. He continued his course directly east, away from Miami.

When he estimated that *Belleau Woods* was approximately twenty miles from Miami, with the cutter just over a mile behind,

Morgan turned the boat sharply to starboard, pushed the throttle to the maximum position and headed due south.

Belleau Woods rose higher in the water and flattened its running angle. The Liberty V-12 screamed as all four hundred-fifty horses spun the drive shaft at full revolutions and the four-bladed propeller bit deeply into the ocean water and thrust the craft ahead at fifty knots. Spray flew from the sides and a narrow strip of frothy bubbles peeled from beneath the hull. Heated exhaust water spewed in twin horizontal columns from the chrome exhaust pipes.

Morgan held his southerly course until the cutter turned and adopted an intercept direction, taking them further from the land. Then he turned and dashed directly for the entrance to Biscayne Bay, south of the Miami inlet, certain he would be out of sight before he entered the protected waters below Miami and arrived at the rendezvous point on the remote far shore.

*   *   *

"We were beginning to wonder if you boys were coming," the tall, bearded man dressed in dirty shorts, a tattered shirt open at the chest, sandals and a crushed straw hat said.

Morgan nosed *Belleau Woods* against a sandy beach between two stands of mangroves on the deserted west shore of Biscayne Bay, ten miles below Miami.

"We had to outrun one o' dem Revenue Cutter boats," Alrick announced proudly. "Dem boys seemed to be on the lookout for us."

Two more slovenly dressed men appeared on the beach. A narrow-wheeled truck with a canvas-draped rear compartment stood on the shore twenty yards inland.

"Thirty cases as promised," Morgan said as he jumped from the foredeck of *Belleau Woods* and waded ashore in the shallow water.

"And four thousand-fifty dollars as promised," said one of the men holding a bulging bag in his right hand. "When can we have more?"

"We got a barge anchored jus' south of South Bimini," Alrick said expansively. "Rudy Dames be livin' aboard ready to serve whoever runs over dere in his boat. Da price be da same. You tell your friends in Miami we be open fer business day and night."

"I want another fifty cases right here, one week from today," the large man said emphatically. "Can you deliver?"

"If the weather permits," Morgan said, "we'll be here."

"Good. Miami is full of thirsty people. I'd hate to disappoint them."

~ 42 ~

Morgan Early sat on the covered veranda of his three year old house perched high on the ridge overlooking the vast flats to the east of Bimini. Pelicans squatted on the pilings surrounding his one hundred-thirty foot sailing schooner *Semper Fidelis* that bobbed lazily in the water below, tugging gently on her lines. The languid trade wind eased the blistering effects of the relentless sun.

Alrick Brown walked through the house from the path entrance to the west and stepped to the porch from the rear door. He mussed Morgan's hair with a friendly hand before taking a seat beside him. It was the second Sunday in September, 1926, and the two friends relaxed from their week's labors.

Alrick had just returned from a run to New York in the schooner with a cargo of 5700 cases of Scotch and rum. They had paid Clifton Bethel $170,000 for the merchandise and sold it for $342,000, making over one hundred-seventy thousand dollars for the two week journey. In the city the cargo would net $650,000. The voyage was the twentieth for *Semper Fidelis* since her launching in 1924.

Nightly, Rudy Dames sold "hams" to the myriad rumrunners that ventured across the Gulf Stream from Florida seeking liquor. A "ham" was a half case of six quart bottles of Scotch sewed into gunnysacks with the ends bunched together to provide ease of handling for the small boat operators. Morgan's cost for one "ham" was seventeen dollars; he received seventy dollars from the bootleggers who could carry about three hundred "hams" in their boats. Most speedboats

216

made two or three runs in twenty-four hours when the weather was calm. A "ham" sold in Florida for one hundred-twenty dollars.

Competition had sprung up in the liquor business. There were now ten other barges anchored near Gun Cay, nine miles below Bimini, dispensing Scotch and other spirits. Dozens of speedy craft joined *Belleau Woods* running liquor to Florida on a regular schedule.

Bruce Bethel, a one-armed veteran of the Great War and a cousin of Clifton Bethel, purchased an old concrete ship in Miami, *Sapona*, and had it towed by the *Messenger* toward Gun Cay to be used as a liquor barge. Unfortunately, *Sapona* hit the wreck of an old Spanish galleon and came to rest on the bottom of the exposed flats east of Pickett Rock, three miles below South Bimini. Undaunted, Mr. Bethel dispensed liquor from his grounded *Sapona* and began to make plans to turn the wreck into a nightclub.

Ashore, the Bimini Bay Rod and Gun Club, a one hundred-room hotel constructed on the south end of the island, entertained a steady stream of Floridians tired of sneaking around illicit speakeasies and risking arrest every time they wanted to enjoy a drink.

In spite of the competition, Morgan and Alrick remained busy. The insatiable desire in the United States to consume liquor was almost overwhelming, and keeping an adequate supply on hand was the greatest business challenge. Fortunately, with the obscene profits available, financing more purchases was not a problem.

The Bahamas in general prospered as well as those directly involved in the distribution of the liquor. Taxes were collected in Nassau on all the imported products, and the decidedly decrepit look of the capitol improved markedly with the construction of hotels, nightclubs and churches. The doldrums of the Great War were soon forgotten as the lot of the Bahamians rose sharply during the folly of the Prohibition period in America.

"When do you want to make another trip in the *Semper Fi*," Morgan asked casually. His bank accounts in Miami and Nassau were already swollen with more money than he had ever dreamed possible; the challenge of operating a successful business was more compelling to him than the money. Profits seemed to be simply a way to keep score on his activities.

"Clifton is expecting another shipment from England next week," Alrick said. "I'll sail to Nassau and load another 5000 cases and then head back to New York."

"We'll need to keep an eye on the weather," Morgan warned. "September and October can bring serious storms."

Alrick Brown smiled and nodded. "Don't you worry none. I ain't in no hurry to get beat up," he said. "If the weather be lookin' bad, I'll be hiding in some hurricane hole till the wind lets up."

Movement along the beach below the house caught Morgan's eye. A girl was walking deliberately toward the path to his house. She turned to glance at the water and her fair skin and golden hair glistened in the harsh morning sunlight. A wisp of breeze lifted a lock from her forehead, and she raised a bare arm and smoothed the strands behind her ear. The casual motion, thoughtless and brief, backlit as she turned to face the house, riveted Morgan's attention. The girl's sensual features and athletic movements instantly etched in Morgan's mind.

Her long, smooth legs were bare and her feet unencumbered by shoes. She kicked playfully at a tern scooting through the tiny wavelets along the shore and laughed as she sprayed water into the breeze that cascaded back on her body. Her abbreviated navy shorts and her pink sleeveless blouse, tied in a knot beneath her taut breasts to expose her flat stomach, were splattered with droplets of seawater.

Alrick Brown looked from the girl and turned toward Morgan. "I seen you wid plenty girls befor', but I ain't never seen you look at one like dat," he said.

Morgan closed his eyes and shook his head. His mouth suddenly felt dry, and he licked his lips before daring to speak. "She's probably somebody's wife from Miami," he said lamely. "I'll bet she walks right past and doesn't even look this way."

"You be about to lose dat bet," Alrick said. "She be headin' dis way for sure."

Morgan sat straighter in his chair and focused on the girl. She was indeed heading directly up the incline toward his porch.

"I tink I be goin'," Alrick said with a laugh as he pushed up from his chair. "Dis business don't need me around. I tink I'll go clean da boat or somethin'."

Morgan stood and reached for Alrick's hand. "Wait. Aren't we going to lunch later? You can't leave me like this."

"You a big boy," Alrick chuckled. "Dem Hun over in France didn't scare you none. Dem Revenue Cutters or, what dey call 'em now, da Coast Guard, dey don't scare you none. You tellin' me you scared of dis little girl walkin' up your beach?"

Morgan's mouth opened but no words issued.

"I'll see you later," Alrick said with a wave as he disappeared into the house and exited by the front door.

*   *   *

"Are you Mr. Early?"

Morgan spun at the sound of the mature voice. The girl, so youthful and carefree appearing as she frolicked along the water, was in reality a young woman, perhaps only a year or so younger than Morgan's twenty-six years. Her skin was clear and her eyes sparkling blue. Her nose was abbreviated and slightly turned up at the tip.

"I'm Morgan. What can I do for you?"

"I was told you own a horse, and I was wondering if I could rent him this afternoon."

"Why don't you step up on the porch?" Morgan suggested with an extended hand. "It's cooler than standing in the hot sun."

"Thank you," the young blonde woman said as she easily mounted the deck and reached out her hand. "My name is Anne. Anne Roberts."

"Nice to meet you, Anne Roberts. Would you like something to drink?"

"That would be great. Is this your house?"

"Yes," Morgan answered. "I built it a couple of years ago."

Anne looked around briefly. "It's lovely. It's big for Bimini. Do you live here alone?"

Morgan smiled. "Yes."

Anne Roberts blushed as she realized the implication of her question. "I just meant...I didn't mean to ask...it's none of my business..."

Morgan laughed. "Have a seat. I'll get you a lemonade in the kitchen and be right back."

Anne eased into one of the cushioned chairs and stretched her legs on the coffee table. Her eyes cast toward the three masted *Semper Fidelis*.

"Here," Morgan said as he handed her a tall glass with ice and lemonade. "This will cool you off."

"Is that your boat?" Anne asked pointing down to the sleek, black-hulled schooner tied in the bay.

"Yes. Would you like to go for a sail?"

"I thought I was here to rent a horse."

Morgan spread his hands and lifted his shoulders. "Why not do both? But I have to tell you, Buck isn't for rent."

"Buck?"

"My horse is a buckskin, and I don't rent him. But perhaps I could persuade him to let you aboard. I'm the only one who has ridden him in twelve years."

"Bimini doesn't seem like a great place to horseback ride."

Morgan nodded. "You're right. But Buck and I came from Arizona to Colorado. Then we went to Mexico for awhile before coming to Florida. I guess you could say Buck and I are sort of retired here. Our serious riding days are over."

Anne Roberts took a long sip of her lemonade and looked at Morgan for several seconds before responding. She hadn't paid serious attention to him when she entered the porch. A two day growth of blonde whiskers covered his cheeks, upper lip and chin, and his sun-bleached hair was in need of a good cut and grooming. His shirt was faded and torn in several places and his khaki pants were cut off above the knees and sported numerous stains, several of which were most likely blood.

Beneath his slightly disheveled appearance, his face was handsome and his body was firm and toned. He spoke as though educated in the finest Boston schools without the Brahmin accent.

He was undoubtedly successful in whatever his enterprise in order to own a splendid house and an enormous yacht. Perhaps most appealing to Anne was the fact that her father would instantly hate him because he hadn't been born to the right family in the northeast.

"Let's go meet this horse of yours," she said at last. "Perhaps he'll take a liking to me."

"Where are you saying on Bimini?" Morgan asked.

"My father dragged me here as a graduation present from college," Anne said. "We're staying at the Bimini Bay Rod and Gun Club. But I think they should rename it the Bimini Bay Drinking Club. That's all they do day and night, and it's been frightfully boring for me."

"Well, Anne," Morgan said standing, "Let's go say hello to Buck. He's quite a good judge of character. I'll be interested to see if you're up to his standards."

Anne pulled back in mock anger and lightly punched Morgan on the upper arm, surprised at her own boldness, and astonished at the hardness of his bicep. "I have a feeling things might become a little more fun around here," she said with a hearty laugh as they walked off the veranda and headed for Buck's stable in the shade of several tall pine trees.

~ 43 ~

Morgan pushed the throttle forward and the powerful Liberty V-12 engine thrust *Belleau Woods* on plane. Within seconds Morgan and Anne Roberts were rocketing down the inner harbor of Bimini and heading south toward the access to the sea. The emerald waters along the beach paled to white across the sandy bar protecting the entrance before darkening as the depth dropped into the Gulf Stream.

Anne's blonde hair streamed behind her as the swift boat passed thirty knots. A broad smile of joy spread across her face and she threw her arms skyward in exhilaration.

"This is great," she screamed to Morgan. "I didn't know boats could go this fast."

"Not many can, luckily for me," Morgan said with a chuckle.

The day before Morgan and Anne had spent riding Buck around the north end of Bimini, exploring the moribund sisal fields that no longer justified cultivating, and collecting shells and sea glass from the pink sand beach.

Morgan had cast his fly rod at cruising bonefish in the shallows off the shore. He had hooked three, and as the magnificent silver fish melted line from the reel with a powerful run, he had handed the rod to Anne who cheered and shouted with delight as she battled to regain line before finally releasing the determined foe.

They had eaten a late lunch of fried fish and conch fritters at a tiny shack in Baileytown on the upper bay overlooking Mosquito

Point. Morgan delivered Anne to the Bimini Bay Rod and Gun Club aboard Buck as the sun was dropping toward the ocean only after she had extracted a promise from him to take her for a boat ride the next day.

*   *   *

"Where are we going?" Anne called.

"There's a beautiful beach on the north end of Gun Cay, about seven miles south," Morgan replied. "It's called Honeymoon Beach."

Anne tilted her head and opened her eyes in feigned shock. "I don't recall us getting married," she laughed.

Morgan lifted his hands from the steering wheel and held them aloft, palms outward. "Oh, I didn't mean..." he began in an apologetic tone.

The first instant he saw Anne walking toward his veranda, Morgan had been struck by her grace, beauty and vivacity. A subliminal spark of mischief and daring and adventure shimmered not far beneath the surface of her personality. Morgan had been with several women in the years since he had left Denver, but Anne Roberts was the first female to strike such a resounding chord in his soul. He had heard of love at first sight, but he had never encountered anything that he might consider such an experience. Could this be it? Could he have fallen in love the moment he first saw her kick at the water and splash herself and laugh?

Morgan's understanding of women had slowly progressed from his initial bewilderment at the actions of Ardyth Calhoun. He had arrived at an appreciation of their distinct view of the world. But he had never considered that a woman could become a genuine friend and an equal partner as well as a mate. Anne Roberts exuded all the attributes and hinted at the promise of such a woman.

"Oh my, you're blushing," Anne laughed.

Morgan wanted to grab her and squeeze her and kiss her. He wanted to taste her lips and feel her firm body against his own. But Anne Roberts was a sophisticated woman. She was college educated, and although Morgan had never heard of Radcliff, he assumed it was a wonderful school, not a one-room shack in the desert. His own formal education had essentially stopped when he was fourteen. Anne's family, obviously wealthy, apparently was important in the Boston area. His family...the best that could be said was that he had none. What chance would he have of wooing this young woman from such a different and superior background?

Honeymoon Harbor opened in a wide horseshoe expanse as Morgan turned *Belleau Woods* back on to the flats from the open ocean. He eased the throttle and idled the boat toward the deserted beach. Twenty yards from the shore, with only two feet of water beneath the propeller blades, he cut the engine and lowered an anchor overboard. The boat drifted momentarily until it gently fetched against the anchor line and began to bob softly in the large cove.

"I've never seen such a beautiful place," Anne gasped. "How deep is it? Can we go ashore?"

"You brought a bathing suit, didn't you," Morgan asked.

"Those bathing suits today are ridiculous," Anne replied with a dismissive wave of her hand. "They're like a dress with pant legs. I'll just swim in my shorts and shirt."

Morgan's lower jaw dropped with astonishment. He marveled at the refreshing idea that a woman would be willing to cast aside the foolishness of one of society's ridiculous dictates.

"If you're ready, let's go," Morgan said as he peeled his shirt from his bronzed chest and stepped to the deck. "Dive shallow; it's only a couple of feet deep."

The words were barely past his lips when Anne hopped to the gunwale of the boat and performed a perfect, flat dive into the crystal water.

They walked the beach for half an hour, stopping to examine tiny shells and pieces of detritus that had washed ashore. The sand was the consistency of sugar and the color of pink roses. It oozed between their toes when they walked near the lapping water.

The languorous breeze cooled their skin as the sun dried them from their swim. Their wet clothes clung uncomfortably to their salty, sticky bodies.

"Are you getting cold?" Morgan asked. "I have a couple of towels in the boat."

"Yes," Anne replied as she looked deeply into Morgan's eyes. "I'd like to take these wet clothes off. Why don't you swim back to the boat and get those towels."

The stirrings Anne felt the day before had intensified at night as she lay in her bed and reflected back on the gentle but strong young man riding his horse in front of her, pointing out the features of the island he so obviously loved. In the morning, seeing Morgan again, she became convinced her attraction was more than a momentary infatuation. She had engaged in a few trysts while at Radcliff, but never had she felt such a powerful allure to a man. Could she actually be falling in love?

Morgan stroked quickly to the boat, boarded and grabbed the two towels he had stowed in the compartment below the helm seat. He jumped back into the water, holding the towels aloft and dry, and paddled back to the beach. He climbed the slight incline from the water and stepped on the wet sand and looked up.

Anne Roberts unbuttoned her shorts, dropped them to her ankles, and stood naked before him. Her alabaster skin glistened with traces of salty residue. Her narrow waist and tight abdomen gave way to firm hips and long, toned legs. A tiny gust of wind fluttered her flaxen hair, and Anne reached with two hands to push the strands slowly from her forehead. Her breasts rose with the action. Her lips parted in a broad smile.

Morgan blinked once in disbelief. Then he stepped quickly forward, dropped the towels and fumbled with his shorts until they fell to the sand.

*   *   *

"Where you be goin' so fancy dressed?" Alrick asked as he banged open Morgan's front door and entered the living room.

Morgan stood before a mirror brushing his hair. His full-length slacks showed a crease down the front and his cotton, collared shirt was sparkling clean.

"Anne invited me to dinner at the Rod and Gun Club," he replied. "She wants her father to meet me."

Alrick raised his eyebrows toward the ceiling and opened his mouth in horror. "You knows what dat means, don't you?" he said. "Dis girl be serious 'bout you."

Morgan shrugged his shoulders. "I'm just going to dinner and meet her father," he said. "It doesn't mean anything."

"How many fathers of da other girls you taken out have you met?"

"None, I guess," Morgan confessed. "But Anne...she seems different."

"How she so different from da other girls?"

Morgan paused. "She's just not like other girls," he began fitfully. "She's not afraid of things. She sticks her foot in the stirrup and mounts Buck without hesitation. She jumps on the boat and doesn't ask for a hand. She dives in the water without asking if it's cold. She shows up on time. She doesn't fuss with her hair or worry if she doesn't look perfect every second. She's interesting to talk to and just plain fun."

Alrick Brown nodded with each recitation of Anne's virtues. "Dis girl sound more like a man than a woman."

"Yeah," Morgan laughed. "Except she's every bit a woman, I promise."

"Dat I could see. So what you gonna do?"

"I'm going to dinner," Morgan said simply. "That's what I'm going to do."

"You knows what I mean," Alrick prodded. "If I was you, I'd be tinkin' 'bout keepin' dis one around."

"I believe her father is taking her back to Boston in a week or so," Morgan said. "I'll just enjoy her company while she's here and say goodbye. We're from two different worlds. She can't have any real interest in me other than a horseback ride or a walk on the beach."

Alrick shook his head and sighed. "You be one o' da smartest people I know, but some times you jus' blind as a bat. Dat girl in love wid you. How come you can't see it?"

"She's a proper woman from a high-class family. She'll return to Boston, marry some banker, and have tea parties every afternoon for the rest of her life," Morgan said. "Five minutes after she leaves Bimini she won't remember my name."

"Now you bein' da dumbest man I ever know," Alrick said as he playfully grabbed Morgan's shoulders and shook them. "I need to shake some sense into dat head o' yours."

*   *   *

Morgan walked down the long concrete path leading to the Bimini Bay Rod and Gun Club. Swaying palm trees on either side of the paved walk formed an archway that added a feeling of exotic majesty to the enormous, four-story building perched on a slab elevated fifteen feet above the sand dunes.

Twin stairs ascended gracefully on both sides of a lower portico and led to a grand, pillared door beneath an overhanging balcony.

Morgan had walked on the sand road, past the stately building, hundreds of times since its opening in 1920, but had never ventured on the grounds. Admission to the hotel was strictly by invitation. Bahamians entered only to report for work.

Anne Roberts stood nervously at the entrance. She was dressed in a demure, coral colored dress with a white lace collar. A tall, heavy-set man with a full beard and flowing mustache stood beside her. The man's florid face and bulbous, roseate nose glistened with a faint sheen of perspiration. He was attired in black, chalk-striped pants held aloft around his copious belly with red suspenders. A white silk shirt, open at the neck, strained to stay tucked in his trousers.

"Father, this is Morgan Early, the young man I rented a horse from the other day," Anne Roberts said with a slight crack in her voice. "Morgan, this is my father, Cyrus Roberts."

Morgan extended his hand and noticed a tinge of moisture in the palm of Cyrus Roberts' strong grip. "Nice to meet you, sir," Morgan said.

Cyrus Roberts narrowed his eyes and looked down from his two-inch height advantage. "What did you said his name was, my dear?"

"Morgan, father," Anne repeated. "Morgan Early."

"I don't know that I'm familiar with that name," Roberts grumbled as he retrieved his hand. "Well, come along you two. They're serving drinks on the back porch. The sunsets here are wonderful. We don't want to miss it."

"Another of the same, Mr. Roberts?" the white-coated Bahamian asked as Morgan, Anne and her father took seats overlooking the ocean.

"Yes, another of the same," Roberts replied. "And for you dear?"

"May I have a champagne, father?"

"Of course, my dear."

"Hey, Morgan," the waiter said with surprise. "What you doin' here?"

Morgan looked slightly embarrassed. "I'm joining Mr. Roberts and his daughter for dinner."

"You want a beer?" the waiter asked.

"Please," Morgan replied.

"No champagne for you?" Cyrus Roberts asked with a slight hint of sarcasm. "Have you ever had champagne before?"

"I tried it once when I was in France, sir," Morgan replied calmly. "It didn't agree with me."

Cyrus Roberts leaned forward. "So, you were in France. How did you find the country, aside from the champagne, that is?"

Morgan swallowed and replied in a measured tone. "I found our reception by the occupants to be rather hostile."

"Hostile? The French?" Roberts snorted. "I've always found them to be rather receptive, especially the ladies."

"I meant the Germans," Morgan said simply.

Anne sat upright in her chair. Her eyes sparkled with interest. "So that's the reason for the name of your boat, *Belleau Woods*. You were there? I remember reading about the battle when I was a teenager."

Morgan nodded silently.

"You were a soldier?" Anne continued slightly breathless.

"No," Morgan said pensively. "A Marine."

"Did you see combat?" Anne asked. "Were you wounded?"

"That was a long time ago," Morgan said quietly.

"Dis boy be a hero," the waiter volunteered as he placed a glass of champagne in front of Anne and a tall Scotch in from of her father. "Dey make him an officer."

"Now, dear," Roberts interrupted. "Don't bother the young man about that. Tell me, where are you from? I'm not familiar with the name Early."

"I'm from Wilcox, Arizona," Morgan said after taking a sip of his beer.

"What was your mother's maiden name?" Roberts asked. "Perhaps she was from the east and a family I'm familiar with."

"Her only name was Samantha James," Morgan said. "I doubt you ever heard of her. She worked in a saloon and died giving birth to me."

Cyrus Roberts rubbed his chin in confusion. "So, your mother was never married? Then that makes you..."

"Father!" Anne screamed. "Stop this right now."

"Yes, dear," Roberts said holding his hands palm out. "I'm sorry if I troubled you."

"Troubled me?" Anne growled. "What about poor Morgan?"

"Oh, I'm sure the boy knows I meant no harm," Roberts said cheerfully. "I was just curious about his background. By the way, what do you do here in Bimini?"

"I'm a bootlegger," Morgan replied in a flat tone. "In all likelihood, you've enjoyed the fruits of my labor while you were back in Boston."

Cyrus Roberts sat straight in his chair. A look of indignation swept over his face. "Are you implying I break the laws of the United States of America when I'm home?"

"Mr. Roberts, dinner is served," the waiter said into the stilted silence that had enveloped the small table. "May I carry your drinks inside?"

~ 44 ~

Tears dripped from Anne Robert's chin as she slumped in a chair on Morgan's porch. She dabbed at her nose with a saturated handkerchief and rubbed her reddened eyes with a fist.

"I'm so ashamed," she sobbed. "My father is a complete idiot and a hopeless bigot."

Morgan waved away the criticism with a dismissive shrug. "Forget about your father," he said. "I'm only interested in what *you* think of me."

"He wouldn't acknowledge anything you've done, even being a hero in the Great War."

"I never said I was a hero," Morgan said shaking his head. "Where did you get that idea?"

"The waiter who knew your name," Anne said. "He mentioned it while he was serving drinks last night, and I talked to him again this morning. He said you were decorated for saving somebody's life and made a lieutenant."

Morgan lowered his head. "I served with many Marines who deserved medals. A lot of them died."

Anne reached out and lifted Morgan's chin with her fingers. "It must have been terrible," she said. "I won't ask you about it any more."

"Sometimes I feel I should talk about it," Morgan said in a faraway voice. "I want to forget how horrible the carnage was, but I never want to forget my friends who were wounded and died in that reeking, smoking, blood soaked woods."

Anne placed her other hand on Morgan's cheek. She turned his face and looked directly into his eyes. "My father is taking me back to Boston the day after tomorrow. I heard him make a reservation on the Chalks seaplane flight to Miami."

Morgan closed his eyelids and dropped his head.

"My father wants me back in Boston," she said. "There's a man there he wants me to marry. He's the son of the owner of a rival bank. It's all been discussed between the two families."

"I understand," Morgan said with resignation. He released a long sigh and sniffled once. "I know I'm not what any proper father wants for his daughter. I've done terrible things. I allowed the wonderful woman who raised me to be killed. I've disappointed others and allowed a kind and gentle man to be killed."

Anne wiped her eyes and wrinkled her forehead in wonder. "Maybe these things weren't your fault."

"I've killed men," Morgan continued without acknowledging Anne's remark. "I've killed men and not just Germans in the war. Your father is right. Go back to Boston and marry a proper man and live a happy life."

Anne gripped Morgan's hands and squeezed them. "I don't care what you've done in the past. I know you had your reasons, and one day maybe you'll feel ready to tell me all about it."

"But there's so much you don't know..."

"I'm sure you're right," she said firmly. "But this I do know; I'm not going back to Boston with my father. I'm staying here in Bimini."

Morgan looked into Anne's eyes. He sat frozen momentarily, unable to frame a response, stunned by her words. "Where will you stay," he began at last. "What will you do?"

"I'll stay with you, silly!" she said with a laugh. "I want to find out if what I'm feeling is really love. You've started a ripple; I want to see if it becomes a swell."

A broad grin spread across Morgan's face. "I believe you're serious," he said. "I was hoping we could find the time to know each other better. The ripple you've experienced is approaching a tsunami inside me."

Anne looked into the living room of the house. "Are you expecting your friend soon?"

"No," Morgan replied. "Why?"

"I was wondering if you'd show me around the house. I haven't seen the bedroom yet."

Morgan chuckled and jumped to his feet. "How could I have been so thoughtless?"

*   *   *

Anne kissed Morgan passionately on the lips. "I love you," she said. "You're stuck with me now. I'm going back to the hotel and tell father I won't be leaving with him for Boston."

Morgan returned the kiss and smiled. "I love you, too," he said. "I hope your father doesn't take your decision too hard."

"He'll fight me," she said. "But my mind is made up."

Morgan pushed to his elbows and glanced out the window. A strange calm had descended on the flats to the east. Not a single ripple disturbed the water as far as he could see. The sky had taken on an unusual tinge of gray.

"I don't like this weather," he said as he rolled from the bed and walked to the barometer hanging on the bedroom wall. "The pressure has dropped significantly in the last hour. I think a storm may be on the way."

"Could it be serious?"

"In September, any drop in pressure should be considered serious," Morgan replied. "After you talk to your father, tell the people at the hotel they should prepare for a storm. I need to find Alrick and get our boats to safety."

"I'll be back," Anne said. "Will you be here?"

"After I take care of the boats," Morgan said. "If I'm not here, stay near the house. This is one of the highest points on the island; you'll be safer here than any other location. Look to the east. That's where the storm will come from."

Morgan dressed and ran from the house to find Alrick. Anne departed for the hotel and an unwelcome confrontation with her father.

~ 45 ~

The wind began to increase in intensity about 3:00 in the afternoon. A thick blanket of dark clouds slid across the sky blocking the sun and painting the afternoon a sinister shade of charcoal.

Alrick Brown arrived with his parents Jessica and Jackson. Alrick's mother, a jolly woman with sparkling eyes and a ready smile, was laden with loaves of sweet, baked bread, an enormous cherry pie and a huge bowl of conch chowder.

"We ain't gonna starve if dis storm hit," Jessica said proudly. She immediately began to fill every container in the house with fresh water.

"If we lose da electricity, we still got water to drink and bathe," she observed.

Morgan and Alrick escorted Buck inside the house and closed the lower half of the French door to the guest room where he took up residence. A substantial pile of oats helped occupy the animal who sniffed nervously at the wind and stomped a hoof to signify his displeasure with the coming hurricane.

"Do you think the boats will be okay?" Morgan asked.

Alrick nodded but raised his hands with concern. "We done tied 'em up best way I know how in da mangroves," he said. "Da schooner gots three anchors out. Da speedboat gots eight lines on her."

"You towed the barge in tight to the beach?"

"She be safe as I knows how to make her." Alrick replied. "Rudy say he would stay on da barge for da storm, but I told him go on home an' be wid his family."

"Good," Morgan said. "We should be okay here. I know the walls are thick enough and the roof is tight."

"Your lady frien' comin' back here? Dat hotel ain't so strong as dey tink."

As if on cue, Anne Roberts banged open the back door and shook the rain from her windbreaker. "It's starting to pour," she said. "The sky is turning blacker by the minute."

Morgan helped her with the wet garment. "Did you talk to your father?"

Anne nodded and leaned her body against Morgan's chest. "He was furious," she said simply. "He said if I stay on Bimini and don't return to Boston with him he would disown me."

"Nobody should own anybody," Morgan said.

"This storm is going to be bad, isn't it?"

Morgan nodded. "It looks like it'll be bad, but we'll be safe here. Are they getting ready at the hotel?"

"Everybody is planning to head down to the basement," Anne said. "I guess that's the safest place."

"It should be," Morgan said. "Your father didn't want to come here with you?"

"He doesn't want to see either one of us," Anne said. "He didn't look very well when I left."

"Say hello to Alrick's parents Jessica and Jackson," Morgan said. "They're going to ride out the storm with us."

"Along with Buck, I noticed," Anne added with a small laugh as she pointed to the guestroom. "The more the merrier."

*   *   *

By nightfall the wind had increased to over one hundred-fifty miles per hour. Palms strained to stay upright in the inexorable, double hurricane force onslaught, but the shallow root system and the paucity of soil defeated many. The crash of toppling trees punctuated the relentless screeching of the wind as it howled across the ridge and around Morgan's house.

The five occupants huddled in a room on the south side of the house, away from the thrust of the raging winds. A sporadic broad palm frond flew past the house, torn asunder from an upwind tree. Roof shingles, shutters and assorted debris sailed through the torrential rain-saturated air, occasionally crashing first against the walls of the building.

Anne peered intently into the gloomy night toward the east. Thick drops of rain blew horizontally across her line of vision. "I think the bay is rising quickly," she said. "The water appears to be approaching the house."

Morgan joined her at the window and stared into the blackness. Periodically a flash of lightning followed almost immediately on the heels of an ear-splitting thunder clap. The jagged bolt of electricity illuminated the slope below the house.

"The water's above the docks and climbing quickly," he observed. "I hope the Saunders women have taken shelter somewhere. Their house is right on the beach."

"Da ocean be crashing on da rocks jus' below da King's Highway path," Alrick said as he returned from a peek out a window to the west. "If it get any higher, da waves be landin' on da roof."

Throughout the night the wind velocity hovered above one hundred-fifty miles an hour with periodic gusts approaching one hundred-seventy. The electricity failed shortly after full dark and wouldn't be restored for four days.

At the Bimini Bay Rod and Gun Club guests and several employees took refuge in the basement. They sat around kerosene lanterns and listened while the Killer Storm of 1926 ripped the roof from the hotel and blew out all the windows. Most rooms were destroyed, with the furniture smashed and the carpets and mattresses soaked.

Sometime after midnight Cyrus Roberts, drinking heavily and smoking cigars non-stop, felt a suffocating pressure in his upper body. A deep, black pain knotted the area in the center of his chest, and numbness drifted down his right arm. He clutched at his throat and fell heavily to the concrete floor, knocking over his Scotch glass and smashing a burning lantern.

"My goodness," one of the female guests screamed. "I think the man is having a heart attack!"

235

A concerted effort to make Cyrus Roberts comfortable occupied the guests, and eventually the area of heart muscle deprived of oxygen died, relieving the pain and allowing Anne's father to fall asleep.

*   *   *

In the morning Morgan and Alrick cautiously ventured from the house and surveyed the damage. The ocean had risen almost to the top of the dunes on the west side of the King's Highway. The bay had flooded across the lower Queen's Highway and lapped just two feet below the foundation of Morgan's house.

The wireless station was destroyed; there was no way to call Miami for assistance. Even if communication had been possible, the Killer Storm of 1926 had proceeded to Miami and destroyed virtually every boat in the city.

Jessica Brown built a fire from driftwood within a circle of coral rocks and heated the conch chowder. "Dis gonna' be a long day," she said pointing at Morgan and Alrick to dissuade dissention. "You boys got to eat something befor' you go check on dem boats."

Anne led Buck from his guest room stall and turned him loose on a dry section below the house. "Your corral is flooded," she explained sympathetically to the buckskin. "But it looks like the water is receding."

"We're going to paddle the dinghy over to South Bimini," Morgan said as he dipped a thick slick of bread in the remains of his chowder. "I've got to see how the boats made out. Why don't you ride Buck down the King's Highway path to the hotel and see how they made out there," he said to Anne. "I'm worried they didn't fare as well as we did."

"I'm nervous about father," Anne confided. "I told you he didn't look well when I left him. He was drinking heavily, too."

"Be careful," Morgan cautioned. "I'll meet you there after I get back from South Bimini."

*   *   *

Wise to the dangers of hurricanes, only seven people of the more than six hundred on Bimini died when the Killer Storm struck. The four Saunders women perished in the ferocious hurricane.

Others managed to survive by hanging on to the trunks of coconut trees and crawling inexorably upward as the water rose, sustaining painful lacerations in the process.

Virtually every dock on the island was destroyed. Most boats, with the exception of Morgan's sloop, his speedboat and the barge were heavily damaged. Many houses were ruined, especially those close to the water. The Bimini Bay Rod and Gun Club received significant damage and never opened for business again. The few surviving furnishings were moved to Miami. The property was guarded for a while to discourage looters, but eventually the ruins were abandoned.

Morgan anchored *Belleau Woods* in the bay near the Rod and Gun Club Hotel and waded ashore. Alrick had elected to remain aboard *Semper Fidelis* and sweep away the hundreds of scattered mangrove branches and wash the remains of driven seawater from the deck. The stout barge *Thirst Quencher* remained unscathed where it was tied near the shore. No damage appeared evident to the vast inventory of bottles.

The walk from the shore to the hotel was greatly abbreviated. The bay had risen across the sand path in front of the building and almost to the foundations. On the ocean side, the sea lapped against the first floor of the structure.

Anne ran from the hotel and fell into Morgan's outstretched arms. Tears stained her cheeks and her words came in halting sobs.

"My father had a heart attack," she managed as she buried her face against Morgan's shoulder and squeezed him with both arms.

"He's alive?" Morgan asked with genuine concern.

"Yes, he's alive," Anne replied. "But he's very weak, and he needs me to take him back to Boston as soon as possible."

"Of course," Morgan said. "We could take him to Miami in the *Belleau Woods*, if you didn't think the pounding would be too difficult. We could go slowly."

"I'd rather he flew on the Chalks plane, but there's no way to contact Miami. Somebody told me the wireless station was destroyed," Anne said.

"We'll wrap him warmly and make the trip immediately," Morgan offered. "He needs to see a doctor as soon as possible."

"It's my fault," Anne wailed as she pushed back from Morgan and looked directly at him. "If I hadn't been so selfish and told him I was staying with you, this would never have happened."

"You can't blame yourself," Morgan said firmly. "The stress of the storm and all the drinking and the cigars..."

"No!" Anne said definitively. "It's my fault. I'm selfish and heartless and the cause of my father's heart attack. I've got to return to Boston with him."

"Your mother..." Morgan began weakly. "What about your mother?"

"She left us years ago. I'm the only one father relies upon. And I let him down."

Morgan's heart sagged with sadness. After years of frustration and confusion about women and a final, reluctant reconciliation that he would never meet a woman he wanted to marry, Anne Roberts had entered his life and changed his mind completely. At last he had found a woman he could love unabashedly and completely. Now, the object of his passion was departing to fulfill an obligation and assuage a feeling of guilt to her father.

He shook his head and emptied his lungs with a deep, mournful sigh. "Let's find some dry blankets and a pillow," he said. "The boat has plenty of fuel. We can be in Miami in a couple of hours. With the hurricane past, the sea will return to calm quickly and the ride shouldn't be too bad."

~ 46 ~

On a perfect Indian summer afternoon in late September following three days of the rainy remnant of the Killer Storm of 1926, Giuseppe Provenzano, boss of bosses of the Chicago Mafia, sat alone at the table farthest from the door in Luigi's Sicilian Restaurant. A fresh red and white checkered cloth covered the small table. An enormous white napkin was tied around Giuseppe's neck, and two bright splotches of red marinara sauce attested to the necessity of the accoutrement.

A heaping pile of spaghetti, smothered in a homemade, red tomato paste with garlic and onions, steamed on an oversized plate. Giuseppe gripped a fork in his meaty right fist and plunged it into the stack of pasta. He twirled the utensil until the strands surrounded the tines and offered hope of remaining mostly in place, then shoveled the thick ball of food toward his mouth. A third glob of marinara flopped to the bib.

Giuseppe chewed quickly, burped, and reached for the bottle of Chianti. He splashed the remains of the basket-covered decanter into his glass and managed to slurp the entire contents down his throat without spilling more than an ounce.

Two tall, barrel-chested men stood silently behind the boss of bosses. They were dressed in dark suits with black silk shirts of insufficient size to button around their thick necks. Curly tuffs of black hair sprouted from the openings of the collars. Each held a Thompson submachine gun at port arms.

239

A third bodyguard stood watch at the front door. Every other table in the restaurant was empty. Luigi would not open to the public until Giuseppe concluded his repast.

A hesitant knock at the outside door bestirred the front guard. With a disdainful expression he turned slowly and released the lock.

Vittorio Bagarella entered. He was attired in a dark suit with thin chalk stripes, a broadcloth cotton shirt and a wide, purple necktie. Starched white cuffs fastened with diamond links protruded exactly an inch from his coat sleeves.

He walked deferentially toward the rear of the restaurant. He slowed as he neared the table, approached Giuseppe and bowed slightly. He reached with unthreatening fingers, lifted the boss of bosses' hand, and brushed a light kiss across the hairy knuckles.

"Giuseppe Provenzano, I am in your service," he said in a low, reverent voice.

The boss of bosses grunted an acknowledgment and pointed to the opposite chair.

Vittorio Bagarella pulled the chair from the table and sat. "How's the marinara?" he asked. "Luigi got more of that in the kitchen?"

Giuseppe sat back and extracted a long, fat cigar from his inside pocket. He pulled the cellophane wrapper from the Cuban Montecristo and snapped his fingers. A flaming match appeared instantaneously at the tip of the cigar. Provenzano drew deeply and released a long stream of smoke toward the ceiling.

"I didn't ask you here to eat, Vittorio," he said in a strained, raspy, wheezing voice.

Bagarella looked chagrined and held up his hands in surrender fashion. "I'm sorry, boss," he said quickly. "I meant no dishonor."

"You know what that kid of yours did last night?" Giuseppe asked simply.

Vittorio closed his eyes briefly and nodded. "I heard this morning. He messed up a speakeasy."

"He messed up a speakeasy and he put Diego Gambetta's nephew in the hospital. The boy may not recover."

"I didn't hear about the boy."

"We talked about this last month," Giuseppe Provenzano said in a scratchy voice through a dense cloud of smoke. "You run the

240

south side of town. That's your territory. You don't mess with the north side. That belongs to Diego Gambetta."

"I understand," Vittorio Bagarella said. "That's the agreement you made among the bosses."

"You understand," Giuseppe said pointing the smoldering end of his cigar at Vittorio, "but your kid don't understand."

"I'll straighten him out," Vittorio said. "It won't happen again, I promise."

The boss of bosses shook his head. He waved the Montecristo to emphasize his disagreement. "It's too late. You said that the last time when your kid robbed one of Diego's delivery trucks. Now I got to whack him."

Vittorio Bagarella lowered his head. He swallowed once and licked his lips before speaking. "He's my only son. Gaetano is *la stessa cosa*. He's the same thing as you, a Mafioso like you."

"No, he ain't," Giuseppe said in his hoarse voice. "He don't understand the code. You don't mess with another man's territory after it's been decided."

"Please, Giuseppe," Vittorio pleaded. "You and I have been friends since childhood. We grew up together. Don't whack Gaetano. He's the only child I have."

Giuseppe reached across the table with a hirsute hand and patted Vittorio's arm sympathetically. "I got no choice. I got to whack him if I want to keep discipline in the families. Diego Gambetta in the north side is demanding it."

Vittorio reached down and pulled a corner of the checkered tablecloth to his face. He dabbed at tears in the corners of his eyes. "Let me do it," he managed between increasing sobs. "Let me do it."

Giuseppe Provenzano held his cigar aloft. A heavy ashtray suddenly appeared on the table beneath his upraised hand. He placed the Montecristo in one of the corner indentations and sat back pensively.

"How many years we been friends?" he asked in a gravelly voice.

"Fifty years," Vittorio replied without looking up.

"I honor that fifty years by allowing you to whack your own kid."

Vittorio raised his eyes and pawed at the tears trickling down his cheeks. "I owe you for this," he said as he slid his chair back and stood. "I'll never forget this favor."

*   *   *

Vittorio Bagarella slammed the door open to his son's bedroom. He brandished an enormous revolver in his right hand. Gaetano Bagarella was sprawled on the mattress, the sheets tangled around his legs. An unclothed female was sleeping beside him.

"Wake up," Vittorio bellowed.

Gaetano vaulted to a sitting position. The girl opened her eyes and screamed at the sight of the gun.

"You," Vittorio hollered at the girl. "Get out!"

"But I ain't dressed," the girl protested as she attempted to cover her breasts with a corner of the covers.

Vittorio leveled the barrel of the weapon at the girl's face. "I said get out!"

The girl leaped from the bed and fled, screaming, through the door, naked as the day she was born.

Gaetano raised his hands and pushed them palms out toward his father. "What's going on?" he beseeched.

"Why did you hit that speakeasy on the north side last night?" Vittorio growled. "That's not our territory."

Gaetano relaxed his hands and smiled. "They aren't pushing enough booze," he said. "I can get them to sell more and we'll supply the stuff instead of Gambetta's boys from the north side."

"I told you, it's all been decided. We have the south side. The north side belongs to Diego Gambetta and his crew."

"They ain't doing the job!" Gaetano argued.

"Is that why you robbed one of their delivery trucks last month?"

"We was low on booze ourselves. I figured we could help ourselves to some of theirs and not have to pay."

Vittorio swept the back of his hand across Gaetano's face. The sound of the vicious slap resounded from the stark walls of the room. "Giuseppe told me he had to whack you to keep peace in the families. Gambetta is demanding it."

"Whack me?"

"I begged Giuseppe to allow me to do it."

"You're going to whack me? My own father?"

Vittorio reached in his pocket. He pulled out a thick roll of bills. "Here's twenty thousand," he said. "Get out of town immediately. Go far away. Go to Miami. But never show your face back in Chicago again. If you do, Giuseppe will kill you and he'll have to kill me, too."

Gaetano looked at his father. He swung his legs off the bed and stood. Unashamed, he hugged the old man tightly.

"Go," Vittorio said at last. "Don't call. Don't write. If anybody discovers you're alive, it will be the death of us both."

~ 47 ~

A bone-chilling December wind blew across the driveway of the Roberts estate. Anne Roberts scurried from the house and entered the rear door of the family Cadillac held open by the chauffer Lawrence Tuttle.

"Good evening, Miss Roberts," Tuttle said in a merry voice.

"Good evening, Tuttle," Anne replied. "And a merry Christmas season to you and your family."

"Thank you," Tuttle said. "You look simply beautiful this evening. I understand we're going to the Country Club."

"Yes, and thank you," Anne said before turning to her father huddled in the back seat wrapped in a thick blanket. "Are you comfortable, father? Are you sure you're warm enough?"

"Yes, my dear," Cyrus Roberts nodded. His once robust appearance had taken on a pale, sickly cast since his heart attack three months previous.

"Father, I must talk to you about something very important," Anne said as Tuttle closed the rear door and walked to the driver's entrance.

"Not now, my dear," Roberts said. "I'm afraid my strength isn't sufficient for a serious conversation."

"You must allow me to talk to you," Anne persisted. "I've been trying to tell you something for a month, but you've repeatedly put me off."

"Now, now, dear," Roberts said as he put his hand solicitously on his daughter's knee. "Not with Tuttle in the car. And besides, I've invited young Archibald Buckley to join us for dinner at the Country Club. I insist you pay him close attention this evening. Last time you hardly acknowledged his presence. He would make a wonderful husband for you. You're not getting any younger, you know."

Anne gritted her teeth and looked out her window. Fat, wet flakes of snow began to fall from a low, leaden sky. The Cadillac's headlights illuminated the cascading flakes that sparkled in the black night ahead.

What is Morgan doing tonight, she wondered for the hundredth time since she and her father had hurriedly departed Miami in September. Anne's emotional turmoil at the time of her father's heart attack had been the most paralyzing she had ever experienced. She was positive she was genuinely in love with Morgan Early. She was convinced staying in Bimini to pursue the relationship would ultimately bring her complete happiness. Not once did she doubt the veracity of her feelings.

However, Anne recognized the selfishness of her action. Her father depended on her. Telling him so abruptly of her decision to remain on Bimini undoubtedly instigated his heart attack. She could never have lived with herself if she hadn't returned to Boston with her father and assisted with his recuperation.

But six weeks after their return home, a new ingredient entered the equation. Anne at first hesitated to discuss the situation with her father until he regained more of his strength. Later, her efforts to engage her father in a discussion met with categorical refusal to listen.

To exacerbate the situation, her father began to campaign vigorously for her to become serious about Archibald Buckley. The young man was handsome; Anne could not deny that fact. However, every time she was with him, she immediately began to compare him with Morgan. The comparison was inevitably unflattering to Buckley and reinforced her conviction that her love for Morgan was genuine and everlasting.

"Have a wonderful evening," Tuttle said as he opened the Cadillac's rear door at the entrance to the Country Club.

"Thank you, Tuttle," Cyrus Roberts said as he struggled to swing himself from the back seat of the vehicle. His strength and stamina were markedly reduced since his episode in Bimini.

"Mr. Roberts!" Archibald Buckley called as Cyrus and Anne made their way through the entrance and into the bright lights of the Country Club. "How wonderful to see you!"

"Good evening, young man," Cyrus Roberts said as he nudged Anne with his elbow. "Give a proper greeting to Archibald, my dear."

Anne leaned toward Buckley and turned her face to direct the moist kiss to her cheek.

Cyrus Roberts beamed with contentment.

What would her father's reaction have been, Anne thought with a smile, if he had seen her kiss Morgan Early so enthusiastically on the beach with her clothes lying damp in the sand?

"Your special table is ready," the maitre d' said with a broad grin and his hand out to receive the ten dollar bill discreetly passed by Cyrus Roberts.

"Thank you," Cyrus said.

"Did I tell you about my squash game this afternoon?" Archibald said as they were seated and enormous linen napkins placed in their laps by a zealous waiter.

Anne looked at Archibald Buckley with bewilderment. "No," she said. "I don't think so."

"Simply marvelous," he continued, barely pausing for Anne's response. "I was magnificent. My serve was unreturnable."

"That's good..." Anne said.

"But you've never played the game, have you?" Buckley addressed to Anne.

"I guess I haven't," Anne replied. "Have you ever caught a bonefish, Archibald?"

Buckley looked askance at Anne. "A *what* fish?" he said with a derisive smirk. "A bunch of foolishness in my opinion, fishing, when you can send one of the servants to purchase all the fish you want at the market."

Anne blinked once and looked briefly at the shimmering chandelier hanging majestically from the tall ceiling. Her thoughts flashed to the day Morgan had hooked bonefish and handed her the fly rod with the line screaming from the reel. Her heart jumped as she recalled her excitement and her appreciation of Morgan's patient instructions while he carefully talked her through the battle.

"Yes, you're right," Anne said dismissively. "Fishing probably is foolish."

"How is your job going with the bank?" Cyrus asked.

"I'm impressing my superiors every day," Archibald said simply with a condescending shrug of his shoulders. "I'm sure they report on my performance to father. Why just yesterday I told them we should raise the rates we charge for mortgages. After all, if borrowers don't have money of their own to purchase property, they should be thankful we're willing to deal with them at all. I can't imagine not being able to afford a house."

Anne turned and looked at Archibald Buckley in disbelief.

Buckley appeared momentarily unnerved when he saw Anne's reaction to his statement. Then his demeanor brightened. "Oh, I see," he said. "Don't worry; understanding business isn't a woman's concern. Just leave the issues of business to us men."

"Would you like something to drink, my dear?" Cyrus Roberts asked as a waiter hovered behind his shoulder expectantly.

Anne pursed her lips and drew a small breath. What was that concoction Morgan ordered for her in Bimini that was so delicious? Was it a Bahama Mama?

"Yes, father," Anne said with an amused smile. "I'll have a Bahama Mama."

"A Bahama Mama?" Archibald repeated with his forehead wrinkled in confusion. "Who ever heard of such a ridiculous drink?"

"I had one...several, actually...in the Bahamas last September. They were delicious," Anne said. "Apparently you've never heard of one."

"No, I haven't," Buckley said with a casual wave of his hand. "And I venture to say I haven't missed anything."

"I'll have a glass of water, please, father," Anne said quietly.

"Have you heard of buying stocks on margin?" Archibald Buckley directed to Cyrus Roberts. "I've begun to delve heavily into the market. My broker only requires ten percent down and allows me to borrow the balance. That means I can purchase *ten times* the number of shares! With the market certain to rise in the future, I'm guaranteed to make money at a fantastic rate. If a stock rises only 1%, I make 10% on my investment. It's brilliant, don't you agree?"

"The stock market is guaranteed to rise?" Anne asked. "What happens if your shares fall below the price you've paid for them?"

Archibald Buckley shook his head in annoyance. He reached toward Anne and patted her hand with exaggerated condescension. "It's okay if you don't understand," he said in a sympathetic tone. "Really, darling, it's okay."

*   *   *

"Father," Anne said firmly when they had closed the front door and hung their coats in the closet. "Go to the library, fix a drink and sit. I have something to talk to you about."

"Really, my dear," Cyrus Roberts protested. "You don't have to be so dramatic."

"I'm pregnant," Anne said simply. "Now would you like a drink?"

Cyrus Roberts clutched at his heart.

"You're not having a heart attack," Anne said. "I've talked to your doctor. He says you can live a full life if you moderate your drinking, give up those foul cigars and get some exercise. But right now I think a drink is required. I'm not finished."

"You're pregnant?" Cyrus Roberts stammered. "How do you know?"

Anne looked directly at her father. "I'm twenty-four," she said with a slight shrug. "I know."

Confusion initially wrinkled Cyrus's face but quickly was replaced by comprehension. "You've been with Archibald Buckley! I should have known! That's splendid, actually! I was convinced he was the right choice for you, especially now that he's working at his father's bank."

"Archibald?" Anne repeated with a laugh. "I wouldn't touch that solipsistic moron if he were the last man on earth."

"The father isn't Archibald?" Roberts asked in surprise. "Then who have you...?"

"Do you remember the rumrunner you dismissed so rudely in Bimini?" Anne asked. "The heroic Marine you refused to acknowledge who won a commission and a medal fighting the

Germans in France? The man who drove us to Miami in his boat so you could receive medical attention?"

"That island bum is the father of your baby?" Cyrus Roberts said in amazement. "You...you can't marry him! Why, he's...he's nobody. I've never heard of his family! They're not even in the Social Register."

"Well, he never heard of you or our family either," Anne said defiantly. "And it doesn't seem to have diminished his life too greatly."

"This is a tragedy!" Cyrus moaned.

"I'm sorry you feel that way, father," Anne said. "But I love him, and I'm returning to Bimini. If you care for your daughter at all, you'll hope Morgan Early forgives me for leaving him and that he's willing to take me as his wife."

"But what about me?" Cyrus Roberts asked petulantly. "Who will care for me?"

"You're a man, father, and I love you. But I'm not your wife and I'm not your servant. You can hire a housekeeper. I deserve a life of my own, and I'm going to Bimini to seek it."

(Archibald Buckley's naïve confidence in the stock market soon proved misplaced. On September 29, 1929, the Dow Jones Industrial Average peaked at 381.17. On Black Thursday, October 24, 1929, 12.7 million shares traded and the market tumbled. On Black Monday the Dow lost another 13% of its value. The following day, Black Tuesday, 16 million shares traded, a record not broken for 40 years, and the Dow lost yet another 12%. In all, 30 billion dollars of wealth vanished, more than ten times the budget of the federal government. The Dow closed on July 8, 1932 at 4.22. (No, this is not a misprint: four point twenty-two.) The total decline in value was 89%.)

~ 48 ~

Anne Roberts boarded the train in Boston with a simple valise of warm weather clothes. Cyrus had exhausted his litany of entreaties for her to remain in Boston and finally reconciled to her departure.

"Here's one thousand dollars," he said at breakfast. "Please don't refuse the money. You'll need funds to travel and for the baby. After all, the child will be my first grandchild."

Anne hugged her father and promised to call from Florida. "I believe there's a wireless on Bimini," she said. "I'll get you a message when I arrive there."

"You convince that young man to marry you," Cyrus said with a sincere laugh. "Somehow I will attend and give you away. Tuttle may have to drive me, but I'll be there."

"Thank you for finally understanding," Anne said. An enormous burden had lifted from her heart when she realized her father was at last supportive and excited at the prospect of becoming a grandfather.

The train wended its way through the snowy Connecticut countryside, offering occasional glimpses of the Long Island Sound. Following a one-hour stop at Grand Central Station and another at 30th Street Station in Philadelphia, the train proceeded down the western shore of the Chesapeake Bay through Baltimore and Washington.

The wintry conditions relaxed and the forests and farmlands of Virginia passed serenely before yielding to the low country of the Carolinas and Georgia. At the Florida border vast stretches of grassy land unfolded for three hundred miles before finally a hint of the tropics appeared in the form of palm trees and orange groves.

Almost forty-eight hours after boarding the train, Anne stepped to the sand surrounding the Miami station and searched for a taxi to take her to the port.

"I'm looking for a boat to take me to Bimini," she informed the kindly driver who reached to assist her with her bag.

"There ain't no regular schedule boat," the man informed Anne. "But there be plenty of private boats willin' to carry somebody who can pay. It ain't that far, and the day look to be pretty calm."

"If you would be so kind as to drive me to the docks where I can hire a boat, I'd be appreciative."

"Yes, madam," the driver said. "I know just where to go."

"And on the way, could you please stop where I can make a long distance telephone call to Boston. I promised my father I would let him know when I arrived in Florida."

"Certainly. I believe the Continental Hotel near the docks will allow you to connect to a long distance operator."

*   *   *

Gaetano Bagarella, locally known by his new name Guy Bags, timidly approached the lobby telephone in the Continental Hotel. He had downed two stiff rum drinks in the sequestered men's locker that served as a daytime drinking place for the hotel guests. Sufficiently fortified, he was about to risk his own life and that of his father by calling Chicago and begging for a fresh infusion of money.

Guy Bags vividly recalled his father's admonition about further contact once he departed Chicago. He was dead. He had read about his own funeral two days after he left in a Chicago newspaper that had found its way to the railroad station in Jacksonville, Florida. The only way he could remain alive was to remain dead.

But Gaetano was penniless. He hoped he had enough money, after the rum drinks, to pay for the call to his father.

He had arrived in Miami with more than nineteen thousand dollars in his pocket. Women and whiskey were everywhere, and after a week of intense acclimatization to his new home, Gaetano's bankroll had dwindled to a mere fourteen thousand.

Business would be Gaetano's salvation. He knew the whisky trade backwards and forwards, so he purchased a speedboat and made his initial run to Bimini with a fistful of cash to make a purchase. Unfortunately, Gaetano's navigational skills were completely lacking, and nobody had informed him of the three-knot northerly set to the relentless Gulf Stream between Miami and the islands. Consequently, the nascent rumrunner missed Bimini entirely and landed nine miles to the north on the uninhabited rock formation of Great Isaac where he spent two days wandering about, cursing the Bahamas in general and the Bimini residents in particular, for moving without informing him.

For one thousand dollars, Gaetano finally convinced a passing turtle fisherman to guide him back to the Florida mainland where he immediately posted a FOR SALE sign on his boat for half the price he had paid.

Guy Bags drew a deep breath and approached the black telephone. Anne Roberts beat him to the instrument by a stride.

"Oh," she said. "Did you want to use the telephone?"

Gaetano Bagarella stopped in his tracks and looked at the stunning blonde. Two days of travel and two nights of sleeping in a stuffy compartment without a shower had done nothing to dull Anne's radiance. The thought that she was hours from seeing her beloved Morgan again, and that she was embarking on this journey with the blessing of her father, spread a glow of happiness that shone through the thin tinge of weariness.

"No, no," Gaetano said hurriedly. "You go first." The idea of a delay was not unwelcome, given the possible consequence of somebody discovering he was residing in Miami instead of a grave in Illinois.

"Thank you," Anne said with a bright smile. "I won't be long."

"Take your time," Gaetano said as he took a seat within earshot of the telephone, slightly curious as to who the gorgeous lady might be calling.

*　　　*　　　*

"I want the Commonwealth Bank of Boston," Anne said to the long distance operator. "And please have them connect me to the chairman's office, Mr. Cyrus Roberts. Tell them it's his daughter Anne on the telephone."

After several moments of switching and clicking and bursts of static, and routing past two secretaries, the familiar voice of Cyrus Roberts came on the line.

"Father," Anne said excitedly. "I'm in Miami and about to hire a boat to take me to Bimini."

Gaetano Bagarella's ears perked up at the mention of Bimini. Not long ago he swore he never wanted to hear the name again, but with the impressive credentials of the recipient of the woman's telephone call broadcast so clearly, a plan to avoid his own call began fermenting in his devious and desperate mind.

"Yes, the weather's warm," Anne said in a breezy conversational tone.

"No, the train ride wasn't too bad. The cars sway and clatter a lot, but I was able to sleep in spite of my excitement.

"The food was pretty awful," Anne continued, "but I got off in Philadelphia and bought some fruit and nuts to tide me over.

"I haven't seen the ocean yet, but there doesn't seem to be much wind. I'm hoping the ride to Bimini won't be too rough.

"I know," Anne laughed after listening to her father's comment. "I probably wouldn't wait if there were a hurricane.

"No, don't send any more money. I'll contact you from Bimini on the wireless when I get there."

With this pronouncement, Gaetano's embryonic plan was committed. He wouldn't have to call his father and put both their lives at risk. A solution to his impecunious situation had fallen into his lap.

"I love you, too. You can never know how happy I am you've given your blessing to my crazy adventure.

"Thank you, father," Anne concluded. "I'll be in touch soon." She replaced the receiver in its cradle and turned with a huge smile on her face.

"Excuse me," Gaetano said with a slight bow of respect. "But I couldn't help overhearing that you were looking to hire a boat for a trip to Bimini."

"Why, yes," Anne said. "I'm heading to Bimini to meet my fiancé."

"I happen to have a nice boat that I would be more than happy to charter at a reasonable price. The ride would be very comfortable, and we could leave at your convenience."

Anne looked closely at Gaetano Bagarella. He was dressed in clothes that appeared somewhat worn and unkempt although the fabrics had a look of quality. Perhaps attention to garments in the tropics was less important than in Boston. His eyes seemed to be a little too close together. Maybe, Anne guessed, he wasn't the sharpest tool in the shed. A further disconcerting feature was his pronounced single eyebrow that ran in a continuous line like a caterpillar across his lower forehead. He seemed polite, though, and Anne did not feel threatened. Why not hire a boat from this young man? After all, she was going to Bimini with a stranger regardless of whom she ultimately selected.

"Where is your boat?"

"At my private dock not far from here," Gaetano said. "I have a car."

"Excellent. I'll dismiss my taxi and ride with you to the boat."

"I'll wait for you here," Gaetano gestured. "My car is around the back of the hotel."

~ 49 ~

Anne Roberts lay on her back with her wrists and ankles bound tightly to the four corners of the bed. Gaetano had forced her into his house at the point of a revolver and tied her securely in the guest room of his rented house on the Miami River.

"Don't bother screaming," he said as he locked the door. "The closest neighbor is almost a quarter mile away."

"You'll never get away with this," Anne protested as she tugged without success on her restraints.

"If your father comes up with the money, you won't be hurt," Gaetano said. "If he refuses or if he involves the police..."

"Let me go now," Anne said calmly. "I have some money. You can have it all."

"I already have your thousand dollars," he said. "That's not what I need. You should be worth one hundred thousand dollars to your rich father."

"How is my father going to get you that kind of money?" Anne asked. "How do you know where my father is?"

"I heard you on the telephone," Gaetano replied with a shrug. "I only have to call the Commonwealth Bank in Boston and ask for the chairman. What could be easier?"

*   *   *

Gaetano placed his telephone call to Cyrus Roberts and was put through immediately. His mention of the chairman's daughter assured a prompt response.

"Mr. Roberts, I have your daughter," he began. "If you ever want to see her alive again, bring one hundred thousand dollars to Miami on the next train. If you contact the police, your daughter will be killed."

Cyrus Roberts sat in stunned silence in his office. "Young man," he managed after a long pause, "if this is a prank, I fail to find the humor."

"Believe me, I'm not joking."

"How do I know you have my daughter?"

Gaetano described Anne and the clothes she was wearing. He also mentioned the one thousand dollars he had retrieved from her valise. "What else do you need to be convinced I have your daughter?"

"Where was she going after Miami?"

"To meet her fiancé in Bimini," Gaetano said. "If you're waiting for a wireless communication from her, I wouldn't hold my breath."

"I'll need time to collect that much cash," Cyrus Roberts said. "I'll have to take the morning train. I'll be in Miami in two days. How will I find you?"

"You won't," Gaetano replied. "I'll find you. When you arrive, check in to the Continental Hotel and wait."

Cyrus Roberts jotted the name of the hotel on a notepad. "I want to talk to my daughter."

"You can't. There's no telephone where I'm keeping her. But I can promise she won't be hurt unless you involve the police."

"I just want my daughter back safely," Roberts said, the desperation in his voice palpable.

"Her safety depends on you," Gaetano said. "If you follow my instructions, your daughter will not be harmed. If you do not..."

"Please don't hurt my daughter. She's the most precious thing in my life."

"Just bring the money," Gaetano concluded as he dropped the receiver in the cradle.

*   *   *

"He insisted we not involve the police," Cyrus Roberts said to Lawrence Tuttle as he packed his toiletries in a bag in preparation for the journey to Miami the next morning. An innocuous satchel with twin leather handles sat on the bed. One hundred thousand dollars in fifty and one hundred-dollar bills resided inside.

"Kidnapping is a local crime," Tuttle said shaking his head. "Alerting the Boston police wouldn't help us in Florida. And if we call the Miami police, we really have no clues to help them with an investigation."

"Can the two of us handle this?" Cyrus Roberts sighed in frustration and sorrow. "I can't lose my little Anne!"

"Why don't I contact her fiancé?" Tuttle suggested. "From what I understand from Anne, he is a most resourceful young man."

"That's an excellent idea," Roberts said with a hopeful smile. "Anne mentioned that there is a wireless station on the island. Perhaps you can discover a way to leave a message for him with the operator."

"I'll attend to it immediately," Tuttle said. "Meanwhile, why don't you attempt to get some sleep? I'll wake you in plenty of time to drive to the station."

*   *   *

Debbie Weech knocked on Morgan Early's door at three o'clock in the morning. Rubbing sleep from his eyes, he padded to the entrance and opened the door.

"You never tol' nobody you was engaged?" she said.

Morgan yawned and stretched his arms. "Nobody told me, either," he said. "Now can I go back to sleep?"

"Well somebody tinks you engaged," Debbie said, "an' dey done kidnapped your fiancé."

"Would you like a glass of cold orange juice?" Morgan asked as he wandered toward the icebox in the kitchen. "It might sober you up so you can explain what all this nonsense is about."

"I ain't drunk," Debbie Weech retorted with hurt in her voice, "least ways not now. But I gots a message on the wireless from a gentleman in Boston. He say your fiancé was kidnapped an' he on the way with a Mr. Roberts to deliver the ransom money. He say

257

they to check into the Continental Hotel when they git to Miami. He tink maybe you can help get your fiancé back."

"Did you say Mr. Roberts sent the wireless?"

"No. Dis gentleman named Turtle or some such. He gonna travel wid Mr. Roberts."

"Did the message mention my fiancé's name?" Morgan asked with increasing anxiety. "Was her name Anne?"

"Nobody said nothin' 'bout no Anne. She the one you so struck by when the hurricane hit las' September? The one you been so mopish about ever since?"

"When are Roberts and his friend arriving?" Morgan asked.

"Dey leavin' Boston on da train dis mornin'," Debbie said. "What's dat take, two days?"

"I think so," Morgan said as his mind began whirling with the implications of the information Debbie had delivered.

Was Anne on her way back to Bimini? Had she changed her mind and was now willing to marry him?

"Was there anything else? Think, Debbie. This could be important."

"Da message say no police," she said. "Dat repeated several times."

"Okay," Morgan nodded. "Is there any way to contact Turtle or Roberts? Are they planning to contact me again?"

"Dere wasn't nothin' about another message. Jus' that dey was checkin' in to the Continental."

Morgan put a gentle hand on Debbie Weech's shoulder. "Thanks for waking me," he said. "I appreciate it."

"I would have come sooner, but nobody came to relieve me 'til jus now."

~ 50 ~

"**D**is way, gentlemen," Alrick Brown gestured as Cyrus Roberts and Lawrence Tuttle stepped off the train at the Miami station. "I have your car ready to take you to da hotel."

"It appears as if you are expecting us," Roberts said in surprise.

"I be expectin' you," Alrick said. "Don't look 'cross da way, but Morgan Early over dere and he recognized you from las' time you be here."

"Why doesn't he come forward?"

"He afraid da kidnapper be watchin da train," Alrick explained. "He tink it better if da kidnapper don't know he be about jus' yet."

"It might be a good idea to have a hidden ally here in Miami," Tuttle said after brief consideration.

"Dat's what Morgan tinks," Alrick confirmed. "We don' know how many dey be or what dey look like. Here, let me take dem bags."

Alrick drove carefully through the crowded streets of Miami, mindful to avoid challenging his limited skills behind the wheel of a motor vehicle.

"Morgan say da kidnapper gonna contact you when you check into da hotel," Alrick said. "Soons you hear from dis guy, Morgan say to find me an' tell me what he say. I'll get da message to Morgan."

"Young man, just what is your connection to Morgan," Cyrus Roberts asked. "You seem very committed to helping us."

259

"Morgan be my boss in several business ventures," Alrick said proudly. "Also, he be my best friend. Anyting he need, I'm dere for him."

"I admire your dedication," Roberts said sincerely.

"It ain't no problem," Alrick said with a casual wave of his hand. "When Morgan went to fight da Hun over dere in France, he left ever'ting to me, includin' da boat and da sisal fields and his horse."

"You two appear to have a wonderful relationship," Tuttle said with admiration.

"Don't you worry none," Alrick said. "We gonna get dat girl back for you. Morgan done flipped da first time he laid his eyes on her walkin' up da beach."

"I can't tell you how thrilled I am to hear that news," Cyrus Roberts said, the relief apparent in his voice. "My daughter has decided to marry your friend, and I was hoping the sentiments were mutual."

*   *   *

Cyrus Roberts approached the front desk and placed his business card in front of the attendant. "I have a reservation for two rooms," he said. "Mr. Tuttle called from Boston two evenings ago."

"Yes, sir," the man said. "We've been expecting you. We have your rooms ready, and we have a message for you."

The desk clerk passed a sealed envelop to Roberts.

"My good man," Tuttle interjected. "Did you perhaps get a look at the person who delivered this message?"

"Actually, I did," the clerk reported.

"You did?" Tuttle responded with excitement. "Please describe him. This could be very important to us."

"But it wasn't a man. It was a little girl," the clerk said. "I remember distinctly because she was sucking on a lollipop and had several more in her other hand."

Tuttle nodded with understanding. "Perhaps our adversary is more clever than we gave him credit for initially."

Cyrus Roberts opened the envelope and stared at the childish block letters scrawled on the lined paper.

SET YOUR WATCH BY CLOCK IN LOBBY
BE AT FLOWER STORE ON
NO. MIAMI AND 2ND STREET
EXACTLY NOON TOMORROW
POLICE MEANS DAUGHTER DIES

Alexander Tuttle waved to Alrick Brown. "Please tell your friend we're instructed to be at a flower shop on North Miami and 2nd Street exactly at noon according to the clock in the hotel lobby."

"Yes, sir," Alrick said. "I'll get him the message. You fellows try to get some rest this evening."

*   *   *

The following day Morgan observed Tuttle and Cyrus Roberts exit the car driven by Alrick Brown and approach the flower shop on the designated corner. He glanced at his watch and noticed they were exactly on time. Morgan had been sitting at a corner table of the café across the street since eleven o'clock reading a newspaper and sipping on a glass of ice tea. He was confident nobody suspected his involvement with the proceedings in the flower shop.

Several female patrons had entered the shop during his one-hour surveillance, but none appeared in the least suspicious. No man had entered the shop.

Moments after walking into the flower shop, Tuttle and Cyrus Roberts exited hastily and dashed toward the waiting vehicle. They were carrying a coiled length of thin rope. They entered the car and closed the doors. Alrick started the engine and spun the car in a U-turn, halting in front of the café where Morgan sat.

Alrick's hand thrust out the open window. He yelled to Morgan. "Read dis," he yelled. "We gots to get goin'. You want to ride wid us?"

"How far," Morgan asked as he approached the vehicle.

"Ain't far," Alrick replied. "Jus' two blocks over an' two blocks down. The Route One Bridge over da river."

Morgan quickly read the message.

GO TO RT. 1 BRIDGE
EXACTLY 12:15
LOWER MONEY WITH ROPE
NO POLICE

"I have time to walk," Morgan said as he looked at Cyrus Roberts and his chauffer Tuttle. Both men fidgeted nervously in the back seat. "I don't want anybody to think you have help yet. Get going."

Roberts looked at Morgan and managed a wan grin. "How have you been, son? I never got the chance to properly thank you for helping me after the hurricane."

"Don't worry, Mr. Roberts," Morgan said returning the gesture with a warm, encouraging smile. "We'll get Anne back safely."

"This gentleman is my chauffer, Alexander Tuttle," Roberts said. "He's been kind enough to accompany me here from Boston to assist."

"Nice to meet you," Morgan said offering his hand.

"So this is the reason for Miss Anne's trip to Florida," Tuttle said as he shook Morgan's hand with a knowing twinkle in his eye.

Alrick motored away and Morgan began walking rapidly toward the Miami River.

* * *

From a vantage point tucked out of sight of the river, beneath the underpinnings of the bridge, Morgan watched the boat traffic carefully. A long, flat barge carrying lumber stretched behind a thick hawser towed by a stubby tugboat. Heavy diesel smoke spewed from its abbreviated stack. A rusty packet freighter passed under the bridge heading toward Dodge Island and the Miami inlet. A cluster of tiny sailboats pointed toward a racing marker anchored off Brickell Key.

Morgan checked his watch. The time was 12:13. No suspicious boats attracted his attention. He peered intently down the river and witnessed only the stern of the freighter and the fleet of children's sailboats. He looked upriver and saw the lumber barge disappearing around a corner.

Then he saw the small speedboat round the same corner and head slowly down the river.

A single person stood at the helm and appeared to consult a wristwatch.

Morgan focused on the driver's face as the craft approached. The man was in his mid-twenties and dark-haired. His eyes appeared to have an unusual proximity and there was a dearth of separation between his brows.

The boat neared the bridge. At exactly 12:15, Morgan saw a bag lowered by rope from the bridge and dangled a few feet from the water.

The driver of the speedboat maneuvered his craft directly at the suspended satchel and pulled the engine out of gear. As he drifted under the bridge, he quickly untied the rope from the handles of the bag and affixed an envelope to the bitter end of the hanging line with a piece of tape.

The moment the satchel was secured inside the boat, the man at the helm shoved the throttle forward and the small vessel rose on plane, exited the Miami River and disappeared around the corner into Biscayne Bay.

*   *   *

As he climbed out from under the bridge and crossed the road, Morgan could sense the disappointment and rage seething inside Cyrus Roberts.

"The man has no honor," Tuttle declared in a voice torn with anger and disgust. "Just look at this."

ANOTHER $25,000 NEEDED
MESSAGE WAITING AT HOTEL
SHE DIES IF POLICE CALLED

"I got a good look at the guy," Morgan said. "I think I could recognize him again."

"Perhaps we should go to the police," Roberts said, the dejection obvious in his voice. "This guy is a step ahead of us at every turn."

Morgan shook his head. "Not any longer," Morgan said. "I know what he looks like, and I know what his boat looks like."

Tuttle rubbed his chin in contemplation. "Perhaps it's not his boat. Perhaps he borrowed the boat. Perhaps the man in the boat isn't the kidnapper, just like the little girl delivering the envelope to the desk clerk wasn't the kidnapper."

"That's possible," Morgan said. "I never saw anybody enter the flower shop with a length of rope, and I guess one of the women who entered could have had it in her hand bag. But I think he's serious about the police."

"You don't think we should go to the police?" Cyrus Roberts asked.

"No, not yet, anyway," Morgan replied. "Alrick should drive you two back to the hotel and look at the next note."

"What you gonna do?" Alrick asked.

"Meet me at the *Belleau Woods* after you drop Mr. Roberts and Tuttle off at the hotel," Morgan said. "I think you and I should spend the rest of the day looking for that boat."

"I have to get to a bank that will advance me $25,000," Cyrus Roberts said shaking his head. "I'm not familiar with any of the banks in Miami. I hope somebody has heard of Commonwealth Bank."

Morgan smiled and pointed to a prominent building a block to the east. "Try that bank," he said. "Ask for Mr. Jeffers and tell him I suggested you speak with him. I think he'll accommodate you."

Cyrus Roberts looked at the young man who was to become his son-in-law with increased respect. "Mr. Jeffers?"

"Yes, he's president of the bank."

~ 51 ~

Morgan Early and Alrick Brown canvassed several of their liquor customers, inquiring about the small speedboat that collected the money dangling from the Route One Bridge. None of the rumrunners knew the boat, and nobody was familiar with a man meeting the description Morgan gave of the driver. All of them expressed their willingness to help in the recovery of Anne Roberts.

"Would any of you be willing to keep watch at the entrance to the Miami River and see if the boat returns?" Morgan asked. "The kidnapper charged out into Biscayne Bay with his money, but it's possible he lives up the river."

Two of the assembled men volunteered to tie their boat near the river entrance for the afternoon and watch for the small boat to return.

"If the boat returns," Morgan warned, "don't attempt to stop him. Don't even follow him. I need this guy alive and well to tell me where he has stashed the girl. If he thinks we're on to him and he gets scared, he might just kill her and disappear."

"Where are you going to look?" another of the rumrunners asked.

"Alrick and I are going to ride around in the bay north of the river and hopefully locate the boat. Maybe he's living around the South Beach area."

"I'll take my boat south toward Key Biscayne," another man volunteered. "We'll meet you back here just before dark."

*   *   *

Morgan and Alrick cruised the entire north end of Biscayne Bay between Miami Beach and the mainland. They nosed *Belleau Woods* into every canal and investigated every hidden dock and possible place to stash a small boat. Their efforts proved fruitless and as evening fell they reluctantly returned to the wharf area where the rumrunners kept their boats.

Morgan was despondent. Alrick was angry. "Why people want to do such tings?" he asked of the stars beginning to appear in the dimming sky above. "Dis guy better not hurt your Anne...," he said with his voice trailing off into the breeze.

"He can't be too smart," Morgan said as his mind whirled with possible scenarios for finding the kidnapper and rescuing Anne. "He could have turned her over today, kept the $100,000, ditched his boat and we probably never would have discovered his identity."

"He be greedy," Alrick said with a nod. "Maybe dat greed what will be his downfall."

Morgan guided *Belleau Woods* gently against the pier and Alrick secured a spring line to temporarily hold the craft. A gaggle of rumrunners were talking animatedly on the dock.

"Morgan, we saw the boat," one of the men called excitedly. "The guy went back up the river about 4:30 this afternoon."

"Really?" Morgan yelled as he stepped to the wooden pier. "You're sure it was the boat I described?"

"We've never seen the boat before," the second man said with conviction. "And it looked exactly like your description."

"What about the driver?" Morgan asked. "Did you get a look at him?"

"He passed less than twenty yards from us on the north side of the river," the first man replied. "He had strange eyes and one bushy brow like you said."

Morgan sat down on a thick, wooden bollard affixed to the pier. He drew a deep breath and raised his eyes heavenward in contemplation. He had to act immediately. Anne had been abducted three days ago. She could be starving or dehydrated. She could be buried or imprisoned with a limited air supply.

The kidnapper's request for additional money was difficult to fathom. Greed was perhaps too facile an explanation. Was the kidnapper so enamored of the process that he wanted further gratification showing off his cleverness at devising ways to transfer ransom money?

One hundred thousand dollars was a princely sum of money. Was the kidnapper accustomed to living a lifestyle that demanded more than that amount to survive for an extended period of time? Who was this guy? Was he armed? Was he operating alone? Did he have an accomplice guarding Anne while he was gathering the ransom money? Would he surrender Anne and give himself up if confronted? Or would he kill Anne and fight?

Apparently the kidnapper lived up the Miami River. He probably lived in a house on the water with a dock. Was Anne there at that location?

The number of unanswered questions was overwhelming, and all of them were essentially unanswerable. To ponder the myriad possibilities, and form contingencies for every option, was not productive.

Morgan decided on his course of action. He would cruise up the river and find the boat. He would reconnoiter the adjacent house and attempt to ascertain if Anne were held captive inside. He wouldn't risk injury to Anne in a fiery assault on the property. If Anne were not in the house, he would enter, capture the kidnapper, and extract the information about her location. Morgan was confident he could make the kidnapper talk. The loss of a few fingers by dull knife blade would loosen any tongue. If an accomplice was present, that person would simply be dispatched as quickly as possible.

"Does everybody have a weapon?" Morgan asked the assembled rumrunners when he had finished developing his strategy for the rescue of Anne Roberts.

"I have a shotgun," one of the men volunteered.

"I have a good pistol," another said.

"Excellent," Morgan said as he jumped aboard *Belleau Woods* and retrieved his Colt Peacemaker from beneath the dashboard. He thumbed open the access to the cylinder and rolled it across his palm. The weapon was "cowboy-loaded" with five rounds of .45 caliber bullets.

"Are you going after this guy tonight?"

"Yes," Morgan answered. "Anne was seized three days ago. There's no telling what she has suffered. I can't wait."

"How about the police?" one of the men asked. "Shouldn't we alert the cops?"

"Da man say 'no police'," Alrick interjected. "He say he kill da girl if we involve da police."

"Based on the success the police have chasing us, I don't have much faith in their ability anyway," another man said with a laugh that was echoed by the other rumrunners.

Morgan smiled in spite of the seriousness of the situation. "No police," he said. "I may have to provide some persuasion to this guy to get him to reveal Anne's location. The police may not like my methods."

"I'll go with you," the first man said. "You may need help. This kidnapper may not be working alone."

"I'll take Alrick and two others," Morgan said. "You guys surround the house and keep anybody from escaping. I'll go in alone. That's the best way to ensure Anne isn't harmed."

"What time do you want to take this guy," another of the men asked.

Morgan looked at the sky. Darkness had fallen in the cool December evening. The stars shone brightly and a half moon was rising in the east.

"Everybody involved get some rest and eat some dinner," he replied. "We'll meet here at one o'clock in the morning and start searching the river. If we're lucky, we'll locate the boat and I'll hit the house between two and three."

"Dat's a nice time of da night," Alrick said. "Da moon be up and da kidnapper be sound asleep dreamin' of his next twenty-five thousand."

~ 52 ~

Bands of striated clouds floated across the dimness of the night as a half moon cast pale shadows on the Miami River.

Morgan and Alrick motored quietly up the shoreline, the Liberty V-12's exhaust burbling in the still air. Two other rumrunners in a second boat followed in their wake that showed brightly as the churning propeller stirred the sparkling phosphorescence in the water.

The four men intently studied every craft along the river's banks, seeking the one vessel that fit the description of the speedboat piloted by the kidnapper.

The search continued inexorably as the river narrowed and the warehouses and commercial buildings on shore gave way to more open space and residential housing.

More than two and a half miles from the Miami River's mouth at Biscayne Bay, on a stretch of sandy bank that rolled gently into a heavily wooded area devoid of lights, Morgan spotted the small speedboat belonging to the kidnapper. The craft was tied to a rickety dock of warped planks that extended fifty feet from the shore.

"You see a house up dere in da woods?" Alrick asked in a whispered voice.

"No," Morgan replied in a similar hushed tone.

"What we gonna do?"

269

Morgan pointed to the far side of the dock. "We'll tie up there," he said. "You stay here. If anybody you don't recognize comes running from the woods, stop them."

Alrick's face broke into a twisted grin and he patted the pistol jammed into his pants. "Ain't nobody gonna get past me."

"Don't shoot to kill," Morgan advised. "We may need to talk to them later."

Alrick nodded his understanding.

The driver of the second boat shut off the engine and drifted alongside *Belleau Woods*. His companion lashed the two boats together with a length of rope. "Where do you want us?" he said.

"You two come with me," Morgan replied. "I suspect there's a house in those woods. I want you to cover the doors and stop anybody from leaving."

"You can count on us," the second man said as he climbed quietly from his boat on to *Belleau Woods* and stepped to the narrow dock carrying a double barrel shotgun. "Anybody trying to flee from that house will need to be able to outrun this buckshot."

"Stay behind me," Morgan cautioned, "and walk quietly. Surprise is going to be our greatest ally."

*   *   *

The low silhouette of the roof of the house broke the vertical lines of the dense trees in the woods. Morgan motioned the two men to spread apart and surround the structure. He bent forward and lowered his profile and scooted toward the closest corner of the one story building. His footfalls were nearly soundless as he landed softly on his toes and eased his heels to the ground.

Morgan reflected briefly how quickly his Marine Corps training in silent movement returned to him. He noted, too, his absence of nervousness and the steady, unhurried rhythm of his heartbeat. He realized with a sudden cognizance how much he loved what he was doing. He was a combatant. His act of vengeance against the man who killed his foster mother was not an aberration. His shooting of the rim-rocker was not an anomaly. His instantaneous grasp of the military situation fighting with Pancho Villa was not an accident. His success in The Great War was not providence.

Morgan was purely and simply a warrior. As horrifying and bloody and grotesque and ghastly and sickening as the details of war might be, he knew he was born to be a soldier. And he recognized with perfect clarity and a distinct lack of guilt his love of battle.

A screen porch fronted the river. At the back of the porch a single door flanked by curtained windows filled the wall. Morgan guessed the interior room was a common living space. He moved swiftly and silently around the corner and assessed the side of the house. Single windows high in the wall suggested a kitchen. The front of the house contained a wide double door with larger windows close to the ground on either side.

The final side of the house contained a small single window centered in the wall with larger, lower windows on either side. Could these be two bedrooms flanking a centered bathroom? Where would the owner sleep, closer to the river? Would the kidnapper confine Anne to the other bedroom? Could there be a criminal cohort in the second bedroom?

Questions swirled in Morgan's mind. Answers were unavailable. No light shone from the house. No sound issued from the dwelling. No hint of either Anne's or the kidnapper's presence was forthcoming from the abode. The time for planning was over. The time for action was nigh.

*   *   *

Morgan crept back to the front door. He paused to listen for sounds emanating from inside before twisting the handle. He pulled gently. The door didn't budge. A dead bolt locked the entry in place.

He returned to the two windows. He pushed carefully on the panes but was unable to slide either one upward.

Morgan silently eased to the side of the building that he believed contained bedrooms. He pushed at the lower mullions of the windows. The effort was in vain; the windows were secure.

He stealthily returned to the rear of the house. With the blade tip of a small knife he slit the screen enclosure beside the doorknob. He reached through the parted mesh, flipped the locking tab, and spun the handle. The door opened.

Moving cautiously and with minimum sound, Morgan crossed to the entrance of the house. He gripped the knob and twisted. The handle refused to turn.

A dilapidated couch was visible in the moonlight against the wall. Morgan cut a large section of material from one of the cushions and wrapped it multiple times around his hand. He stood directly in front of the door and withdrew his fist. A quick punch to the glass above the knob burst the pane. A single muffled thump accompanied the blow, followed by a tinkle of glass on the interior floor. Morgan shed the protective cloth and turned the door handle from the inside. The house was open.

He moved swiftly past a sitting area and a kitchen. Pale, flat light filtered through the windows facing the descending moon to the west. Morgan turned toward two closed doors on either side of an open door that suggested a bathroom. He gingerly reached for the first handle and twisted. It was locked. Was this Anne's prison? Would a man lock himself inside his own bedroom inside a locked house?

Morgan moved to the second door, the one closer to the river. He touched the knob and gently, imperceptibly, rotated his hand. The knob moved a quarter turn. The latch retreated from the mortise. The door cracked an inch. Morgan stepped to the side of the entrance, away from the opening, and pressed his back to the wall. He reached and placed the tip of his index finger against the closest panel of the door and pushed.

The twin barrels of a ten-gauge shotgun simultaneously discharged in the absolute silence of the night. The door shattered. Wood splinters and heavy steel shot flew through the opening. A flash of flame lingered momentarily in the bedroom. The acrid smell of discharged gunpowder tumbled toward Morgan's nostrils.

The sudden roar of the powerful, deadly weapon startled Morgan. His left forearm, exposed to the blast as he reached and pushed the door, screamed with pain.

Morgan spun to face the opening to the bedroom. A perfect hole, chest high and shoulder width, gaped through the thin wooden door. The silhouette of a man stood, clutching a shotgun, framed against the dim light issuing through the bedroom window.

Morgan whipped his single action Colt from his holster and squeezed the trigger. He raised his bloody left arm, extended his fingers, and fanned his flat palm three times across the hammer of the weapon. Three shots spat from the ten-inch barrel. Narrow tongues of flame briefly illuminated the small room as cordite filled the air.

Morgan watched as a look of astonishment wrinkled the single eyebrow on the face of the occupant of the room. The man lowered his tightly spaced eyes and stared incredulously at the three red stains blossoming on the front of his shirt. He opened his mouth to speak and lifted a heavy hand to staunch the flow of blood pouring from his chest.

"How did you...?" Gaetano Bagarella gurgled as a stream of bright arterial blood erupted from his mouth.

"Where's the girl?" Morgan said simply.

Gaetano sagged slowly to his knees. "Next door," he said weakly. "I never touched her."

The son of the Chicago Mafia boss tumbled face first to the floor, dead at last, three months after his funeral.

"MORGAN!" Anne screamed from the second bedroom. "Is that you?"

"Anne," he called as he walked deliberately to the adjacent bedroom. Without hesitation he kicked sharply at the doorknob. The door flew open and he rushed to the bed.

"It's over," he said as he leaned over and kissed Anne Roberts tenderly on the lips.

"Oh, Morgan," Anne wept silently, tears dampening her soiled cheeks. "Oh, Morgan."

"There's nothing to be afraid of now. You're safe with me."

*   *   *

Morgan Early and Anne Roberts were married in an Anglican church on Bimini the following Sunday. Cyrus Roberts proudly walked his daughter, resplendent in a hastily created white gown, down the aisle. Morgan's bandaged left forearm, where four shot pellets had ripped skin from the bone, was hidden by the sleeve of his suit jacket.

Alexander Tuttle ushered the two hundred guests to their seats with impeccable dignity. Alrick Brown stood at Morgan's side as his best man.

The reception was held at Morgan's house and the liquor flowed unceasingly until dawn.

"Would you be interested in starting a family soon," Morgan asked Anne as they collapsed on the porch when the last of the guests departed.

Anne turned to Morgan and burst into a broad smile. Her white teeth sparkled in the flickering light of a dozen candles. Her blue eyes blazed mischievously. "We've already started," she said with a laugh.

"We've already...what?" Morgan repeated in confusion before the meaning of his bride's words registered.

"I didn't want to tell you before," Anne said. "I didn't want you to marry me for the wrong reason."

Morgan lifted his head and roared with laughter. "There isn't a reason in the world why I wouldn't marry you."

"That's the best wedding present I could ever want," Anne said.

"Speaking of presents," Morgan said. "Your father offered me the $100,000 we recovered at the kidnapper's house as a wedding present. I thanked him, but I refused."

Anne laughed again and patted Morgan on the shoulder. "I know," she said. "He told me. But I didn't."

"You didn't what?"

"I didn't turn him down. I took the money. I have a feeling the rum running won't last forever," Anne said. "America will wake up soon and decide they can't legislate something like drinking. You'll have to think of another occupation."

"I already have," Morgan said. "Alrick and I are going crawfishing."

"Crawfishing?"

"Lobsters," Morgan said. "They may never replace Scotch, but we can make a nice living right here on Bimini."

~ 53 ~

The 21st Amendment to the Constitution of the United States of America, repealing the Volstead Act, was ratified by the U.S. Congress on December 5, 1933. For all Bahamians it was a sad day and ended the most prosperous period the islands had experienced since the glory days of "wrecking" passing ships prior to the installation of lighthouses.

Morgan and Alrick, with the instigation of Anne, had made preparations. The three-masted *Semper Fidelis* was sold for a price four times the cost of construction. The liquor barge was sold in 1932 to Mr. H. F. Duncombe and his wife Helen for a profit. The beautifully weathered planks were to be used in the construction of their twenty-three-room hotel on Bimini named the Compleat Angler. The magnificent structure was completed in 1933, and the famous author Ernest Hemingway spent many nights drinking copiously at the bar. Contrary to popular belief, Hemingway never spent a night in the Compleat Angler. Mrs. Duncombe considered him an obnoxious drunk and therefore branded him an unwelcome guest.

The virgin waters of the Gulf Stream, sweeping less than half a mile from the sandy shores of Bimini, and teeming with huge marlin and giant tuna, began to attract fishermen from the Unites States.

In 1936 Morgan took delivery of a single engine, thirty-seven foot Wheeler sportfishing boat. He fitted the craft with a stout fighting chair in the open cockpit. When he wasn't crawfishing in the original thirty-foot sloop, Alrick Brown manned the cockpit and

275

assisted the paying customers. Morgan's son, James, born in June of 1927, guided the fighting chair to keep it square to the hooked prey while the angler strained to wind in his catch.

"Are we going fishing today, Dad?" James yelled as he dashed to the breakfast table from his bedroom one day in 1937. "I just know we're going to catch a big marlin!"

Morgan tousled his son's blonde hair with his hand and grinned. The boy had been a complete delight from the day of his birth. At age ten he had grown to five feet three inches tall with broad shoulders, well developed muscles and a trim waist. Anne took charge of his schooling because her formal educational background was vastly superior to Morgan's, but the boy and his father studied the lessons together in the evenings. James was proficient in history, geography and mathematics far beyond his age.

In the daytime, Morgan, Anne and James fished and swam and explored. The three were inseparable, and Morgan had never been happier. Anne, for all her structured upbringing in Boston and immersion in country club living, was thrilled with her new life on the island. "Another perfect day in paradise," she said every morning at breakfast.

Anne walked from the kitchen with three plates of fresh fruit and a stack of Bimini toast. "If you boys are going fishing, you need your strength," she said with a smile. "James, go get the three glasses of juice in the kitchen."

"What are you doing today?" Morgan asked.

"I promised Buck I'd take him for a ride," Anne said. "He's slowing down some, but he still needs his exercise."

"I wonder how much longer he has," Morgan mused. "He's almost twenty-seven now."

"I'm not sure how long horses live," Anne replied with a broad grin. "But living here is probably healthier than chasing Mexican bandits around the Rio Grande like you made him do in the old days."

Morgan laughed. "I'm sure you're right," he said. "But we had fun while it lasted."

"How much fun was that jail?"

"Oh, yeah. I forgot about that part of it."

*   *   *

"I'm Henry Cromwell," the Miami man said as he boarded Morgan's fishing boat *Gallivant*. "And this is my son, Jason."

"It's a pleasure to meet you," Morgan said extending his hand. "And this is my son, James. He'll handle the cockpit today. Our regular mate, Alrick, is lobster fishing."

Morgan started the engine from the helm station atop the cabin, and James untied the lines from the pilings. *Gallivant* idled away from the rickety dock and headed south toward the harbor entrance. The tide was high and the ocean water inside the bay was gin clear. The sky was cloudless and only a slight breeze drifted across the surface from the southeast. Every feature of the sandy bottom was visible, and three spotted eagle rays gently flapped their wings ahead of the boat.

"The tide will be falling soon," Morgan observed to Henry Cromwell. "There's an excellent chance we'll catch a marlin just off the entrance."

Gallivant proceeded past the south tip of North Bimini and along the deeper channel between the beach bordering South Bimini and the prominent sand bar. At the southern terminus of the bar, Morgan turned toward the west and pushed up the throttle.

The light blue of the channel and the pure white water over the sand bar quickly gave way to turquoise as the depth dropped to fifty feet. One hundred yards further, the water turned cobalt as the bottom fell away to six hundred feet.

"Put out the baits," Morgan called to James.

"We're fishing here?" Jason Cromwell asked in disbelief. "I thought you had to travel far to catch big fish."

"Most places that's probably true," James laughed. "That's why Bimini is the best place to fish."

"Wow, Dad," Jason called to his father. "I could almost swim to shore from here."

James opened a cooler packed with ice and lifted two four pound bonefish rigged with 12/O hooks and long wire leaders.

"That's our bait?" Jason exclaimed with astonishment. "What's going to eat that?"

"A big marlin, I hope," James answered as he attached the leaders to the fishing line of the stout rods and star-drag reels.

James carefully slid the baits over the transom and released line until they were positioned on the seventh wave of the wake.

"When a fish appears," James instructed, "I'll feed him the bait and set the hook. Whoever is going to catch the fish, rush to the fighting chair and sit down. I'll bring you the rod."

"It sounds like you've done this before," Henry Cromwell said with surprise.

"My dad and I have been doing this for over a year," James replied. "It took us a while to learn how to catch these big fish, but we've got the hang of it now."

Morgan adjusted the *Gallivant's* speed until the baits skipped enticingly in the wake. The bonefish's shiny silver scales gleamed in the pounding sunlight, and the action of the rigged bait produced a smoky trail of bubbles when it sipped air and then wiggled inches beneath the surface.

Morgan steered *Gallivant* in a weaving pattern toward the south, into the current, maintaining her position in water depth he believed ranged between six hundred and fifteen hundred feet. He scanned the surface of the ocean looking for weed lines and current rips that he suspected gathered bait and enticed the large pelagic fish like the tunas and marlin.

Henry Cromwell wiped the perspiration from his face with a broad handkerchief and looked at the sky. "How will we know when we get a marlin or tuna?"

James laughed. "Oh, you'll know," he said. "My dad will see him, and he'll be screaming with excitement. I'll see him, too, and I'll be able to point him out to you."

An hour passed. The engine exhaust droned in an uninterrupted monotone. The bow wake splashed repetitively alongside the hull. The pristine wake fanned with tedious regularity from the transom. Jason retired to the shade of the open cabin and sprawled on the bench seat inside. Henry Cromwell's eyes began to droop. He looked helplessly up at Morgan who was intently searching for likely holding zones for big fish. He opened his mouth to issue a remark, but decided to hold his comment. James maintained his vigil in the cockpit.

~ 54 ~

"Flying fish showering ahead," Morgan called from the cabin roof. "Stay alert."

James moved to the side of the boat and looked ahead. Small fish with gossamer wings glided over the surface of the purple ocean. *Gallivant* slid relentlessly past the disturbed area. Nothing appeared in the wake...until a dark shadow loomed behind one of the skittering bonefish.

"Blue marlin," Morgan sang out from the helm. "Left bait."

James was already in motion dashing toward the correct fishing rod. "He's a good one, too," he said to Henry Cromwell, the admiration obvious in his voice as he hefted the heavy rod and reel.

Jason stumbled into the cockpit and rubbed his eyes. "What's everyone yelling about?"

Henry Cromwell rotated his head between the two baits. "I don't see anything," he said.

The surface of the ocean split behind the left bonefish. An enormous pointed dorsal fin protruded atop a wide, dark body that carried a row of electric blue stripes fanned down the length. A pair of glowing pectoral fins protruded from each side.

"I see him," Henry Cromwell yelled. "Look! Look!"

A wide rapier bill broke the surface of the water and slashed at the bait. A gaping maw appeared below the pointed bill. A tall, sickle-shaped tail slashed once behind the long body, and the bonefish disappeared.

James held the heavy rod in his left hand. His right manipulated the large reel. Line peeled from the spool as James kept the reel in the free position. When he calculated the marlin had swallowed the bonefish, and turned his body to continue hunting, he snapped the chrome lever forward, engaging the drag. The rapidly spinning spool slowed. The line tugged grudgingly off the reel against the heavy friction of the drag mechanism.

An explosion tore the ocean. The marlin, feeling the hook for the first time, burst from the surface.

The reel continued to turn, more quickly, as the drag pressured the huge fish into activity. James lifted the rod sharply once, twice and a third time. He struck the marlin, sinking the sharp point of the hook deep into his jaw.

Henry Cromwell sat in the fighting chair, his mouth slack with disbelief. James placed the rod butt in the holder between the man's legs. "Grab the rod above the reel with your left hand," he instructed. "Hold the reel handle with your right. Rest your feet on that wooden box."

Henry Cromwell seized the fishing rod properly, and James released his grip.

The rod bent abruptly as the marlin began a rapid series of leaps away from the boat.

"I can't hold him," Henry Cromwell gasped. "He's getting away."

"You can do it," James said gently. "This is what you came here for, isn't it?"

"How big is this fish?" Henry Cromwell grunted as the fishing rod bowed in his hand and the line ripped from the reel.

James looked up at his father and smiled. "How big?" he called. "Eight hundred pounds?"

James wound in the second bonefish bait and stored the rod.

Morgan slipped the engine into reverse and began backing toward the greyhounding marlin. "He's at least eight," Morgan confirmed with a huge smile on his face.

"Dad's backing up," James noted. "When the fish stops jumping, it's time for you to go to work."

The marlin made a final vault into the air, clearing the surface of the sea with its tail, heaving frothy droplets from its majestic head, before sounding.

"Lift the rod to gain slack," James said. "Then wind down to retrieve line."

Henry Cromwell raised the rod and turned the handle as he lowered the pole. Twelve inches of line grudgingly returned to the spool.

"That's it," James said encouragingly. "Keep that up."

"You'll never get him at that rate," Jason said. "Look at all the line the fish took."

*   *   *

The sun baked the cockpit. Henry Cromwell's shirt was soaked with perspiration. Sheets of sweat poured from his forehead. His left hand was cramped around the rod, and his arm screamed with pain from the constant pulling and lifting. Bolts of agony flashed up his spinal column. Previously unused muscles throughout his body barked in protest. But a grim determination overcame the suffering.

"I'm going to catch this fish," he sputtered between gasps of breath. "This is the most exciting thing I've ever done. Did you see that fish in the air, Jason?"

"I saw him, father," Jason nodded. "He scared me."

"How long has he been on the line?"

"Only about an hour," James replied. "I suspect it'll be a while yet."

"How's he holding up?" Morgan called from the helm.

"Mr. Cromwell is doing fine," James yelled back. "He's getting the hang of it."

The line suddenly grew slack. Henry Cromwell was able to wind without lifting. "It's getting easier," he called. "Is the fish giving up?"

"No!" James yelled. "He's *coming* up. Wind! Wind as fast as you can. You can't give him slack."

Suddenly the immense blue marlin rocketed into the air twenty feet behind the boat. Water flew as if a bomb had exploded inches beneath the surface. The pectoral fins burned bright blue in the sun. Neon stripes glowed in rows down the dark body. The huge, round eye of the fish rolled toward the cockpit and fastened on the angler. The body of the fish hung suspended in the air, until finally it fell into the sea, splashing water into the cockpit.

"Wind!" James hollered. "Wind!"

The ocean flattened after the magnificent leap. The marlin began a relentless run for freedom, pulling nearly all the line from the reel. Finally the fish tired and Henry Cromwell was able to resume pumping and winding, gaining inches at a time. Precious, hard-won, line slowly built on the reel as the minutes mounted and inexorably turned to hours.

"He's close," James mouthed to his father after a long period of steady gain.

"Get the gaff," Morgan called. "Get both of them."

James nodded and disappeared into the cabin, returning immediately with two long, sharp gaffs.

Morgan put the engine into neutral and climbed down from his helm station atop the cabin. He slid thick welding gloves on his hands and handed another pair to James who wordlessly tugged them on his own hands.

"What's going on?" Henry Cromwell asked when he ventured a brief look at Morgan and his son making preparations in the cockpit. "Who's driving?"

"Keep gaining line if you can," James said. "We're getting ready to take your fish."

"You're going to bring that thing in the boat?" Jason asked with concern in his voice.

"Maybe you better go up on the top," Morgan offered. "You can see better up there."

"Okay," Jason said, not needing a second invitation to leave the cockpit.

The junction of the fishing line and the heavy leader appeared above the surface of the water. Morgan reached out, grasped the wire leader and wrapped it once around his palm. "Stop winding," he said to Henry Cromwell over his shoulder. "I have the fish."

Morgan braced his knees under the covering board of the cockpit and pulled. His hand lifted with gained leader. He reached with his other hand, took one wrap, and pulled again. He pulled three more times, exchanging grips on the leader, and snatched a quick look at James. "There he is."

James lifted a gaff and held it over the transom. "Two or three more pulls," he whispered. "I don't have a shot yet."

Morgan tugged steadily, attempting not to rip the hook from the fish with a violent movement. Suddenly, the thick body of the marlin broke the surface. "Stroke him," Morgan said to his son. "Stick him right in the shoulder."

James positioned the gaff over the marlin and turned the point back toward the body. With a smooth, practiced tugging motion he pulled the sharp end of the gaff into the meat of the fish.

The marlin felt the gaff sink deep into its flesh. The magnificent fish summoned a final burst of energy and sprang from the water, away from the transom. James tightened his grip on the gaff handle, refusing to release the fish, and was pulled from his feet. Morgan, standing immediately beside his son, the wire leader wrapped around his right hand, curled his fist toward his chest to stop the marlin, and simultaneously reached with his left to grab his airborne son around the knees.

The combined pressure of the clenched leader and the restraint of Morgan holding James, who was holding the affixed gaff, folded the gigantic fish back toward the boat.

Water cascaded into the cockpit. Henry Cromwell screamed with surprise and fright. James slammed back to the cockpit floor and Morgan released his grip on his son. With his free hand, Morgan seized the second gaff and burled it into the marlin's thick midsection.

Father and son braced their feet and pulled in unison. A second later a thirteen foot long, eight hundred and fifty pound blue marlin crashed to the cockpit floor, shaking the braces beneath the deck.

"Congratulations, Mr. Cromwell," Morgan said as he hugged James and slapped him on the back.

"Nice going, Dad," Jason called from the top of the cabin. "You did it."

"You weren't going to let go of that gaff, were you?" Morgan said to James with a broad grin.

"I was not going to let that fish get the best of me," James laughed. "Now let's go weigh this monster. I'll bet it's the biggest of the season."

~ 55 ~

"Alrick is going to take a couple of days off," Morgan Early announced at dinner one evening in October, 1939. "Why don't the three of us take the sloop and go crawfishing?"

Twelve-year-old James looked up from his heaping bowl of conch chowder. "Yes, Dad," he said enthusiastically. "Can we? Can we?"

Anne Early rubbed her fingers in her son's blonde hair. "Are you sure you want your old mother tagging along?"

"Of course," James said. "She'll have fun, won't she, Dad?"

"You've caught crawfish, but you've never seen how it's done from the sloop," Morgan said to his wife. "I think you should come along. Besides, we'll miss you if you stay behind."

"You just want me to feed you," Anne chided.

"Oh, no," Morgan said. "You're going to help us catch the lobsters. This is a money-making trip."

Anne shook her head and smiled patiently. "You barely make enough money crawfishing to justify the cost of the sloop," she said seriously. "What do they pay in Miami recently, isn't it down to three cents a pound?"

Morgan nodded and shrugged his shoulders.

"You only keep the crawfishing operation alive to give Alrick an income," she said. "We have enough money to last three lifetimes after the rum running days and selling the schooner and barge."

"He's been a good friend to me," Morgan said simply.

"I know he has," Anne said as she leaned over and kissed Morgan lightly on the cheek. "I just want you to know what a wonderful man I think you are."

*   *   *

At dawn Morgan pulled on the halyard and the sail slid easily up the tall mast of the thirty-foot sloop. The gentle morning breeze caught the large canvas sheet and puffed it to starboard. James hauled the mainsheet rope and pulled it tight.

"Trim it a little more," Morgan called from the front deck. James retrieved more line and wrapped it twice around a cleat. The sprightly sailing vessel heeled slightly and picked up speed as it headed south down the channel.

"Wheeee!" James yelled with excitement. "We're flying!"

Anne guided the sloop toward the ocean. "Get ready to jibe," she called as she ducked her head and pulled the tiller arm sharply toward her to spin the boat one hundred-eighty degrees to the north. "Jibe ho!"

The bow of the sloop turned away from the wind and the long boom swung quickly across to the port side of the boat. The canvas flapped noisily for a second before the wind filled the sail and snapped it tight. Momentum was restored and the vessel took up a steady course north.

Anne maintained the sloop in fifty feet of water until she rounded North Rock. Then she began a series of long tacks into the wind across the shallow bank. Grassy bottom covered the twelve-foot depths, and contours and swales could be distinguished through the clear water.

"Sail east for about three hours," Morgan suggested. "That's where the most productive bottom has been for the last month."

Crawfish, or spiny lobsters, unique from their cold-water cousins residing in the northeast of the United States, have no large claws. They inhabit the shallows of the Bahamas, seeking refuge in the coral reefs along the edge of the ocean and depressions and fissures in the sandy bottom of the expansive flats.

Fishermen often place barrels or cinder blocks in strategic locations to create artificial homes for the crawfish, saving them the problem of finding natural hiding places.

Shortly after ten o'clock, Anne headed the sloop directly into the wind. The sail luffed and flapped slowly as Morgan uncleated the halyard and lowered the main sheet to pile atop the boom. James dropped an anchor from the bow and the boat soon fetched tight against the line.

"This looks like a good place to try," Anne said. "I can see many undulations in the bottom and a few coral heads that should hold lobsters."

Morgan and James stripped to their shorts and grabbed their "bully" nets, which were used to scoop the lobsters. Anne strapped the tiller in place and peeled off her shirt and pants to reveal a tight bathing suit.

"Where's my 'bully', she laughed. "Are you two going to have all the fun?"

Morgan draped a rope ladder over the side of the sloop to facilitate reentry. James handed his mother a third "bully" net. "Come on, Mom," he called. "I'll bet I can catch more lobsters than you can."

"Figure out which way the tide is running," Morgan cautioned. "Work into the tide so that when you have a full net and need to head back to the boat, you can drift along and not have to work too hard."

"And let's all stay close," Anne said. "I want you two in my sight at all times."

"Your mother's right," Morgan repeated. "Don't swim off."

James rolled his eyes at the admonishment. "I know, I know," he said happily as he approached the side of the boat and jumped into the warm water.

Anne swam along the top of the ten-foot depth with her face in the water, surveying the bottom. A grassy flat gave way to a white hole with a distinct undercut along the edge. She drew a deep breath and dove gracefully beneath the surface. At the bottom, she pressed her stomach to the sand and looked up into the recess below the slight overhang. Two dozen pairs of fourteen-inch long feelers waved before her eyes.

She surfaced and looked for James and Morgan. They were nowhere in sight. Suddenly two heads bobbed above the water.

"Have you seen any?" she called.

"Not yet," James shouted.

"Come over here," Anne yelled. "I've found a honey hole."

James stroked toward his mother with his "bully" net in tow. "Where are they?"

"Right below me," Anne said as she pointed beneath her feet.

James jack-knifed toward the bottom with a huge grin on his face. The moment he saw the sandy hole, he swam for the more pronounced edge which experience told him was the most likely hiding spot.

He dropped to his knees and stared for a moment at the hoard of lobsters. With the handle of his net, he reached into the recess and gently wiggled the stick behind the lobsters. Three of the crawfish, nervous at the intrusion of their lair, moved to vacate their hiding place. James pulled the net back, spun it in his hand, and scooped them into the mesh.

Anne dove to the bottom and watched with pride as her son captured the three crawfish. James turned to display his catch, and she nodded her approval and waved congratulations.

Both returned to the surface for a fresh breath, and Anne called, "Nice going, James."

"I'm going to get them all," he yelled. "Come on, you catch a few."

"I'll watch," Anne replied. "I'd rather you have all the fun."

James dove three more times, adding to his haul with each excursion, until his net was overflowing with panicked, struggling crawfish, each giving off silent signals of distress through the water.

The sensitive lateral line of the bull shark, tuned through eons of development to receiving subliminal messages of terror, immediately homed on the vibrations racing through the water. Eyesight was unimportant to the three hundred pound shark. Smell and sensitivity directed his relentless search for food. Wounded and distressed fish commanded special attention from this ancient carnivore that feasted on the oceanic weak and wounded.

"Let's take those lobsters back to the boat," Anne suggested. "Your net is almost full."

"One more dive," James begged. "There's still more crawfish under that ledge."

287

Anne opened her mouth to object, but James disappeared beneath the surface.

A rhythmic undulation of the massive tail brought the bull shark inexorably toward the sandy hole, tracking directly at the waves of terror broadcast by the frenzied lobsters. Anne dove down to watch proudly as her son scooped another four lobsters into his net.

James was facing the ledge, his back to the approaching killer. Anne's heart momentarily stopped and her blood felt cold in her veins when she spied the gray monster approaching her son. She didn't think. She didn't hesitate. She didn't waver. She swam directly at the shark and poked her "bully" net at the animal's nose with all her strength.

The resistance of the dense water slowed the blow to a mere tap, but the shark, intent on the net of frenzied lobsters, was surprised and veered sharply away. James sensed the commotion behind his back and turned. His eyes widened as he saw the bull shark circle and his mother maintain her defensive posture.

Together mother and son surfaced and blew their lungs clear. "Swim," Anne shouted. "Swim for the boat."

Anne recognized the additional vulnerability of remaining on the surface. Under the water, she could see and keep the shark in front of her. On the water, her visibility was distorted and her dangling, churning limbs were further enticements for the shark to attack.

She dove after insufficient time to replenish her oxygen. Her lungs immediately screamed with the build-up of carbon dioxide, but she forced herself to scull backward, beneath the water, her back to her paddling son, facing the menacing bull shark.

The shark turned and darted directly toward Anne. She withdrew her net and waited. At the last second, she lunged out and stabbed the shark in its unblinking, black eye with the net handle.

The blow brought pain and confusion to the instinct driven animal. It turned away and hovered briefly ten feet from Anne who surfaced and sucked at the air. She looked around quickly and saw Morgan swimming rapidly toward her, his head in the water, twenty yards away.

Anne forced panic from her mind and concentrated on recovering her breath. She gulped a lungful of air and slid below the surface, searching for the shark. The bull was slowly moving toward her, caution dictating its methodical approach. Anne held her net in readiness as she watched Morgan swim swiftly into view. He held a knife in his hand.

Anne ceased her movement, inviting the bull shark closer, concentrating its attention on her presence. She kept both eyes focused on the shark, but watched Morgan with her distant vision.

Morgan dove under the shark's tail and reached up. He drove the point of the knife into the shark's vulnerable belly and ripped backward with all the strength he could summon.

Blood billowed into the water from the fissure Morgan sliced in the shark's stomach. Tendrils of intestine fell through the opening. The shark turned from Anne, disorientated and wounded, further confused by the sudden loss of the panic signals as James climbed aboard the sloop, lifting his "bully" net of lobsters from the water.

Anne and Morgan surfaced together, grabbed breaths of air and dove again. The bull shark was swimming slowly fifteen feet from them, the former aggressiveness replaced with an apparent lassitude of behavior.

Two additional sharks appeared on the periphery of their vision, darting back and forth with sharp, purposeful movements. The blood trail streaming from the wounded bull shark, combined with the signals of vulnerability, riled the new arrivals. The most audacious of the two invaders launched an exploratory attack and ripped a chunk of flesh from the bleeding animal. The second, emboldened by the success of the first, charged the bull shark and sunk its teeth into the exposed stomach.

A cloud of blood blurred further sight of the receding carnage. Anne surfaced beside Morgan and pointed toward the boat. Together, stopping to look back frequently, they swam to the sloop and climbed aboard.

"Wow," James yelled with excitement. "Did you see that?"

Anne dashed to her son and hugged him tightly. Morgan joined his wife and son and threw his arms around them both. The parents remained speechless for several minutes. James couldn't stop recounting the exciting events.

*   *   *

Following lunch, Morgan and James dove near the boat and netted more lobsters while Anne kept a vigil from the bow. When they had nearly two hundred crawfish aboard, they sailed leisurely back to Bimini where they deposited their catch in one of their specially built wooden structures called a "car" that was anchored in the harbor in less than two feet of water. The eight foot long, six foot wide, two-foot high "car" kept the lobsters alive until enough were gathered to justify a trip to Miami.

When the crawfish were to be transported to Miami, they were removed from the "car" and wrapped in wet sacks that kept them alive until delivery. Crawfishing was an important segment of the entire Bahamas economy from approximately 1925 until the Second World War caused a temporary halt in the activity.

*   *   *

The news of Hitler's invasion of Poland in September 1939 returned Morgan's thinking to war. He had been blissfully happy the last thirteen years on Bimini with Anne and James. He never for a moment regretted marrying the woman he considered his best friend as well as the most wonderful and beautiful person in the world. But Morgan was convinced his country could not long remain out of the conflict raging in Europe.

A war had broken out. The United States would soon be involved. He was a warrior, and he was very good at the bloody business of war.

Morgan had the highest admiration for the Marine Corps. He loved the traditions, the stiff-collar dress uniforms which were a direct salute to the original "leather-neck" Marines serving on ships in stiff, leather collars to protect them from decapitation by sword when they boarded an enemy vessel. He loved dedication to service and the camaraderie of the men. In the depths of his heart, however bizarre, he even loved combat.

Morgan passed many hours thinking of the coming conflict and ruing the fact the war might pass him by.

~ 56 ~

"Who's Lieutenant Colonel Bennett?" Anne asked when Morgan walked through the door and sat on the porch with a bottle of beer in his hand the first week of January, 1942. The debacle of Pearl Harbor was one month old.

Morgan looked at his wife with genuine confusion. "Colonel Bennett?" he repeated as he searched his memory. "I don't think I know a Colonel Bennett."

"He seems to know you," Anne said simply.

Morgan rubbed his chin in contemplation. He lifted the dewy bottle of beer and placed it to his lips. "I knew a Captain Bennett in France," he said vaguely. "But that was over twenty years ago."

"Jim Bennett?" Anne continued. "Does that ring a bell?"

Morgan wiped a drop of moisture from his chin and placed the bottle on the coffee table. "I think the captain's name *was* Jim. Why?"

"Colonel Jim Bennett called today. He also sent a telegram," Anne said holding a yellow envelope aloft. "He says you saved his life in Belleau Woods."

Morgan shrugged and opened his hands. "I remember bringing him back to our lines after he was knocked unconscious. I'm not sure I saved his life."

"The colonel wants you in Washington next week," Anne said. "He has recalled you into the Marines."

"I've been recalled into the Marines? Can he do that?"

Anne responded by handing Morgan the telegram.

BY ORDER OF THE COMMANDANT US MARINE CORPS STOP LT MORGAN EARLY THIS DATE REACTIVATED US MARINE CORPS STOP REPORT TO LT COL JIM BENNETT WASHINGTON, DC, SOONEST STOP IMMEDIATE PROMOTION TO MAJOR STOP

"Is this legal?" Morgan asked. "What did Bennett say?"

"We talked for several minutes," Anne replied. "He simply said that he needs you."

Morgan sat without speaking, his mind awhirl. Confusion and uncertainty rarely entered his thought process. He was a man of black and white thinking, able to immediately identify the correct moral path and unhesitant to move forward. But the telegram from his former commanding officer tore him with conflict.

Morgan had served his duty to his country once, with great distinction. He had a wife and young son. How could he leave them to fight another war? It was unfair to draft him again, after more than two decades, to fight the Germans a second time. He would refuse to go to Washington! His loyalty and responsibility clearly lay with his family.

Yet...how could he not heed the call of the country he loved. Yes, he lived in Bimini, but America was his birthplace and ultimate home. He was needed, and being needed was a concept always foremost in his mind. Morgan served when called, regardless of the circumstances.

"Why are you sitting there with such a glum expression?" Anne asked finally.

Morgan swallowed and shifted uncomfortably in his chair. "I won't leave you," he said at last. "My first loyalty is to you and James. I'll just call the colonel and tell him..."

Anne smiled and stood. She walked to her husband and sat smartly on his lap, turning her head to face him. "I've known who I was going to marry from the first day I met you," she said simply. "I know your feelings about the Marine Corps. I know you can't say 'no' when someone asks you for help."

Morgan opened his mouth to protest. Anne placed her index finger gently across his lips to silence him. "I appreciate that you're thinking of James and me," she said. "We know that you love us. But we know you."

Morgan began to shake his head. Anne held his cheeks between her slender fingers and leaned forward to kiss his mouth.

"Now finish that beer and go pack," she said firmly. "How many times have you told me? Once a Marine..."

*   *   *

Morgan strode quickly to Lieutenant Colonel Jim Bennett's desk and snapped to an awkward position of attention. He was dressed in civilian slacks and shirt with a sweater he had purchased during a train stop in Norfolk, Virginia to blunt the effects of the winter weather. He did not salute the colonel as his head was bare.

"Morgan Early!" Colonel Bennett said in a robust voice when he looked up from the pile of papers on his desk. "At ease!"

Morgan spread his feet precisely eighteen inches and locked his hands behind his back.

The colonel pushed from his chair and walked briskly around his desk. He reached for Morgan's right arm, pulled it free and shook his hand vigorously.

"How have you been?" he asked sincerely. "You don't look a day older than that time in the woods when you single-handedly overran the Hun and pulled my sorry butt back to our lines."

"I...I've been well, thank you, sir," Morgan replied, slightly overwhelmed by the friendly, unmilitary, reception he was receiving from the colonel.

"Good," the colonel said, nodding with approval and pointing to a comfortable chair. "Sit down. Sit down."

Morgan broke his stiff posture and eased into the padded seat. "You spoke to my wife," he began hesitantly.

"Yes," the colonel admitted. "I thought a telegram from the commandant was a little cold."

293

"Can I really be recalled into service?" Morgan asked. "I never knew that was possible."

Lieutenant Colonel Bennett lifted his hands and shrugged. "For officers, yes, it's possible."

"I guess I'm confused," Morgan began. "If you want me to serve, I'm more than willing to do what I can. But I don't see how I can be of service. I haven't been a Marine for over twenty years. I don't know anything about the modern weapons. Certainly there are younger officers that can be of assistance."

Colonel Bennett tapped his cheek with his index finger as Morgan was talking. A wide grin slowly spread across his face and he shook his head with polite disagreement. "Morgan, you still have the innate ability to totally discount your talents that you constantly displayed in France."

"But sir..."

The colonel held up his hand for silence. "You're a natural leader. The men all looked up to you in the company. You have an inherent ability to understand the flow of a battle among the chaos and confusion of combat. You never panicked when panic was fully justified. You simply assessed the situation and moved forward. This type of leadership is rare and will be vital for the role the Marine Corps has drawn in this war."

"The Hun were a formidable opponent in the Great War," Morgan conceded. "I imagine they'll be even more determined this time."

Colonel Bennett closed his eyes briefly and waved his hand. "The Germans will be the army's problem this time. Our job will be the Japs."

Morgan sat quietly for a moment. "I don't know anything about fighting the Japanese," he said slowly.

"Neither does anybody else," Bennett said. "We're going to have to figure out how to succeed at the most difficult military challenge of all: direct frontal invasions of heavily fortified islands in the Pacific."

Morgan shifted in his chair and re-crossed his legs. "I read about the invasion of Galippoli by the Brits, the Aussies and the New Zealanders in 1915," he said. "It was an unmitigated disaster. They suffered nearly 175,000 causalities and finally had to withdraw."

"I've studied that campaign," the Colonel said sadly. "You have an accurate recollection of the battle."

"The Brits invented self-firing guns that they left in the trenches to keep the Turks from realizing they were evacuating," Morgan said shaking his head. "That's the only frontal invasion from the sea I know about."

"And that's the only model we have to study," Colonel Bennett said. "That's why we have to develop another way to conquer defended beaches from the sea."

Morgan drew a deep breath. "I don't know enough about our capabilities to help develop such a strategy," he said. "This is beyond my expertise."

"I agree with you," the colonel said. "The development of the techniques is not why I asked for you. Your responsibility will be the preparation of the men for this difficult task."

Morgan opened his mouth, but Bennett silenced him with a shake of his head. "You know combat in all its horror and terror. I need you to train the men in my battalion to overcome their fear, survive the initial shock of combat, storm those defended beaches, and throw those Japs from their positions."

"There won't be any cover on the beaches," Morgan observed, already thinking of the terrifying problem of rushing from a small boat against rifle and machine gun fire.

"We need those islands," the colonel said. "The Pacific is enormous. To conquer Japan we need bases all the way across the ocean. You have to develop men willing and able to hit those beaches and win."

"Where will we be training?" Morgan asked.

"I am the commanding officer of the 2nd Battalion, 2nd Regiment of the 2nd Marine Division," Lt. Colonel Bennett explained. "You, Major Early, will be my executive officer. You and I leave by military transport tonight for Camp Elliot, California."

"I haven't unpacked from Bimini, colonel," Morgan said. "I'm ready to fly."

"Make me proud of my troops, major," Bennett said as he rose and extended his hand. "We've a war to win."

Hank Manley

(What's a self-firing gun? British soldiers attached an open container to the trigger of a rifle by a lanyard through a pulley. They punctured a canteen and allowed water to slowly drip into the container as they departed their positions. When a sufficient weight of water fell into the container to overcome the natural resistance of the trigger mechanism, the trigger pulled and the weapon "self-fired".)

~ 57 ~

Major Morgan Early stood with the commanders of the four companies of the 2nd Battalion, 2nd Regiment, known as the 2-2 in Marine parlance. The group was on a sand dune overlooking a shallow ditch near the Pacific Ocean at Camp Elliot, California, home of the 2nd Marine Division.

At the far end of the depression a .30 caliber M-1919A4 air-cooled, belt-fed, light machine gun was mounted on a concrete slab. The barrel rested on a horizontal piece of pipe that was held rigidly in place by two vertical uprights so the weapon could traverse fire but not aim toward the ground.

At the near end of the ditch a platoon of nervous Marines with their lieutenant, dressed in 1941 sage green, herringbone twill, utility combat uniforms, awaited Morgan's whistle. The famous "bird-on-a-ball" was stenciled above the black letters USMC on the left breast of each shapeless jacket.

Strewn in the trench through which the Marines were about to crawl, live machine gun bullets rattling inches above their heads, were the bloody guts and squishy intestines of four dozen chickens.

"Gentlemen," Morgan addressed the four captains standing, fascinated, by his side. "I wish to make our training of these young Marines as realistic as possible. Everything we can do to make them inured to the horrors of combat will increase their chances of survival."

Morgan placed the whistle in his mouth and blew.

The platoon of Marine riflemen dropped to their knees and elbows and began crawling through the wet, mushy entrails of the butchered chickens. Their M-1, .30 caliber, Garand semi-automatic rifles, capable of firing eight rounds, were held tightly across their forearms. The Marines' initial instinct was to lift slightly to avoid facing the grisly mess on the ground.

Following Morgan's nod, the machine gun rattled.

The Marines' intuitive reaction was to bury themselves lower in the grotesque innards of the butchered fowl.

A young Marine gagged as his face pressed into a bloody intestine. He rose on his arms to avoid the vomit pouring from his mouth.

"Stay down," Morgan screamed. "If you raise your head, you will die. Your job is to kill Japs, not become casualties."

Another Marine stopped crawling. A whimper of revulsion and fear issued from his mouth. He closed his eyes and cursed his stupidity for joining the Marine Corps.

"Keep moving," Morgan yelled. "If you stop, you will die. The only way to live is to advance and kill your enemy."

One of the captains observing the exercise turned to his fellow officers and indicated Morgan with his thumb. "Who is this guy?" he mouthed. Morgan's sudden appearance at the Marine base had come as a surprise to the other officers in the battalion. Nobody knew him, and nobody knew his background.

Morgan had been friendly while observing strict military courtesy with his fellow officers. He had not discussed his previous Marine Corps experience or his relationship with Lt. Colonel Bennett.

"What's inured?" another asked with a chuckle behind an open hand over his mouth.

"Isn't this drill a little crazy," another captain ventured in a half whisper. "Chicken parts?"

The platoon crawled through the length of the trench and emerged blood stained, revolted and shaking.

Morgan sliced his hand across his throat, and the machine gun ceased firing. He turned to the four captains. "How many of you have ever been shot at?" he asked casually.

None of the four answered in the affirmative.

"Then there's no time like the present. Get to the beginning of that enfilade," Morgan said.

"You want us to..." one of the captains began.

"Stand at attention, captain," Morgan replied without rancor.

The captain braced and stood rigidly at attention. His eyes bored straight into the hot California air.

Morgan walked directly in front of the officer. He pressed his face inches from the captain. "I don't know where we're going. I don't know what we'll be facing. But when we get there, and I give you an order, you'll only have one response. That response will be 'aye, aye, sir'. Is that understood?"

The captain blinked and swallowed. "Yes, sir."

"Now, get to the beginning of that trench. All four of you," Morgan barked. "You will never order your men to do something you won't do."

"Yes, sir," the four captains barked in unison.

"That's better," Morgan said. "Come on. Follow me. We're going for a little crawl together."

*　　*　　*

I understand you made quite an impression on the captains of the 2-2 companies," Lt. Colonel Bennett said to Morgan at a corner table of the officers' club.

"I hope so, sir," Morgan replied. "Leadership has its responsibilities. If the men don't respect the officers, they'll never follow them into combat."

Bennett smiled and sipped on his Scotch. "I believe you're beginning to understand why I wanted you to train these men," he said with a small laugh.

"Sir," Morgan began. "Do you have any idea where they're going to send us?"

"If I knew, I couldn't tell you," Lt. Colonel Bennett said.

"I understand, but if I had an idea of the island, sir," Morgan continued, "I could study the terrain and better prepare the men for the invasion."

"Believe me, major. I wish I knew where we were going as much as you do. I suspect we won't be told until we're aboard ship."

Morgan lifted his bottle of beer and drained the remains. "If I was the Japs, and I was going to defend an island," he mused after swallowing the last of his beer, "I wouldn't be *on* the island. I would be *in* the island."

The colonel wrinkled his brow and looked inquisitively at Morgan. "You'd be *in* the island?" he repeated.

"Yes, sir," Morgan continued. "I'd dig fortifications and fight from underground bunkers and pillboxes."

"Impervious to a pre-invasion barrage," the colonel reflected. "Very difficult to attack."

"With your permission, sir," Morgan said. "I'd like to concentrate on attacking buried fortifications. I want to train the men to concentrate suppressing fire on ground level firing positions while others advance with satchels of explosives and flame throwers."

"If you're right, Morgan," the colonel said pensively, "the only way to neutralize such positions is as you suggest."

"That's my idea, sir," Morgan said as a waitress delivered another round of drinks.

"Proceed as you recommend, major," Lt. Colonel Bennett said reaching for his fresh Scotch.

"I plan to emphasize a great deal of individual initiative in the training," Morgan said. "No invasion will proceed according to plan. Units will be separated while attacking the beach. Commanders will be cut off from their platoons. The men must be taught to think and act on their own."

"The men must be taught to obey instantly, under the most difficult conditions," the colonel stated.

"I agree, sir," Morgan said. "But what if the platoon leaders and company commanders are killed? What if the sergeants are killed? The men must advance even if leaderless. They can't be paralyzed because their leaders are not available."

Lt. Colonel Bennett leaned back in his chair and raised his eyes to the ceiling. The chain of command was paramount in the Marine Corps. Instant, unquestioning obedience to orders was ingrained in every Marine. But what if there was nobody to give the orders?

"I approve your idea, major," the colonel said. "Proceed with the training."

"Thank you, sir," Morgan said. "I hope I'm right."

"I do, too, Morgan," Lt. Colonel Bennett said. "I've already bet my career on it."

*　　*　　*

The Marines and officers of the three rifle companies of the 2-2 knelt in the sand below a dune stretching inland from the California coast. At the crest of the rise a plywood gun emplacement was barely visible fourteen inches above the surface. From a ten-inch slit in the horizontal face of the fortification the cylindrical barrel of a .30 caliber machine gun was visible.

"Traverse the weapon," Morgan called to the Marine manning the mock pillbox.

The Marines watched as the barrel of the weapon swung left and right to the limit of the opening.

"Fire with tracer rounds only," Morgan ordered. "Traverse left to right and back again."

The machine gun abruptly barked RAT-A-TAT-TAT, RAT-A-TAT-TAT, RAT-A-TAT-TAT. Green colored rounds spit from the end of the barrel, allowing the huddled Marines to witness the direction and pattern of the weapon's fire.

"Cease fire," Morgan yelled when the machine gun had passed back and forth across the slot.

He turned and addressed the young Marines. "I don't know what the Nips will have on the beaches," he said. "But if I were to defend an island, this is an example of what I would use."

The Marines looked apprehensively at one another.

"When you hit the beaches there will be confusion. There will be smoke. There will be deafening noise. There will be wounded. There will be dead bodies," Morgan said as he paced slowly in front of the assembled Marines. "You may be separated from your unit. Your officer may be dead or wounded or missing. Your sergeant may be nowhere in sight. There may be no one to give you orders."

The assembled young men shuffled nervously.

"But I am giving you orders here, today," Morgan said. "You will move forward and you will engage the enemy. You will not stay in one place. You will attack!"

Turning to three of the privates in the front row, Morgan pointed. "You three," he said as he lobbed a square canvas sack roughly

301

the size of a baseball base. "You have five seconds to formulate a plan to knock out that fortification. You have your rifles and hand grenades. And you have that satchel of explosives. Now move!"

The three young Marines looked stunned. "But sir," the first protested. "We've never been trained to knock out a machine gun."

"And when you hit that beach, you'll see things you haven't been trained to deal with, private. That's why you have to use your own initiative and act with speed and decisiveness. Go!" Morgan ordered.

The private holding the simulated satchel of explosives waved to his comrades. "Lay down suppressing fire on that emplacement," he yelled. "I'll crawl forward and toss these explosives."

"Open fire," Morgan called to the machine gunner. "Blanks and tracers."

Immediately the .30 caliber, air-cooled, light machine gun began to rattle blank shells interspersed with green tracer rounds.

The two Marines dropped to prone positions and fired blank rounds from their M-1 rifles toward the slot of the plywood pillbox.

The first Marine private began a frenzied crawl toward the simulated enemy position.

"Stay outside the lateral range of the machine gun," Morgan called. "Pick a line wide of the tracers."

The Marine with the satchel of explosives scooted sideways, beyond the spread of tracer rounds.

"Excellent, private," Morgan called. "Excellent."

The two Marines supplying suppressing fire both stopped shooting at the same time and reached for fresh clips of bullets.

"Stagger your fire," Morgan called. "Don't run out at the same time. You've got to keep the Nips occupied so your buddy can advance."

"Yes, sir," the Marines acknowledged together.

The two privates thumbed new clips of eight rounds into their weapons and began a measured, alternating, series of fire. The first Marine slithered toward the edge of the slot in the plywood fortification and heaved the satchel through the opening.

The Marine manning the machine gun stood and executed a dramatic death dive over the short fascia of the pillbox. The entire assembly of Marines laughed and cheered the performance.

Morgan walked forward. An enormous smile creased his face. "Outstanding," he said. "I pity those Japs when you guys hit the beaches."

~ 58 ~

Morgan folded his weekly letter to Anne and placed it in the envelope. He licked the flap, sealed it, and flipped it into his "out" basket. In the morning the 2nd Division was scheduled to ship out to Wellington, New Zealand.

My Darling Anne,

We have finished our training here and will depart by ship to a destination I cannot reveal because of the censors. However, I can tell you I am looking forward to our next base with new zeal and enthusiasm.

We have not been told of our mission,

but the men have responded to my training. I pity the Japs when we finally engage them. These are wonderful men that I have the privilege of serving with.

Please give James my love and a hug. I miss you both terribly, but I feel I may be making a small contribution to the war effort.

I will write weekly, but I'm uncertain how frequently the mail will be delivered. Please keep up your letters. They are very important to me.

All my love,   Morgan

Lt. Colonel Bennett knocked on Morgan's door and entered his office. He flopped in a chair in front of the

Morgan's desk and lit a cigar.

"Are the men ready?" he asked.

"I believe so," Morgan said.

"We'll be in New Zealand for a few more months," Bennett said as he blew a stream of tobacco smoke toward the ceiling. "Keep at the men. Don't let them lose their edge. I suspect we'll be in combat before the end of the year."

Morgan looked at his commanding officer and nodded slowly. "Do you have any idea where we're going?" he asked.

Colonel Bennett shook his head. "I don't," he said. "But I'm hearing we'll be guinea pigs, responsible for executing new beach landing tactics that will be needed for the conquest of Japan and Europe."

Morgan nodded. "I understand, sir," he said. "The men will be ready. I promise. They're a fine group."

"We'll be commencing amphibious assault exercises at a place called Hawke Bay," the colonel said.

Morgan drew a long breath and slowly released it. At last the fight was close. The months of training were coming to an end. The time was near when his efforts to harden the men and prepare them for the most horrendous experience of their lives would be tested. Victory was the only acceptable outcome. There was no provision for retreat from a bloody beach.

*   *   *

"New Zealand's own Marine Division", as the country had proudly proclaimed the 2nd, sailed away from Wellington on November 1, 1943. Elaborate plans were made to disguise the real nature of the departure. Rumors were circulated that the division was simply off on another landing exercise to Hawke Bay. The truth was far more grim. The 2nd Division, destined never to return to New Zealand, was headed for a small atoll in the Gilbert Islands called Tarawa and a tiny island named Betio (pronounced Bay-sho) located only eighty miles north of the equator that measured a mere one square mile. At its widest point, Betio was a scant 800 yards wide and only two and a half miles long. At its highest point, the island was only twelve feet above sea level.

There were two justifications for landing American Marines on this pathetic dollop of sand: to secure the 4000 foot runway needed by the Army Air Corps, and to test invasion methods that would be needed later against Japan and Fortress Europe.

Betio was surrounded by a coral reef that extended between 800 and 1200 yards from the shore. Much attention had been paid to the reef in the planning of the invasion. A group of sixteen English, New Zealand and Australian expatriates who had lived and worked on the island were gathered and queried about the tides. During the lunar cycle, there are two types of tides that occur: spring tides and neap tides. Both tides have highs and lows with the neap tides having less depth than the spring tides. Neap tides occur during the first and third quarter of the moon cycle. Betio was to be attacked on November 20th, during the neap tide phase.

In certain parts of the world, the Tarawa Atoll included, there are "dodging" tides. A low dodging tide is lower than a neap tide, and a dodging tide was a distinct possibility on the day of the invasion.

Major Frank Holland, one of the "Foreign Legion" of sixteen advisers who had lived on Tarawa for fifteen years as resident commissioner, vehemently advised that the tides would be too low on November 20th for the landing craft to reach the beaches. He had made elaborate studies of the tides during his time on the atoll, and he was convinced a dodging tide would occur that would leave no more than three feet of water over the reefs. Tragically for hundreds of Marines, Major Holland's protestations were ultimately ignored and the assault was ordered to proceed as planned. The Marine corpses that would float bloated and bloody in the surf would remain as silent testimony to the intransigence of the commanders.

The 2nd Marine Division consisted of approximately 20,000 men. The core of the division's fighting strength was provided by the 2nd, 6th and 8th Marine regiments. Each regiment officially carried 3,242 men, roughly divided into three battalions plus a headquarters, a service and a weapons component.

Each battalion consisted of a headquarters company, a weapons company and three rifle companies. The rifle companies had a headquarters element and three rifle platoons that, at full strength, numbered forty-two men.

Opposing this invasion force were 4,836 elite Japanese, most either of the Yokosuka or 7th Sasebo Special Naval Landing Force –

the *rikusentai* or "Imperial Marines". Fourteen heavy coastal defense guns, forty to fifty medium field pieces and more than thirty single and twin-mounted heavy machine guns were located around the perimeter of the tiny island. Well prepared emplacements consisting of palm trunk logs, concrete, and heaped sand, and coral, along with barbed wire entanglements, anti-tank ditches and mine fields fortified Betio and hid the defenders from artillery and naval fire. The Japanese were literally *in* Betio rather than simply on it.

The Japanese commander, Rear Admiral Keiji Shibasaki, issued unequivocal orders. The defenders were "to wait until the enemy was within effective range and direct fire on the enemy transport and destroy it. If the enemy starts a landing, knock out the landing boats with gunfire, then concentrate all fire on the enemy's landing point and destroy him at the water's edge."

> *My dearest Anne,*
> *Tomorrow we attack. I don't know if this letter will ever reach you, or if I will ever see you again. There is talk the landing will be only lightly opposed. We could see the island for the first time yesterday, and it is tiny. Perhaps there are few Japanese defenders.*
> *My only fear is that I have not prepared the men sufficiently. There really is no way to prepare for combat.*
> *Should this be my last battle, I want you to know how much I love you and cherish the years we have spent together. You have truly made me the happiest man in the world. Hug James for me.*
> *All my love to you both,   Morgan*

Lt. Colonel Bennett approached Morgan as he stood at the railing of the transport ship. The sun was fading beneath the horizon to the west and the faint outline of Betio was cast in relief eleven miles to the east. The ship's engine, throbbing quietly beneath the heavy deck plates, provided the only sound. Dim glimpses of the other seventeen troop carriers in the convoy appeared as they maneuvered to hold position under strict blackout conditions.

"You've done a wonderful job with the men," Colonel Bennett said. "There's nothing further you can do. Why don't you go ashore with me in the morning? You don't have to go with the first waves."

Morgan turned slowly and looked at his commanding officer. He pursed his lips and drew a long breath that he held in his lungs for several seconds before releasing. The colonel was giving him a chance to live. He was being offered an opportunity to see his beloved Anne again. He would be able to see his son grow to become a man.

Morgan closed his eyes. Anne's indelible image flickered across the screen of his imagination. His wife smiled and beckoned as she skipped along the pure white beach in front of their house in Bimini. Her eyes danced with mischievous humor as she mouthed "follow me" into the gentle fall breeze. Morgan felt his heart squeeze tight with longing and love.

He opened his eyes and looked down at the camouflage cloth covering his M-1 steel helmet, a uniform affectation that had already become a Marine trademark. Tormented ambivalence raked his mind. Should he go ashore with the colonel on a later, safer, landing craft and enhance his chances of going home to his family? Or should he fulfill his commitment to his men and join them in the initial assault.

"I appreciate your thoughts, sir," Morgan said at last. "But I told the men I would be there for them when they needed me."

"There's no disgrace in coming with me," Colonel Bennett said.

Morgan shrugged. "It's getting to be a little late to put me in an early grave, sir. I'll go ashore as planned."

~ 59 ~

At 4:41 AM on the morning of November 20, 1943, a single red star shell zipped into the sky from the center of Betio. The strange occurrence was witnessed by thousands of Marines who had commenced disembarkation from the troop carriers, ending any hope that the Japanese had abandoned the island.

Twenty minutes later the assembled battleships and cruisers swung into position and began a bombardment of the island. Sixteen-inch guns fired massive shells weighing over two thousand pounds at tiny Betio. Within a minute massive explosions erupted on the island as an ammunition dump exploded. Flame-tinged black clouds ballooned toward the sky, momentarily silhouetting the multitude of palm trees on the shore.

Morgan stood with his men alongside the railing. The Marines were dressed in a combination of the old 1941 sage green utilities and the new 1942 camouflage-printed herringbone twill uniforms. Ankle length brown "boondocker" boots covered their feet. The canvas web leggings, which extended from the instep to the calf, had been largely discarded as the men considered them hot and difficult to remove in order to treat a wound.

Each Marine carried his "782 gear" which consisted of the basic web fighting harness and haversack. The rifle belt contained ammunition clips in the eight snap-fastened pockets, a field dressing pouch, steel canteens in web carriers and a K-bar knife. Suspenders supported the web belt and were linked to the haversack, which contained combat rations, eating utensils, spare underclothes, extra ammunition and a soft utility cap. A folding entrenching tool that acted as a shovel or a spade and a bayonet were hooked to tabs from the haversack.

Nervous sweat poured from the men in the early hours of the morning. Apprehension about the coming battle churned the glands in each Marine. The heated air from the relentless bombardment added to the natural discomfort of Betio's close proximity to the equator. The burden of carrying over one hundred pounds of equipment – in addition to their own packs and weapons the men carried radios, mortars, disassembled machine guns, flame throwers, demolition charges, and huge quantities of extra ammunition for the crew-served weapons – sapped the strength of even the most fit Marines.

"Over the side," Morgan yelled when the order for his battalion to disembark was issued. His voice was barely discernable over the unimaginable noise of the battleships' guns that sent salvo after salvo of deadly explosives whistling toward Betio in the most concentrated pre-invasion bombardment in naval history.

The men struggled awkwardly over the railing and proceeded unsteadily down the cargo nets, careful to grip only the vertical ropes to avoid trampling by the boots of the man above. Each Marine focused a jaundiced eye on the gap at the bottom of the net that continually opened and closed like the yawning maw of a deadly monster as the landing craft bobbing below alternately slammed against the hull of the troop ship and then bounced wildly away.

"There can't be a living thing on that island after this bombardment," one of the Marines noted as another series of explosions erupted on the island with a monstrous flash.

"Them navy boys promised to obliterate the island," another laughed. "It looks like they're going to keep their promise."

*   *   *

Morgan jumped the last five feet from the dangling cargo net that was slapping wildly against the side of the hull. He landed on the deck of the plywood Higgins boat designated a LCVP – Landing Craft Vehicle/Personnel.

The first three waves of Marines were aboard amphibian tractors known as "amtracs", with caterpillar tracks that would allow them to crawl unimpeded over the reefs. Forty-two LVT-1s, each carrying eighteen Marines, and forty-five LVT-2s, carrying twenty Marines, churned toward the beaches of Betio. Fifteen hundred young, scared, wet and queasy Marines, attempting the first successful frontal attack in history against a fortified beach, plowed relentlessly toward a hostile enemy held island.

The Higgins boats, making up the fourth, fifth and sixth invasion waves, formed up in the rendezvous area three and a half miles outside the lagoon at 8:30 am. They proceeded at an agonizing four-knot pace behind the amtracs until they reached the line of departure. The landing craft then wheeled toward Betio and began to chug the final three miles to the designated beaches.

Morgan peered over the top of the blunt steel ramp of the LCVP. The naval gunfire was to continue until the first assault craft were one mile from the shore. Fire and smoke engulfed the island. Airplanes were diving to deliver heavy bombs on suspected defense fortifications. Japanese heavy machine guns began sweeping the unarmored boats with menacing fire. Seawater splashed over the sides of the Higgins from the confused wake of the amtracs ahead. A chalky cloud of dust hung over the entire island from the coral rock pulverized by the shelling. A blazing fuel dump threw a thick column of oily smoke hundreds of feet into the air.

A Marine kneeling on the deck of the Higgins boat stood to vomit his steak and scrambled eggs overboard. The wind blew the detritus of his breakfast back into his face.

Morgan tapped a lieutenant on the shoulder and pointed. A patch of coral lay drying in the sun when the landing boat was still seven hundred yards from the beach. Instead of the four or five feet of water over the reef that had been expected, only three feet existed. The amtracs would be able to claw their way over the reefs; the Higgins boats were destined to ground.

"Keep the men spread out if we have to wade ashore," Morgan shouted. "Don't give the Japs a concentrated target."

The lieutenant blanched. "We can't get out here, major," he yelled back. "It'll be suicide."

"It'll be suicide to stay if the boat runs aground," Morgan called.

311

Machine gun fire punched through the plywood sides of the Higgins boats. Artillery exploded in the lagoon, showering water into the bobbing craft. An amtrac wallowed in the churned water, its driver dead at the controls. Bullets found the unarmored fuel tank and the boat burst into flames and exploded. An LCVP ten yards from Morgan's boat was blown apart by a direct hit from a shore battery.

Morgan's Higgins lurched to a sudden stop, solidly aground five hundred yards from their objective, Red Beach 2.

"Get out," Morgan shouted. "Everybody get in the water!"

*   *   *

Morgan rolled over the side of the Higgins boat with his M-1 carbine held over his head. His feet hit the coral bottom and the water came to his chest. A Marine landed five feet behind him and vanished into a depression in the reef. He drowned before Morgan could pull him to the surface, tangled in his heavy equipment. A corporal paused at the lip of the landing craft before jumping. A hail of machine gun fire ripped across his chest and he slumped over the hull side, leaking blood into the lagoon.

"Move!" Morgan shouted. "Stay spread out, but move toward the beach!"

Bullets stitched the surface of the lagoon, raising tiny plumes as they pierced the water. Morgan waded as rapidly as possible along the periphery of the fields of fire toward Betio. Men struggled to walk in the water under their burdens of arms and ammunition. Japanese fire raked across the advancing Marines, puncturing bodies and tearing vital organs. Men staggered and fell, their cries of agony drowned in the sea.

Morgan plowed through the lagoon as the water sucked at his boots and dragged against his equipment. Machine gun rounds sprayed the surface. Explosions erupted, sending geysers of incarnadine water into the air. Morgan tripped over a submerged corpse pressed to the bottom by the weight of his rifle and ammunition and a radio strapped to his back. He fell to one knee, barely keeping his carbine dry, before trudging relentlessly forward another three hundred yards through a hail of lead, shrapnel and flames.

312

Dozens of dead Marines lay along the beaches, blood clouding the water around their bodies. The hulks of exploded, burning and disabled landing craft, twisted and akimbo on the reefs, littered the shoreline.

Ahead, Marines crouched behind a coconut log seawall that rose three feet above the beach. Morgan sloshed from the water and fell on the sand behind the safety of the wall.

He turned to the six men huddled beneath the logs. "We can't stay here," he yelled. "We've got to advance and knock out those Jap positions."

"They're murdering us, major!" one of the Marines whimpered.

"Check your weapons," Morgan shouted over the cacophony of the battle raging all around. "We're going over this wall and do some killing of our own."

"I lost my M-1 on the way in, major," another Marine said.

Morgan turned and pointed to the beach. Eight dead Marines washed in the surf with the waves. "Get one of those Garands," he ordered. "Grab that satchel of explosives and all the hand grenades you can find."

The six Marines crawled toward the dead bodies, stripped them of their grenades and weapons, and rejoined Morgan.

"You three deliver covering fire over the wall," he yelled. "You others come with me. Do not stop until I stop. Understood?"

The corporal and two privates nodded apprehensively.

"As soon as you see us arrive at some shelter," Morgan continued, pointing to the first group of three Marines, "get over that wall and join us. We'll lay down fire to cover your advance."

"Shouldn't we wait until others join us?" one of the privates protested. "There's only the seven of us."

"Look out there," Morgan snarled as he pointed to the debacle in the lagoon. Landing craft were burning. Enemy shells were exploding. Marines were wading ashore through sheets of machine gun fire and rifle bullets and dying. "Unless we kill these Japs, nobody else is getting ashore."

"The major's right," the corporal said. "I'm tired of sitting here. It's time we did some killing."

"All right," Morgan said. "Start firing."

313

The three Marine privates pushed cautiously upward until they could see over the log wall. They positioned their M-1 Garands on the ledge, selected targets and began firing.

Morgan, the corporal and two privates slithered over the wall and began crawling rapidly inland under the cover of the rifle fire delivered by their comrades. The sand stuck to their wet uniforms. Their haversacks and entrenching tools and bayonets weighed heavily on their backs. Oily smoke invaded their lungs. The hot, tropical air sucked perspiration from their skin. Continuous explosions assaulted their ears. The smell of death and rapidly decomposing flesh choked their nostrils.

"This way, major," the corporal yelled as he pointed toward a mound of sand topped by two fallen palm trees that offered a modicum of cover.

The four men scrambled behind the natural barricade and took up firing positions. To one side and in front, Japanese machine guns blazed toward the lagoon, seeking targets of opportunity as more Marines trudged through the water from destroyed and grounded Higgins boats.

"See that bunker?" Morgan called to the corporal. He pointed to a narrow slit covered with logs and sand thirty yards in the distance.

"Cover me," the corporal yelled as he grabbed a satchel of explosives just as the three Marines from the seawall dove into the position.

Morgan pulled a hand grenade from his front pocket, yanked the pin and tossed it toward the Jap machine gun. The grenade sputtered through the air and exploded in front of the horizontal opening.

"Fill that slit with fire," Morgan directed to the three new arrivals.

The corporal crawled toward the Jap position with the satchel strap locked around his elbow. Five Marines methodically poured .30 caliber rounds into the enemy bunker.

A Japanese soldier appeared from behind the bunker and trained his rifle on the prone corporal. He squeezed his trigger and a red blotch appeared on the back of the Marine's leg. The corporal screamed with pain and clutched the wound.

Three M-1 Garands swung to the enemy target. The soldier's chest exploded as five rounds plowed into his body.

The corporal released his hand from his leg and continued crawling. He pulled the lanyard that activated the explosive charge, threw the satchel like a discus into the opening, and rolled away from the slit.

The concentrated explosion blew apart the coconut logs framing the bunker opening. Sand mushroomed upward from the covering and then fell into the resultant hole.

Morgan stood and charged the exposed position with his carbine ready. A Japanese soldier stood, blood dripping from his ears. Morgan flattened him with two shots to the head. Another struggled to reach his knees and groped for his weapon. Morgan shot him in the heart.

"How are you, corporal?" Morgan asked as he looked at the leg wound of the Marine who had delivered the deadly charge of explosives.

"It's just a scratch, major," the corporal replied. "A million dollar wound."

"You're a good Marine," Morgan said as he patted him on the shoulder. "I'll see if I can find a corpsman."

"Just keep the men moving," the corporal said as he rested against the side of the enemy bunker and reached for a cigarette in his pocket. "There's lots of other bunkers on this spit of an island that need attention."

"Rest easy," Morgan said. "Semper Fi."

"Go get 'em, major."

Morgan turned to the other Marines and waved them forward. "Come on," he called. "We're not finished yet."

One of the privates approached Morgan. "Is there any water, major?" he asked through cracked lips. "My canteens are empty."

Morgan turned to face the private. He reached behind his web belt for one of his canteens and held it out. The Marine stepped forward then suddenly stopped with a bewildered look on his face. A pulpy red spot appeared on his forehead where a Japanese bullet had entered his brain.

The reality of the desperate situation struck Morgan with acute intensity. The pre-invasion bombardment had accomplished little beyond providing spectacular pyrotechnics. The Japanese defenders had hunkered deep in their interconnected tunnels and survived the shelling without appreciable causalities. The brief suspension of fire before the amtracs hit the beaches afforded the enemy a precious ten-minute respite to man their weapons and begin a murderous fire on the landing craft.

The brutal, tropical sun beating on Betio had sucked the energy from the Marines, many already dehydrated from continuous vomiting as they circled for hours at the rendezvous point in the bobbing assault craft. Drinking water was critically lacking on the island. The small force of six enlisted men Morgan had assembled was reduced to four. He understood that no continuous line of advance had been established. Small groups of Marines, operating independently, comprised of disparate units, would have to carry the fight to the enemy.

Communication with the ships offshore was impossible. The bulky radios carried by the Marines were largely ineffective after a heavy salt water dousing.

Command and control of the forces ashore was nonexistent. Few Marines landed on the correct beach. The landing craft drivers instinctively steered through the smoke toward the perceived direction of least enemy fire. Units were scattered, and communication between the few commanders surviving the landing and their scattered men was reduced to direct verbal contact.

Morgan's belief that the ultimate success of the invasion would depend on the ability of the individual Marines to overcome their revulsion of the massacre imposed on them by the Japs, and act independently to strike back, was about to be put to the definitive test.

~ 60 ~

Five thousand Marines had clamored out of landing craft on D Day, November 20th. As many as two thousand had died or been wounded. Almost no artillery had arrived on the beaches, and only seven tanks had successfully negotiated the lagoon.

During the course of the afternoon, Morgan assembled almost two hundred Marines, some from his own 2nd Battalion and others from the 1st Battalion that was supposed to land to the west on Red Beach 1.

He directed the Marines to blanket the enemy bunkers and fortifications with covering fire and neutralize the positions with hand grenades, satchels of explosives, Bangalore torpedoes and spewing flamethrowers. By evening they had destroyed more than a dozen strong points and advanced to the first taxiway of the airport, approximately three hundred yards inland.

"Dig in here," Morgan ordered as the oppressive heat of the day began to fade. "The Nips are sure to launch a *banzai* counterattack tonight. Shoot anything that moves."

By nightfall of D Day, the Marines' hold on Betio remained extremely tenuous. The 3rd Battalion occupied a tiny corner of Beach Red 1. Marines of the 2-2 and 1-2 occupied the eastern half of Beach Red 2. Beach Red 3 was partially occupied by elements of the 2-8 and 3-8. Most of the units were without their heavy weapons. There was no continuous line of defense. The Marines dug individual fighting holes, occupied destroyed bunkers and enemy trenches, and waited for the Japanese to counterattack.

Morgan did not sleep the night of D Day. He roamed between the men's positions, encouraging them to remain alert, inquiring about their rations, water and ammunition.

"We'll try to get some drinking water up tomorrow," he repeated from foxhole to foxhole. "We'll get some more ammunition soon. Tomorrow we'll push these Nips back and get off this hell hole of an island."

Inexplicably and miraculously, the night banzai charge never materialized.

The morning of D+1 broke bright and steamy with the addition of a sickening stench of rotting flesh pervading the entire island. One thousand yards offshore, in landing craft that had been waiting at the line of departure since mid-morning of D Day, the six hundred Marines of the 1-8 detected the smell of decomposition as they prepared to bob around for another ten hours.

"Major, what happened to those Nips last night," a lieutenant asked Morgan as the men began to stir when the sun cracked the horizon. "If they had attacked, they could have walked through us like shit through a Christmas goose."

"I don't know, lieutenant," Morgan replied. "We may never know. But in my opinion it was a mistake that will cost them this battle."

(To this day, historians debate the reason a banzai attack was not launched by the Japanese defenders. The most likely explanation is that a fortunate shell during the naval bombardment landed in the command bunker killing Rear Admiral Shibasaki and his staff. In contrast to the Marines, blind obedience to the Emperor was emphasized rather than individual initiative. When commanders were absent, the Japanese rarely acted aggressively and often committed suicide rather than risk capture, the ultimate humiliation. On the island of Apamama, 75 miles southeast of Tarawa, the Japanese commander, while addressing his men, accidentally shot himself in the head with a pistol. The distraught soldiers, unable to make decisions on their own, dug their own graves and killed themselves.)

* * *

"Grab something to eat," Morgan ordered as he walked between the groups of exhausted Marines. "We're going to take that airstrip."

The scattered Marines of the 1st and 2nd Battalions gathered ammunition and explosive charges and prepared to move out.

"Major," a Navy corpsman called. "I don't have any medical supplies.

"Send a few men to the beaches," Morgan advised. "Gather first aid kits from the dead."

"Aye, aye, sir," the corpsman said as he scurried off in the direction of the invasion beach.

Morgan called the three lieutenants and two sergeants together. He knelt in the sand, exhaustion drooping his shoulders as he sketched the outline of Betio with the tip of his bayonet.

"Here's the Burns-Philp wharf," he said drawing a long line pointing north into the lagoon. "We landed here on Red 2. Here's our position near the taxiway, and here's the runway going east and west through the middle of the island."

He looked up and surveyed the faces of the three officers and two non-commissioned officers. Fatigue pulled at their jowls. Their eyes were bloodshot and slightly glazed. Each had a thirty-hour growth of whiskers on his face, and each looked parched and pale.

Morgan pointed to the south, across the island. Bare palm trunks stood starkly against the blue sky, their tops sliced away by shrapnel, the fronds lying in piles at the base. Broken trees littered the surface in twisted disarray. Craters of sand surrounded deep pits blown into the terrain by the gigantic battleship shells. The condensed scene of destruction and chaos emphasized the amount of ordinance expended on the tiny island.

"We're going across the island," Morgan declared. "We won't stop until we hit the south shore. Form the men for a frontal assault and tell them to keep running until we get to the other side."

"How far do you think it is, major?" one of the lieutenants asked.

"No more than five hundred yards," Morgan replied. "Remember, no stopping, even if somebody's hit."

"Aye aye, sir," the men responded in unison.

Half an hour later, Morgan signaled for the attack to commence. Two hundred Marines rose from their positions and began to charge across the taxiway and then traverse the main airstrip. Machine gun fire fanned through the ranks. Individual rifle shots popped, but the energized Marines raced through the resistance and kept running until they killed the unprepared Japanese in the trenches along the south shore and took possession of their positions.

Casualties among the Marines were surprisingly light due to their aggressiveness and use of surprise.

Morgan bent over in the safety of a shell crater and panted to recapture his breath. "Have the men prepare for a counterattack," he shouted to the officers in a neighboring trench.

The three lieutenants jumped from their position and scattered to prepare the men.

The Japanese didn't wait long. Hordes of enemy soldiers appeared from covered fortifications and rushed, shouting and waving swords, toward the Marine line. Garand M-1 rifles snapped .30 caliber rounds in measured beats. The Japanese attackers fell in waves, their frenzied screams buried in the sand as they pitched forward.

Morgan shouldered his carbine, aimed and fired. Japanese *rikusentai* fell with every pull of his trigger. He fanned the barrel of his weapon across the field of attackers, careful to shoot the closest to his crater first.

An enemy soldier crawled behind a fallen palm tree within ten yards of Morgan's position. The man stood, his slightly protruding front teeth visible as he opened his mouth to scream. He raised his sword and charged.

Morgan fired at the rushing man, hitting him in the stomach. The bolt on his semi-automatic weapon flew open and remained in place. The carbine was empty. Morgan had exhausted the twenty round magazine.

The wounded Japanese soldier leapt at Morgan, his sword pointed straight ahead. Morgan swept the barrel of his weapon at the man's head to divert the point of the sword from its path, which was aimed directly at the center of his chest. The effort was only partially successful. The long, razor-sharp steel blade buried in the hollow of Morgan's right shoulder, beneath his collarbone.

Morgan grunted and fell back against the far wall of the crater, his steel helmet toppling from his head. The Japanese soldier crashed against Morgan's body, driving the sword nearly to the hilt. He released the handle of his saber and brought his two hands to Morgan's throat. He buried his fingers into Morgan's windpipe and squeezed.

Thick blood poured from Morgan's shoulder. His right arm turned numb and refused to move. The Jap grimaced from his own wound but increased the pressure of his choking grip. Morgan could smell his enemy's foul breath and the stench of his body odor.

Morgan reached behind his back with his left hand for the bayonet hanging in a sheath from his haversack. He clutched the handle of the weapon and pulled, but the pressure of Japanese soldier's body pinned the bayonet against the sandy wall of the crater.

Morgan felt his strength ebb. His eyes seemed to cloud and confusion swept across his consciousness. Was this the end? Would he never see his beautiful Anne again? Would he never again see James?

Morgan stretched his neck away from the Japanese soldier and pressed the back of his head against the sand. When he had achieved several inches of separation, Morgan snapped his head forward with all his remaining strength and smashed his forehead into the enemy soldier's nose.

Over the roar of explosions, the rattle of machine guns, the blasts of hand grenades and the snapping of rifle shots, Morgan heard the cartilage in the Japanese soldier's nose crunch. The enemy soldier removed his hands from Morgan's neck and released his pressure from Morgan's body as he pulled away in agony. Morgan tugged his bayonet free, swept it under the Jap's chin, and swiftly drew it across the soldier's neck.

A sheet of bright red blood cascaded from the vicious slash and poured across Morgan's chest. Morgan pushed the gagging, sputtering man from his body and fell back against the crater. His eyes fluttered. Darkness shrouded his vision. He reached for his right shoulder and crumpled to the bottom of the sandy crater.

(The turning point in the battle for Betio occurred shortly after the charge across the island on D+1. Significant numbers of Marines landed on Green Beach at the western end of the island and established a strong, continuous position by nightfall. Bloody fighting to eliminate individual Japanese strong points dominated much of D+3 as the Marines advanced east across Betio. At noon on D+4 all hostilities ceased. Marines killed in action numbered 47 officers and 790 enlisted men. In addition, there were 2,449 wounded. Of the Japanese garrison of 4,836, all but 17 were killed.)

~ 61 ~

Anne Early stood at the end of the Queen's Highway in Bimini facing the seaplane ramp. It was a blustery day in February, 1944, and a cold front had worked across the Gulf Stream sending temperatures plummeting on the island. Tears cascaded down her cheeks. She scrubbed her hands together in anxious anticipation as the pilot of the Chalk's Grumman Goose revved the twin engines to thrust the arriving plane from the water and up the concrete slope. The yellow Labrador puppy at her feet yelped uncertainly and wagged his tail with a mixture of excitement and confusion.

The cumbersome plane waddled across the street, seawater dripping from the hull and landing floats, and spun one hundred-eighty degrees to face the bay. The engines stopped and a door swung open. A narrow set of steps unfolded to the tarmac.

A gaunt figure appeared in the doorway, and Anne released a scream that caused the other Bahamians milling around the plane to look with concern in her direction.

"Morgan," she shouted as she bounced on her toes and waved vigorously. "Morgan, Morgan, Morgan!"

Morgan stepped carefully down the steps and thrust his left arm toward his wife. His right was encased in a cloth sling.

"You're home!" Anne yelled. "Oh, I was so worried. But now you're home, and I'm never letting you out of my sight."

"I missed you so much," Morgan said as he smothered Anne's face with kisses. "I'm never leaving again."

323

"I don't know whether to hug you to death or kill you," Anne said when she withdrew her head from Morgan amorous assault. "Colonel Bennett told me how you insisted on going ashore on that infernal little island with the fourth wave instead of waiting with him."

Morgan patted Anne's shoulder and managed a wan smile. "My men..." he said weakly. "I couldn't..."

Anne shook her head and muttered. "I know, I know. It's always 'your men' or 'your duty' or 'your friend'," she groused feebly as she tried to restrain the respect in her voice. "It's who you are, and I love you for it. But we've had a lifetime of it. Now it's my turn to be completely selfish."

Morgan smiled. "And it's my turn to devote all my attention to my family. By the way, where's James?" he asked looking around the landing area.

Anne lowered her head and brushed at a tear. "I couldn't tell you on the telephone," she said. "The doctors advised me not to upset you when you were recovering from your wound."

"Something has happened to James?" Morgan shouted as he faced Anne and gripped her shoulder with his left hand. "Tell me what happened."

"He's fine," Anne said hurriedly. "But he's not here. He's in Hawaii."

"Hawaii?" Morgan said in confusion. "What's he doing in...? Oh, no!"

Anne confined her sad response to a simple nod.

"You let him join the Marines? Why, darling?"

"I didn't let him join," Anne said defensively. "He read everything in the newspapers about the Marines on Guadalcanal, and he read about your unbelievable assault on Tarawa, and he took off for Miami and joined."

"Honey," Morgan began. "You shouldn't have let him go. It's not like what they write about in the newspapers. It's...it's more horrible than anybody can imagine. It's..." Morgan couldn't finish the sentence.

"He's so proud of you," Anne said simply. "You are all he talks about. He just wants you to be proud of him."

"I am proud of him," Morgan said slowly with a spreading smile. "But I don't know whether to hug him to death or just kill him for joining the Marines."

Anne squeezed Morgan's arm affectionately. "We'll call James when we get home. He's anxious to talk to you."

"And who's this little cutie bouncing around your ankles?" Morgan asked as he bent to scratch the Labrador puppy behind the ears. "He doesn't look like a regular scrawny Bimini dog."

"He's yours," Anne said with a sparkle in her eye. "He's your new canine companion. I thought you needed a pet after old Buckskin passed away."

Morgan squatted on the tarmac and reached out to rub the dog. The blonde Labrador licked Morgan's left hand enthusiastically and shook its rear happily. Suddenly the dog stopped and cocked his head uncertainly. His eyes focused on Morgan's damaged right shoulder, and he began to whimper and sniff and scratch the ground with a paw.

"That's strange," Morgan said. "It's almost as if he knows something's not right with my shoulder."

"I think you'll find your new dog very interesting," Anne said. "I've taught him to open the refrigerator and fetch a bottle of beer. He'll pick up your keys if you drop them and hand them to you."

"He opens the refrigerator?" Morgan repeated in amazement.

"Yes," Anne said. "I drape a towel through the handle, and he pulls on the towel to open the door."

"Hey, old man," Alrick Brown yelled as he jogged down the street toward Morgan. "How you doin'?"

"Hello, partner," Morgan called back as he extended his left hand in greeting.

"Anne tol' me you was comin' in today," Alrick said as he shook Morgan's left hand and hugged him warmly. "I cut short da fishin' trip an' put up da boat so I could see you firs' ting."

"What's this?" Morgan said with a loud laugh. "Is that gray I see popping up in your beard?"

"An' how 'bout dat white stuff on your head sprinkled in wid da yellow? Dat ain't gray hair, is it?"

Morgan placed his arm around Alrick's shoulders and squeezed gently. "We're just not the kids we used to be."

325

"What 'bout dat arm?" Alrick asked, his voice turning serious. "What you gonn' do 'bout dat?"

"The doctors told me they're not certain how it will heal," Anne said placing her hand tenderly on the damaged area. "Morgan just has to be careful for a while."

"The pain is pretty bad," Morgan conceded. "That Jap tore up a lot of flesh with his sword. It's difficult to move. But I still have one good arm to hug you with."

"Come on home, darling," Anne said as she reached for Morgan's Marine seabag. "Your war is over."

*   *   *

Morgan removed the sling from his arm and carefully eased his body to the bed. He grimaced with pain as he lowered his head to the pillow. His new companion, the blonde Labrador, sat on the floor beside Morgan and raised his moist nose in the air. His tail scribed slow arcs across the wood planking. Suddenly the dog jumped on the bed and walked toward Morgan.

Anne screamed at the dog. "Off the bed. Be careful of the shoulder."

The dog flopped to the sheets beside Morgan's right side and lowered his head gently to Morgan's right shoulder.

"Doesn't that hurt?" Anne asked in alarm. "I haven't been able to touch your shoulder once without drawing a pained reaction."

Morgan looked quizzically at Anne. He paused before speaking as if unsure of his response. "It...it doesn't hurt," Morgan said in a near whisper. "I was expecting pain, but it doesn't hurt at all."

Anne pushed to one elbow and stared at her husband lying peacefully, without pain, with the blonde Labrador's head directly on the angry, purple scars of his surgically repaired shoulder. "I can't believe it," she said. "Fetching a beer is one thing, but this..."

"I think I'll call him 'Doc'," Morgan said with a firm nod. "Doc Holliday. He certainly has a pleasant bedside manner. Welcome to the family, Doc."

"Doc Holliday?" Anne said quizzically. "Isn't that the tubercular dentist you told me about who was involved in the famous gunfight?"

Morgan nodded. "He was controversial, but he was a loyal friend to my uncle."

"I know," Anne said with a laugh. "And I understand how much loyalty means to you. You may be much more like your uncle Wyatt Earp than you realize."

~ 62 ~

The knock on the door in late February, 1945 surprised Anne Early as she stood at the kitchen sink scrubbing the lunch plates. Doc Holliday barked a friendly greeting and stood at the door wagging his tail expectantly.

Anne and Morgan had enjoyed heaping bowls of conch salad, generously sprinkled with locally caught shrimp and wafer thin medallions of raw tuna saturated with a tangy Tabasco sauce.

Morgan had kissed Anne affectionately and begged her forgiveness for leaving the dishes as he hustled to gather his fly rod and join his friend Cordell Rolle for an afternoon bonefishing on the flats.

Anne knitted her eyebrows in wonder. She couldn't recall the last time anyone had knocked on her door in daylight hours. Before evening, neighbors typically walked into the Early home and announced their presence with a hearty "hello".

Anne walked to the front door and paused. A cherubic brown face with downcast eyes stood nervously outside the screen.

"What's the matter, Clifton?" Anne asked as she opened the door. "You know you don't have to knock when you come calling during the day."

"Yes, Mrs. Early," the youth said without lifting his eyes from the stoop. "I gots a telegram for you."

"Well," Anne said cheerfully. "Let me see it, or do I have to guess what's inside?"

Silently Clifton handed Anne the small, yellow envelope with the cellophane window. He immediately turned and fled without making eye contact.

Anne stared at the telegram in her hand for several seconds, perplexed by the young boy's uncustomary behavior, and unnerved by the possible meaning of his timidity. Had Clifton seen the message at the telegraph station before it was placed in the envelope? Did a telegram ever contain good news?

With trembling fingers Anne peeled open the flap and withdrew the yellow parchment with pasted strips of type.

THE COMMANDANT OF THE MARINE CORPS REGRETS TO INFORM YOU OF THE DEATH OF YOUR SON CORPORAL JAMES EARLY STOP CORP EARLY WAS KILLED IN ACTION THIS DATE IWO JIMA STOP HE DIED HEROICALLY LEADING HIS SQUAD AGAINST ENEMY POSITION STOP CORP EARLY TO BE BURIED ARLINGTON NATIONAL CEMETERY STOP

Anne Early's legs buckled and she cascaded to the floor like a marionette with the strings suddenly severed. A groan of anguish poured from her throat, and she quickly gasped for air as she felt her head spin and wondered if she would faint.

Doc Holliday bounced to his feet from his customary position beside the door. A low growl of concern sounded deep in his throat. He approached Anne cautiously and placed his damp muzzle against her cheek.

With enormous effort, after several minutes lying prone on the floor, Anne crawled on hands and knees to the porch and looked through her tears toward the bay where Alrick Brown was cleaning the thirty-foot crawfish sloop.

"Alrick," she called in a desperate, cracking voice. "Alrick!"

Doc Holliday barked sharply twice, echoing Anne's plaintive call for help.

Alrick Brown looked toward the house with a furrowed brow. Was that Anne's voice? The timbre was familiar, but he had never heard such desperation and pain from Anne who was consistently strong and resolute. He was certain the dog had barked which was also very unusual.

"That you callin', Anne?" Alrick yelled back. "Sounds like you in trouble."

"Alrick, please come to the house," Anne beseeched in a fading voice as hysteria overcame her and she fell back to the floor.

"What's da matter?" Alrick screamed as he jumped from the boat, splashed through the shallow water, and dashed up the path toward the house.

Anne lay staring at the ceiling, unable to speak as her sobs choked off her words.

"You sick, Anne?" Alrick asked with panic in his voice when he banged open the screen door and saw Anne on the floor weeping uncontrollably.

"Get Morgan," she managed weakly through her tears. "He's fishing with Cordell."

"What is it? What's wrong wid you?"

Anne could only shake her head. "It's not me," she finally croaked. "It's James. He was killed on some god-forsaken island in the Pacific."

Alrick dropped his head into his hands and burst into tears. "I loved dat boy like he was my own," he blubbered into his palms. "I's so sorry, Anne," he said. "Oh, I can't tell you how sorry I is."

"Yes," Anne said, barely able to nod her head in recognition of Alrick's compassion. "He loved you, too."

"I'll go get Morgan," Alrick said after several awkward moments. He welcomed the chance to leave the house, but he dreaded the assigned task. "You want me to tell him?"

"No," Anne groaned. "I have to do it. Just get him back here. But tell him I'm okay."

"Dis ain't gonna be easy," Alrick said. "He gonna want to know what's wrong."

"Help me into a chair," Anne said. "I know it isn't going to be easy. This might be the hardest thing I've ever done."

*　　*　　*

Morgan pushed through the door without breaking stride and dashed to Anne's side. She was collapsed in a chair, her normal strong posture folded and shrunk with her grief, her shoulders rounded and her head hanging.

"Alrick wouldn't tell me what's wrong," he said as he knelt beside the chair and grabbed one of Anne's hands. "It's James, isn't it?"

Anne looked toward Morgan with puffy, red eyes. Her upper lip was moist from her running nose. She nodded and pointed to the telegram sitting on the cocktail table.

Morgan reached for the tattered yellow paper and held it in front of his face. His eyes focused on the first words then glazed over with tears. He was barely able to distinguish the last several lines, but their meaning was of no importance. Everything that needed to be said was contained on the first pasted strips.

Morgan crushed the telegram in his hand and threw the balled missive violently across the porch. He slumped back on his rear, lowered his head into his hands, and howled with pain and agony.

Anne reached for Morgan's shoulder and pulled him toward her in the chair. She wrapped her arms around her husband's chest. Her hot tears fell unabated from her cheeks.

"It's all my fault," Morgan wailed. "Why did he want to be a Marine?"

"Because your son loved you and wanted to be just like you."

"But he didn't need to join the Marine Corps," Morgan howled. "Why...why...why?"

"Because he thought you were the finest man on the face of the earth," Anne said through her sobs. "Just like I think you're the finest man in the world."

Morgan turned and lowered his head to Anne's shoulder. They embraced awkwardly and together they cried long into the dark, merciless evening until they had no more tears to shed.

~ 63 ~

Nicholas Early was born in November, 1945 exactly nine months after the death of the brother James he never knew.

Morgan welcomed the arrival of his second son with unbound enthusiasm. From the moment the boy was able to walk, he and his father were inseparable. Morgan taught his son to swim and fish and catch lobsters. Together they explored the island of Bimini every day the weather allowed, visiting the mythical Fountain of Youth where allegedly Ponce de Leon had discovered the secret to eternal life, and the Healing Hole where the tannic waters purportedly cured a myriad of ills.

Morgan's shoulder had healed completely. The blonde Labrador puppy Doc Holliday had slept with his head on Morgan's damaged shoulder every night for a month after his return. Each day Morgan reported greater mobility and less pain.

Neither Anne nor Morgan were ready to subscribe the result to a miracle, but they were unable to offer any other explanation except the mysterious healing powers of the warm, unquestioning companionship of the loving dog.

*　　　*　　　*

In 1952 Morgan commissioned Ansil Saunders, a local boat builder of excellent reputation and exceptional skills, to construct a fifteen foot long, extremely lightweight, fishing boat that could be poled across the flats in a mere seven inches of water. Morgan

332

announced his availability as a bonefishing guide, and for the next eighteen years worked diligently at that trade, charging visiting tourists to hunt and release bonefish in the shallow waters east of the island.

Nick Early studied at home with Anne and proved to be an exceptional student. He excelled at math and history, as had his father under the auspices of Widow O'Brien. The boy completed his high school equivalency with honors at the age of seventeen.

There was much discussion in the Early household about where Nick should attend college. Morgan campaigned vigorously for a school in the northeast to give his son a broader view of the world and increased competition studying with students from other parts of the country.

Nick steadfastly held out for a school in south Florida.

"Your son adores you," Anne reminded Morgan. "He doesn't want to be too far away from either of us. At vacation time he wants to be able to come home to Bimini and fish and swim with you."

Morgan listened patiently to the entreaties of his son, which were echoed by his wife. He shook his head in disagreement. "There is so much more Nick should experience than bonefishing and diving for lobsters," he argued. "He needs a great education in order to get a fulfilling job. He can't expect to make a living on Bimini."

"Nick wants to emulate you," Anne said simply. "You're his hero."

"That's what I'm afraid of," Morgan said. "That and..."

Anne moved closer to Morgan. "You don't have to say it," she whispered. "I know, I know."

"It seems like everyone I've been close to all my life, from my foster mother to Con Ira Calhoun to my squad in France and my men on Tarawa, have suffered and died because of their proximity to me. Even you were kidnapped trying to find me."

"Oh, my darling Morgan," Anne said soothingly. "We've had this conversation one hundred times before. You can't blame yourself for all these calamities. In fact, you've probably saved more people in your life that any ten other men. I might be dead if you hadn't found me in that shack up the Miami River. The police would never have rescued me."

Morgan sat silent for several seconds. He knew his training and leadership in combat had undoubtedly mitigated the loss of hundreds of lives. Yet violence seemed to follow him and spread to others near him. James' surprise enlistment in the Marine Corps in 1943 was honorable and on a certain level flattering. But the pitiless loss of his first son still stung as bitterly seventeen years later as it did the night he read the callous telegram.

*   *   *

Nick Early entered the University of Miami as a freshman in the fall of 1962 and, unbeknownst to his parents, signed up for the Marine Corps Platoon Leader Program. When news of the decision was revealed as Nick was about to board a Chalk's flight back to school on January 2nd, 1963, Morgan registered his strenuous objection.

"Please," Morgan pleaded. "You don't have to do this."

"I know, Dad," Nick retorted. "But, I wanted to sign up. If the war in Viet Nam ever gets bigger, I'm sure I'll eventually be drafted. At least this way I'll be an officer and lead men I can be proud to serve with."

Morgan's heart sunk, but he was powerless to reverse the decision.

Nick spent six weeks during the summers of his sophomore and junior years at the Marine Corps base in Quantico, Virginia completing his officer training. In the fall of his final year at the university, Nick fell desperately in love with one of his classmates, Mary Osborne.

Morgan and Anne tried in vain to talk the young couple out of marriage until Nick completed his obligation to the Marines, but they were unsuccessful.

Nick graduated from the University of Miami in his handsome dress blue Marine Corps uniform in June, 1966 with bright gold 2nd lieutenant's bars on his shoulders. Two weeks later he and Mary were married in Bimini in the same church that hosted Morgan and Anne.

Mary's mother Elaine Osborne traveled from her home in Lakeville, Connecticut for the occasion. The bride's father had left the household a decade previously and was not invited.

"You certainly live in a quaint place," Elaine commented to Anne as they wended their way up the Queen's Highway toward the Early house.

"It may not be for everyone," Anne admitted with a laugh. "But Morgan and I find it very interesting."

Mary was beautiful in her wedding dress, and the local boys heavily pursued her four classmates serving as bridesmaids during their weeklong stay on the island.

Nick wore his Marine dress blues and cut a dashing figure that swelled Morgan with pride even as he swallowed his trepidations about the coming commitment to the Corps. The Vietnam situation showed unmistakable signs of significant escalation.

Nick's four groomsmen managed to put a serious dent in the beer supply on the island as they caroused nightly in the Compleat Angler Bar and the sand floor End of the World Saloon.

*   *   *

Nick left for the first phase of his Advanced Infantry Training three months later, in September of 1966. Before he departed, he and Mary announced they were expecting a baby. Mary returned to her hometown of Lakeville to live with her mother, await the birth of her child, and the completion of her husband's tour of duty.

Nick Early, now fully trained to lead a platoon of Marines in combat, boarded an airplane for Vietnam in November, 1966.

Anne began a business raising Labrador puppies and teaching them to assist disabled veterans with simple tasks around the home. Her dogs were so helpful and so much in demand, the business blossomed into a thriving, but unprofitable, enterprise. Anne's charitable spirit continually persuaded her to give the dogs away when the recipient could not afford the cost. Morgan never protested when he was asked to replenish the continuously dwindling account; he, more than anyone, knew the value of a canine companion.

Morgan and Anne flew to Hartford, Connecticut in May, 1967 for the birth of their first grandson, Morgan II, named in honor of the proud grandfather. Nick arrived home on leave two weeks later, and he and Mary managed to escape for a few days while Anne and Elaine took over nursing duties.

Hank Manley

Morgan and Nick never discussed the war or Nick's involvement after one truncated conversation.

"Why don't you come home after your first tour?" Morgan urged. "Nobody has to serve more than a year over there."

Nick looked at his father and shook his head. A strange sensation overcame Morgan as he stared at the ruggedly handsome face of his son, his piercing eyes, square shoulders and powerful physique. Morgan suddenly felt he was looking in a mirror that possessed the bizarre power to transcend time and propel him back half a century.

"I can't leave my men," Nick said. "They depend on me."

Morgan opened his mouth to respond, but instead drew a breath and remained silent. At that moment Morgan realized with absolute certainty how much his son resembled him.

"I love you, Nick," Morgan said after several seconds. "I'm so proud of you."

~ 64 ~

Erwin von Hempsted knocked impatiently on Morgan Early's door on a calm morning in May, 1968. He was impeccably dressed in a starched fishing shirt, tan shorts and a broad-brimmed hat. "Is anybody about?" he called through the screen.

"We're on the porch," Anne Early replied. "Come in!"

Von Hempsted tentatively pushed the door open and walked slowly through the house toward the sound of the voice.

"Excuse me," he began hesitantly. "My name is Erwin von Hempsted. I was scheduled to fish with one of the guides, but unfortunately he took sick. I'm told you might be an adequate substitute, Mr. Early."

Morgan looked up from his breakfast and pointed to a vacant chair. "Would you like some eggs or coffee," he asked.

Von Hempsted looked surprised at the unexpected hospitality. He opened his mouth, but Anne spoke first.

"It wouldn't be any trouble," she said pushing back from her chair. "I have all the ingredients out."

"Please," von Hempsted said quickly, waving his hand for Anne to sit. "Don't trouble yourself. Besides, I've had breakfast. I was hoping to enlist you as a guide this morning."

"Are you interested in bonefish?" Morgan asked as he took a bite of toasted Bimini bread slathered with orange marmalade.

"I've caught large trout all over the world," von Hempsted replied. "I've heard about the fighting ability of your bonefish, and I want to see if they're as tough as reported. I have my doubts."

"They're a fine fighting fish," Morgan said simply.

"Have you ever caught large trout, Mr. Early? Say on the Colorado River?"

Morgan nodded. "I have."

Von Hempsted raised his eyebrows in surprise at the positive response. His attempt to establish a superior position in the debate between trout and bonefish appeared thwarted. "Well, could I interest you in a day of fishing?"

"Do you have your own rod and reel? I assume you want to fly fish."

"I have the finest five weight outfit built in Europe," von Hempsted said contemptuously. "Some people consider me one of the most accomplished anglers on the Continent."

"And what do the others think, Mr. von Hempsted?" Anne asked as she stood and gathered dishes before heading to the kitchen.

Von Hempsted looked puzzled for a moment. "What do the others think about what, Mrs. Early?"

"Nothing," Anne said as she brushed past. "Nothing at all."

Erwin von Hempsted refocused his attention on Morgan. "Are you available today?" he asked with a touch of impatience.

Morgan glanced at his watch. "The tide started out about two hours ago," he said. "We could still get to the fish and have some good wading if we leave soon."

"Excellent," von Hempsted said. "I hope you can find some fish for me. This is my only opportunity. I must leave for New York tomorrow."

Anne reentered the porch and smiled. "I believe you'll find my husband rather more than adequate," she said. "Although I can't say the same for your three weight rod. I suggest you let Morgan outfit you."

Von Hempsted sniffed his reply. "I have full confidence in my equipment."

"Yes," Anne chuckled. "I have no doubt. But my money's on the participant at the other end of the line."

*   *   *

Morgan sped across the bay in a northeast direction, heading directly for the solid wall of mangroves on the far shore. The water was less than two feet deep, more than adequate for his custom-built, fifteen-foot skiff. He passed three fiberglass stakes to port, delineating the very shallow area below a dense shrub island. Von Hempsted looked with consternation into the water.

"There's almost no water here," he said with a hint of alarm in his voice. "Are we going aground and become stranded?"

"I've come this way a time or two," Morgan said. "Don't worry."

"But it's getting shallower."

"And it will continue to do so. Get ready to duck your head."

Morgan turned directly for the shore and increased power to lift the engine higher in the water.

Von Hempsted turned to Morgan and pointed at the rapidly approaching mangroves. "We're going to crash."

"Duck down," Morgan said in a soothing voice. "Everything's okay."

Morgan pushed the tiller arm on the 90 horsepower Johnson and the boat bent slightly to starboard. A small opening in the dense mangrove thicket was suddenly apparent, and the boat scooted under overhanging branches and entered a narrow, shallow trail. Exposed mangrove roots delineated the watery path that carried no more than fourteen inches of water in its twisty channel.

Von Hempsted scrunched low in his seat and peeked at Morgan. His face had lost considerable color and a sheen of perspiration glistened on his top lip.

Morgan guided the boat through the circuitous path at high speed. To slow the boat and bring it off plane meant the certain impossibility of resuming travel except with a push pole.

The mangroves opened and the little boat sped across a small lake with a brown bottom. A trail of disturbed mud issued behind the craft as the depth decreased slightly and the blades of the churning propeller spun rapidly a mere inch from the silt.

Morgan pointed the boat at a tiny opening in the corner of the lake, and again the skiff was in a tight, serpentine passage, weaving between stout mangrove shoots, and forced to negotiate ninety-degree turns.

Finally the skinny waterway broadened, and Morgan cruised the craft close to the south bank, forty yards from the distant stand of mangroves to the north. The verdant foliage broke away to starboard and suddenly the skiff was in a deep-water slough with a narrow sandy beach to port.

Morgan weaved through the twelve-foot channel, passing over several large sharks and two spotted eagle rays cruising the depths. He slowed as the boat approached a broad, gleaming white sandy flat that stretched endlessly to the east and seemingly all the way back to Bimini, now visible to the west. He nudged the front of the skiff up on the flat, jumped into the six-inch deep water, and placed an anchor on a long line ahead of the bow.

"We're here," Morgan said simply. "Hop out."

"Didn't I see large sharks and some other huge animals just back there?" von Hempsted asked with concern as he pointed at the foamy trail of bubbles that remained in the skiff's path.

"That's a good sign," Morgan said. "The sharks often follow the bonefish schools."

Von Hempsted looked dubiously around the beached skiff. "We're going to walk?" he asked at last.

"Yes. The bottom is all sand. You'll be fine in your sneakers."

*   *   *

Morgan and Erwin von Hempsted walked slowly along the edge of the deep slough. The water varied from four to ten inches in depth depending on the pocked contour of the bottom.

Von Hempsted repeatedly glanced toward the slough.

Morgan fanned his hand across the vast flat. "The bonefish will be in the shallow water," he said. "There's no need to watch the slough."

"I was just keeping a wary eye out for the sharks," von Hempsted replied.

"You don't have to worry about them," Morgan said. "They won't bother you. If one comes close, just kick him away."

Von Hempsted looked at Morgan quizzically, not certain if the answer was honest or fatuous. He kept silent as they continued to wander.

"Pull some line from your reel," Morgan suggested. "Trail it behind you. Hold the fly I tied on your leader in your hand. When we spot a fish, I want you ready to cast."

Von Hempsted complied slowly, as if doubtful of the eventual need to cast. "I don't see anything," he said. "Are you sure there are fish here."

Morgan pointed. "There's a pair of stingrays working sixty yards away. That's hopeful. I see two small sharks circling eighty yards ahead. That's a boxfish off to the right. Stay alert."

The two men continued easing along the slough until Morgan reached out and placed a restraining hand on von Hempsted's arm. "Three fish about fifty yards," Morgan said in a whisper. "See them, about two o'clock?"

"I can't see anything," von Hempsted said, frustration creeping into his voice.

"There," Morgan said as he crouched down and pointed. "Can you see their tails flashing in the air when they feed in the sand?"

"I...I think so," von Hempsted said uncertainly.

"Cast," Morgan said quietly. "They're heading directly for us."

Erwin von Hempsted lifted his five-weight trout rod and began a series of false casts, waving the rod back and forth."

"Throw," Morgan hissed. "All that false casting will just scare the fish."

Von Hempsted cocked his rod back to an almost horizontal position, beyond the point where the shaft could bend and add velocity to the line when whipped forward. He heaved the rod ahead, in the direction of Morgan's pointing finger, and the line traveled softly through the air, losing momentum in the slight breeze, until it fell in a heap fifteen yards in front of the fish.

"Damn wind," von Hempsted grumbled, as it was immediately obvious his cast was short of the fish and the fly was surrounded by slack leader.

"You have to haul the line," Morgan said easily. "I guess you haven't needed to haul on your trout streams.

"Haul? What's that?"

"Let me show you," Morgan said without rancor. "Come around to my left side so I can make a cast."

Von Hempsted surrendered his five-weight rod and re-positioned himself on Morgan's left side.

Morgan snapped the rod just past the vertical position, lifting the tumbled line from the water. His left hand tugged downward on the fly line above the reel, increasing the speed of the returning line.

"Watch my left hand," Morgan instructed. "I haul the line with my left to increase the velocity of the line through the guides.

When the fly line had passed beyond the nearly vertical rod, causing the shaft to bend back, loading it with energy, Morgan snapped the rod forward. He simultaneously hauled the line again, completing the double haul motion, and sent the line whistling straight ahead. As the line came tight on the reel, stopping the forward progress of the cast, the leader gently unfolded and the fly landed softly on the water five feet in front of the lead bonefish.

Morgan paused a moment to allow the fly to sink to the bottom. Then he stripped the fly line with his left hand in a three-inch tug. The fly popped from the sand and jumped to a new position. The action caught the attention of the hungry bonefish that wiggled its tail and darted ahead to nose down and inhale the artificial crustacean in its under-slung mouth.

Morgan saw the bonefish race to the fly and watched as the tail popped above the surface of the water. He felt the fish gobble the fly through the vibrations of the line. With his left hand he "strip-struck" the fish with a sharp pull on the fly line.

The eight-pound bonefish immediately sensed its predicament and began a run across the flats, parting the water with its back and leaving a visible wake.

Morgan handed the rod to von Hempsted. "Hold the rod high," he cautioned. "Keep the line out of the water as much as possible to avoid any little coral rocks or shells."

Von Hempsted obeyed and shot a quick glance at Morgan when he felt the power of the departing fish and noticed the line melting from his small trout reel.

"I don't know if I can stop him before he takes all my line," von Hempsted commented with deep concern in his voice.

"That's probably true," Morgan said as he watched in admiration as the bonefish raced across the flat.

"I've never had a trout do this to me before," von Hempsted continued breathlessly.

"I believe that, also," Morgan said suppressing a grin.

(The route Morgan took Erwin von Hempsted through the mangroves to the bonefishing flat is the exact path my good friend Ansil Saunders used when he took Martin Luther King, Jr. fishing. Dr. King became so enchanted with the beauty and serenity of the area, he implored Ansil to stop. After several moments of contemplation, Dr. King took out a piece of paper and a pen and in Ansil's boat composed his Nobel Peace Prize acceptance speech.)

~ 65 ~

The sun broke above the horizon of the glassy flats east of Bimini and poured on the porch of the Early home. It was the first day of June, 1970, and excitement and anticipation crackled the air. Nick Early, now a 1st lieutenant in the Marine Corps and serving his third tour of duty, was scheduled to return home in a month. His wife, Mary, and their three year-old son Morgan II, were arriving from Lakeville and planning to stay until Nick's arrival on the island.

Anne walked from the kitchen with a large plate of scrambled eggs, three crisp pieces of bacon, and a stack of locally baked toast. She kissed Morgan warmly. "You sit right here on the porch and eat your breakfast," she said. "I'll ride down and meet the Chalk's flight and bring Mary and little Morgie back."

Morgan reached for the steaming plate of food and set it carefully on the coffee table in front of his comfortable chair. He reached up with his sun burnt arms and liver-spotted hands and gently placed his arthritic fingers on his wife's face.

"Have I told you today how much I love you?" he asked with a mischievous smile.

Anne looked in her husband's face and tilted her head. Her eyes appeared to mist momentarily with a look of unadulterated joy. "No, you haven't," she answered with a little tease in her voice. "But after all, it is only seven o'clock in the morning."

"Well, I apologize for being so forgetful," Morgan said in a mock, self-deprecating tone. "It won't happen again. But I do love you. You've made these last...how many has it been...forty-seven years...the most wonderful any man has ever enjoyed."

"It's been everything I wished for, darling, when I ran away from home to come to Bimini to marry you," Anne said.

"Even when I left in 1942?"

Anne touched Morgan's cheek affectionately. "I knew who I was marrying when I left Boston," she said. "I wouldn't have expected you to deny your country when you were called upon. You have established a legacy of honor, and our sons have been faithful to it."

Morgan lifted Anne's hand from his face and placed his lips on her knuckles. He held her fingers tightly and closed his eyes. His embrace continued for several seconds, and for a brief moment Anne worried that something might be wrong with her husband.

"Is everything all right?" she asked tentatively.

Anne was still, at age sixty-eight, the most stunning woman Morgan had ever seen. Her blonde hair was shot with gray, and tiny wrinkles highlighted the corners of her eyes. But he still could not look at her without feeling twinges of desire. "When you're near me, everything's perfect."

Hesitantly, Anne slid her hand from Morgan's grasp. "I'll be back soon with our daughter-in-law and grandchild," she said. "Eat your breakfast and enjoy the sun."

*   *   *

Morgan heard the car start and back from the covered port as Anne departed for the short drive to the south end of the island and the seaplane ramp where the Chalk's planes pulled ashore.

He had not seen his namesake since he and Anne had traveled to Connecticut for the birth of the boy, and he was anxious to spend time with the lad. Was he old enough to enjoy bonefishing? Could he swim yet? Would he like to drive the old *Belleau Woods*?

Morgan flexed his right arm. The numbness he had been experiencing for the past few weeks was particularly acute this morning. He shook his shoulder and massaged the limb, but the feeling of weakness persisted. He felt his forehead turn clammy and the return of a deep, piercing pressure in his chest.

Perhaps he was just hungry. The strange sensations in his right arm undoubtedly were the residual effects of his shoulder wound. He picked up his fork and plunged into the pile of eggs on his plate with forced gusto. At seventy years of age, weird feelings were bound to manifest themselves.

The knock on the front door surprised Morgan. Had Anne returned so quickly from the seaplane ramp with Mary and Morgie? He had hardly begun his breakfast.

Morgan locked his hands on the arms of his chair and pushed. His body hefted forward but sank quickly to the seat. He took his napkin and dabbed at his face, curious when he discovered substantial dampness on the cloth. With renewed determination, Morgan pushed himself to his feet and shuffled toward the door.

"Mr. Early," the eager boy at the door said when Morgan appeared. "I got's a telegram for you."

"Why, thank you, son," Morgan said. "Would you like to come in and have something to drink?"

"No, thank you, sir," the boy replied. "Dey tell me I gots to keep goin' wid my deliveries."

Morgan reached in his pocket and removed an American dollar bill. "Here, son," he said. "For your troubles."

"Thank you, sir."

Morgan trundled back to the porch and sat heavily in his chair. He looked at the small, yellow envelope with the cellophane window and frowned with curiosity. He hadn't received a telegram since... since 1945 when the Marine Corps informed him of the death of his son James on Iwo Jima.

Could this be another...?

With trembling hands Morgan turned the telegram over and peeled the flap open. He closed his eyes and let his hands sink into his lap. The numbness had disappeared briefly when he started his breakfast, but the initial sensations began to return. He swallowed and fought the dark tightening beneath his breastbone.

Morgan shook his head, snapped open his eyes and commanded his fingers to extract the thin sheet of paper from the envelope. He blinked and forced his eyes to focus on the tiny block letters glued in strips to the parchment.

*　　　*　　　*

The sun bore down on Morgan in his chair. Crispness and clarity devolved to blurry, nebulous images. The water of the flats shimmered in front of his eyes. Enormous bonefish swam past, close enough that he could touch them with his hands. Was he in the water? Why wasn't he wet? Morgan struggled to comprehend. He reached for the fish but his outstretched hand passed through the chimera image.

Morgan blinked deliberately to clear the confusion from his mind. The water immediately receded and a dense, tangled forest appeared. Silence reigned over the sylvan scene. Morgan relaxed in the serenity of the calm woods.

Without warning a mortar shell exploded directly in front of his chair. The mangled torso of a Marine turned and gushed blood over the coffee table. Was it his son James? Was it Michael Houlihan?

I remember this girl; she had blood all over her. It was a dying shame!

What was Private Houlihan doing on his front porch?

Stars sparkled in Morgan's eyes. How could it be night already? His plate of eggs still sat on the table. Where was...what was his name...oh, yes, little Morgie? Wasn't he supposed to visit today? How could anyone ever forget his grandchild's name?

The trees disappeared in an oily plume of black smoke. The acrid smell of cordite washed across Morgan's senses. He looked down at his chest. I'm not wounded, he thought. Why am I unable to move?

A large American flag taped to a drainage pole snapped in a stiff breeze. Morgan's son James appeared and raised his arms triumphantly, his left hand clutching an M-1 carbine. The corners of his lips curled in a sardonic grin, and he flipped a salute with his fingers as a mortar exploded at his feet.

"James..." Morgan muttered into his chest. "You didn't have to leave..."

The cloud of exploded ordinance drifted away. Pale white sky glistened before Morgan's watery vision. The angelic face of the widow O'Brien appeared, wavering and indistinct against the shiny background. "How are you feeling, Morgan?" she asked with genuine concern.

The background darkened and Morgan's foster mother faded from view. By twos and threes, other figures materialized from the distance and trudged across the suddenly re-emerging shallow flats and approached the porch. Some were without arms. Others stood on stumps or balanced on their torsos. All dripped blood on the floor. Incomprehensively, their faces radiated calm and peace and understanding.

Darkness closed on the porch. The wounded and dead turned and departed. A star flickered high in the sky and the widow O'Brien peered around the perimeter and smiled kindly.

*   *   *

Three year-old Morgan Early II pushed through the screen door and charged into the house. "Grandpa," he yelled with excitement. "Grandpa!"

"Try the porch, Morgie," Anne called as she struggled into the house with Mary and several bags of luggage.

"Grandpa," the boy called as he bounded on to the porch. "I've decided when I grow up I'm going to be a Marine just like you and daddy."

Morgie skidded to a halt in front of Morgan. He stepped tentatively forward and placed his little hand on Morgan's arm. "Then I'm going to be a boat captain," he continued more slowly. "Like you were when you met Grandma."

The boy looked down and wrinkled his face in confusion. "Will you let me drive the *Belleau Woods*?" he asked in a near whisper. "Mommy says I'm old enough."

Morgie removed his hand and stared at Morgan for several seconds. He looked closely at his grandfather before backing away.

"Mom," he said slowly in a voice cracking with confusion and fear. "Grandpa isn't moving."

Anne Early stepped to the porch and groaned in disbelief.

Mary Early stood in the doorway. She gasped in fear and her right hand flew involuntarily to her lips. With her left she reached for her son and pulled him from the porch into the house.

Anne's shoulders slumped and she fell to her knees, her initial sobs racking her chest as she descended.

"Morgan!" she shouted. "Morgan! Oh, no. Please!"

Her hand slid to his chest but she could detect no heartbeat. She pressed her lips against his mouth but felt only the desiccation of his bloodless skin.

The crumpled telegram on Morgan's knee caught her eye as she dropped her head with resignation into his lap. Terror stabbed her heart. For several moments Anne was unable to move, but slowly, reluctantly, fearfully, she lifted the paper and read the message.

THE GOVERNMENT OF THE UNITED STATES REGRETS TO INFORM YOU OF THE DEATH OF YOUR SON 1ST LT NICHOLAS EARLY STOP LT EARLY WAS KILLED IN ACTION VIETNAM MAY 28, 1970 STOP REMAINS TO BE RETURNED TO UNITED STATES STOP LT EARLY TO BE BURIED ARLINGTON NAT'L CEMETERY STOP

Anne Early closed her eyes and screamed. Her body heaved with choking, blubbering tears. Her grief upon finding Morgan, beyond any sorrow she had previously experienced, instantly doubled as she now mourned her son as well as her husband. She clung to Morgan's inert body as if her warmth and love could restore his life and resurrect her son from the body bag where he rested half way around the world.

"Anne," Mary called from the interior of the house in a trembling, hesitant voice. "Is Morgan...? Is Morgan...okay?"

"Take Morgie down by the water," Anne sobbed against Morgan's chest, unable to raise her head. "I need to be alone here for a while."

"Is there...is there anything I can do?" Mary stuttered, the realization dawning that her father-in-law was dead, and that she needed to remove Morgie from the tragic scene quickly.

"No," Anne managed. "Just go. I'll find you after a while."

"Come with Mommy," Mary said as she seized Morgie's hand and pulled him in the direction of the front door. "Let's go down by the water and see if we can find some conch shells."

"Is Grandma okay?" Morgie asked, looking up at his mother with sad, troubled eyes. "Why is she crying?"

"Grandma needs to be alone with your grandfather. Come along," Mary said firmly, bravely fighting her own sadness to temporarily shield her son from the tragedy.

Anne lifted her head and sniffled back a fresh spate of tears. Her cheeks shone with moisture from her initial gush of mourning. "You were the best man I ever knew," she whispered. "You blamed yourself when you couldn't save everyone near you, but you were wrong. You saved hundreds of lives, including mine. You always did the best you knew how, and it was better than most men could do. I hope you know that now, and I hope you think it was enough."

A black hole of agony imploded inside Anne. Her heart felt as if it were squeezed and strangled inside her chest. Her breathing grew shallow and she pressed her eyes tightly closed as if to wring away the reality of the loss of her husband and son.

For a moment Anne was unable to sustain a coherent thought. Finally, she surrendered to her grief and melted against Morgan's inert body, consumed by her pain and misery.

*   *   *

The brutal fact of Morgan and Nick's deaths slowly seeped into Anne's consciousness. She had no idea how long she had spent in Morgan's lap pouring tears. Had she fainted? Had her mind shut down to mitigate the unbearable sorrow? Awake again, with the tortured knowledge that she was alone in the world except for her daughter-in-law and grandson, a harsh understanding suddenly arrived. Anne had to inform Mary that she too was now a widow.

Anne struggled to her feet and almost collapsed as her legs wobbled and her knees quivered with instability. Her head pounded and her temples pulsed and for a moment her eyes clouded. She licked her lips and felt extreme dryness in her throat. A brief moment in time flashed across her memory. Anne recalled her devastation when she had read a telegram informing her that James had been killed on Iwo Jima. A fresh dagger of pain stabbed at her tortured heart. How many sons must a mother sacrifice for her country?

Distantly cognizant of her duty to Mary and Morgie, Anne trudged from the house in a near trance and descended the slope toward the bay. Mary sat on a large rock with her head cast down, her feet in the pristine water, her eyes red and puffy. Little Morgie was one hundred yards down the beach, joyfully chasing juvenile fish at the water's edge.

"I'm so sorry," Mary said as Anne approached. "He was such a wonderful man. Nick absolutely worshipped him and Morgie loved him dearly."

Anne nodded in acknowledgement of the sentiment, unable yet to frame words for her impossibly difficult task.

"Yes, he was a very special man," Anne said finally as she sat beside Mary on the rock and gently placed her arm around the young girl's shoulder. "He was...he was...oh, Mary," Anne stammered. "It's not just Morgan. It's..."

Mary initially turned to comfort Anne and then jolted back as her mother-in-law dissolved into fresh tears, unable to speak the unspeakable words. "What do you mean 'it's not just Morgan'?" she asked, her senses suddenly alert. "What could be...oh, no! Is it Nick? It's Nick...!"

Anne could only nod.

The two women clutched together and howled in pain, their tears cascading over each other's shoulders.

Little Morgie looked up as the sounds of grief tumbled down the beach. He stopped running and kicking the wavelets and began a cautious jog toward his mother and grandmother. Confusion and trepidation immediately replaced his unrestrained joy. What had happened to cause Mommy and Grandma to cry so intensely?

"What's wrong?" Morgie called apprehensively as he approached the weeping women with a measured, reluctant step. "What's the matter?"

With pounding heart, little Morgie walked along the shore toward the wailing women, the last of the Early men.

About the Author

Hank Manley has traveled the Bahamas by boat for thirty years. He has written two books on fishing, A Grand Quest and Beyond the Green Water. He lives with his wife, Gretchen, in North Palm Beach, Florida.

Printed in the United States
139339LV00002B/2/P